URBS ANTIQUA FUIT STUDIISQUE ASPERRIMA BELLI

CANCELLED

Nimrod's Shadow

CHRIS PALING

Portobello
BOOKS

Published by Portobello Books Ltd 2010

Portobello Books Ltd
Twelve Addison Avenue
London
W11 4QR

This is a work of fiction. The characters, incidents, and dialogues are
products of the author's imagination and not to be construed as real. The author's
use of names of actual persons, living or dead, and actual places is incidental to the
purposes of the plot and is not intended to change the entirely fictional
character of the work.

A CIP catalogue record is available from the British Library

9 8 7 6 5 4 3 2 1

ISBN 978 1 84627 233 2

www.portobellobooks.com

Text designed and typeset in Garamond by Patty Rennie

Printed in the UK by CPI William Clowes Beccles NR34 7TL

For Paul and Ann

Shadow is the diminution alike of light and of darkness, and stands between darkness and light. A shadow may be infinitely dark, and also of infinite degrees of absence of darkness. The beginnings and ends of shadow lie between the light and darkness and may be infinitely diminished and infinitely increased. Shadow is the means by which bodies display their form. The forms of bodies could not be understood in detail but for shadow.

Leonardo da Vinci

ONE

Reilly, Mountjoy and the Small Matter of the Exhibition

HAVING AT LAST CONVINCED MOUNTJOY TO EXHIBIT HIS WORK – the exhibition just five days away now – T. F. Reilly was painting day and night to ensure he would have sufficient finished pieces to cover the walls of Mountjoy's coffee shop. But on this bright September day nothing was going right. The artist was working with a fresh flesh tint of ochre, white and vermillion that he had graded into four fine tones by adding increasing quantities of white. The small pots sat beside him on his makeshift shelf. He was currently dipping his sable brush into the third of these pots but the more he worked at it the more ludicrous the skin tone of the reclining woman appeared so he left his studio (the room directly under the roof of the lodging house where he painted – where he slept, where he ate, where he washed, where he cooked, where Nimrod – his Jack Russell – also ate and slept) and he went down the stairs, down a second set of stairs (uncarpeted, like the first), down a third set of stairs (where the carpet clung to the treads like fur on an old alopecic lion), down a fourth (where the stair carpet was intact but greasy), along the dark hallway corridor, negotiating the unused hat stand, and out, through the old heavy door, into the street. Here he paused and blinked in the sunlight. Summer! Of course. Late summer. Reilly drew in a deep breath, and was immediately assailed by the smell of horse manure, recently deposited in the road by a passing hansom.

The artist, as he acquainted himself with the day, heard an insistent scratching from the interior of the lodging-house hallway. He opened the door. There Nimrod waited, sitting back tautly on his haunches, eyeing his master with his habitual eager disdain. Reilly apologized. Nimrod emerged from the damp shadows of the hallway and, head high, set off for Mountjoy's coffee shop which was, to his mind, the obvious destination. Reilly tugged the door shut and followed on obediently. He was aware of the pavement through the halfpenny-sized hole in his right brogue, but it had been there so long that his exposed sole had hardened to the consistency of leather.

Down the narrow street they paraded, Nimrod pausing at the greengrocer's to sniff at the naked leg of a trestle table. While Reilly waited for him to finish he observed the cherries, and was, in turn, observed by the greengrocer's daughter, Amy Sykes. Reilly was more notorious than celebrated in the vicinity of Old Cross. There was a suspicion that he would play fast and loose with the hearts of the local women, that he would run up credit at the local stores and then vanish in the night – unfounded, as he had few needs beyond his meagre daily ration of food, seven eggs a week (which he used to make the tempera mix with which he painted) and bones and scraps enough for Nimrod. He ordered his paint pigment by post and it arrived on the second Thursday of each month. Amy watched Reilly with fondness – twenty-four years old, young in years and hopes, old in expectations, with luminous blue eyes and the lanky gait of a butcher's boy. She took a glance over her shoulder. Her father the greengrocer was in the back of the shop with his spiders. 'Take some, darling,' she called to him, *sotto voce.* The endearment rang out like a bell.

Reilly, who was unaware he had been observed, cut round and when he saw Amy he blushed; the handsome, ungainly girl bounded out from the shop door, took up a brown paper bag, palmed a handful of cherries into the bag and offered them to Reilly, whose blush was now as fierce as the colour of the fruit he had been given.

'Here. Take them.' She pressed a kiss onto his warm cheek.

Reilly had nothing to offer in return but his thanks, which he gave, but the gift of the fruit left him with an awkward debt not to the girl but to her father, the notoriously stern and parsimonious Sykes. He would borrow the money from Mountjoy and settle the bill on his way back from the coffee shop. Nor did he like cherries. He was staring at them only in an attempt to discern how many hues of scarlet there were in each drupe. Nimrod watched and waited for his own reward. But Amy had eyes only for the artist and the artist only had eyes for her.

'When will you paint me as you promised?' the girl asked him.

'You know I paint only from memory.'

'Oh – well, remember me and then paint me.'

'Perhaps that's what I'm doing.' Reilly smiled.

'A portrait of me!'

'Perhaps.'

The picture on Reilly's easel was, indeed, of Amy Sykes but he was superstitious about discussing his work in progress. He held the belief that the mystical process of coaxing something into life with paint demanded a monastic vow of silence. Subjects, if discussed during this process, tend to get their own back on the garrulous artist by refusing to come to life.

'If you are painting me, don't make me look old.'

'I promise,' the artist said. Now he was aware of Nimrod, whose expression had shifted minutely from expectation to impatience (via a fleeting diversion into disappointment). Few would have registered these changes but man and beast spent so much time in each other's company that they communicated more effectively than many long-married couples. Nimrod adopted the subservience of a dumb animal only when the artist was in the company of others. The artist had found him one winter's night shivering on the street corner, frozen, beaten and virtually starved. Wrapping him in his coat Reilly carried him to his room, laid him on his mattress and encouraged him to eat. He had lodged with Reilly ever since.

'Grieve is very thin. Are you starving him?' Amy said, at last taking notice of Reilly's companion. Nimrod of course had borne witness to those afternoons when the lovers tangled on Reilly's mattress; he had watched them shed their outer skins and roll pink and naked in each other's arms.

'He's no longer called Grieve.'

'Why?'

'He didn't answer to the name when I called – and then Mountjoy told me the story about Edward Elgar, and that seemed to suit him.'

'What story?'

'Something along the lines of one of his variations – the tenth or eleventh – supposedly portraying a dog paddling in the River Wye, having fallen in. I liked the notion, but I couldn't call him "Number Ten" or "Number Eleven" so I called him after the ninth – Nimrod – which is also the hunter, as I'm sure you know.'

'And does he hunt?'

'I'd say he's more of a collector than a hunter – aren't you, old chum?'

Nimrod looked up and stared at Reilly in puzzlement.

'Hello, Nimrod,' cooed Amy Sykes.

At the third unrewarded mention of his name, Nimrod put politeness aside and set off once more for the café.

'Thank you again. For the cherries,' Reilly said and followed Nimrod up the road. The girl watched them go. She regretted the gift of the cherries now but she didn't regret the afternoons spent with Reilly and neither, she was sure, did he.

❧

Nimrod arrived first and waited at Mountjoy's matt grey door for Reilly to catch up. For some time the exterior of the coffee shop had been in the process of redecoration. Three months previously the door and the frame of the window had been stripped of their old paint, the rotten wood removed, the holes faced up with putty and rubbed down, and the expanse primed. The following weekend the painter had fallen from a ladder and the work had halted. Rumour was that he was now fully recovered but Mountjoy, always careful with his money except for what he considered to be good causes, chose to wait for the man to re-establish contact. Until he did, the work would remain incomplete, the bill unpaid.

Reilly pushed open the door and Nimrod led the way in. There were two customers in the boxes: a cadaverous old man in a threadbare coat sitting by the window reading a newspaper and a muscular young Adonis in ragged clothes and heavy boots, dusty-haired and -shouldered from stonemasonry work on the local church, at his feet a nut-basket of tools. Applying himself with vigour to one of Mountjoy's breakfasts, he forked the food into his mouth like fuel into a furnace. For the price Mountjoy charged the breakfast was considered a bargain – two fried eggs, two sausages, two slices of ham, one tomato (halved and fried in old beef dripping), two slices of bread, thickly buttered, and a large tin mug of best mocha. Much of Mountjoy's business came from local men employed in the trades and older men and women who saw no reason to spend two or three times what Mountjoy would charge them on lunch in a local eating-house. At half past four Mountjoy turned the key in the lock and at a quarter to five the coffee shop was dark and quiet (a full day's work, as he opened at five o'clock to cater for the underground engineers from the local depot on their way home after a night shift, some early carpenters carrying tool-bags of saws and planes, bricklayers en route to the new terraces, and the occasional exhausted whore). Mountjoy greeted them all with the same enthusiasm. The coffee shop was a happy democracy. There were no delineations of age, race, class or intelligence; everybody was accorded equal respect and Mountjoy's customers generally felt better for having visited his establishment.

Reilly had been a customer there for three years, the length of time he had been resident in Old Cross, having arrived from completing his studies in Paris. Although on his first visit Reilly had enough in his pocket only for a cup of mocha, he could not resist the lure of the open fire in the small grate and the warm yellow glow from the dim gas mantles. When he first pushed open the door Mountjoy greeted him as though he had been expected. He instructed the artist to take a seat close to the fire, ignored his order for a twopenny cup of mocha and his protests that he had insufficient funds to pay for any food, and brought over a plate of mutton pie, grey boiled potatoes and tinned marrowfat peas. Reilly's debt to Mountjoy was thus established, and it was in the hope of paying it off that he had convinced Mountjoy to allow him to exhibit his paintings.

Mountjoy wasn't in any way typical of a coffee shop owner – men who tend either to be small and at the mercy of their large wives, or well-built, bare-knuckle fighter types: utterly imprisoned or deliriously free. He seemed instead to have been diverted from another, more obscure profession – a part-time shifter of pianos, for example, or a man who owned a shop selling fishing tackle. Facially, in repose, he seemed a content individual. His eyes shone with perpetual delight and occasionally, when registering interest or enthusiasm, the rest of his face would spring to life like that of a circus ringmaster announcing an act (another profession attracting those who seem merely to be marking time). Physically he was above average height. His skin was slightly olive. Over his clothes he sported an apron – fresh each day. He lived alone above the premises.

Today Mountjoy was glad to see Reilly. He had been afraid that the threat of an exhibition was proving too much for the maestro's fragile temperament and he had taken to his bed. The coffee-shop owner looked on the artist like a fond and proud parent, cajoling him towards a seat at the window with the promise of food. Nimrod was granted a tin plate of cold pork sausages, which he dispatched quickly, and then fell asleep beside the counter.

As was his habit, while Reilly sat by the window and ate, the artist indulged himself by bringing to his mind's eye his latest completed work. The picture was of a boy sitting on a wooden bench. The bench was on a stony beach. In the foreground was a shallow, rectangular, penned-in expanse of seawater. Discernible beneath the water was a submerged rowing boat. The bespectacled boy was looking with some concern towards the boat. Behind him the sky rose in rich layers of duck-egg blue, creamy white, salmon pink, carnation pink, gold, white and royal blue. The hue of the picture was, however, a chilly grey. There was, as in all of Reilly's works, a sense of melancholy, menace and a number of questions unanswered. When Reilly's work was first remarked upon, the critic Gower suggested that he represented those small moments before the larger, more significant moments of our lives. Reilly would not have disputed it. He would occasionally have liked to represent the larger moments, but these never seemed to come to him.

Reilly's pie now finished, Mountjoy came over, enthusiastically inhabiting the seat across the table from him.

'I've been making enquiries,' Mountjoy said, rippling the fingers of his right hand with the motion of a fish passing through weeds.

'Concerning what?'

'Your exhibition.'

'And what did these enquiries concern?'

'Well,' Mountjoy leaned forward, 'we need to drum up interest. Make a splash. I've spoken to the local newspaper and they're sending a photographer.'

'A photographer?'

'Yes. And a newspaper reporter.'

'But surely there's nothing to report.' Reilly pictured the tired man wearily pretending an interest in his paintings; he knew there was no creature on earth more wretched, jaded and resentful than the local hack. At least the photographer would perhaps make no pretence at either understanding or appreciating his work; a selfish witness stealing an image for his own glory and financial reward, nothing more.

'You underestimate yourself, Reilly. This is your first exhibition. That's something the world has a right to know about.'

'I'm not sure about that. Art is rarely newsworthy and I'm not sure the world will be at all interested in my paintings.'

'Of course it will! You're a genius. All we need now is for the world to acknowledge that, and you'll be rich.'

'I'm not a genius and I have no desire to be rich, only to pay off my debt to you.'

'Well, of course you are – and of course you do. Every man wants to be rich.'

'I don't. Not at all. I just want to be left alone. To work.'

'Then you'll have your wish. Being rich won't get in the way of that. I promise you.'

But however much Mountjoy tried to convince him, beyond paying off his debt Reilly refused to accept that the exhibition would do anything to improve his circumstances, with which he was content. He had, it was true, come to the attention of the critic Gower when one of his paintings had been accepted for a prestigious summer show some three years before. But the interest unsettled him. He heard the critic's praise ringing in his ears when he next tried to paint and eventually discarded two efforts because they seemed like pale imitations of the piece he had entered for the show. The experience was akin to suffering a long and debilitating fever.

'...We need to settle on the price of each painting,' Mountjoy was saying.

'The price, I expect, should represent the cost.' Having never once sold a painting Reilly had no idea what to charge. The two men had reached an agreement that Mountjoy would take a fifth share of the sale proceeds.

'Yes, of course it should,' Mountjoy agreed. 'But when you mention cost...?'

'The cost to me – for the work done.'

'The physical endeavour?'

'In part. And the mental.'

'Physical and mental. Yes. I see. Of course the price should reflect both. I imagine there's a price you have in mind – taking both of the above into account?'

'Not at all,' Reilly said. 'Not at all.'

'Well, this must be resolved.'

'Yes, I expect it must. What would you suggest?'

'Five pounds?' Mountjoy tried. 'For an average sized canvas?'

Reilly's vanity flared. 'Five pounds! What do you take me for? Even a house painter would receive more than five pounds for two months' work.'

'Of course he would,' Mountjoy hurriedly agreed.

'Not that I'm suggesting that I'm in any way superior to a house painter.'

'As a house painter I'm sure you'd do very well. I doubt many house painters would achieve an equivalent result as an artist.'

The two men fell silent until Reilly said, 'Well, perhaps we should estimate what a house painter would charge for a similar period and use that as a yardstick. That at least would lead us towards the value of the physical effort expended.'

'Seven pence per hour.'

'Per hour?'

'Minimum.'

'Seven pence per hour, at forty hours for the week, multiplied by eight comes to...?'

Mountjoy fetched a pencil and a piece of paper and applied himself to the calculation, concluding that on that rate a house painter would receive almost ten pounds.

'Ten pounds, then, for an average sized painting?' Reilly tried. 'For the physical endeavour alone. Then, say, five pounds for the mental effort?'

'So fifteen pounds?' Mountjoy stroked his chin. 'Yes. I see. Fifteen pounds.' The price, worked out against the hourly rate of a house painter, seemed fair, but he knew few, if any, of his clientele would have that kind of money to spare.

Seeing Mountjoy's embarrassment, Reilly relented. 'Perhaps even fifteen pounds seems excessive to you. But for two months' work...'

'Of course...' If he was honest, even five pounds seemed excessive to Mountjoy, but he knew that this was probably not the time to say it.

'I imagine...' Reilly started warily.

'What?'

'I imagine we could approach Gower. I'm sure he'd have an idea of the market rate.'

'Gower?'

'The critic.'

'I know who he is. I'm surprised you mention his name. That's all.' Remembering that he had heard Gower's name invoked only disparagingly in the past, Mountjoy was surprised that Reilly had brought him up. The name wounded him, as if he could feel some of Reilly's pain. But he acknowledged that Gower was probably the best man for the job and might even bring some much-needed attention to the exhibition. But Mountjoy was unhappy with the suggestion knowing, as he did, that this was the first faltering step Reilly had taken on his own. Soon he would stand on his own two feet and surely then it wouldn't be long before he would be lost to him and to Old Cross forever.

So, with a heavy heart, Mountjoy accepted the task of contacting Gower and asking him to value Reilly's work. Reilly thanked him and left the coffee shop with Nimrod in tow. Mountjoy cleared the pans from the range and put up the closed sign. He looked at the bare, filth-blackened walls of his coffee shop and tried to visualize how they would appear with Reilly's work on them. For the first time the walls looked very drab and the grey undercoat of the door and window frame seemed to chide him for his penny pinching. Whatever the season, the exterior of the coffee shop would always belong to the winter.

TWO

The Critic Calls

TWO DAYS LATER GOWER'S APPROACH ALONG THE STREET WAS signalled by a cry of alarm. He had stumbled slightly as he turned the corner, lost his footing, and taken a sudden sideways step into the narrow road. The cab barely missed him, the cabman shouting more in surprise than anger. Nevertheless, Gower waved the tip of his malacca cane at the departing hansom to indicate that because he was an invalid the driver should have given him a wider berth. The driver, looking back over his shoulder, glimpsed the black-clad critic in his sealskin-trimmed coat and silk hat. He looked like an angry jackdaw, one foot up on the pavement, the other in the gutter. The cabman returned his attention to the street ahead of him. When next he cast a quick look back, the man was on the pavement, leaning on his cane, his spine arched, peering up towards the sky (this being a poor, dense district, views of the clouds were limited).

In fact Gower was not peering towards the sky. He was looking for Reilly's window, wanting to fix the moment in his mind so that he would have something to put down later when he wrote up his journal. Since he had first encountered Reilly's work three years before he had waited for the artist to re-emerge, knowing beyond doubt that when he did the world would acknowledge him as a figure of importance, and there were few living painters about whom such a claim could be made. In the intervening period he had on many occasions held himself back from making anything but the most casual contact. He did not want to scare Reilly off. Gower had sent two letters to Reilly inviting him to exhibitions (only one of which was answered, with a polite refusal), and he had asked his publisher to send notice of the publication of his own journals (Volume Three: 1906–10), along with an invitation to the artist to attend the launch. Gower hadn't expected him to accept the invitation and indeed he didn't.

Reilly had received the invitation some days before he had finished what he considered the most important work of his career to date. It was a large piece (roughly five feet wide and four feet high), representing the view from a rear first-floor window of a substantial farmhouse built of Cotswold stone (not derelict, but neither in particularly good order). From the window a greenhouse dominated the scene and stood at the end of a short flagstoned path, just beyond the reach of the shadows. Beyond the greenhouse were the russet brick walls of a kitchen garden, the cement between the brick an ice-cream colour. The impression was of early afternoon. Some of the panes of old glass in the greenhouse were greened with damp, some were broken, and the light through these broken panes Reilly had managed to represent as distinct from the sunlight piercing the intact panes. One of the great benefits egg tempera brings to the practised painter is its ability to render subtle distinctions of light and shade. In the greenhouse, on a wooden bench, stood a large galvanized iron watering can. This lay just to the right of the centre of the canvas. Sitting beneath it on the warm paving stones, slightly dwarfed by the can because of its dominance in the perspective, was a boy in shirt sleeves and brown britches. He was looking up through one of the broken panes of glass, the impression being that he was staring towards the observer of the painting; the boy was hiding in the greenhouse, aware that the observer of the painting had seen him, but seemed to be imploring the observer not to give him away. The boy was Reilly. He titled the painting *The Crime.*

Gower's journals had not sold well, but then nobody expected them to. They were, however, as his publisher assured him, an important historical document and they would remain in print for as long as he was at the helm of the company. Publishers enjoy nautical metaphors, spending so much of their time away from the office, occasionally at sea. Volume Four (1910–12) was nearly complete, and Gower intended his discovery of Reilly to be the climax of them. Fitting then, perhaps, to have walked away and left the story hanging there – the inference available to be drawn by the reader. But Gower was not Reilly, had nothing of the complexities, insecurities and contradictions of an artist about him, so he rang the bell and waited to be let in. Nobody answered. He rang again. Still nobody answered. Joseph, the young academic who tenanted the room closest to the front door, had made it known that he was not interested in the job of unpaid doorman, hence would only interrupt his studies and answer the door if he was expecting a guest himself. As a result, unless an appointment was made with one of the tenants, visitors rarely found their way in.

The door remaining unanswered, Gower, an impatient and intolerant individual, would under any other circumstances have walked away. But he was excited at the prospect of seeing how Reilly's work had developed. Although he was intending to offer a fair valuation, he was hoping to secure some of the best pictures for himself. He maintained his lifestyle not by the paltry rewards of criticism but by investing in the early works of artists he promoted.

Gower's gouty leg ached. He had passed a small drinking den at the corner of a street but the sound of the polyphone from the Saloon Bar told him all he needed to know about the clientele. He would never get out of there alive. But just as he was considering how undignified it would seem to rest by sitting on the pavement, the front door opened, and a woman emerged with a small, foul-smelling bundle of child in her arms – one of the second-floor tenants. She hurried away, glancing towards the critic as if his presence had in some way impeded her journey. Gower existed in a small world where decency and deference (to him) were the usually observed courtesies. When he ventured beyond this world and encountered anything resembling hostility it unsettled him. He was, however, always drawn to the women who frequented these far boundaries of society; another reason a visit to Old Cross was not entirely unwelcome.

Gower entered the hallway and was assailed by the smell of damp walls, foul lavatories and stale food. From the brief correspondence he had had with Reilly over the summer exhibition he knew that he lived and worked at the top of the building, so he prepared himself for the climb. At each landing he paused for a few moments to get his breath back. When he reached Reilly's door he waited, composing himself. As a critic he was conditioned to view those he encountered in both his private and professional life with disdain. This would not do in the presence of genuine talent. He heard a movement behind the door, a creaking of floorboards, the urgent padding of a dog. He heard the rush of water as a tap was opened. He heard a voice. He knocked. A pause. That voice again. Footsteps on boards. Then the door was snatched open and Reilly was revealed – his face older, but more alive than Gower remembered, his eyes wide with expectation. In his left hand a teacup of water, in his right, a brush. A thin, mangy dog cowered behind the protection of his legs.

'Good evening, Reilly,' Gower said, transferring his cane from his right hand to his left before advancing towards Reilly with his free hand outstretched.

'Yes. Yes, Gower. It's you.' Reilly put down his brush, wiped his palm on his trousers, took the critic's hand and shook it. He had been interrupted at his work and he always emerged from it as he did from a dream. He shook his head to rid himself of the wild energy of creativity.

'Should I come in?' Gower asked him.

'Do. Please. Yes. Do.' Reilly stood aside and Gower walked in. The first thing he saw was the back of the easel, which dominated the room. The rear of the panel Reilly was currently working on was visible. To the right of it was a tall makeshift shelf on which stood several jam jars of sable brushes and tiny glass pots. A mattress lay at the edge of the triangle of space afforded by the sloping roof. Gower looked round and took in the struts of the roof, the chimney breast stained by russet patches of damp, a wash stand, a gas burner (new) on which stood an old kettle, a mahogany cupboard and a wooden table scattered with coins and crumbs as if the artist intended to lure birds to it. The mahogany veneer of the table surface was lifted by damp. The only thing competing with the easel in size and dominance was a large rack of unfinished wood, built into the right eaves of the roof. Ranged in the rack, just the edges visible, were, to Gower's excitement, a number of boards – perhaps thirty or forty. The room was a study in neat, barely controlled chaos.

'You've been working hard, Reilly,' Gower said with approval, approaching the rack.

'It's… all I have. All I am.'

'Indeed.' Gower, his gout forgotten, placed his hand on Reilly's arm and guided him to the only chair in the room. Then he set his cane against the chimney breast and slid one of the smaller panels out from the rack. He held it at arm's length; almost no weight at all. Autumn. A grey walled garden some time late in the day. A street light (on closer inspection a gas light), unlit. Muted colours of the autumnal garden. The promise of winter in the empty flowerbeds. Melancholy as life. It spoke to Gower just as Reilly's first canvas had done: driving hard and direct into his heart. Now it was Gower's turn to sit, and Reilly allowed him the flimsy chair. Nimrod watched as the two men seemed to have become overwhelmed by grief. Reilly rarely cried, except occasionally at the completion of a canvas and sometimes at night, but never in company. It was beyond the animal's understanding, so he sat and waited for the emotion to pass, unsure what bearing it would have on his next meal.

When Gower finally composed himself, he said: 'You studied under Hart?'

'Yes. Yes, I did. I was at L'Académie Julian for a while but I didn't get on with Laurens – and then another student suggested Hart could help me, so I attended one of his *croquis* classes.'

'He inspired you?'

'I'm… I'm unsure whether I liked him much. But his enthusiasm… I particularly valued his pictorial composition class. We all did. He'd set us a subject the previous session and then gauge our efforts, placing the one he considered the most successful on the easel closest to the door. The others were ranked accordingly along the wall – only those that had, in his opinion, achieved balance, proportion, rhythm, earned a place on the easels. The others were left on the floor.' Reilly's eyes strayed to the boards in the rack, all carefully replaced by Gower.

'I imagine he'd have a great deal to say about your recent efforts. Tempera is a demanding medium.' Gower stood, buttoned his bulky coat, and took his cane from where it rested.

'Thank you for coming to see me,' Reilly said.

'The pleasure was mine. You'll hear from me tomorrow.' Gower took one more look around the room, patted his chest, nodded twice and, carrying the impression of the room with him, left Reilly's studio for the first and last time.

THREE

Reilly, the Agony of Creativity and the Arrival of the Authorities

'WELL?' MOUNTJOY DEMANDED WHEN REILLY ARRIVED AT THE coffee shop two days later. But the artist didn't reply. Instead he walked stoop-shouldered to his favoured seat at the window and slumped into it.

'Well?' Mountjoy addressed Nimrod more lightly, but Nimrod seemed as out of sorts as his master. His tail did not wag. His eyes were dull and lifeless. He lay down disconsolately on the floor beside the counter, rested his jaw on his crossed forepaws and stared into space, his breathing slow. Mountjoy waited, anticipating some ruse cooked up by them both – one in which both Reilly and Nimrod would suddenly spring to life, Reilly brandishing a price list in the air. But artist and companion seemed to have been blighted by the same terrible experience.

Mountjoy filled a teapot from the kettle. There was nothing to be gained by rushing Reilly. He had encountered him in such a mood many times before – it often prefigured a major breakthrough in his work. Only tea could save him now – coffee was much too brutal a remedy for a man in his condition. On the hob bacon sizzled wetly in a frying pan. A tiny jet of fat ejaculated from a frying sausage, bringing the sausage briefly to life. It rocked on its belly with mirth and then settled again. Mountjoy closed the pot, placed it on a small tin tray, found a cup and saucer and took the lot over to Reilly, who continued to stare at the wall.

'Are you unwell?' Mountjoy asked.

'Me? No, I'm not unwell.'

'Out of sorts, then?'

'Oh, yes. Very much out of sorts.' Reilly looked at the pot as if he had some vague memory of its function but to operate it was beyond him.

'Would you prefer to be left alone?'

'No. Sit down.'

So Mountjoy sat and poured the tea. He slid the cup across the table into the harbour of Reilly's arms. Reilly watched the silver steam rise from the brick-brown liquid. A hansom passed along the street and the liquid shuddered. Reilly thought of underground streams, caverns beneath the earth and the brevity of life. He lifted the cup and felt the heat of the tea through the pads of his fingers.

'Has something occurred?' Mountjoy prompted.

'Yes. Yes it has.' Reilly put down the tea cup, looked directly at Mountjoy and said: 'I've had no word from Gower.'

Mountjoy waited, but that seemed to be the full extent of Reilly's concern.

Reilly went on: 'He called. Two days ago. He took some notes, measurements and suchlike. And then he left with the promise that he would return the following day with the valuation. Since then, nothing.'

'So you anticipated the valuations yesterday?'

'That was the promise he made to me. Yes.'

'I'm sure there's an explanation.'

'Of course there is. That's the issue. The explanation is that he found the work unworthy of valuation.'

'No!'

'I'm afraid so.'

'Did he give any indication of his thoughts when he came to see you?'

'None. Critics are well versed in obfuscation. Few are prepared to trust their judgement alone. I imagine he returned home, called up his inner circle. They met. He described the work and shortly afterwards – by common agreement – my reputation was in tatters. I tell you, Mountjoy, the whole thing has paralysed me. I'm fit for nothing now. You might as well dig a hole in the floor and bury me now. My life is over.'

'But...'

'I wouldn't expect you to understand. How could... how could anybody understand who hasn't been through this whole tortuous, agonizing, solitary process?'

'Well...'

But Reilly needed no further prompting. 'Three years. Longer. Five years. Longer still. Working alone, day after day, dredging for inspiration, picking away at any old scab I can find. Each day the terror that it's all over. Finished. That I have nothing more to say. Can you imagine?'

'I...'

'But worse than that. Much worse, the fear that what I do have to say is no good: old, tired, said before but much better... each day confronting that fear but pressing on. Do you begin to understand?'

'I do. And I'm sorry.'

'I can't begin to describe the daily agony of facing that canvas and wondering if the gift (such as it is) has disappeared in the night. Every day begins with having to relearn what you were confident you knew only the night before. Picture yourself facing a similar predicament.'

Mountjoy did so.

'…I tell you, Mountjoy, it is agony. Small wonder most serious artists drown themselves in drink and barely sleep.'

Mountjoy was now genuinely concerned for Reilly, but there was nothing in his experience he could call on to help him. The coffee-shop door opened, triggering the bell. A policeman entered.

'Forgive me, Reilly. I have a customer.'

Reilly nodded – he had no further use of an audience. Nimrod pretended a lack of interest towards the customer but when the policeman reached down and ruffled the fur at the nape of his neck he stood, shook himself, and seemed to have returned to life.

Mountjoy, now back at the business side of the counter, looked up at the man, who seemed to be at least six and a half feet tall. His uniform was standard issue of the Metropolitan force but he wore it well. The trousers were crisply pressed and his brass buttons gleamed. It seemed to Mountjoy that the man was also wearing scent, although it might only have been a perfumed soap.

'I'm looking for a man called Reilly,' the constable announced. 'An artist. I understand he frequents this coffee shop?'

'You're looking for Reilly?' Mountjoy said, loudly enough to ensure the artist had heard the mention of his name. Reilly looked up guiltily.

'Yes. Do you know him?'

'I do. Very well. Can I ask what this is in connection with?'

'You can ask but unless your name is Reilly I can't tell you.'

'I see.' Stalemate. Mountjoy didn't want to make any trouble for himself; equally, if Reilly was in trouble, he felt he owed it to him to buy him some time. He therefore waited for the artist to identify himself. He had no plans beyond that, should Reilly choose not to. Thankfully, at that moment, Reilly stood and approached the constable, saying, 'I'm Reilly.' The arrival of the authorities had distracted him from his misery.

The policeman took a quick inventory of Reilly's appearance, mentally checking it against what he knew about the case. 'I have a number of questions. Would you prefer to address them in private?'

'No. I have nothing to hide from Mountjoy.'

'Very well. Perhaps we should take a seat, then.' The policeman at this point deferred to Mountjoy. Figures of authority are usually sensitive to the limited authority of others, and occasionally nurture it. The effect of this flattery is rapidly to win people over, and sure enough Mountjoy emerged from the counter, cleared a table in the centre of the room, wiped it with his filthy cloth and encouraged first the policeman, and then Reilly to sit down. He moved away, but remained just within earshot as the policeman took out a notebook and opened it.

'You're a painter, I understand?' the policeman asked.

'That's right,' Reilly said firmly.

'You make a living?'

'I live, as many artists do, relying in part on the charity of others.'

'By which I take it you mean you don't make a living?'

'Not in the sense that I earn sufficient from my paintings to pay for my few needs.'

'Then how do you pay for those needs?'

'Does this have anything to do with why you're here?'

'Possibly. Possibly not.'

'Am I obliged to answer?'

'Not if you choose not to.' The policeman smiled sadly, and Reilly regretted the tone he had taken. The police are prone to melancholia, having witnessed more depravities than many of us. But the opportunity for Reilly to win him over had gone.

He glanced briefly at his notebook before asking, 'Do you know a man called Gower?'

'Gower?' Reilly said.

'Yes. Gower.'

'I do know a Gower, yes.'

'For the moment we'll assume it's the same gentleman.' The policeman again looked at his notebook, then said, 'A critic, so I understand.'

'Yes.'

'And you know him how?'

'Strictly in a professional capacity.'

'Nothing beyond that?'

'No.'

'And have you seen Gower recently?'

Reilly paused, wondering if for some reason admitting to Gower's visit would incriminate him. 'Why are you interested in what I know about Gower?'

'We'll come to that in a moment. After you've answered the question.'

'Yes,' Reilly said, 'I have seen Gower recently. Two days ago. He visited me in connection with a forthcoming exhibition of my work. I haven't seen him since.'

'A business meeting?'

'I expect you could put it that way.'

'And roughly what time would you say he left your rooms?'

'Room.'

'Room.'

'Around, I don't know, around seven?'

'P.m.?'

'Yes.'

'And that was the last you saw of him?'

'It was.'

'And how did he appear to you?'

'He seemed… at ease.'

'At ease.' The policeman made a laborious note in his notebook then offered Reilly a wincing smile, as if he was suffering a sharp pang of indigestion. He placed the book on the table and looked around the room. When his gaze alighted on Mountjoy, the coffee shop owner smiled encouragingly. He had heard every word of the conversation.

'Well?' Reilly said.

'I've heard tell of this place,' the policeman said. 'And it more than lives up to its reputation.'

'But, Gower. You were asking about the critic.'

The policeman's attention swung sharply back to the artist. 'Disappeared.'

'Disappeared?'

'Having left home two days ago he failed to return. Your name and address were found in his engagements book.'

It's at such moments that the experienced policeman changes tack, offering no further information, asking no further questions, relying instead on the interviewee to steer the conversation. But Reilly had fallen silent.

'In the light of this you have nothing to add?' the policeman asked.

'Nothing.'

The policeman reviewed his notes. 'You suggested Gower was "at ease" when he visited you. You stand by that?'

'I do.'

'At ease when he left?'

'Indeed.'

'A cordial visit?'

'Yes.'

'So he gave you no indication he was intending to go away?'

'None.'

'Very well,' the policeman said, standing. 'There may be further questions as the investigation proceeds.'

'Of course.' Reilly stood too. The policeman nodded to Mountjoy and left the coffee shop.

'Disappeared, then?' Mountjoy said. He had never met Gower and felt nothing for him.

'So it seems,' Reilly replied. Having met Gower, he felt more for him than Mountjoy, but his shock was rooted in the gratitude he felt on hearing the news; at his own callousness. So Gower had not considered his work unworthy of valuation; he had disappeared before he had been able to commit that valuation to paper.

In the silence that followed, Mountjoy and Reilly examined the effect of Gower's disappearance on the forthcoming exhibition. The critic's support would unquestionably have guaranteed Reilly's work attention – might even have catapulted him to immediate acclaim – and the valuation would have been useful, but other than that they imagined the exhibition, just three days away now, would be unaffected. They could not have been more wrong.

Gower, languishing in the chill waters of the canal, was beyond caring.

FOUR

Samantha Dodd in Soho

IT IS TIME FOR REILLY, MOUNTJOY AND NIMROD TO RETURN TO their graves for a while because we must now advance nearly a century and introduce another individual. We encounter the young woman on the route she takes each day from her Soho office to the café where she buys her daily sandwich, two packets of crisps and two bars of chocolate; a walk which takes her along Lexington Street and past a gallery where she has a habit of pausing and looking in. She has never found the courage to enter. The paintings in there she assumes to be well beyond the range of her meagre salary and she isn't the kind of individual who would, as she considered it, waste the gallery owner's time by simply browsing. Although she was only twenty-two years old, Samantha Dodd's attitude to life had already hardened. True, she had inherited something of this attitude from her mother, but a kind and loving companion could have nurtured the gentleness and softness that lay within her. Having never found such an individual, she had begun to believe she never would. But few people see themselves as others see them, and there are as many versions of ourselves in the world as we have acquaintances. Samantha had been known well by her mother, less well by her one close school friend, and was known not at all well by her flatmate and the three other women with whom she worked in the outer office of the law firm where she was employed as a secretary. Samantha had a good eye for detail and was therefore valued by the partners. While it would be going too far to suggest that this keen eye of hers led to resentment on the part of the other women in the office, it certainly didn't endear her to them. But they would have forgiven, perhaps even applauded her abilities, was she not also regarded by them as stand-offish and disdainful. She turned down the offer of drinks with them, explaining that she didn't much enjoy pubs, didn't much like alcohol, and would prefer to go home, cook a meal and read her book. Between the women of the office her size made her a target for derision. It never occurred to Samantha that she was overweight, or that, despite her size, without exception the men in the office found her physically appealing, just as it didn't occur to her that since her mother's recent death she was regarded as being lonely or that her posture would be improved by a better-fitting bra. What did get her out of bed in the morning was the sense that there was some bigger role in the world waiting for her, something that her life up to this point had been preparing her for. So, when she returned home to read each night, she was happy to fold her legs beneath her on the large comfortable chair, her teacup and chocolates within reach, as she sat warmly under the cone of light from the standard lamp.

It was the habit of the Lexington Street gallery to feature a single painting on an easel in the window. Each week that painting would be changed for another in the exhibition. Exhibitions tended to run for a month which meant that, over their course, four paintings by a single artist would be available for close inspection from the pavement. For one month a year, however, often September, the gallery would mount a more eclectic show featuring the work of a selection of artists that had come into the possession of the gallery owner during his travels. Some of these canvases would be contemporary, some older, having been bought at auction.

This being 1 September, Samantha was peering in at the new exhibition for the first time. She had a habit (such was her orderly mind) of beginning her inspection at the far right top corner of the gallery wall. She would then examine the paintings mounted highest along the right hand wall, then return her gaze, like an old-fashioned typewriter carriage, to the centre of the right hand wall, make a second sweep, and then do the same with the paintings mounted on the lower tier. This is not to suggest that the canvases were hung in orderly rows and were a uniform size. The gallery owner (Keith Blake) had a good eye for showing art and tended to hang pieces sympathetic to one another. He would even go so far as to guarantee a painter which of his works would sell first solely by how he had arranged them on the wall. One of his other tricks was to put something eye-catching in a small alcove at the rear of the shop. The alcove was large enough to house a medium-sized canvas and was the only part of the gallery that needed strong light. Samantha always saved this painting for last – as a treat. She would rarely allow herself an opinion on her first visit. She believed that art needed to be slept on, allowed the distance of time, so that one could judge not just the impact it had on the conscious mind but how deep into the subconscious it had penetrated. She adopted the same approach with books, eschewing those she picked up and felt the author urging her, by the sly withholding of detail, to turn the page. Not that she disapproved of plot, she just didn't like too much of it cluttering up the lives of the characters.

So, on this day, 1 September, having seen all but one of the paintings in the new exhibition, she finally turned her attention to the piece in the alcove. It was a small picture, no more than a foot square, which made the detail of it difficult to discern from a distance. But immediately she felt compelled to press her face closer to the gallery window so that her forehead was resting against the cold glass, her breath flaring the pane. What she saw was a grey walled garden late in the day. A street light (on closer inspection a gas light), unlit. Muted colours of the autumnal garden. The promise of winter in the flowerbeds. Melancholy as life. It spoke to Samantha Dodd as no other painting had done: bypassing her intellect, driving hard and direct into her heart. She wanted that painting, whatever it took. In a trance she stepped away from the glass, approached the door of the gallery and for the first time went in.

The girl at the desk looked up from her screen and saw Samantha sleepwalking towards her. So intent was she, the girl thought it unwise to challenge her. The girl was filling in before college so didn't adopt the superciliousness of many who work in galleries when confronted with visitors who clearly don't have the means to pay for the work on the walls. She watched the young woman approach the painting and stand some three feet away from it; she seemed afraid to take her eyes from it in case it disappeared.

Politely, but without deference, the girl at the desk said, 'It's a beautiful picture, isn't it?' She rose and came to stand beside Samantha, who was three inches shorter and considerably broader.

'It's wonderful.'

'Egg tempera on gesso ground. It's called *Damp Path*.'

For a moment there was silence until Samantha asked, 'Who is it by?', her voice reverential.

'The artist is T. F. Reilly.' The girl had filled the long hours of inactivity in the gallery logged into Facebook. Out of curiosity and boredom she had, however, devoted some time to learning the names of the artists of all of the pieces on the walls.

'Riley?'

'I'm afraid I don't know anything about him. I did Google him but I couldn't find anything. I'm sure Keith will. He'll be here tomorrow if you'd like to ask him.'

'...And how much is it?'

The girl returned to her screen, leaned down and consulted the price list. 'Seven thousand four hundred pounds.'

Samantha had known the price would be beyond her reach but she thanked the girl anyway, left the gallery and returned to work. The afternoon passed slowly, the only thing on her mind how she was going to get hold of the money to buy Reilly's painting. She was so distracted that Anita, the kindly receptionist at the office, commented that she looked unwell. For the first time in her professional life she lied, and took the opportunity Anita offered her to leave work early. She returned to the gallery. But the gallery was closed, as it occasionally was in the afternoon, the opening hours being eccentric. For half an hour Samantha stood at the window peering at the painting, which seemed now to be calling out to her with a sense of abandonment she could hardly bear.

Then she returned home. There were two things occupying her now. The first was how she could raise the money to buy the painting. The second, how she could find the artist. This was the quest she had been waiting for.

FIVE

Taking the Skin for a Walk

REILLY WAS WORKING AT HIS CLUTTERED TABLE, A SINGLE LANCE of sun through the skylight illuminating and warming his right knuckle. Nimrod was lying on the floor beside him and chewing the fold of cured skin he'd brought back from his walk three evenings before. Surrounding Reilly were his pictures propped against the walls, the legs of the easel, the door, the sink, and the roof; images from the multi-coloured world conjured by the artist's fertile imagination. On the floor at his feet were several crumpled pieces of manuscript paper he'd discarded during the three hours he'd been sitting at the table, his temper worsening.

'This is all extremely difficult,' Reilly said. Nimrod indicated a flicker of interest by briefly raising his head. He then returned to his chewing, and Reilly to the creamy paper on his table, running his pen nib down the list and counting. He then, silently, but moving his lips, counted the canvases in the room, in turn pointing the wooden stem of his quill pen towards each one.

'Thirty-seven,' he announced. 'And thirty-seven on the list. Good. The numbers tally. Well, it's the best I can do, though how any artist can be expected to give a true valuation of his worth is beyond me.' Exhausted by his endeavours, Reilly yawned, picked up the paper, blotted it, folded it in half, then put it into the inside pocked of his jacket and stood.

'We'll need assistance getting these to the coffee shop. I doubt Mountjoy will have given the matter any thought.' Reilly stretched out his arms, scratched the back of his head with his fingernails and approached the board on the easel. He tended to approach his work with caution, sometimes with deference, occasionally with awe. This wasn't arrogance or even vanity, it was a simple matter of objective fact.

The painting on the easel was the finished study of Amy Sykes reclining on Reilly's mattress, fully clothed, the shadow of Nimrod in the bottom right corner. He felt he had caught Amy's insouciance well and had not, as she had requested, made her look old. But when Reilly had taken the board from the easel the picture seemed to be demanding further attention, so he returned it there. No work of art after all is ever truly complete, only abandoned, often in frustration. Reilly, however, couldn't now see what it was about the painting that seemed to need mending, so he spent a few moments longer admiring it, then took it down and leaned it against the wall. It was at that moment he realized he hadn't given the picture a title. Sometimes paintings coalesce around a title; more often than not a title is awarded on completion. The shadow of Nimrod caught his eye, so, in pencil, he named it on the rear of the board. As an afterthought he wrote 'For Amy Sykes', though he had no intention of presenting the portrait to her, only that she was the dedicatee.

Nimrod raised himself to his feet, strolled over and took a brief look at the picture. He then returned to the warm spot on the floorboards and lay down again. On the floor beside him was a thick, folded rectangle of leather – approximately four inches by three inches – of a mahogany colour, tentatively chewed.

'I imagine we could borrow a barrow,' Reilly mused. 'But we'll have to post a guard while we carry the paintings down the stairs.'

An opinion seemed to have been sought so Nimrod, still lying on the floor, chose to offer an encouraging wag of his tail. The root of it thumped against the floor.

'And if we are to borrow a barrow we should set about procuring one soon.'

It was then that Reilly noticed the brown rectangle on the floor.

'What have you got there, old chum?' Reilly asked, leaning down and picking it up. 'A wallet?' Unfolding it, he pulled out a thick wad of coloured notes. 'Good grief! Where on earth did you get this?' Reilly fanned out the notes. Nimrod dutifully stood and offered another vigorous wag of his tail before looking coyly towards his master.

'Where did you get it?' Reilly repeated.

It wasn't often that Reilly's questions of Nimrod demanded anything but the animal's vague assent or a general indication of interest. Nimrod put his head on one side, then the other.

'Where?' Reilly was now gesticulating towards the hallway with the wallet. 'Show me where you found it, old chum.' Now he opened the door: a clear signal he was expecting Nimrod to follow him. Reilly left the room. Dutifully, Nimrod trotted after him down the stairs. They reached the street door. Reilly led the way out. It was a chilly, grey summer's afternoon. Autumn approached. Reilly closed the door behind them and pushed the skin towards Nimrod's face, then drew it back and gestured first one way up the street and then the other.

'Where did you find it?' Reilly said. 'Where?'

Nimrod led off in the direction of the canal and Reilly fell into step behind him. He proceeded at a gentle pace because he knew his master was easily diverted; whenever they went out together they tended to stop at least four or five times so that Reilly could peer into a shop window, lean down to tie his shoelace, or sometimes pick up a twig, a pebble, or an occasional coin from the gutter. They crossed two narrow street junctions, turned left along the appropriately named Canal Street, went down the damp steps by the bridge (always in shadow), and set off south along the canal towpath. A rat plopped into the water and the echo sang from the brickwork of the bridge. They paused to watch it sculling across to the far bank, its feet chalking quivering lines on the surface of the water. A short distance farther along the towpath Nimrod stopped and looked around.

'Here, old chum?' Reilly asked him, looking up and then down the towpath. 'You found it here?'

Nimrod had paused because there was, close at hand, a source of food: flesh, something animal, the faecal tang of decay, river water, mud, fresh blood. Reilly seemed to have become aware of it, too, because he was now standing on the edge of the bank and looking down the three-foot drop into the canal. Nimrod joined him. Their reflections (thin, poorly dressed young man, elderly thin dog; a poignant study in loneliness) quivered as the breeze idly tousled the water. Below them, from somewhere in the lee of the bank, there came a commotion of high-pitched squeals of anger and gluttony.

'What on earth is that?' Reilly continued to peer into the water but he could see nothing. 'Rats?' He shivered with revulsion, then, without warning, he started off, back towards the bridge, calling, 'Come along. We'll go and see Mountjoy. Kill two birds with one stone: I'm sure he'll be able to advise us on the wallet, and I can deliver the price list to him.' Reilly patted the pocket of his jacket to ensure the list was still in there, then set off. Nimrod fell obediently into step, leaving the rats to go about their macabre business in peace.

When they got to the coffee shop a sign-writer on a tall ladder was engaged in painting Mountjoy's name onto the fascia. The cornice, pilaster, mullions, sills, stall riser and the doorway itself had already been given a fresh coat of green. Inside, Mountjoy could be seen standing on a bowed plank suspended precariously between two stepladders. Over his shirt and trousers he was wearing a bibbed overall. In his left hand he held a pail of whitewash. He was applying the whitewash to the wall with a wide brush and little finesse, which pained Reilly as he watched. He knocked on the window. Mountjoy turned, cheerfully gestured his brush towards the artist as if for some reason Reilly couldn't work out for himself what he was doing, climbed down one of the ladders and let them in.

'I'm preparing the establishment for the exhibition,' Mountjoy announced grandly. The walls, previously mustard in colour with decades of smoke and grime, were now streaked with unevenly applied white-wash. Because he hadn't troubled to wash down the walls first, the patchy whitewash, drawing out the filth, was already discoloured. The floor was awash with paint and the ladders and board looked like they had been left outside in a snowstorm – as did Mountjoy.

'Perhaps, when the wash has dried…' Reilly said.

'Indeed. Indeed.' Now it was Mountjoy's turn to look at the walls and, from this distance, see them as they really were. He had, as so often in his life, been carried along by his good intentions, fully expecting his enthusiasm to override his shortcomings. 'I'll allow it to dry, and then apply another coat.' Mountjoy looked again at the far wall, his face now pinched with disappointment.

Reilly couldn't bear to see his agony. Mountjoy's face exhibited the world's bruises too vividly. 'I have the list of prices,' Reilly said, in an attempt to cheer him up. He drew it from his pocket.

'Still no word from Gower?' Mountjoy rubbed the palm of his paint-specked hand on his overall knee and took it from him.

'Nothing.'

Mountjoy ran down the list of titles and prices. He was pleased to see that there were three paintings at two pounds and ten shillings, which he thought might actually have the chance of selling, given a bit of luck. He had no hopes for any of the others unless the newspaper coverage attracted a better-heeled clientele than the regulars at the coffee shop, few of whom brought in much over two hundred pounds a year. When he looked up again, ready to praise Reilly for his efforts and his penmanship, he saw the artist taking something else from his pocket and placing it carefully at the centre of the table.

'What have you got there?' Mountjoy asked. From the way Reilly had got it out, he was immediately on his guard.

'A wallet,' Reilly announced as if the object was a rarity.

'Yes,' Mountjoy concurred. 'I can see it's a wallet. Presumably not your wallet?'

In reply, with some drama, Reilly opened the fold and Mountjoy saw the white wad of notes against the leather like the flesh inside a halved fruit.

'That's a… a great deal of money,' Mountjoy said, his mouth suddenly dry. 'Where did it come from?'

'From the canal bank. Nimrod found it.'

'Did he?'

Hearing his name, Nimrod came to stand beside Reilly's chair.

'With more than a hundred and fifty pounds in it.'

Mountjoy nodded and repeated the sum.

'We should take it to the police station, I expect,' Reilly suggested.

Mountjoy didn't much like the way he'd immediately become a conspirator, but he expected no less of Reilly. 'I'm sure you should,' Mountjoy said. 'Peculiar, though…'

'What?'

'The owner of the wallet – a man of such substance – walking the canal towpath. In fact a man of such substance walking anywhere.'

'I hadn't considered that,' Reilly said. 'Perhaps he was up to no good.'

'Yes, and perhaps he was attacked as he was up to no good.'

'…And fled, losing his wallet in the process?'

'Indeed. Indeed. In which case…'

'What are you suggesting?'

'I'm suggesting nothing.'

'I thought you might be suggesting...'

'What?'

'Surely you can understand the temptation...'

'Of course.'

'...Because if the fellow was up to no good then perhaps the money wasn't his after all.'

'Stolen?'

'Or extorted.'

'No,' Mountjoy said with some force. 'No, Reilly. It won't do. You must take this wallet immediately to the police station and hand it in.'

'Of course. Of course. That was my intention all along.'

Why then, at that moment, as the police constable walked into the coffee shop, did Reilly snatch the wallet and put it into his pocket? He would later argue that it was because he felt ashamed that he had even considered keeping the money for himself – that he was afraid that handing it to the policeman would somehow imply he had taken it. After all, what was he doing sitting talking to Mountjoy when he should already be at the counter of the police station reporting the finding of a wallet on the canal bank? As for Mountjoy, he would later argue that had he been the one to mention the wallet to the constable, this would have reflected badly on Reilly. Reilly, having found the wallet, had to be the one who handed it in.

Both men, then, looked suitably guilty as the tall policeman approached them.

SIX

Samantha Dodd Changes Employment

AFTER FALLING IN LOVE WITH REILLY'S PAINTING, SAMANTHA WAS to be found most mornings staring through the gallery window, again at lunchtimes, and again in the evening. Each time she returned there she expected the gallery to have reopened but since the day she had first encountered Reilly's painting it had remained closed. In her fanciful imagination it was as if a door to a magic kingdom that had once been open had now swung shut again. The worst of it was that the gallery remained dark save for the single light illuminating the painting on the window easel. It was this alone that gave her hope. If the business had been sold, or become bankrupted, or had some tragedy befallen the owner, then surely the light would have been turned off.

Samantha continued to turn up for work, but her eye for detail seemed to have deserted her. Mistakes mounted. She was called in to see the senior partner, the elderly and appropriately named Tubman, who had intended to counsel her kindly, but because of her disdainful attitude, ended up rebuking her, telling her to buck up her ideas, and giving notice that this was a formal warning and if her work didn't improve then she'd find herself looking for alternative employment. She forced herself to concentrate on her duties not through any sense of loyalty but because she needed the income.

By the time the third week of September came around and the mail had mounted high behind the gallery door Samantha decided to take matters into her own hands. She did what she should have done at the beginning. She wrote down the telephone number painted on the gallery door and at lunchtime, after the other women had gone out for their soup, she called it from her office. The number rang six times and then clicked to the answerphone. A man's voice informed her that there was nobody available to take her call and invited her to leave a message. Just as she was about to do so, as an afterthought, the man suggested that should the caller need to reach him urgently they could 'do worse' than try his mobile. Samantha wrote down the number. The voice on the answerphone was undoubtedly that of Keith Blake, the gallery owner. He sounded, she thought, somewhat chaotic, but there was an archness in his tone that appealed to her. And any man with the sensitivity to find and display such a painting as T. F. Reilly's was surely worth getting to know. It is said that women fall for men who make them laugh, men who can cook, men adept at playing musical instruments. Keith had courted Samantha with the careful selection of paintings he displayed in his gallery. Slowly but surely he had won her over. So when she dialled the mobile phone number she was nervous because there was more than the ownership of a painting invested in the outcome of the call.

The phone rang twice and was then answered. 'Yes?… Oh, just a minute. Wait a moment, please.'

Samantha heard the phone being put down onto a hard surface.

There was a pause and then three loud sneezes, a curse, then a wracking cough. The phone was picked up again and Keith, weakly, defeated, said, 'Yes?'

'You poor man,' Samantha said. 'You're ill.'

'I am ill. Dreadfully ill.'

'How long have you been ill?'

'Nearly four weeks. In another week I believe I qualify as an invalid.'

'And are you alone?'

'Utterly.'

'Well, you shouldn't be alone. Not in your condition.'

'I asked for the doctor to call, but you know how hard it is nowadays to lure any member of the medical profession out of the surgery. The receptionist told me I was over-dramatizing. Me! I told her she clearly didn't know me.'

'So the doctor didn't call?'

'Of course not. I was allotted two minutes of his valuable time over the telephone. He informed me I had the flu. That I should stay in bed and drink plenty of liquids. Wretched man.' There was a pause, after which Keith finally got round to asking who was calling. The woman on the line seemed to know him and was being dutifully sympathetic – which was an endearing trait, implying, as it did, a certain malleability and eagerness to please – but he couldn't place the voice.

'My name is Samantha Dodd.'

'I see. Samantha Dodd. Well, as you can hear, it's doubtful I'll be able to help you with whatever you're calling about – at least for the foreseeable future.'

'No. But I could help you.'

'Could you? In what way?'

'Well, do you have any cough medicine?'

'None at all. I've run out.'

'I'll bring some round for you.'

'But why should you want to do that? Are you auditioning for the social services?'

'No. I'm a secretary.'

'A secretary?'

'…Hello?'

'Yes, I'm still here,' Keith said. He had been wondering, uncharitably, snobbishly, as was his wont, what his mystery caller looked like.

'…And it's not entirely unselfish. I want to talk to you about one of the pictures in your gallery.'

'Well, if it's business, I suppose…'

'I won't stay long. I promise.'

'All right.'

'Can I have your address?'

Keith gave it. Samantha wrote it down, telling him she'd be there after work. Keith thanked her and put down the phone, only then wondering how wise it had been to invite a complete stranger to his home. Beyond discovering the woman's name and profession, he hadn't the faintest idea of who he'd been talking to. She was a secretary. It seemed an outdated profession, like lamplighter. He thought it unlikely that a secretary would be able to afford any of the work in his gallery. But it was a measure of how depleted he had become that he didn't unduly care why she wanted to see him. He needed to see another human being. He craved love and attention and he didn't care where they came from.

Samantha was unsurprised she hadn't had to explain herself any more fully to Keith. They had talked as if they had known each other all their lives. Following the death of her mother she had always known she would be capable of caring for another human being; only now had she perhaps found somebody worthy of her care. So, after the agonizingly long afternoon, she walked past the gallery to the Underground station and caught the Tube to Old Cross, which necessitated a change at Paddington. She emerged from the Underground station into a suburb of London she had never before visited. The air seemed two or three degrees warmer than the district in which she worked. The shops, too, were more eccentric and individual than those in her locality, all of which gave her the sense of getting off a plane in a foreign country. Outside a grocer's were vegetables she'd never encountered before: multi-coloured, huge and comically phallic. Several corpulent sacks of rice lolled beside them on the pavement. From the dim interior the smell of spices was a tantalizing mix of the exotic and illicit. Next door to the grocer's, there was an Internet café with ill-painted window frames. A card Blu-tacked to the window offered 'Mobile phone unlocking'. Inside were twenty or so student-aged multinationals sitting in three ranks and concentrating on their screens as attentively as if they were taking an exam. A woman sat at the top table, seemingly invigilating. Keith had mentioned the Internet café as a landmark. A Polish delicatessen was next door, and beyond that a more traditional café. The exterior of the building seemed to be undergoing refurbishment; it was clad in scaffolding and a man loitered on the top boards, smoking a cigarette and looking out across the rooftops towards the salmon-coloured dusk. Inside the café were two customers, a man and an elderly woman. The man was wearing a shiny cheap suit of silver grey cloth, cut very tight to his body. The woman, leather shopping bag at her feet, was rubbing the fabric of his sleeve between finger and thumb. She was smiling. For a change her son had done something to warrant her love in him. That, at least, was how Samantha Dodd chose to read the scene. Passing the café, she turned left as Keith had directed on the phone, turned right at a pub (The Dog Tray), from which she could hear the sound of sports commentary from a large television, and then she walked down Canal Street. She was immediately aware of the moisture in the air as a welcome softness against the toxins on her palate. Keith's house was on Ladysmith Road, second left off Canal Street. The houses were neat, terraced, red-bricked and Edwardian. Soon she was standing at his front door, the unused knocker sticky with old cobwebs. Only then did her nerve falter. But she struck the knocker three times and heard several sneezes from inside in response. The lean man who opened the door was wearing a blue quilted dressing gown and red scarf. He looked to be in his mid to late forties, with thinning black hair. With a full head of hair he would have been passably handsome and might have looked ten years younger. His face was angular; rakish.

'Keith Blake?' she said. 'I'm Samantha Dodd.' She offered her hand to be shaken. She knew it was an absurdly formal gesture, and she could see he did, too, but as he hadn't taken the initiative she felt it was up to her. Keith took it, unsmilingly (his was rather clammy, his fingers long and fragile like a piano player), and stood aside, inviting her in. She paused in the hallway as he closed the door, deciding that it was probably best to explain her reason for being there. She didn't want any awkwardness to cloud her first visit. So she told him as briefly as she could about the visit to the gallery, and seeing Reilly's painting for the first time, concluding, 'I just… fell in love with it, really. It's never happened to me before.'

'Well, I can understand why. It's a wonderful picture.'

Samantha could see that Keith approved of her reaction to it. For the first time he showed pleasure on his face, though it stopped short of a smile.

'And I'd like to buy it.'

'Good.'

'But I just don't have the money. Not at the moment.'

'…Ah.'

'And I was worried, you see, because since that day the gallery's been closed.'

'Yes, well, there's an explanation for that. Please, come in,' Keith said, expending his remaining reserves of energy in leading them into the sitting room. He no longer seemed suspicious of her motives but now there was no prospect of a sale, nor did he seem to feel the need to act as host. Perhaps that was her fault. She had volunteered to help him so perhaps she should now be volunteering to make the tea. Keith slumped onto the scuffed leather sofa, which was scattered with used tissues, and pulled a tartan rug over his pyjama-clad legs. On the floor beside the sofa Samantha counted seven tea mugs, three crumbed plates, a number of brown apple cores, several broadsheet newspapers and an open, empty biscuit tin. Choral music emanated politely from a large digital radio, also on the floor. There was no television in the room and all of the alcoves were taken with bookshelves. Samantha took the single chair beneath the front window, removing from it a pile of auction catalogues. She sat primly, her hands clasped in her lap.

'The girl, Terry, or Billy, or something, went off to France, or Greece, or somewhere,' Keith explained. 'One of these young people who travel everywhere carrying a huge bottle of water with her. Do you know the type I mean? It's not as though we live in a desert region. Not yet, anyway.'

Samantha smiled. She wasn't sure whether Keith wanted an audience or if she was expected to join in.

'She claims she told me but I swear she didn't,' Keith went on. 'I mean under normal circumstances I'd have gone in the following day and taken over myself, but then I was struck down with this bloody flu and therefore couldn't. Nor could I find a replacement – so the gallery is closed until further notice.'

Samantha was aware that as Keith spoke he was using the time to look her up and down. The words, she now knew, were a wash, nothing more than something to fill the silence. What she didn't know was whether this was one of Keith's traits – whether he was a habitual people watcher – or whether he'd singled her out for special treatment. It crossed her mind that he might be gay – the way his look lingered on her shoes, her knees, took in the details of her rather utilitarian and shapeless turquoise coat still buttoned tightly to her neck. Was she being written up as a story he would share with his friends at some later date – the earnest girl who had forced her way in to his sickroom with her awful clothes, he having amused himself by encouraging her to stay for a while? She shrugged the hem of her coat down as he seemed to be looking at her legs.

'...afford not to. I'll be bankrupted.'

'I'm sorry?'

'I was saying that I can't afford to leave the gallery closed for much longer. I'll be bankrupted. I mean, my sister volunteered to come down from Yorkshire to help out, but I got the feeling that her husband wasn't all that keen to be abandoned alone with the boys and I didn't like to press her.'

'I could work in your gallery,' Samantha offered, surprising herself as much as Keith.

'Work for me?'

'Yes.'

'But you said you were a secretary.'

'I am.'

'And presumably working for a reasonable wage?'

'Yes.'

'Well, why on earth should you want to come and work for what I could pay you?'

'I don't know. I just... I just think I must.'

'You think you must? I see,' Keith drawled. 'I see.'

'Yes.' Her enthusiasm built: 'There are moments in your life when you have to follow your instincts. I mean, literature is full of stories of people who haven't – and ended up miserable. So... yes, please. I'd like to work in your gallery. I know I'd be good at it. I'm very organized and I'm good at pretending to like people and I won't steal from you and I'll always open the gallery on time and never close until half past five. And I have no family left so there won't be a family crisis to deal with. I'm never ill so you won't have to worry about that.'

'But I don't even know you. You could be anybody.'

'You can trust me. I promise. I can get references from where I'm working if you want.'

'But the money…'

'Pay me what you paid Charlie or Terry or whatever her name was and give me commission on everything I sell. Say ten per cent. I'll be a good salesman.'

'Two.'

'Seven and a half.'

'No. I couldn't possibly go beyond two.'

'All right. And I have to serve a week's notice.'

'I can accommodate that.'

'Good… Well, should we shake hands or something?'

'I suppose we should.'

So they did, and then Samantha returned to the shops close to the Underground station to buy the cough medicine, some fruit and orange juice. She'd offered to prepare a meal but Keith told her he wasn't up to it. When she got back again, he was dressed and showered and had opened a bottle of wine. He met her at the door with a glass, which she took through into the kitchen where she put the juice into the fridge. He looked on for a while, leaning against the kitchen wall, but standing up exhausted him and, after an epic coughing fit, he returned to lie on the sofa. She administered the cough medicine. They talked. The time passed quickly. Soon it was ten o'clock and Samantha said she must leave. She allowed Keith to help her into her coat then turned, offering her hand for a final handshake. Instead he kissed her cheek. For the first time she noticed he had a small gold stud in his right ear. It seemed uncharacteristic; a sign of uncertainty. She was glad of it. As she left she paused and said, 'Goodbye, Keith.'

'Goodbye, Samantha. It has been a pleasure.'

'I'll send the references and call you next week.'

'All right.'

Keith smiled and closed the door.

SEVEN

Incidents on the Day of the Exhibition

AUTUMN HAD COME OVERNIGHT TO OLD CROSS BUT WINTER, TOO, had sneaked an early visit under the cover of the season's change. On the day of the exhibition Reilly woke chilled to the bone. He had also, it seemed, become partially paralysed from the waist down. He flexed his knees but something seemed to be constraining their movement. Perhaps he had been stricken with rheumatism in the night. He tried again. This time they moved more freely. There was then a sudden draught of foul air against his face and a rasp of damp sandpaper against his cheek. He opened his eyes to find Nimrod standing beside his mattress, keen to embark on the adventures of the day; the feared rheumatism, the weight of the dog sleeping across his legs.

'We really must do something about your diet, old chum,' Reilly said, sitting, stretching, scratching, emerging from the cocoon of his sheets into the chill of the room. He walked naked to the pile of clothes on the table. He no longer discarded them on the floor since the day he had found two mice in his trouser pocket while grubbing in there for coppers. Reilly bent, stretched and stamped his body into his clothes and cold shoes. Nimrod watched his master's exertions with fondness. Each day began with this jerky, angular dance, and when the dance was over the maestro was no longer pink and naked, but shrouded from neck to foot.

Reilly found his matches and lit the new gas burner – the delivery of which had been a rare concession by his landlord to his tenant's comfort. It had taken a further four months before the gas was connected to the attic. Reilly watched the flames lick the sooty base of the old kettle. It usually took him half an hour or so to achieve full wakefulness and he was more than capable of falling asleep for brief periods while standing up. The flames, though, led his thoughts to Mountjoy's blackened cooking range, the range led him to the coffee shop and once the coffee shop was established in the salon of his mind he was jolted fully awake by the realization that today was the day of the exhibition. He would need to shave. He left the kettle to boil while he took the piss-pot to be emptied in the back-yard privy, on the way letting Nimrod out of the front door to perform his morning toilet. The privy door was bolted. Boots were visible beneath so Reilly waited in the chilly yard listening to the exertions and eruptions of the occupant. When the chain was pulled and the owner of the boots emerged Reilly was distressed to see it was the third-floor tenant: Easton, the drayman, who filled the stinking lavatory not only with his own foul gases but also with clouds of pipe smoke. Easton nodded (pipe in mouth) as they passed in the yard. His newspaper was clamped beneath his left arm, leaving his hands free to button his fly. Water dinned into the lavatory cistern. The chain swung. Reilly took a breath, held it, and then entered the foul lair. He emptied the pot into the foetid bowl, pissed, and dashed out before he had to draw breath again. Days before, Mountjoy had promoted the benefits of wealth. At the time the artist had protested there was little he needed in the way of material comforts. Perhaps a room in which he had a lavatory solely for his own use was something he should aspire to.

Reilly led Nimrod back up the stairs. When the kettle had boiled he poured hot water into his teapot and also into the pail on the wash stand. While the water in the pail cooled and the tea brewed he returned his thoughts to the coffee shop and the paintings now hung on the walls. The position of each of them was fixed in his mind. It had taken almost no time at all to hang them to his satisfaction, to achieve the right balance of subject matter, perspective and colour. His unconscious mind had done the job of arranging them for him, distracting his troublesome conscious mind with worries over Gower and the price of each picture. The only concern he had was the wall closest to the door. He rearranged the paintings, which ran in a line from the door to the counter, a number of times but the balance was wrong. Almost as if there was a painting missing – a stepping-stone of logic short. He had counted the pictures: thirty-seven, so they hadn't lost one on the way there. The previous day Reilly had borrowed the grocer's truck to transport the paintings. Mountjoy had helped him carry them down from his room to the street and Nimrod had stood sentry over the barrow while it was unattended. When they pushed the laden barrow through the district an enthusiastic cry of 'Good for you!' came from a short-sighted old man who seemed to think they were performing an impromptu circus act. Others, who knew Mountjoy, came up and asked him what he was doing, which allowed him to promote the exhibition and introduce Reilly to them. Some of course knew the artist, but many only by sight. Mountjoy saw how deferential the locals were to him, as if he was party to their deepest secrets. Reilly was not rude to them but made little conversation, doing no harm to the enigma that already surrounded him.

When they arrived at the coffee shop it was apparent that Mountjoy had given the walls another covering of whitewash, which had improved the look of the place, although Reilly would have preferred it if he had applied a final, thicker coat. But his mood was robust and he was fully committed to making it a success. When the paintings were mounted on the walls Mountjoy went outside to gauge the effect from the street. He called Reilly outside. The two men stood side by side on the pavement as the light of the day faded. Reilly's work, stealing a gloss from the flames of the fire and the gas lights on the walls, pulsed with life. The coffee shop looked as if it was a living, breathing thing, colourful as a fairground, as enticing and comforting as the velvet walls of a womb. Mountjoy reached out and embraced Reilly, though Reilly felt it should have been he who had initiated the gesture. Without Mountjoy he might never have shown his work to the world. But Mountjoy's hug was more than congratulatory, and not entirely selfless. It was an acknowledgement that he had been vindicated in his support of a genius.

Having shaved, Reilly set off for the coffee shop, catching Nimrod unawares. They would rarely leave the house in the morning, it being Reilly's preferred time to work. But a change in routine was always welcome, so he left Reilly to take the lead, unsure where they were heading. On the expedition of the previous day Nimrod had proudly led the barrow through the streets, pausing occasionally to accept the congratulatory pets and strokes of the locals as Mountjoy talked and Reilly stood impatiently by. It had been a long and tiring day.

When they reached the coffee shop, they paused at the window and stared in. Mountjoy saw Reilly and bowed. Reilly pushed open the door and entered.

'I've spoken to the newspaper man,' Mountjoy announced before they reached the counter. Nimrod pushed ahead of Reilly and Mountjoy obliged him with a stroke.

'He's decided not to come?'

'On the contrary. He was here early. I explained to him how excited everybody in the district had become over your exhibition and he said he'd better take a walk around and speak to some of the locals before he returns to meet you.'

'But nobody has yet seen the pictures.'

'No. I'll grant you that – but he's reporting on the excitement surrounding the event as much as the paintings themselves.'

'I'm unconvinced that anybody in the neighbourhood will have anything charitable to say about the exhibition. You've always made it clear to me that I'm viewed at best as some sort of curiosity – at worst an out and out vagabond.'

'You underestimate the pride the people have in Old Cross. If you do make your reputation with the exhibition, believe me, they'll be the first ones to claim you as their own.'

'We'll see,' Reilly said, walking over to one of the pictures and straightening it. Technically the exhibition was now open but none of the five men, bent over their breakfasts, seemed to be showing any interest in it.

'It's early days yet, Reilly,' Mountjoy called cheerfully, sensing the artist's frustration. He watched Reilly survey his paintings, tilting his head from side to side, walking, pausing, stepping back, then forward again, leaning close, licking a finger and removing a speck of soot. Mountjoy was by nature an optimist. Only now did he allow himself a moment of concern over the damage it would cause to Reilly should none of his paintings sell. He had gone along with the idea of the exhibition, imagining only good could come of it. But while Reilly's work remained out of the public's gaze, he was secure – his talent untested. What if none of it sold, and Mountjoy had to accompany him back through the neighbourhood with a full barrow? What if the journalist took against him and chanced his arm as a critic, heaping scorn on his paintings? Mountjoy watched Reilly take his seat at the window then cast a look round the room before sighing hard, making a fist of his right hand and pushing it into his left, turning it like a ball in a socket. He then rested his elbows on the table and leaned his chin on the brace of his clasped hands, staring intently into space.

Mountjoy's silent prayer for something to come along and distract Reilly from his introspection was answered when the door opened and Pardew, the journalist, arrived. He was a lean, impatient man in his late twenties. Mountjoy had hoped that having canvassed the views of the locals, the scorn evident on his face earlier that morning might have softened. Unfortunately, it hadn't. He was a man of modern ideas and Mountjoy was unsure of himself in his company. Pardew was already looking round the coffee shop – for Reilly, Mountjoy assumed – and when none of the six men in there showed any interest in him he strode to the counter and demanded to know why the artist had chosen to keep him waiting. He was a busy man. If they were to make the deadline for the evening edition he needed to get on with it. Reilly, being more attuned than usual to the atmosphere in the room, had seen Pardew enter. Seen his cursory, dismissive glance at the paintings on the walls. Seen him stride to the counter and admonish Mountjoy. He knew immediately that the journalist had arrived. He had met people like Pardew in the salons of Montparnasse – young, self-important, opinionated; educated well enough to know their limitations and how to disguise them – usually by scorn or disdain, or impatience, all of which were effective weapons when employed against those not entirely sure of themselves (in other words, the great majority of the people Reilly encountered). He prepared himself to do battle as Mountjoy, smiling broadly to compensate for Pardew's disdain, led him to the window table. Reilly stood and shook Pardew's hand while Mountjoy effected the introductions, then withdrew to prepare them tea.

Each immediately recognized the strength in the other. Pardew was not entirely displeased when he saw Reilly. He had expected a deferential, pale-faced individual, prepared to agree to anything he might choose to offer by way of criticism or praise, but he saw Reilly's eyes narrow minutely and knew that he was on his guard. It might be an enjoyable interview. He knew every journalistic trick there was to make people pay for their pathetic vanity. The first skirmish between them was fought over who would sit first, and thus momentarily be towered over by the other. Reilly made the decision that he should be the one to defer, so although he was technically the host, he sat. The second battle was over who should begin the conversation – and how it should be done. Reilly could flatter Pardew by soliciting his opinion. Pardew, if he chose, could make it easy on Reilly by singling out a piece of work for praise.

In the event, Reilly broke the silence by asking what Pardew had discovered on his walk round Old Cross. He was genuinely interested whether anyone was aware of the exhibition. Pardew offered Reilly a cigarette from a pewter case, warm as flesh. Reilly declined with a shake of his head. Pardew lit his cigarette, shook out his match with impatience, and embarked on a diatribe against the locals; their characteristic narrow-mindedness, their reluctance to acknowledge anything that set any of them apart from their fellows. He was, however, careful not to ascribe these characteristics specifically to the denizens of Old Cross – but Reilly didn't notice. He said that it didn't surprise him. He had not expected Old Cross to welcome the exhibition. As yet, Pardew had not mentioned the exhibition.

'As narrow a bunch of individuals as I've come across,' Pardew concluded, reaching across the table to tap a maggot of ash into the tin ashtray.

'I couldn't offer an opinion on that,' Reilly said.

'You wouldn't deny it, though? This narrow-mindedness?'

'I doubt I've spoken long enough to more than a handful of them, except Mountjoy here, to form an opinion.'

Pardew nodded and noted something down in the book he had opened on the table. 'I did, however, come across a good-looking, rather boisterous girl who did speak highly of you. Poorly dressed but neat. The daughter of the greengrocer.'

'Sykes,' Reilly said.

'Yes.' Pardew consulted his notebook. 'Amy Sykes. She suggested…' He glanced again at the book, turning over a page. 'She suggested you were fond of cherries.'

'That's what she imagines. She made me a gift of them.'

'You didn't pay for them?'

'No. I didn't. They were, as I said, a gift.'

At that moment they were interrupted by Mountjoy bringing over a tray with a teapot, two cups and a small plate of slightly burned jam pastries.

'Thank you, Mountjoy,' Reilly said.

'Yes,' said Pardew, looking disdainfully at the pastries and assessing how wise it would be to drink tea in this establishment. '…She seemed fond of you.'

'But, the exhibition,' Reilly said. 'Should we discuss that?'

'Of course. And leave the issue of the paternity of her child to another time.'

'Child? She's having a child?'

Pardew seemed satisfied with the reaction he'd provoked. But he couldn't capitalize on it because at that moment a scruffy, urchin lad ran into the coffee shop, looked quickly round and dashed to their table. The boy stood, panting with the exertion of having run from the newspaper office and, without pause or permission to speak, said, 'Mr Henry says as you should get down the canal sharpish.'

'Take your cap off and start again, boy,' Pardew snapped, blowing a cloud of cigarette smoke towards the child. The jug-eared boy, whose name was Grubb, was thin, the legs below his shorts grained with conker-brown filth. His corduroy shorts matched the fabric of his cap. The boy tugged it off and, now dancing from one foot to the other with excitement, said, 'Mr Pardew, Sir, Mr Henry tol' me to come fin' you and tell you to get down the canal as quick as you like.'

'Exactly where on the canal, and why?'

'He says close to the Old Cross bridge an' he says 'cause there's been a body fetched out an' he says he's been told it's not jus' any old body but word is it might be the man they been looking for. And he says you's to get there sharpish because he wans it writ up for the firs' eve'ing edition.'

'He says that, does he?' Pardew got to his feet, collecting his notebook, picking up his hat from the table, then his cigarette from the ashtray. He put it to his lips, took a long final draw, then leaned down and ground it out. Reilly stood too, and Mountjoy, who had been out of earshot, came over to see what the fuss was about.

'Well, Mr Reilly, I'm afraid we'll have to return to the subject of your exhibition at a later time,' Pardew said, shooting his cuffs.

'What's going on?' Mountjoy asked.

'A body – in the canal,' Grubb told him. 'All bloaded they say, Mr Pardew is writing it up for the firs' eve'ing edition, arencha Mr Pardew?'

'Be quiet.' Pardew didn't miss the look of alarm that passed between coffee-shop owner and artist. He stored it away in his mental file along with the other gratifying winces of guilt and embarrassment he'd wheedled from Reilly. Yes, he was building up quite a nice picture of debauchery – and he knew there was nothing like debauchery to sell the evening edition. He hadn't even got round to asking him about his time in Paris – though mention of the French capital was enough to lead readers to their own conclusions about the people who chose to spend their time there.

Mountjoy closed the coffee shop. His announcement to the five remaining customers that a body had been discovered in the canal was enough to clear the room. So Pardew, Grubb, Reilly, Nimrod, Mountjoy and the customers set off towards the canal. The boy, having got his breath back, raced along in front with Nimrod, who tried to outpace him but couldn't. Reilly and Mountjoy walked together, with Pardew keeping two steps' distance behind them. The customers had already banded together in boisterous solidarity. They trooped five abreast, spilling out from the pavement into the road. The sight of the procession excited interest and questions from the people they passed, so by the time they turned into Ladysmith Road the group numbered more than twenty. Concerned that the sight of such an unruly mob might cause the police to close off the canal bank, Pardew hurried to the front, pushing past Mountjoy and Reilly, still deep in conversation, and led the way down the steps to the towpath, where a crowd had already gathered. A short distance beyond them, veiled by the morning mist which was always reluctant to leave the canal, he saw the body covered by a tarpaulin. Pardew impatiently elbowed his way through the mass, who were keeping a deferential and respectful distance from the corpse. Two uniformed constables immediately barred his way, but a senior man saw Pardew, met his eye, and called him through. Reilly and Mountjoy followed. The rest of the new mob, already quipping and speculating wildly about the victim, were kept back by the linked arms of the two constables and swelled the more sober ranks of those already there. Nimrod nipped between the two policemen and

Grubb dodged after him, receiving a sharp cuff on the ear. He took his place next to Mountjoy, who became aware of him because of the smell of damp compost that emanated from him. It was not too dissimilar from the smell of rotting vegetation that lingered on the canal bank through the autumn and winter.

On the walk there, Mountjoy and Reilly had conducted a hurried and hushed conversation, the occasional phrase drifting back to Pardew, who followed them closely. His hearing was acute, as was his ability to pretend otherwise. Mountjoy was clearly perturbed; Reilly was the one offering a calming reassurance. The discussion concerned the ownership of a wallet that seemed to be in Reilly's possession. Pardew added it to his mental file, which was now bulging nicely. He would use the procession as the opening gambit in the story about the discovery of the body in the canal. The journalist had a way of drawing in his readers with a telling, teasing detail: 'What terrible occurrence drew a mob from the dismal coffee shops and dens of Old Cross this chilly September morning? How were they to know, as their numbers grew, and children and mothers joined the throng, that they were to confront a corpse so bloated by its time in the stinking water of the canal that the man was unrecognizable? Foul play is suspected, robbery the obvious motive in this poor district where only today, a notorious local artist chose callously to open his new exhibition, knowing full well that the life of a man had been cut brutally short. A blow to the head? A knife between the ribs? Soon we will know…' But perhaps he would save Reilly's exhibition for tomorrow; use it to stoke the speculation over the killer before the excitement was tempered by the sober report of the police surgeon. 'Murder!' A grand term more suited to the burlesque theatre than the ill-lit rooms and alleys where the act was usually performed.

'Let the dog see the rabbit!' a wag called from the crowd. A laugh went up. This was the crowd that used to gather at Newgate, Pardew reflected, and it was comments like that that ended the public hangings there. For those despicable creatures at the bottom of the pile there is little to be celebrated – the only gift they have, their miserable existence – which raises them only above the dead: hence the laughter and joy at the public hangings, hence the jollity here on the canal bank.

Macreadie, the Chief Inspector, was dressed for lunch and cursing the mud on his shoes. The victim must have been some figure of significance to draw Macreadie away from the lure of the tantalus at his club. He beckoned Pardew over. The journalist paused, not wanting to miss anything. It wouldn't be long before the body was removed and the scene trampled by the crowd. He could see the trail of light grass where the body had been dragged. He could see the top of the ladder against the canal bank and the constable in rubber trousers standing on it, waist-deep in the brown water, poking about in the mud with a trowel. Pardew looked back towards the bridge and the steps. What was the man doing on the canal bank – and had he been there of his own accord? Maybe queer and looking for a friend who'd take down his trousers for a shilling. Or had one of the local doxies lured him down with a promise of a good time under the bridge?

Nimrod could have told them. Nimrod saw it all.

EIGHT

The Genius of Vulgarity

PERHAPS IT WAS THE CALL FROM THE WAG IN THE CROWD THAT LED Chief Inspector Macreadie to the body; that led him to kneel down on a borrowed cape to preserve his trousers and, with some ceremony, peel back the tarpaulin. Those closest to the corpse pantomimed a collective drawing-in of breath. Those farther back pushed forward to get a clearer view. Mountjoy and Reilly turned their heads away, but the image was already established in their minds. Pardew's attention stepped nimbly from the corpse to Mountjoy, then to Reilly. The artist was calm. He nodded, as if to say to himself, 'Of course, yes, of course.' But it was left to the boy – as it often is – to state the obvious: 'His eyes is gone! Where's his eyes?' Pardew was already wondering if the vulgar detail could be used in the evening edition. He had heard of, but never come across, such cases before. Rats, he knew, were partial to eyes, even over flesh. There was a line of Gissing's he had noted down when he had been called on to write the novelist's obituary almost ten years previously. Gissing had died just before the New Year. The newspaper was short-handed so the young, promising Pardew, who had been at his desk even on Christmas Day, was called upon for a rapid 800 words. He dashed out and found a one-volume copy of Gissing's most popular work (second edition) in Mudie's and rushed back, speedily reading it as he walked. He turned down the corner of a page when he found a phrase he felt compelled to record: 'To please the vulgar you must, one way or another, incarnate the genius of vulgarity.' Soon it became Pardew's motto. The obituary ran in the second evening edition.

The corpse on the canal bank was, of course, that of the critic Gower. They had all heard of his disappearance, and the police were on the alert, so they knew it could only be a matter of time before the reason for it was revealed. Whatever the reason, Pardew's editor knew it would be newsworthy. A critic whose eyes were devoured by rats. There were many who would have seen it as fitting.

❧

Mountjoy, Reilly and Nimrod made a sad and sober return to the coffee shop. Grubb tagged along, Mountjoy expressing concern to Reilly that the boy might suffer nightmares provoked by the sight of the corpse. Reilly couldn't muster any concern for the waif. He had initiated no conversation since they had left the towpath, and had answered Mountjoy's questions with weary brevity. Mountjoy, retaining his generosity of spirit even under such trying conditions, was more worried for Reilly than he was for himself. Not just because of the wallet – circumstantial evidence at best, should things proceed as he knew Reilly feared they would – but because he sensed that Reilly had somehow foreseen this event. Perhaps not in its fullest detail, but the anxiety he knew Reilly lived with was perhaps that his life would somehow change through such an event. Was that what gave his pictures their melancholy; that sense that although he was a young man, he was already into the winter of his career? But how to broach the subject with his old friend? How to reassure him that he would do all that he could to help him?

Mountjoy gave up offering his reassurances. He could see that they were now irritating Reilly, whose pace had slowed as they approached the coffee shop. Mountjoy was afraid he would leave and go back to his room, and this provoked his own anxiety. If they could all stay together then surely nothing ill could befall them. Look at the sky, Mountjoy wanted to shout. Look at the sun trying to break through. Look at Nimrod walking keenly towards the coffee shop where, inside, your wonderful work lights up the walls. Look at the boy trotting happily along the road with Nimrod. Let's not part yet, because together we are safe.

They reached the coffee shop door, Nimrod arriving there first, Grubb shortly after. The boy, immediately bored, plunged a finger into his right nostril and searched around him for distraction as he waited for Reilly and Mountjoy to catch up. Mountjoy took the key from his pocket, turned it in the lock and pushed open the door. The fire was low, a pursed mouth of orange in the grim face of the grate. The vermin scattered as Nimrod and Grubb dashed in, the boy immediately going behind the counter to look for food. Mountjoy had no objection; the urchin looked as though he hadn't had a square meal for weeks. But Reilly didn't follow him. Instead he went to the window and looked in through the glass, just as he had done the day before after they had hung the pictures together. Today Mountjoy saw something quite different on the artist's face: he saw an appreciation of the work that hung there, as if it had been painted by a stranger. Now his pictures belonged to the world. The separation was complete.

Reilly took a step away from the window. 'I shan't come in,' he said.

'No. I thought you might choose not to.'

'If Pardew comes looking for me, I'll be in my room.'

'Of course.'

Reilly nodded. Soberly he offered his hand to Mountjoy, who took it. 'Thank you,' Reilly said. 'Whatever befalls us. Thank you.'

'All will be well,' Mountjoy assured him, but he couldn't help but add, 'Reilly…'

'Yes?'

'Take good care.'

'I will, Mountjoy.'

Reilly turned and walked away. Mountjoy entered the coffee shop. Grubb had found a crust of bread and made a sandwich with bacon. Mountjoy's warning shout stilled the boy's hand just before the raw meat reached his mouth. Nimrod jumped in alarm, then looked round for his master. Concerned, he padded to the door. Mountjoy opened the door to release him, and Nimrod set off home.

❧

Reilly walked slowly through Old Cross, Nimrod dogging his heels. Neighbours who hadn't spoken for years were standing on their doorsteps discussing 'the murder'. At street corners people gathered in twos and threes, rubbishing reputations, pointing the finger; a collective joy that on this day there was a man (it must be a man) in worse circumstances than their own. When Reilly passed each conversation paused, only to begin again when the stooped figure was out of earshot. Somehow the news that the dead man had been visiting the artist had become common knowledge and opinion was now divided between those who saw Reilly as the most obvious suspect and those (in the minority) who saw him as unlikely to have committed the murder. The former's arguments tended not towards malice aforethought but to an accidental killing (an argument, a fight, the younger man pushing the older man, a stumble, a head striking a table edge...); those standing up for Reilly pointed to the fact that if he had done it he was most unlikely still to be in the neighbourhood – and there were many more likely candidates who had, over recent days, disappeared. Reilly rehearsed the arguments as he walked. All he was guilty of was keeping the wallet. It was now too late to return it. He had no choice but to dispose of it. Only Mountjoy knew he had it and he would trust Mountjoy with his life. Tonight, under cover of dark, he would take it to the canal, return to the point on the towpath where Gower had gone in, and drop it into the water. If the search continued the following day and the wallet was discovered, all well and good. If not, then no matter. All that did matter was that the wallet would no longer be in his possession. Now was the most dangerous time, made more so because, after returning from Mountjoy's coffee shop, he had hidden the wallet in the lavatory cistern. The act itself he knew would be seen as an admission of guilt, and no explanation he could offer would remove the taint – even the honest truth. And what was the truth? The truth was that he did intend to take the wallet to the police station, but only after a few days had passed. He was intending to argue that Nimrod had lately found the wallet in his room (under this mattress? Beneath the boards?) and he had immediately returned it. What he would never admit even to Mountjoy was that there was a part of him that had no intention of returning the wallet. He would leave it in the cistern and in a year, even two or three years' time, when even Mountjoy would have forgotten its existence, get it out again and perhaps ease his penury with a note or two of the critic's money. Gower, he knew, would not have objected.

Reilly felt better. In the court of his conscience he was an innocent man – foolish, but innocent. Soon the matter would blow over, Gower's death would be written off as accidental or the killer found, and the district could once more return to its own parochial concerns. He and Mountjoy could then concentrate on the exhibition. Life would go on, seeming more valuable for its ordinariness. For days, even weeks, he would revel in the mundanity of his routine. Perhaps Gower's death would excite interest they could capitalize on. He dismissed the unworthy thought, justifying it by the pressures of the day and the shock at seeing the critic's bloated body on the canal bank. He was still trying to rid himself of the dreadful image of Gower's savaged face when he reached Sykes's stall and saw Amy start as she caught sight of him. In a moment she was gone, away into the back of the shop – and only then did Pardew's words come back to him. Amy Sykes was carrying a child. Could he really be the father?

He knew he should stop and talk to her. In a moment he would know. But she had never run from him before; what further evidence did he need? Reilly liked himself less for walking by. He looked down at Nimrod, who always seemed to know it all, but never judged him. How lonely the world if we were party to each other's consciences.

'What will become of you, old chum?' Reilly said as they reached the front door. He unlocked it, and Nimrod led the way inside.

NINE

Engineering Works and the Half-Hour Man

SAMANTHA DODD, HAVING SERVED OUT HER PERIOD OF NOTICE with Tubman's firm, was due the following day to begin work at the Lexington Street gallery. A week had gone by; she had expected Keith to have recovered from his flu but when, as arranged, she telephoned him the day before she was due to start, the phone went unanswered. She dialled the number again and still there was no reply. An hour later, when she had tried the number for the third time, Samantha began to wonder whether she might have acted too hastily in resigning her job. But then her phone rang and a voice she barely recognized croaked, 'I was asleep.'

'Keith?'

'Yes.'

'It's Samantha Dodd. You sound terrible.'

'I feel terrible. I've taken to my bed. I'm so ill I was even granted a visit from the GP. Not my GP, I hasten to add, some callow youth on a motorcycle who attends the sick at night, presumably after his pizza delivery shift has finished.'

'And what did he say?'

'He said I should rest. So that's what I'm doing. Continuing to do.

But I'm terribly weak. Terribly. No appetite at all. And I still have the most dreadful cough.'

'I'll come round.'

'There's really no need.'

'I don't mind. I'll need the key, anyway.'

'Key?'

'For the gallery.'

'Of course. I'd quite forgotten. You're starting tomorrow.'

The Underground was closed due to Sunday engineering work which meant it took Samantha nearly and hour and a half to reach Old Cross. When she got there the spare key to the door, as Keith had promised, was under the mat. She went in, immediately feeling the chill. There was no light on in the hallway, and when she tried the switch nothing happened. She heard a cough from upstairs, then another, more wracking. She approached the stairs and made her way up. The third tread creaked.

'Who's that!' Keith called in terror.

'It's all right, Keith. It's me: Samantha Dodd.'

'Thank God. But do be careful. The lights have fused again. I really need to get this place rewired. You'll need to press the button thingy in the box in the kitchen. Come and get a candle. Turn left at the top of the stairs. I'm in the front room.'

So Samantha continued her careful climb of the dark stairs, her right palm against the wall to guide her. When she reached the top she navigated her way along the landing by the dim glow from beneath the door of the front room. When she entered the bedroom she saw Keith's pale, thin face on the pillow illuminated by the candle on the bedside table. She closed the door behind her and the breeze bent the flame, which then righted itself.

'There's a chair over there,' Keith said hoarsely. 'Pull it up and come and talk to me. I haven't seen a soul bar the doctor for a week. You are real, aren't you? Not a ghost.'

'No. I'm not a ghost.' Samantha fetched the chair and set it by the bed. She didn't feel that she could remove her coat. There was a presence in the room that chilled the air.

'I've been having the most dreadful dreams. Fevered dreams. I wake covered in sweat and frozen stiff. Surely this isn't simply the flu?' Keith tried to sit, but he was too weak and his head fell back onto the pillow.

'You don't look at all well.'

'And here. Here. Look.' Keith held out a bloodied tissue. 'Now I'm coughing up blood. Surely, surely, that can't be right.'

'I'm going to call the doctor again. You can't go on like this.' Samantha opened her handbag and felt inside for the mobile phone.

'He won't come. I've told you.'

'Leave it to me. What's the number?'

'Use my phone. It's under Q for Quack.' Keith extracted an ill-smelling arm from his bed and passed over his mobile telephone. Samantha dialled and Keith was impressed to hear her clinical instructions to the woman at the answering service, making it clear that she expected a doctor to call within the hour and, no, she didn't need to speak to him over the phone first. Perhaps he once had that authority, but he was finding it hard to remember anything of his life before the illness struck him and took over his whole being.

Samantha turned off the phone and said, 'I'll wait with you until he comes.'

'You're kind. I don't know what I'd have done without you. It's at times like these you learn who your friends are.'

'I'll make you a drink and then you can tell me what I need to know about working in the gallery.'

'I've written it down – here.' He fumbled for an envelope on the bedside table and passed it to her. 'You'll find the key in here, the code for the alarm and the password for the computer. I've also written a brief précis of how to take payment.'

Samantha put the envelope in her handbag and went down to the kitchen to make Keith's drink. Despite his fever all he wanted was a cup of tea. When she returned he was asleep, although he was so still and pale that for a moment she wondered if he was dead. He opened his eyes in terror.

'Another dream?'

Keith nodded.

'A bad dream?'

'I feel as if I'm being punished for something. But I don't know what it is I've done. Perhaps that's what illness is, the way we punish ourselves for our bad deeds. Did I say that out loud?'

'It's the fever. Don't worry.' Samantha settled herself on her chair, the teacup and saucer balanced on her knee. 'Is it always the same dream?'

'I don't think so. Perhaps it is. I find myself by the canal. Something dreadful has happened but it's unclear what. I approach a group of people and then… then I look down into the water and I see a painting floating there.'

'And do you recognize the painting?'

'No. It's face down. I can see only the back of it.'

'You're anxious about the gallery. That's what your dream is about.'

'You think so?'

'Drink this.' Supporting Keith's head, she tipped a little of the tea into his mouth.

'God, this is worse than *The Diving Bell and the Butterfly*, isn't it?' Keith's lips were dry and cracked, his tongue white. But as he tried to swallow his neck arched and his body convulsed. He then emitted a lung-splitting cough that projected a flume of tea and blood across the bed cover. 'Oh God! Forgive me,' Keith cried, continuing to cough.

Samantha felt only pity when he picked up a tea towel from the floor, put it to his mouth and spat blood into it. After that, the coughing subsided and he slipped back into sleep. He woke briefly every five or so minutes and each time he did it was like a drowning man coming up for air. She could do little but mop his brow with a damp towel and stroke his head. Finally the doorbell rang, and by then she was so distressed she tore down the stairs and pulled open the door in tears.

'Thank God you're here,' she said to the doctor. But the squat, neck-less, moon-faced man on the doorstep didn't look like a doctor. He was dressed in the dusty work clothes of a jobbing builder.

'That's nice,' the man said cheerfully. 'It's not often my customers are so happy to see me. You all right?'

'You're not the doctor?'

'No, love. I'm not the doctor.' The man addressed his words towards Samantha's chest, which is where his attention remained. She crossed her arms.

At that moment a car pulled up at the kerb, and a lean young man in a sports jacket and corduroy trousers got out quickly, opened the back door of the car, pulled out his bag, and headed briskly towards them.

'It's not convenient. It's a bad time. You'll have to go,' Samantha said to the man on the doorstep.

'Fair enough. But tell Keith I've found some more.'

'Some more what?'

'Pictures and whatnot. Tell him Brian called. He'll know. Tell him to bell me on the moby.' Brian mimed lifting a phone to his ear.

'Brian. Yes. Fine. Just go now, please.'

By now the doctor had reached them and was waiting politely for Brian to move aside so that he could get in.

'Right, well, I'll be on my way, then,' Brian said. 'Nice to meet you.'

'Please leave.'

'On my way.' Brian stood aside, his jollity undented, allowing the doctor access to the door. 'Stand aside – doctor coming through!' Brian announced, marshalling him past like a traffic policeman. With one more appreciative look at Samantha's breasts, he left, whistling.

'He's upstairs. Front room,' Samantha said to the young man. 'I'm afraid the electrics are out. Be careful on the stairs.'

She closed the door and heard the engine of a Transit van cough into life. Upstairs she heard Keith's cough echoing it, then the deep rumble of the doctor's voice through the floor. Another cough. Keith's higher pitched voice replying, then silence.

The ambulance's arrival twenty minutes later was signalled by blue lights capering around the narrow street. When the paramedics had taken Keith away, strapped into a chair, the doctor spent a moment or so reassuring Samantha that he would be all right but recovery would be slow. He suspected TB. There had been a number of new cases in the area. The disease, having been under control for many years, was making an unwelcome reappearance. Antibiotics would be administered. He would be isolated. Samantha thanked the young man, who paused at the door to ask her whether she was all right. Samantha smiled bravely and told him she was. He smiled back, knowing she was not, but recognized her as one of society's copers, without whom the world would grind to a halt. She watched him get into his car, having opened the back door and dropped his case onto the back seat. He drove away, giving her a brief wave. The way he did it made Samantha wonder if he was a musician. She pictured him on his night off standing on a podium, conducting a chamber orchestra.

When she closed the door she heard a noise upstairs, the sound of light footsteps padding across the ceiling. Perhaps a cat had crept in while the door was open. She felt her way back upstairs. The candle had burned low in Keith's room. She picked up the saucer and ushered light to the four corners of the room but she couldn't see anything. Kneeling down, she looked beneath the bed. Nothing there either.

Having reinstated the electricity by pressing the switch in the fuse box, Samantha boiled a kettle on the stove and washed up the pots stacked on the drainer. She then took a tray and collected the cups from the sitting room and the bedroom, returning to both rooms with a carrier bag, which she used to collect the old newspapers, apple cores and biscuit wrappers. When she left the house she dropped the bag into the empty wheelie bin by the front door, locked the door and replaced the key under the mat. Because of the engineering works on the Underground, she intended to catch a bus back to Paddington and pick up the Tube there so she set off for the high street to look for a bus stop. She found one next door to the café. Since her last visit a plastic rubbish chute had been tethered to the scaffolding that clad the building. Like an exposed digestive tract, the chute ran the height of the building and terminated at ground level in a skip. It emitted a 'whumpf', dust puffed from the joins in the pipe, and there was then a clatter as a length of wood landed in the skip. Having excreted, the device settled back to stillness again.

While she waited for the bus, debris continued to whistle, crump or clatter down the pipe. Samantha's attention strayed around the street and came to rest once more on the café. The window frame and pilasters had been stripped of their paint in preparation for a fresh coat. The illuminated sign had been discarded, revealing the old italic lettering that had been painted directly onto the fascia. The black, gold-hedged letters were still bold, sufficiently old-fashioned to appear contemporary: MOUNTJOY'S.

Samantha mouthed the name silently. It was a habit she had, like looking at clouds and noticing their formations. Details were important to her, which is why she had been so drawn to T. F. Reilly's picture. It felt as though it had been painted by a man with a similar sensibility. 'Mountjoy's,' Samantha mouthed again, at which point she saw the lights go on in the café and a man appear through a door behind the counter, his head bent into a newspaper. When he looked up she saw it was Brian, the cheerful builder she'd sent away from Keith's house when the doctor arrived. Recognizing her, Brian unlatched the door and came out.

'It's a bit late for you to be standing round here on your own,' he said.

'I'm waiting for a bus. To Paddington.'

'Paddington, is it?' Brian's look conveyed that he knew things of Paddington it was best he didn't divulge.

'Yes.'

'I'll keep you company for a mo. I was coming out for a snout anyway.' Brian took a packet of Regal cigarettes from the breast pocket of his grimy tartan shirt, opened it and offered one. Samantha declined with a shake of her head. Brian, she could see, was an easily diverted individual, his good cheer doubtless the product of a sturdy upbringing; a man who fell into the category of those she would be happy to spend half an hour with, though no longer. Her mother, who denied the charges of snobbery Samantha laid against her, categorized people in a similar way. Those in the trades: builders, plumbers, milkmen, electricity meter readers, bus conductors, were all 'half-an-hour people'.

'So, did you tell Keith I came round?'

'No. I'm afraid he's been taken to hospital.'

'Hospital, is it?'

She went on to explain the traumatic two hours she had spent at his house, the visit of the doctor and the diagnosis. Brian expressed sympathy and said he'd 'put the word round', though what word, and to whom, he didn't specify.

'Well, tell him to bell me when he's out. I've got some more stuff I know he'll be interested in. Turned up when I got up into the loft space. Pictures and old newspapers.'

'Do you always work this late on Sunday nights?'

'I work when it suits me. At least on a Sunday you can park round here without getting towed away. Here. Have a look at this. This'll interest you.' Brian darted back into the café for something, Samantha assumed, connected with the local parking restrictions. Instead he returned with an old newspaper. 'There's a chest of stuff up there, old clothes, all sorts of old rubbish. Interesting, isn't it?'

Samantha took it from him and began to read. 'Yes. Yes it is.'

'Look out. Here's your bus.'

'Well, thank you.' Samantha handed back the newspaper.

'Keep it. Show it to Keith if you see him. Give you something to read on the bus. Give it back to us when you come round next time. OK?'

'I'll look after it.'

'I know you will. Don't do anything I wouldn't do. Chirry bye.' Brian smiled and winked.

'Goodbye.'

The doors hissed open. Brian's smile slid away as his attention turned to Samantha's legs as she climbed the step. She turned to wave, then paid the driver and walked to the centre of the bus where she took a seat, having noted that should the elderly or disabled require it she should immediately vacate it. She passed the thirty-minute journey to Paddington undisturbed, reading the ancient newspaper. She began with the notices on the front page. When she turned to the inside her eye was caught by the grisly story of the 'respectable' man murdered in the canal. It began with the report of a witness, Annie Cole: 'I was in my room, up a pair of stairs – the gas-light is over my door. From my back window I can clearly see the canal. I heard a loud splash and I went to the window… I opened my window and saw a figure running off along the towpath. I didn't think any more on it until I came on the crowd yesterday and saw the gentleman's body. It chilled me so I told the police what I saw.'

TEN

The Return of the Authorities

HAVING RETURNED TO HIS ROOM, REILLY COULDN'T SETTLE. HE SAT at the table drumming his fingers then stood and sentried up and down the room: ten strides from wall to wall, a sharp turn and ten steps back. For a while Nimrod trotted obediently at his side but grew bored and went to lay on the mattress, where he was allowed to rest if Reilly wasn't using it. Reilly returned to the table, at the centre of which was a damp, oilcloth-covered package. He sat and contemplated it for a while, before reaching out and undoing it.

'Well?' he demanded of Nimrod, picking up the wallet from the table. 'And what do you suggest we do with this?'

There was no response.

'Hide it, I suppose is the obvious answer to that question.' Reilly stood and took the wallet to the mattress, lifting the corner of it and tipping Nimrod unceremoniously onto the floor. Embarrassed, he stood, and shook himself to retrieve his dignity.

'Under here, perhaps?' Reilly tossed the wallet onto the floor and dropped the mattress on top of it, raising a cloud of dust.

'No. That's no good. No good at all.' Retrieving it, Reilly took it to the wash stand, where he secreted it beneath the pail. But that didn't suit him either. The hiding place he settled on was behind a loose brick in the chimney breast. Reilly's room, being directly beneath the roof, was without a fireplace, but in the winter, when the fires of the other tenants were lit beneath him, the wide chimney breast soon warmed up and so did his room, although he did suffer the soot from the stack, some twelve feet above his head, raining down (literally, in a downpour) onto the skylight. In the winter, therefore, he kept it closed.

The wallet having been hidden, Nimrod stood and approached it, pushing his nose gently against the brick.

'Leave it,' Reilly said sharply. 'Just leave it. You've caused me enough trouble already.'

Nimrod slunk back to the mattress and lay down with a sigh. The bell at the front door jangled on its spring.

'Who can that be?' Reilly said. 'Mountjoy, perhaps?'

The bell rang again and was rung a third time before Reilly reached the front door. A policeman was on the step. 'You'll remember me,' the tall constable said. 'We discussed the disappearance of the critic Gower.'

'I do recall that,' Reilly said.

'You suggested his visit to you was a convivial one. It seems that after this convivial visit he ended up in the canal.'

'So it would seem.'

'I should like to discuss the matter further with you. Now would suit me, if it would suit you.'

'I have nothing to hide,' Reilly said, eliciting a flicker of interest from the policeman. 'What I mean to say is that there's little else I can tell you.' Reilly stood aside to let the man enter the hallway. The PC inclined his head out of habit but the doorway was more than high enough for him to have entered without doing so. Reilly closed the door, marooning them in the darkness. 'There are no lights. I'll lead the way up the stairs.'

'Very well.'

When the policeman walked into Reilly's room he was taken aback by the squalor. The most striking image was the quarter-loaf of bread on the table, ripe with mould. The olive of the mould was the most vivid colour in the grim room, made more dismal because of the copious light flooding in through the skylight. Wooden struts, which supported the roof, partitioned the space, each throwing a slanted shadow across the floor which was roughly boarded. Reilly's garret put the policeman in mind of the steerage deck on a steamer.

Nimrod raised himself cautiously to his feet. The policeman stroked his head. Satisfied with the attention he'd received, Nimrod returned to the mattress.

'Sit down. Please,' Reilly said, drawing the chair from beneath the table.

'I'm happy as I am, thank you.'

'Very well.' Reilly remained standing, too. 'What was it that you wanted to discuss? I'm sorry, I don't think you gave your name when we spoke last.'

'Portch. PC Portch.' The policeman waited. Reilly, he could see, was nervous, nervousness implying guilt. In protesting their ignorance or pleading innocence guilty men often did an effective job of incriminating themselves. It was only a matter of time. 'So, this is where you paint?' Portch asked.

'Yes.'

'The light, so I understand, is important to a painter.'

'Of course. Northern light is preferable. Direct light if at all possible.'

'Light tends generally to be direct does it not?'

'No. It does not.'

'No?'

'We could spend the day discussing the differing qualities of direct, diffused and subdued light, but perhaps another time.'

'Very… colourful pictures, if you'll forgive the observation.'

'You've seen my paintings?'

Portch was content to stand still and solemn at the centre of the room, his helmet under his arm. Reilly, by contrast, was like an actor who had learned his lines but had not yet had his moves blocked out for him on the stage. He couldn't seem to find a stance or position that suited him.

'Yes. I called at the coffee shop. Mr Mountjoy explained that the pictures on the walls were the work of a local man called Reilly and said it was a privilege to have them on his walls. When I told him I had encountered you before he apologized and said it wasn't his habit to forget such incidents.'

'Mountjoy rarely forgets a face.'

'Even those who forget a face rarely forget a uniform.' Portch left it there for a while. A connoisseur of guilt – he had seen it the moment he walked into the coffee shop and knew both men were on their guard. 'I asked you if you made a living from your pictures, if you recall.'

'I remember.'

'And you said, as I remember it, that you live as most artists do, relying in part on the charity of others.'

'Yes.'

Portch cast another look round the garret. 'Can I ask what you pay for this room?'

'Five shillings a week.'

Portch nodded to suggest that five shillings seemed a fair price. 'One pound each month. Fifty-two pounds of charity each year?'

'I'd be happy to discuss my financial affairs with you in detail if that's why you're here.'

Without a change of tone, Portch said, 'You were at the canal this morning?'

'...Yes. I was. As you probably know from Mountjoy.'

'Why should I have learned of your whereabouts from him?'

'We went down there together.'

'He didn't mention it.'

'He had no reason not to mention it.' Reilly chose to sit down. He wanted to gather his thoughts and his strength. 'You said you came to discuss Gower's disappearance with me. Perhaps you'd be good enough to ask what you came to ask. I need to get on with my work.'

'When I arrived at the coffee shop you were painting the walls.'

'Mountjoy was painting the walls.'

'For what reason?'

'Did you not discuss this with Mountjoy?'

'I did.'

'And I expect he told you that he was painting the walls because of the exhibition. Why else should he have been painting them?'

'He asked the very same question. And I answered that I had known walls to be painted, or washed down, for a number of reasons.'

'Oh. I see,' Reilly said. 'I see.'

'What do you see?'

'You're suggesting Gower was murdered in the café and Mountjoy was covering it up.'

Portch allowed a smile. 'Murder? And conspiracy between you two gentlemen? All in one breath. If I hadn't already seen the evidence in your pictures, I would now be remarking on the vividness of your imagination.'

'I know what you're doing. I know exactly what you're doing, Portch. And it won't work.'

'I came here, Sir, to ask if, in the light of the discovery of the body in the canal, there was anything new you recalled about the visit of Mr Gower. That's what I'm doing and I apologize if I've led you to believe otherwise.'

Would this tall, dark statue, this implacable figure, ever leave his room? Reilly told himself again that he was not guilty, that he had nothing to do with Gower's death. Why, then, each time he opened his mouth, did he seem intent on convincing Portch otherwise?

'There is nothing more I remember about Gower's visit,' Reilly said, hoping the weariness in his voice would encourage the constable to leave him in peace.

'I'm sure there isn't,' Portch agreed. 'It's unfortunate when a gentleman such as yourself gets caught up in such matters. I'm not saying that there are those who deserve it, but there are those better suited to dealing with it.'

'Thank you. Then why bring up the matter of Mountjoy painting the walls of his coffee shop?'

'It was an observation. When I arrived, the walls were being painted. Had Mr Mountjoy been singing, or playing the piano, I might have remarked on that. As it was, he was painting the walls.'

'You asked why he was painting the walls. Had he been singing, would you have asked why he was doing that?'

'If I had not deduced the reason for myself.'

'A man paints his walls. There is to be an exhibition of paintings on his premises. He wishes to display them in a fitting manner. That's all.'

'I was happy with his explanation. It's you who seem otherwise.'

'I just sense...'

'Sense?'

'That you're trying to trap me.'

'I'm a policeman, not a poacher. I serve the law. The law serves justice. And the reason I am here today is that it would have been remiss of me not to visit the last place the critic Gower was seen alive. I did not come here to trap you.' Portch looked around the room and seemed about to leave. 'But motive – once a motive is established, a crime such as this is more likely to be solved, justice therefore being served.'

'If, indeed, it was a crime.'

'Indeed.' Portch made a move towards the door.

'It might have been an accident.'

'Oh, I think a sober man is unlikely to find himself in a canal for no reason. Besides which, no wallet was found on the body.'

'No wallet?'

Whether it was by coincidence, or because he had heard a word which had recent associations, Nimrod raised himself to his feet.

'Nor was he carrying any money in his pockets. How, then, was he to pay for his return to his house in Regent's Park? A considerable walk even for a younger, fit man.'

'When I suggested murder you accused me of a vivid imagination.'

'Indeed I did. Though I did not deny the possibility.'

Reilly stood and moved to the door, hoping Portch would take the cue and leave, which had seemed to be his intention. 'Well, I hope I have put your mind at rest, Constable,' he said, opening the door.

'Thank you, but my mind rests very well.' Portch's attention had been arrested by Nimrod, who had padded towards the chimney breast and was now pushing his nose against one of the bricks.

Reilly's heart leaped in his chest. 'Here, old chum. Here,' he called, clicking his fingers, but Nimrod chose to ignore him. Portch did not miss the rise in pitch of Reilly's voice.

'My boy's after having a dog,' Portch said.

'Excellent companions. Excellent. Here, Nimrod. Here!' Reilly knew there was only one thing that would distract Nimrod, but there was no food in the room – even Nimrod would draw the line at the mouldy bread on the table. The brick shifted inwards with a short, dry squeal.

'He's found something there, hasn't he?' Portch said in admiration.

'Oh, Nimrod's always chasing rats and mice. He senses them everywhere – but he won't find any in the chimney breast. Leave it, chum!'

'Indeed not. But he's got something, hasn't he?' Portch continued to watch Nimrod, who was now scrabbling at the brick with his paw. 'He's a persistent fellow, I'll give him that.'

'Yes, indeed.'

Reilly saw with some relief that the face of the brick was now recessed half an inch into the wall. If Nimrod pushed harder it would stick tight and they would need a knife to prise it out.

'...Would you say he required a great deal of exercise?'

'What?'

'Returning to the issue of dogs as pets.'

'I'd say all dogs are different. Nimrod requires a good walk each day.' Reilly pitched his voice louder. 'Walk, old chum?' But Nimrod would not be diverted from his task. He was now nosing at the right-hand end of the brick, the change of strategy paying immediate dividends as the left end pivoted forwards. With a combination of nose, paw and jaw it was now only a matter of time before the brick was out.

'Well,' Portch said. 'I'll discuss the matter with Mrs Portch and a decision will be made. I tend to leave the final decision on domestic matters to the wife.' He smiled in fond benevolence.

'Good, well, please let me know what that decision is.'

'I'll be sure to remember to do so, Sir. And on the other matter, I'll be in touch.'

'Thank you.'

Abruptly, Portch left the room and before Reilly could offer to lead him back down the stairs, he was gone.

Reilly closed the door, leaning against it with a heavy sigh of relief. Immediately the loosened brick dropped out of the wall, landing with a crash onto the floorboards, narrowly missing Nimrod's paw.

'You'll have me hanged. I swear you will,' Reilly said, not without fondness.

Nimrod, having retrieved the wallet with his teeth, now padded back to his spot on the floor and, with one final look towards Reilly, set about chewing it.

He was still chewing it thirty minutes later when the front door bell again rang. Reilly had a good mind to open the skylight window and hurl the wallet out as hard as he could. But he knew the way his luck was playing it would probably land at the feet of Portch, Portch would compare the teeth marks with those of Nimrod and the game would be up. The safest course of action was also the simplest, and the one he chose: tug the wallet from Nimrod's jaw, ignoring his protests and wounded look, put the wallet in his pocket, and dispose of it after dark. He was no longer intending to return to the canal and throw it in; it would be foolhardy to return to the crime scene where a constable might have been posted. Instead he would find a drain to drop it into.

There were few visitors to the lodging house and Reilly knew there was a good chance that again the bell was for him. He was feeling stronger after surviving the visit of PC Portch. Fate, it seemed, was on his side, so he decided to go down and face whatever new challenge now lay in store for him on the doorstep. When he opened the door he found a man, head bowed, cloaked in the fading light of the afternoon. He was wearing a long dark coat and an absurd cap made of carpet. The man looked up. 'It's me.' The shadow cast over Mountjoy's eyes by the cap's brim lent him a rakish severity.

'Mountjoy?' Reilly said. 'Is everything all right?'

Mountjoy took a vagabond's look left, right, then, whipping a newspaper from inside his coat, demanded with a harsh whisper, 'Have you seen this?'

'Seen what?'

'You'd better read it and then we can discuss what needs to be done. If, indeed, anything can be done.'

'What on earth?' Reilly took the newspaper from Mountjoy's outstretched hand.

'If I hadn't agreed to this damned exhibition none of this would have come about.'

'But nothing has come about. Gower is dead, yes. And it's a terrible tragedy, but life must go on.' Reilly gave Mountjoy's shoulder a reassuring clench. 'There's really nothing to become concerned about.'

'Read Pardew's story and then tell me there's nothing to worry about.'

'Surely it can't be that bad.'

'Please. Read it now. Read it here.'

'Very well,' Reilly said, and took up a stance on the step, borrowing the door frame to lean on and the last of the daylight to read the story. Mountjoy looked on, letting out a pained sigh as he saw the face of the artist begin to harden into terror.

It began innocently enough, with the report of a witness, Annie Cole:

'I was in my room, up a pair of stairs – the gas-light is over my door. From my back window I can clearly see the canal. I heard a loud splash and I went to the window... I opened my window and saw a figure running off along the towpath. I didn't think any more on it until I came on the crowd yesterday and saw the gentleman's body. It chilled me so I told the police what I saw.'

The writer of the report, the hack Pardew, avoided mentioning the gender of the figure on the towpath, choosing instead to divert to a sketch of the crowd that gathered there the following day. He mentioned the police and the only two men whose curiosity led them close to the corpse: Mountjoy, the proprietor of a local coffee shop, and T. F. Reilly, a 'notorious' local artist.

'Notorious?' Reilly said out loud. 'Am I?'

'There's more. Read on.'

It was a careful and elegant character assassination. Reilly, it seemed, was in the habit of stealing fruit from a local grocer called Sykes – small wonder, as he had no money of his own to pay for it. And was he grateful, Pardew asked his readers? Of course not. The man who had spent five years in Paris had no intention of paying – and when questioned about his relationship with the grocer's sweet, corrupted daughter, Amy, seemed barely to recall her name.

'That's not true! Not true! And he calls her corrupted! Surely she can sue.'

'Which particular untruth is that?' Mountjoy asked.

'About Amy – poor Amy.'

But Reilly's treatment of Amy was by no means out of character, if

Pardew was to be believed. The artist, he reported, was disdainful of the citizens of Old Cross, 'as narrow-minded a group of individuals as any he'd encountered'.

'But I didn't say that... Oh God... Oh God...'

'Wait until you reach the end.'

Reilly returned warily to the article. There he found himself being attacked for insisting Pardew not only visit, but also praise, his exhibition on the very day that a body had been discovered in the canal – 'forgivable, perhaps, until one considers that the corpse was that of the famous critic Gower, a man who had gone out of his way to support the artist, had visited his lodgings, and had been murdered on his way home to a more salubrious part of the city. Robbery would appear the obvious motive; the critic's wallet is still being searched for by the police. Presumably this would explain why the hushed and excitable conversation between Messrs Reilly and Mountjoy on their way to the canal concerned that very item. Had they found a wallet, perhaps? Here one must be charitable because at that point in the investigation no mention had been made by the police that the critic's wallet was missing. No doubt the police will await a visit from these men to explain their conversation. Inspector Macreadie assures us that an arrest is imminent.'

'...Judge and jury. Judge and jury.' The newspaper fell from Reilly's hands. Feeling weak and faint, he let the door frame take his weight.

'Judge, jury and prosecuting counsel,' Mountjoy said. 'Thank God you disposed of the wallet, that's all I can say.' But then he saw Reilly's hand go to his pocket, saw him draw the wallet slowly out. 'Oh, no,' was all he managed in the moment before they heard voices at the end of the street – and turning to look saw a group of men approaching: a mob, grim-faced, angry, some of them with dogs at their heels. In the vanguard was PC Portch, another constable, a sergeant, Pardew and the well-dressed Chief Inspector.

In the final moment before the mob reached them Reilly took Mountjoy's shoulders and pleaded. 'Look after Nimrod for me?'

'Of course.'

'And my work. All of it. I entrust it into your care.'

'I promise, Reilly. I promise. But the wallet…'

'The truth,' Reilly declaimed, holding high the wallet. 'Only the truth can save me now.'

ELEVEN

Samantha Dodd Hears Reilly's Whisper

SAMANTHA DODD, HAVING READ PARDEW'S NEWSPAPER REPORT ON the way to Paddington, was now in no doubt that T. F. Reilly had whispered across the century and she had been the one chosen to hear it. She was still unsure what the painter was demanding of her but she resolved to be alert to the signals. There were steps she could take, the most obvious one being to return to Old Cross and ask Brian the builder if he would let her see the remaining contents of the café loft. Perhaps there would be more newspapers. Was it possible the paintings he mentioned were Reilly's? She didn't dare hope. But before that she would take custody of Reilly's painting in the gallery. It had been alone in that cold, dark room for three weeks now. She felt it signalling to her; a ray from Reilly's sun, as vivid as the day he took it from the easel. Tomorrow she would be reunited with it; with him. No, tomorrow was too long. She would go there now.

It was after eleven o'clock by the time Samantha reached the narrow Soho street. The tall Victorian buildings were unlit and cheerless. Without the daylight to soften them the contemporary grey, black and olive stuccoed exteriors were unwelcoming. But the street was so narrow that even in the summer the sun never entirely removed the chill. That night even the restaurant (fashionable black-painted stucco, gold italic lettering) was dark and closed. Inside she saw the menacing shadows of the chairs stacked on the tables. The hams hung in the window of the Spanish delicatessen across the street looked like human limbs; battlefield amputations. She shivered. This was a weekday street and it didn't take kindly to weekend visitors.

The portrait on the easel in the gallery window was still lit. She paused to peer inside, beyond it, to reacquaint herself with the geography of the room. It lessened her fear when she turned the key and walked in. The alarm box bleeped. A light flashed. She keyed in the code and the bleeping stopped. The light switches were beside the alarm. Samantha switched them all on, flooding the room with cold white light, but the light was too brutal so she switched all but one off, using it to guide her to Reilly's painting. She was relieved to see that it remained in the alcove at the rear of the gallery and only now acknowledged her fear that somehow the past month – from the moment when she first caught sight of the picture to this moment now – had all been a dream and she would wake and her life would revert to its old patterns. Perhaps there was, even now, another Samantha Dodd living her old life, legs drawn up beneath her, reading her book under the cone of light, chocolates in easy reach, dreading the approach of Monday morning. She reached out and touched Reilly's picture. There – it was real, but different now because she knew something about him and while she hadn't much liked what she'd learned, it made her love his painting no less. The surface of the picture was smooth, almost silky to her touch and warm despite the temperature of the room.

For the first time she noticed the birds in the chilly sky and the shadow on the path. She had assumed the short shadow (at the bottom of the picture, vanishing into the frame), to be the dampness of the path but now she wondered if it could be the shadow of Reilly himself – the artist's head, just visible for those who chose to look closely. Was this the first sign of his presence?

'What are you asking of me, Reilly?' she said, and listened hard for Reilly's voice. If he replied, she couldn't hear it above the distant wash of traffic on the city streets.

Samantha fell easily into her new work routine. She got up at the same time that she had for her previous job. She caught the same bus, she bought her usual sandwiches, crisps and chocolates from the same café (though she ate them in the gallery because when she wasn't there she had to lock the place up – if anybody came into the gallery while she was eating she would stuff the food into a drawer). There were few customers, although she did notice that many people stopped to look in through the window. Like her, they were too intimidated to come in. If she met their eye, they hurried away. Occasionally, when she saw somebody peering in, she would go to the door, apply her friendliest face, and invite them to look round. Some were glad of the offer and one elderly woman promised (with a glint in her eye) to return with her daughter and her daughter's credit card. On Thursday she sold her first painting. It was (in her estimation) an indifferent town scene by Peter Henty, who, Keith's catalogue notes on the computer suggested, was a minor member of the

Camden Town Group. The buyer, an edgy man with very blue, tired eyes, didn't seem to want to chat to her and became impatient when she couldn't get the chip-and-pin machine to work. As she tried it for the third time he took out his BlackBerry from his Burberry mac and held it in such a way that she was afraid he was going to hit her with it. All he would tell her was that he was buying the painting for somebody else and seemed to resent even giving that much away. When she had wrapped it, he took it from her without thanking her, glanced at his watch, and dashed away.

'We didn't like him, did we?' she said when the man had gone. She had taken to discussing her concerns with Reilly when no-one was in the gallery. Wanting to share her triumph over the sale, she called the receptionist at her former workplace, Anita, and invited her and any of the other women in the office to bring their lunch and eat it with her in the gallery. Despite refusing almost all social invitations that came her way, it never occurred to Samantha that Anita would not want to visit her, even at such short notice. And, indeed, Anita (half Greek on her father's side, with her father's stockiness and colouring) and Sonia, the young woman who had replaced Samantha, arrived shortly after one o'clock. Initially overwhelmed by the empty, echoing room, they wandered round, arm in arm, and looked at the paintings. Samantha remained at her desk watching them whisper, and the new girl giggle. She was particularly taken by a nude which provoked raucous laughter. Sonia was young and assertive and tall. She reminded Samantha of a gazelle-like Ghanaian girl who had bullied her at school, but had left at sixteen to become a model. Already she seemed to be in control of Anita (much plainer, much shorter) despite a ten-year gap in their ages. Anita giggled nervously at something Sonia whispered in her ear, then the two women marched up to the desk and Sonia demanded to know what they were having for lunch.

'I'm having my sandwich, I don't know what you're having,' Samantha replied.

'But you asked us for lunch – didn't she?' Sonia asked Anita.

'Well, not exactly *for* lunch,' Anita said.

'Still,' Sonia pressed, 'we're here now. Jacket potato would be nice.'

'I don't have a jacket potato. Only my sandwich. And I asked Anita if she'd like to come because I thought it might be nice to catch up with her.'

'So you didn't want me to come,' Sonia challenged her.

'I'm sure Samantha didn't mean that,' Anita soothed. 'Did you?'

'Well, no, I didn't mean that. But to be quite honest, having met you, Sonia…'

'Oh dear,' Anita said, in the tone of voice she would have used had one of them upset a drink.

'Well, to be quite honest, Samantha Dodd, having met you I wish I hadn't come. I'm not surprised they sacked you.'

'They didn't sack me, I resigned.'

'To work in this dump!'

'It's not a dump.'

'Seems like a dump to me.'

'Well, we'll have to agree to differ on that.' Samantha had now laid down her sandwich.

There was a silence, which Anita broke. 'You'll have to come to the Christmas party, Samantha. The other girls said I should ask you.'

'But it's only October.'

'I know. But they've got decorations up already in some shops and I'm organizing the Secret Santa. Can I put you down? It's ten pounds – we draw the names out of a hat.'

'If she's coming, I'm not going,' Sonia butted in.

'Oh, Sonia, don't be like that. Samantha's lovely when you get to know her.'

'Fat bitch can sod off as far as I'm concerned.'

'Sonia!'

'I'm going to get a jacket potato. And I'm having butter,' Sonia said, storming out and leaving the door open.

'...She's a bit excitable,' Anita said. 'But she's very young.'

'I couldn't stand to share an office with her.' Samantha picked up her salmon sandwich and took a comforting bite.

'I had to bring her. If you want the truth it was my turn. She's only been there three days and already we have to take it in turns to have lunch with her. That way the other two can have an hour of peace. Between you and me I think she's a bit doolally.' Anita sat in the chair at the end of the desk, took off her right shoe and peered at her foot. 'I think I've got a blister coming. I envy you in here. It seems very peaceful.'

'It is. I love it. Here.' Samantha took her other sandwich from the table and handed half of it to Anita.

'I couldn't. It's your lunch.'

'No. It's OK. Please.'

'Well, all right then. Thanks.' Anita took a surreptitious sniff of her hand, then used it to take the sandwich. She took a grateful bite. 'She didn't mean that about Christmas,' she said, between chews.

'I don't care about Christmas.'

'Don't say that!'

'I don't.'

'But it's lovely. It's a lovely time of the year.'

'I know. Of course it is. Or it can be. What I mean is that I just can't put my mind to it in October.'

'You have to plan, Samantha, or all the wine bars get booked up and there's nowhere to have your Christmas party. We might be having an Abba night – or Boney M. Can you imagine Mr Tubman all blacked up like that boy? I used to fancy him. The black lad, not Mr Tubman.'

'Not really.'

'...You've changed, Samantha.'

'Have I?'

'You have.'

'I've only been here a few days. I don't see how I can have changed that much.'

'It doesn't do to spend so much time on your own.'

'I'm not on my own.'

'Yes, you are. I walked past here yesterday and you were on your own. And the day before. Only yesterday you seemed to be talking to somebody.'

'But I don't feel alone.'

'Just because you don't feel lonely, doesn't mean you aren't lonely. I know it's been hard since your mum passed.'

'It's fine.'

'You miss her. You're bound to.'

'I'm not lonely. Honestly.' She had cried appropriately for her mother – but the tears were less for the loss she felt and more for her mother, who had died alone.

'No, Samantha, I know you think you're not. But you can't live in a bubble or you'll end up like those mad old people who don't care what they say, whether they offend people or not.'

'Is that how I seem to you?'

'Yes. It is. A bit.'

'Have I offended you?'

'No, but I know what you're like. Anyway, you know me, "good old Anita". Anita doesn't get offended. I did a questionnaire in *OK!* magazine and it said I was a "people pleaser" – I thought that was a nice thing to be until I thought about it and decided it wasn't. It was actually a very rubbish thing to be.'

'You are what you are,' Samantha said. 'Accept it or change. I knew I had to change when I heard there was a job going here. If I hadn't, I'd have regretted it.'

'But you're a strong person. I'm not… Listen to me, telling you all my secrets. We never talked like this when we worked together, did we?'

'No,' Samantha admitted, 'we didn't.'

They fell into a companionable silence then talked about work for a while.

'So, tell me what you have to do,' Anita said.

'Sit here and sell the paintings. That's all.'

'But you have to know about them?'

'You don't have to. But I like to.'

'What's your favourite?'

Samantha turned round in her chair and faced Reilly's picture. 'That one.'

'Why?'

'I can't put it into words.'

Anita stood and approached the painting. 'Is it paint?'

'Yes. Why?'

'It doesn't look all shiny like oil paint.'

'No. It's egg tempera.'

'What's that when it's at home?'

Now Samantha stood and joined Anita at the painting. 'It's made up with egg yolk and pigment. You have to make up a new batch each day.'

'That sounds a bit fiddly.'

'It is. You have to be a special type of painter to work with it.'

'...The picture – it makes me feel sad,' Anita said, after contemplating it in silence for a while.

'Yes. I know.'

'Is that what it's supposed to do?'

'I don't know. Perhaps when Reilly painted it he wanted to make people feel how he felt... or perhaps he didn't know how to do any different.'

'I hate to feel like that,' Anita said. 'When I do feel like that I know I'm having a bad day.'

'I think something terrible happened to him.'

'What?'

'I don't know. I'm just beginning to find out.'

'Well, if you do find out, don't tell me. I'd rather not know. Is it cold in here, or is it just me?'

'I don't know. I'm used to it.'

'Well,' Anita said brightly. 'I'd better be getting back. No doubt Sonia will be telling everybody what a terrible person I am for making her buy her potato on her own.'

'Thank you for coming.'

'That's all right. You look after yourself, love.'

'I do.'

'You don't. You never did.' For a brief moment Anita's fragile mask fell away. 'Make sure you ring and tell me how you are.'

'All right.'

'At home or at work. I don't mind. You've got my home number?'

'Yes. Thanks.'

'Don't be put off if Paul answers. He doesn't like the phone.'

'I won't.'

The two women embraced. Anita went back to work. Samantha returned to Reilly's painting. Anita's question had stayed with her: if Reilly's painting made people feel sad, was it intentional or was he incapable of portraying the world in a more positive light? Art, after all, was supposed to be uplifting, wasn't it? And sadness was such an easily provoked emotion. Or did he have some premonition of his fate which he had no choice but to represent in his pictures? Until she returned to Old Cross, all she could do was speculate.

When the phone on the desk rang she jumped in shock, but managed to sound businesslike when she answered.

'Keith Blake Gallery. Good afternoon.'

'Samantha. It's *moi.* I'm out. Escaped!'

'Keith?'

'Yes, who else would it be? I thought you'd be pleased to know I'm back at home.'

'So it wasn't TB?'

'Apparently not. Nor fatal. A chest infection. That evening quack didn't know what he was doing. Thankfully I seem to have escaped from the ward without contracting MRSA. Why don't you come round and we can catch up on your first week. Tomorrow?'

'Yes. All right.'

'I'll cook something. Come straight from there. I'll expect you at seven. And bring the mail.'

'All right.'

'...Is something wrong, Samantha?'

'No.'

'Are you sure?'

'No. No, I'm fine. Just – the phone – it surprised me, that's all. I'm fine.'

'Seven, then?'

'Yes.'

Samantha knew she should have been grateful that Keith had been discharged from the hospital, but she wasn't – she was surprised at how disappointed she felt. Now she would have to share what she had found out about T. F. Reilly with him.

❧

The following day she closed the gallery early. It had been the first day she hadn't enjoyed working there, which was less to do with the work itself than the anxiety she felt over visiting Keith in the evening. As the day went on the anxiety grew. There was nobody around to divert her from it, just the empty room and the pictures, which seemed to act as a distorting mirror to her concerns, bouncing them back towards her and magnifying them. She spent much of the afternoon with her chair turned, her back to the gallery, facing Reilly's picture as she would a fire. When she left at half past four she felt cold even though the temperature was no lower than the previous day, and she was dressed no less appropriately. When she got to the end of the street she realized she had forgotten to bring the manila folder of mail for Keith, so she returned for it.

She then went immediately to Old Cross, intending to call in on Brian at the café before arriving for her seven o'clock appointment at Keith's. She had already formulated the white lie she would use – that Brian had contacted her about the paintings and she wanted to assess what he had found so as not to waste Keith's time. She would adapt the lie depending on circumstances. But when she reached the café it was closed. Peering inside and seeing the tables and counter draped in decorator's sheets, Samantha thought it looked to have been out of commission for some days. There was no sign of Brian, no clatter of debris coming down his chute. In fact the skip was now gone, although the space for it was reserved by three red cones. She tried the door. It was locked. Half past five. Unless she could find Brian she had an hour and a half on her hands.

She would use it to look for clues that would help in her search for Reilly. She had brought the old newspaper with her, but she knew the story well, having read it three or four times. It mentioned the canal and made reference to Mountjoy's coffee shop. Reilly's room would have been somewhere within the vicinity, although no indication was given as to exactly where. The canal seemed as good a place to start as any so she made her way there, hoping that she wouldn't encounter Keith on the way.

When she walked down the steps beside the bridge she knew that, of all Old Cross, the canal bank was probably the area least changed since Reilly's day. Conservation restrictions had preserved the exterior of the buildings that backed onto the towpath, if not the industries that once inhabited them. The colour works was now a facilities house for television. Two young women and a young man were standing on the roof balcony, smoking cigarettes, oblivious to the cold. She tried to block the sound of their chatter and laughter, tried to visualize the crowd that had gathered on the bank a century before, held back by the two constables, Gower's body behind them and Mountjoy and Reilly standing close by. She squinted but she couldn't see them. She closed her eyes but they remained invisible to her. Samantha did, however, feel fear; the fear of being alone on an unlit canal side at night. She shivered and hurried back towards the bridge, rushing up the steps to the sanctuary of the lit street.

When she returned to the café she was grateful to see Brian's van, hazard lights flashing, a scrawled note in the window ('Emergency plumber'), parked in the space reserved by the three traffic cones. The café lights were on but there was no sign of life on the ground floor. Samantha backed away from the door and looked up towards the roof of the building. A beacon of light radiated from the hole in the slates. She knew it was unlikely that Brian would hear her but she tried the bell anyway and waited. She tried it again a minute later, then once more to no effect. As an afterthought she pushed at the door and it opened. Tentatively she went in, calling Brian's name as she did so. She heard the sound of an electric drill above her. It stopped, started, stopped, then started again. The door behind the counter was open, and immediately behind it she saw the stairs, so she went up.

She called again on the landing, and this time Brian replied with an 'Up here.' He didn't sound surprised to hear that somebody had wandered into the café. She climbed another flight. On the top landing she was faced with a tall ladder that went up through a loft hatch into the roof space.

'I thought it was you.' Brian's face appeared at the gap. 'Do you want to come up?'

'All right.' Samantha left her handbag, the folder of Keith's mail and her plastic bag beside a hammer and some other tools and climbed the ladder. She felt the chill of the open air when her head arrived in the loft space. It was disorientating – cold outside air inside a house. Looking around, she saw Brian standing by the hole in the roof. He was illuminated from behind by an arc light. The loft floor was boarded and Brian was in the process of nailing plaster boards to the underside of the roof. The space was twenty-five or thirty feet long, cluttered with tools, and higher and wider than she had expected. A dormer window was waiting to be fitted into the gap in the roof. The far end of the room was partitioned off with a plasterboard wall, an unpainted door at the centre.

'Give me your hand,' Brian said, taking her hand and helping her up the final step. 'There.' As he released her hand his attention slid slowly down her body.

'I've brought your newspaper back,' Samantha explained.

'OK.' Brain seemed uninterested. There was something else on his mind, something he seemed to want to convey to her. Something she didn't want to acknowledge.

'...I wondered if you had any more.'

'Plenty.' Brian gestured to a pile covered in dust sheets at the far end of the roof space. He then seemed to brighten and went on to ask after Keith. Samantha filled him in on Keith's progress, although she was impatient to find out what lay beneath the sheets.

'Pictures,' he said. 'Lots of them. More newspapers and some other rubbish.'

'Can I see?'

'If you like.'

She followed Brian across the boarded floor, stepping around tools and cables and a stack of plasterboard. Brian reached down and peeled back the tarpaulin to reveal two opened tea chests. One of them, she could see, contained paintings.

'Do you mind if I look?' Samantha said, approaching the chest.

'Fill your boots. I've got to get on.' Brian returned to the job in hand and Samantha reached in to the nearest chest, taking hold of a black wooden picture frame and gently tugging it out of the clutch of the pictures on each side of it. Grittily it slid out. The dust on the glass obscured the picture beneath. She blew it, but the heavy dust, made damp by the roof's exposure to the air, clung on. She wiped it with her fingers, smearing a small clearing on the glass, and turned it towards Brian's light. As she did so she glimpsed him staring at her. He looked quickly away, returning to his work. The picture was a cheap watercolour reproduction: a bucolic summer scene of milkmaids and cottages. She laid it carefully on the floor and took out another, which slipped out more easily: another rural scene, this time featuring more cottages and a stone bridge. The seven other pictures were on a similar theme. A newspaper had been used to line the chest. No story caught her eye. She replaced the pictures in the order she had taken them out and, still kneeling, examined the contents of the other chest: some pottery, an incomplete tea set, an empty photograph album, a pair of binoculars, a folded Union flag.

'I told you there was more pictures,' Brian called over.

'Yes. You did.'

'Load of old tat, isn't it?'

'I'm sure it has sentimental value.'

'Oh, I'm sure it does. But I know what you're looking for…'

'What do you mean?'

'You know.'

'What?'

He winked. 'Same as what Keith's after. More of the proper stuff. Originals. Not that old crap.'

'And did you find any?'

'Yeah. I'll show you. Just finish this first. You can't expect me to down tools just like that.'

'I'm sorry. If you're too busy.'

'Nah. Never too busy. Never.' Brian's smile re-established itself.

Having nailed up the board he was working on, Brian dropped his hammer noisily onto the floor and opened the door in the partition wall.

'This way,' he said, and led the way into a newly plastered room tricked out with plastic and copper pipes in readiness for a bathroom suite. There was no external window in the room and no light. The room smelt of damp plaster. 'These was up here, too.' He gestured towards three cloth-covered canvases leaning against the only wall that hadn't been plastered. 'I reckon this lot was stored up here and just left. I had a devil of a job to get the loft hatch open. Nobody had been up here for years. Anyway, I found four canvases – the one in the front loft that Keith took off my hands a few weeks back – and then these three at the back when I got that old partition wall down. Oh yeah, and those newspapers in that chest, and that old thing over there.' He pointed to a cube, draped in sheeting. 'Have a look if you like.'

Samantha leaned down, and before she had taken the picture from the cloth she knew she was in the presence of Reilly again. It was a large piece (roughly five feet wide and four feet high); when she unsheathed it it represented the view from a rear first-floor window of a large Cotswold house (not derelict, but neither in particularly good order). From the window a greenhouse dominated the scene and stood at the end of a short flagstoned path, just beyond the reach of the shadows. Beyond the greenhouse were the russet brick walls of a kitchen garden, the cement between the brick an ice-cream colour. The impression was of early afternoon. Some of the panes of old glass in the greenhouse were greened with damp, some were broken, and the light through these broken panes Reilly had managed to represent as distinct from the sunlight piercing the intact panes. But what dominated the picture was the boy staring up towards her; a young boy, eight or nine, pleading for her not to tell. Reilly, at last – imploring her to keep his secret. That was why he had been here for almost a century. He had been hiding – not from her, but from the rest of the world.

'Yes,' Samantha said. 'This is what I'm looking for.' Brian's eyes, she now saw, were on her legs. As she knelt down her skirt had ridden up her thigh and she was suddenly aware there was a good deal of her flesh on display. She stood, smoothing down her skirt.

'Worth anything?' Brian swallowed dryly.

'Oh, yes. Yes. I'm sure.' She carried the canvas through the door. The arc light glossed its surface into silk.

Brian followed her. 'How much?'

'I don't know. You'd have to…' And there Samantha paused. She didn't want Reilly's pictures in Keith's gallery. She didn't want them to be sold to undiscriminating investors like the hurried man who'd bought the Peter Henty. In fact she didn't want Keith to have anything to do with them.

'You'd have to what?'

'…You'd have to leave them with me.'

'So you can talk to Keith?'

'That's right.'

'Unless…' Brian was looking at her the same way he'd done when he helped her off the ladder. She'd chosen to ignore it at the time but she couldn't now.

'…We could come to an arrangement between ourselves,' Samantha said. 'If that's what...' Immediately she regretted the offer, seeing that was exactly what was on Brian's mind.

'Well,' he said, advancing towards her. 'I think I can live with that.'

'A financial arrangement. That's what I meant.'

'Is it?'

'Yes. Of course.'

'You sure?'

'Very sure.'

Now he was close: an outstretched arm away from her. 'I mean, you'd have to forgive a bloke for thinking otherwise. Given you being here on a Friday night, all dressed up and that.'

'Don't be ridiculous, Brian. I'm dressed for work. That's all.'

'Yeah, well... still...'

'Look,' Samantha said, stronger now. 'I'd be very happy to meet you for a drink or something. Who knows, perhaps we could, I don't know, get to know each other better. But I hardly know you. And even if I did, I certainly wouldn't be getting up to anything in this filthy room.'

'Shame,' Brian said. 'Because it's places like this I like. You know? Bit of dirt. Bit of muck on the floors. That's what I like.'

'Don't be ridiculous.'

'You think it's ridiculous, do you?' He advanced towards her. ''Cause I don't.'

'Brian. No.'

'You're just playing with me. You know you want it.' There was an absence in his eyes. She felt his hands on her breasts.

'No!' She shouted, shoving him away.

'No need to play hard to get.' Brian stumbled and reached for her. She pushed him away again. He stepped forward to steady himself but his right foot found space, air, nothingness, and he vanished with a cry and a clatter through the loft hatch. Then there was silence.

Samantha peered through the open hatch and saw, ten feet below, Brian staring towards her. Air was escaping from his mouth. His right leg lay beneath him at a comical angle. Beneath him there was a widening pool of black. With effort he lifted his head from the floor. It fell back softly. He made one final plea with his eyes and then the light went out in them.

TWELVE

Reilly in Chains

REILLY HAD BEEN WAITING FOR TWO HOURS IN A SMALL, STINKING cell beneath the police station. He was cold. They had taken his watch, his shoelaces, his belt and the few coins from his pocket. He had kept track of the time by a distant church bell that chimed the quarter. He could hear the occasional rumble of carriages along the street above him and the rhythmic drip of water into a bucket. The floor was stone. The walls were brick and cold to the touch. The straw mattress of the cot was covered by a rough grey blanket. There were no sheets; nothing in the way of comfort. Reilly lay down and tried to sleep but his mind was busy with the events of the previous few hours. As night fell, Portch had arrested him on the step of his lodging house. The crowd, which included Pardew, had been silenced into respect by the sombre theatricality of the procedure. Reilly had challenged the arrest, protested his innocence, and handed over the wallet to prove it. A day before, even an hour before, the gesture would have counted in his favour. Now it was too late. Portch took him by trap to the police station. Macreadie made his own way there.

'You had your chance,' Portch said to him on the journey. There was no censure in the observation but Reilly knew his case was weakened by not having confessed the wallet on Portch's visit to his room.

'Yes.'

'Somebody looking after the little dog?'

'Mountjoy.'

'Any other arrangements that need to be made?'

'You don't believe I killed him, do you?'

'Thinking doesn't come into it. It's now a matter of evidence, and motive.'

'So what will happen now?'

'You'll be held in a cell. You'll be interviewed and tomorrow you'll be brought up in front of the magistrates.'

'And then?'

'One day at a time. That's the best way to proceed. Take the medicine.'

'What do you mean?'

'You'll find out.'

❧

Reilly heard the bolt being drawn back. The heavy door swung open.

'All right, up you get,' the man said: a huge shadow, a wide-shouldered bruiser, blocking the miserly light from the subterranean corridor. Reilly stood. The man advanced towards him, pulling the door shut behind him. 'Just a few words of warning.'

'Yes?' Reilly could smell stale beer on the bruiser's breath.

'Just a few words of warning.'

Reilly was shoved against the wall. First his body made contact with the cold brick, then his head snapped back. The pain was sharp. He glimpsed the bruiser's fist: swollen fingers strangulated by gold rings.

'Please,' Reilly said, but he expected no mercy.

'Just a few words of warning.'

Reilly was worked over, softened up; discovered what it meant to take his medicine.

❧

Each time a figure walked past the coffee-house window, Nimrod stood and, with a hopeful tail wag, waited for the door to open. When the figure was gone, he settled to the floor with a sigh. Mountjoy, resting at the table closest to the fire, envied his optimism. The gas lights were unlit, the fire low. After the arrest several locals had made their way to the coffee shop to see the murderer's paintings but Mountjoy refused them entry. Instead they peered through the window, their faces pressed to the glass like a grotesque display of death masks. Mountjoy turned off the gas mantles. The masks dispersed, diffusing like ghosts into a fog. Reilly's presence was strong in the room. Mountjoy found a quiet solace in the pictures. Since the arrest, Reilly's work had a new currency. But would the artist want his paintings to be sold under such circumstances – or would he expect Mountjoy to take the paintings from the walls and close the exhibition? It was a question that only Reilly could answer. Mountjoy would try and get word to him.

He heard a knock at the door and looked round warily, expecting another ghoul or, worse, Pardew. He knew, in the shadowed interior of the coffee shop, he was invisible from the street and had no intention of allowing anybody in, but he could see that the visitor was a woman, her head covered by a black shawl. Mountjoy left the table and went to the door. The woman pulled back her shawl: Amy Sykes. Mountjoy turned the key. She hurried past him without a word. He locked the door. Amy waited at the centre of the room, her shawl now low around her shoulders. She was clearly in some distress.

'I didn't know where to go,' she said.

'Sit down, please.' Mountjoy went to fetch a seat from a table, then busied himself lighting the gas.

'No, thank you, I'll stand. Were you there?'

'When…?'

'When they took him away.'

'Yes. I was there.'

'I was so ashamed. He came by. A few hours ago. He came by and I was ashamed and I ran to the back of the shop. How I do wish I had spoken to him.'

'It's Pardew who should be ashamed. The man is a viper.'

'He was only telling the truth.'

'He twisted the truth into a lie. Several truths.'

'That's as may be.'

'…How can I help you?' Mountjoy asked.

It was clear that Amy Sykes's concerns were not over the damage to her reputation. A wildness showed in her eyes; her face was pale and emaciated. 'I didn't know where to go. I've been walking the streets for three hours. Then I passed here and I saw you and Reilly speaks well of you so I…'

'Reilly is a friend. A good friend.'

'You've taken in his dog.' Amy looked fondly down on Nimrod. 'You must be a good friend.'

'Please do sit down,' Mountjoy said. Amy Sykes seemed close to madness. At this bidding she sat, tugging her shawl tight around her, rocking back and forth in short movements. Mountjoy went to the counter, reached beneath it and took out a bottle of port. He poured two glasses. Amy Sykes accepted one as if by right and emptied it in a single swallow. It seemed to calm her.

'Now tell me what it is that I can do for you.'

'What you can do for me?' she said, as if the idea had only just occurred to her.

'Yes. I'll do what I can.'

'Give me a home? Provide for my child? Protect me from my father who seems intent on killing me – and Reilly?'

'Sykes has thrown you out onto the street?'

'With nothing.'

'But surely he'll relent.'

'The way he relented over my mother?'

'Your mother?'

Amy Sykes shook her head. The story of the loss of her mother was for another time. 'I have nowhere to go. I must find a place to stay.' She stood and made for the door.

'Stay here. For tonight at least.'

Amy Sykes paused.

Mountjoy continued, 'It's too late to be out looking for a room.'

'I'll pay you. Not tonight. I have nothing. But I will pay you.'

'You'll pay me by sleeping soundly. It's the least I can do for you – and for Reilly.'

'You're kind. Reilly said you had a good heart.'

'I try to be decent,' Mountjoy said, knowing now that Amy had never had any intention of leaving the coffee shop that evening. Uncharitably, he wondered if she had, indeed, spent three hours wandering the streets or whether she might have run there directly after an argument with her father.

Amy Sykes drifted along the parade of Reilly's paintings, finally coming to her own portrait beside the counter.

'No!' Amy Sykes's hand went to her mouth.

'He didn't tell you he'd painted you?'

'I had no idea.'

Mountjoy allowed her a few moments to contemplate her image, then he asked: 'Is this your life?'

'It's the life I had. The life I had with Reilly. The life we could have had together. That's the woman I see there.'

'There's still a hope, Amy, of that life. So long as Reilly is alive, there's still hope.'

Mountjoy felt a small weight against his right leg. Nimrod was leaning against him, peering up, reminding him of his right to affection. Mountjoy reached down and patted the dog's head. Nimrod settled on his foot. Mountjoy was content to let him rest there as Amy Sykes continued to stare with wonder at Reilly's portrait of her and the fire burned low in the grate.

❧

After the beating Reilly was left alone in the cell with only his fear to accompany him. He felt a terror akin to waking in the night and sensing a presence in the room. The source of his terror lurked behind him and he was fearful of turning over and confronting it. He had entered a lawless world. He was friendless. There was no-one to guide him. All could have been different had he confessed to, or confided in, Portch. Had he done so the police constable, he sensed, would have spoken up for him.

There is no softness in the depths of a police station or the wings of a prison. Every entry and exit is signalled by the percussive opening or closing of a cell door (however well-oiled their hinges, heavy metal doors require brute force to shift them), any moment of reverie shattered by the spyhole guillotining shut. It was the harsh slide and slam of the latter, as rapid as an ancient musket being cocked, that accompanied the entry of a mute warder, who marshalled Reilly from the cell to the interview room where Macreadie and Portch awaited him. Here, at least, were a few vestiges of the familiar world – a wooden table, two wooden chairs, a harsh, unshaded electric lightbulb dangling on plaited flex from the ceiling and the world going about its merciful business outside the window. Reilly glimpsed a constable, bull's-eye lantern swinging, making his way across the street towards the station. Lurching ahead of him, his huge and comical shadow. On the stand beneath the street lamp a cabman dozed on his bench, the reins loose in his gloved hands while his nag shifted in her shanks like a boat at its moorings. Reilly had been in the cell for three hours but already he was mourning the world. How would he bear life in the echoing hell of prison? If, as was famously written, an artist is defined as an individual on whom nothing is lost, Reilly's only hope of survival lay in stiffening those sensibilities; becoming another individual entirely.

The mute warder who had fetched Reilly from the cell was dismissed by Macreadie. The Chief Inspector welcomed Reilly. Portch stood sentry by the door. In the absence of a mirror, Reilly studied Portch's face hoping that he would learn from his reaction how visible the beating had been. But Portch reflected nothing.

'Sit down,' Macreadie commanded. The Chief Inspector was a civilized man, or played the part of a civilized man well. His voice was slow, suggesting a cognitive lag or a weakness for drink. He had a ruler-sharp centre parting; his elegantly cut hair was greased flat. His sideburns were long though it was his moustache that dominated his face. Flecked with grey, it seemed to have been designed to draw the observer's eye from his small brown eyes, the only weakness in his features. Macreadie had removed his jacket and stood in waistcoat and shirtsleeves, his stiff-winged collar and cuffs still spotless, his trousers retaining their morning crease.

Reilly took the chair and waited for the interrogation to begin. Having no experience of such circumstances, he prepared himself to answer as honestly as he could.

'Portch here tells me he understands why you might have killed Gower,' Macreadie began, aiming a look towards the constable.

'I did not kill Gower.'

'...He tells me you seem a decent man. Much taken by your dog, he was.'

'I did not kill Gower.'

'No. I don't believe you did.'

'Well, thank you,' Reilly said, standing. 'If you'd be good enough to let me out…'

'What I mean to say is that I don't believe you killed him intentionally. Sit down.'

Reilly sat.

'Your solicitor will explain to you the distinction.'

'I understand the distinction.'

'Then you'll understand that if you choose to make a statement now to the effect that there was an argument, Gower stumbled, he fell, and drowned – and also, perhaps, that you tried to save him but failed – then we can all go to bed and your visit to the magistrate will be a more conducive one.'

'You're suggesting I plead guilty?'

'To the lesser charge of manslaughter. I'd be happy to support such a plea. We wouldn't therefore need to call on the services of Mr John Ellis in a few months' time.'

'Ellis?'

'The hangman. You could serve out your time in the Model Prison – where the food is not at all unappetizing, where the cells and the chapel are adequately heated, and where you might use your artistic abilities to some commercial end. Many inmates work at the looms, which passes the time quite well. The library, so I understand, is second to none.'

'I did not kill Gower.'

'Mr Reilly.' Macreadie settled against the table, folding his arms and adopting a genial man-to-man tone. 'Let me explain something to you.' He pondered. 'No, first let me tell you of a conversation I had with Mr Ellis when I last encountered him.'

'Mr Macreadie,' Reilly responded, finding some strength at last. 'You can tell me all you wish about your conversation with the hangman but it won't change the fact that I did not kill Gower. And however long we remain in this room, and however many times you threaten me, you won't hear me change that plea.'

'To return to the conversation with Mr John Ellis,' Macreadie continued. 'He was explaining when we last met, I can't remember for what reason, something of the training he undertook. Pentonville is a popular venue to train men of his profession. Along with the calculations of the length of the rope, how to set the drop, pinion the prisoner and carry out a speedy execution using a dummy, he said the most important lesson he learned was how to hang a man who'd cut his own throat (Ellis, of course, is perhaps not a gent you'd choose to spend much time with on a cold and dark winter's night). He suggested that this was by no means uncommon. He was making a plea he hoped we'd pass on: that the condemned man should trust him to do his business, being much better equipped to dispatch the man than the man himself.' Here he paused to allow the image to establish itself in Reilly's mind. 'The point I'm leading to is this. There are two moments in the career of a criminal – after the committing of the crime, and before sentencing – in which the accused can both influence and speed his passage through the legal system. The first comes when he encounters the police constable or detective and is questioned over the circumstances of the crime. A simple admission of guilt at this point would make his life much easier. The second is when he is cautioned and brought to the station. Here he is given a final opportunity to save the time of the police, the courts and those employed in the prisons: all the way from the governor at the top to the carter, the cook and the baker at the bottom. I am now offering you that final opportunity and if you choose not to take it then, tomorrow, I can assure you, your unhappy apprenticeship as a condemned man begins. Ellis's business, I have no need to remind you, is with men who took neither opportunity.'

'I did not kill Gower,' Reilly said.

Macreadie leaned menacingly towards Reilly as if he was going to strike him. Instead, he whipped out a chair from the table and took it to the wall where he set it down. He sat, crossed his legs, lit a cigarette he had taken from a case in his pocket, and Portch came forward to take his place.

'Tell me about the evening Gower called,' Portch began.

'I've told you all there is to tell.'

'Then tell it again.'

'Gower called,' Reilly said with some weariness. 'He looked at my work. He made some notes and he left.'

'But that isn't all there is to tell. You've missed out an important part of the story.'

'Have I?'

'I should think you have. The reason the wallet came to be in your possession.'

'Nimrod fetched it back from the canal bank.'

'Your Jack Russell?'

'Yes.'

'Gower left, the little fellow went out and later returned with the wallet?'

'Yes. Well, Nimrod left at the same time as Gower.'

'They left together?'

'At the same time. When Gower went it was the time for Nimrod's evening walk, so I let him out. He came back and I assume it was then that he brought the wallet back with him.'

'And why should you assume that?'

'Because that was the only night between Gower's visit and the exhibition that he went out alone.'

'And how do you know it was brought back from the canal bank?'

'Because Nimrod showed me.'

'He showed you?'

'Yes. He led me there and… showed me.'

'But the wallet might, of course, have been left in your room by Gower.'

'I suppose it might, but then I'd have noticed it.'

'Would you?'

'Yes, I'm sure I would.'

'Very well, let's move on. Gower leaves in the company of your dog. The little fellow returns with the wallet – but you are unaware he has brought the wallet back?'

'Yes.'

'You didn't notice it?'

'No.'

'And yet you've just informed me that had Gower left the wallet in your room you would have noticed it.'

'But Gower is not Nimrod.'

'I think we can agree on that. But what point are you making here?'

'Nimrod hides things away. You saw him scrabbling away at that brick. He's secretive. It's part of his nature. He brings all manner of things back from his walks. I rarely find any of them until he chooses to reveal them to me.'

'You speak of him as if he's human.'

'If being secretive is only a human trait, then yes, I do. But Nimrod has many traits that are recognizably human.'

'Such as?'

'Well… impatience, joy, sadness, disdain, haughtiness, despair.'

'You discern all of those traits in the little fellow?'

'I do.'

'Next you'll be suggesting that he murdered Gower in a fit of rage.'

'Don't be ridiculous, Nimrod's incapable of such a degree of rage. Had I seen the wallet, had Nimrod not hidden it, I would have brought it straight to you.'

'For what reason?'

'For the reason that Gower had disappeared and the wallet might have provided a clue as to where he was.'

'But you were unaware that Gower had disappeared. All you knew was that Gower had left your room in the company of Nimrod.'

'On that day, yes. But later, when you called at the coffee shop…'

'Let's not get ahead of ourselves. Let's return to the discovery of the wallet. When did you become aware of it?'

'A day or two after Gower's visit. Perhaps three. I saw Nimrod chewing away at something on the floor.'

'But, because two or three days had passed since the visit, you chose not to bring the wallet to the police station?'

'No. I did not. I took it to Mountjoy.'

'For what reason?'

'I... I didn't know what to do.'

'But two or three days before, you suggest that had you found the wallet you would have known immediately what to do with it.'

'Yes. But... but, two days before I wasn't aware that Gower was missing, which changed things entirely. I learned of it when you called at the coffee shop.'

'So when you arrived at the coffee shop with the wallet you were unaware Gower was missing?'

'...Yes.'

'The circumstances, therefore, being the same as two or three days before – when, as you've already said, you would have delivered the wallet directly to the station had you found it.'

'I don't... You're trying to confuse me.'

'And if the circumstances were the same it would seem to suggest that, right from the off, you were aware of the implication of being in possession of that wallet. You visited Mr Mountjoy only because your conscience was troubling you.'

'No. That's not... that's not true.'

'Thank you, Portch. Very illuminating.' Macreadie stood, leaned back, and stretched out his spine. 'I'm sorry to say you've just condemned yourself, Mr Reilly.'

'How? I'm just trying to be honest.'

'I'm sure you are. But you've just admitted this: the wallet was in your possession. Increasingly concerned, knowing it was only a matter of time before Gower's body was discovered, you took it to your accomplice, Mountjoy, to discuss what to do with it.'

'I'd hardly call Mountjoy my accomplice.'

'...PC Portch's arrival at the coffee shop confirmed that Gower's disappearance had been brought to the attention of the police, which increased your concern even further.'

'I don't understand how that changes anything. Two days, three days... what difference does it make? All I'm guilty of is, for a short time, keeping hold of the wallet and, I admit, examining how a hundred and fifty pounds could change my circumstances. I would not have kept it.'

'But you did keep it. And you ask what difference two or three days makes – it makes all the difference. Knowing Gower was dead, from the outset you were aware of the implications of being in possession of that wallet. The discovery of the body confirmed the seriousness of this. You had no intention of bringing it to the police station. Since then you constructed the implausible tale of your blameless dog somehow coming across the wallet on his evening walk and fetching it back. I'd strongly recommend that if you intend to use the story in your defence you discuss the matter at some length with your solicitor. I suspect he would counsel against it.'

'But if, as you say, I was aware from the beginning that it was Gower's wallet, why would I keep it? Surely I would have got rid of the evidence and hidden the money.'

'That would have been the logical step to take.'

'Very well,' Reilly said, in some desperation. 'If I did kill Gower, how did I do it – is there any evidence of foul play? And why would I have taken the risk of doing it at the canal?'

'On the first issue there will be an inquest at which the coroner will present his evidence. On the second, should the jury at the inquest find there to be sufficient evidence, there will be a murder trial. Meanwhile, Mr Reilly, I'm afraid you'll be kept on remand until such a time as, at least, the first issue is resolved. Assuming that tomorrow morning the magistrate agrees. Do we offer one more opportunity for him to change his plea?' Macreadie asked Portch.

'I think so,' Portch said.

'Well?'

'I did not kill Gower.'

Macreadie rapped on the door. The silent man returned and took Reilly back to the cell to see out the night. Macreadie and Portch went to their homes.

A distant bell chimed three o'clock.

THIRTEEN

Dancing Around the Flames

'IT'S ALL RIGHT,' SAMANTHA ASSURED REILLY. 'HE'S GONE NOW. WE'RE safe.'

From the canvas, Reilly looked back.

'I know. I know. We'll have to get you out of here. Don't worry, I'll find a way.'

Samantha's orderly mind struggled to take command of the emotions that fought to overwhelm her: shock, fear, regret, sadness, guilt. She wiped a tear from her cheek. Her heart slowed as she assessed the tasks she faced: remove the paintings from the café, check through the other box and take anything that might be of use, hide the paintings, and get to Keith's house in a little under an hour. There was no perfect solution, but there was an obvious one. She would use Brian's Transit van and hope to return it before his body was discovered. She backed down the ladder to the landing and stood over him. The pool beneath Brian had spread unevenly. Most of the blood seemed to have come from his left side but he was not lying flat. Curious as to why, she knelt down, put her cheek to the floor and peered beneath him. The wound in his back had been made by the upturned claw of a hammer. Had it not been lying there, carelessly discarded like many of his other tools, he might still be alive. His fault, then. Not hers. Nevertheless, she apologized to him as she reached into his right pocket and rooted around, feeling the give of the warm thigh flesh. The pocket was deep. At the bottom her fingers made contact with metal and she tugged out his van keys.

It was an easy matter to get the paintings out of the building and into the back of the van. Only one of the three was large but it weighed very little. She left the others draped, saving them for later, loading them into the van as if she had every right, then returned one final time to the loft to check the contents of the other chest. There were three more newspapers, at least one of which featured the developing 'case of the canal murder'. She decided to take them all and laid them on the floor beside the chest, then took out an Oxo tin. Prising off the tight lid, she was disappointed to see that it contained only buttons. The tin, a silver coffee pot wrapped in newspaper and a bowler hat in its box she returned to the chest. Only one thing remained: the cube beneath the sheeting. She pulled off the sheet to reveal a display case, similar to those she had seen in a museum containing birds and otters and other stuffed animals in carefully contrived natural scenes. This case housed a dog, a Jack Russell terrier. The taxidermist had done his best but the dog, at its death, had been old, his coat dull. A simple brass plaque attached to the side announced the dog's name: 'Nimrod'. She had no use for an old, stuffed dog so she draped the sheet over and, taking the newspapers, backed down the ladder for the final time. At the bottom she stepped back into Brian's blood, but she was careful to wipe the toe of her shoe on the chest of his shirt so as not to leave incriminating footprints. She then collected her handbag, the plastic bag she had brought with her containing the original newspaper, and the Manila file.

When Samantha left the café she turned out all the lights and pulled the door shut, dropping the catch. She had established that one of the Yales on Brian's key ring fitted the café lock. If Brian was missed and anybody went to the café to look for him she hoped they would assume by the locked door, the darkness of the building and the absence of his van that he wasn't there. Samantha got into the van and turned the key in the ignition. The diesel engine started without complaint and ticked over with a throaty grumble. She found the switch for the hazard lights and turned them off, looked in the rear-view mirror, signalled and pulled away. The van stalled. It had been four months since she had been behind the wheel of a car – and that had been her mother's old Fiat when she ferried her back and forth to the hospital. She forced herself to draw in a deep breath before she turned the key again. The van was still in gear. It jumped forward and cut out. Finally she got it started, pulling away from the café with one last glimpse in her mirror. She would park near Keith's, then drive herself home after she had seen him. Somehow she would find the way across North London. She would unload the paintings at her flat then return the van to Old Cross (no reason to leave it near the café). She would then take a taxi home again. The plan was foolproof. Reilly would have been proud of her.

❧

'Oh, there you are.' Keith greeted her at the door as if she was late, though she was, in fact, two minutes early. 'Do I look better?' He touched his palm to his flushed face. He was wearing a blue apron and carrying a tea towel.

'Much better.'

Keith forced out a cough. 'See? I can cough without bringing up a lung. I can't tell you how good it feels. I feel as if I've been released from a death sentence.' He looked up and down the street like a practised busybody. 'Well, don't just stand there. Come in. Did you bring the mail?'

'Yes.'

'Good girl. Pop it on the table, and when you go, take that envelope for me and shove it in the desk drawer in the gallery. Just receipts and whatnot. I'll file them when I next come in.' He waved her inside with a waft of his hand. She paused at the door to the living room.

'Go straight through. We're in the kitchen.'

An uncovered pan of pasta was venting steam into the small room. The windows were opaque with condensation. Sauce bubbled in a small non-stick pan. Lying on the drainer was a bag of Italian salad leaves inflated like a lung. The radio was playing low; a man whispered a smiling introduction, a piano struck up a waltz.

'I didn't know if you were a veggie or not so I've done a tomato and basil sauce. Is that OK?'

'Fine.'

'So tell me how you got on. Wine?' Keith held up a half-empty bottle of red wine.

'No, thank you.'

'Why not? You're not driving, are you?'

'No! No, of course I'm not.'

'Well then, one little glass isn't going to hurt you, is it?'

'I suppose not.'

'Good girl.'

Keith filled a large glass, handed it to her, and then topped up his own. 'Cheers!' he said, clashing his glass against hers.

'Cheers.'

'So tell me how your week's been – and I'll tell you about mine.'

❧

Samantha endured Keith's food and chatter, grateful to find that the wine was dulling her anxieties over the events of the early evening. It had been so long since she had drunk anything that after three or four sips she felt light-headed. It did not, however, lighten her mood. She had always refused to relinquish control to alcohol. Tonight she allowed it in, but only a little way. It lay like a warm flannel over her mind – another sip and she knew she would become another Samantha, and she was saving that version of herself until she was ready to deal with her. Keith's account of his few days in hospital was dull: a litany of sleights, sleepless nights, unsavoury commodes, slack practice and unanswered calls. In return she sketched her week, saving the climax of the sale of the Henty for the end. It wasn't greeted with as much enthusiasm as she'd hoped. Keith seemed disappointed she had sold only one painting. She changed tack, asked him about the other paintings on the walls, picking her way carefully towards Reilly's picture which, of course, was the only one she was interested in.

'The Reilly? It's rather marvellous, isn't it?' Keith said. 'I wish I still smoked.'

'Smoked?'

'Yes. Don't you crave nicotine after a meal?'

'Have one. I don't mind.'

'No. I gave up years ago.'

'But you were telling me about the Reilly painting.'

'Yes. Shall we go into the lounge?' Keith stood. 'Coffee?'

'Well… all right.'

'Go through. Make yourself comfortable. I'll bring it in.'

Samantha waited in the living room while Keith prepared the coffee. A fire burned in the grate. She knelt and looked into the busy orange heart of it, feeling the warmth against her knees. She chose two large pieces of coal from the bucket on the hearth and dropped them on. Fireflies fled up the chimney. The fire quietened and settled. She lost herself in the story of the flames. This is what they told her: We come from fire, not water. Our lives are a dance around the flames. When we die many of us choose to return there. Her mother had made her wishes known. She wanted a quick ceremony at the crem. 'And Samantha, you make sure my friends get a good spread afterwards. Don't let me down.' Samantha did not let her mother down; she had never let her mother down. She had been warm and welcoming, a good host, and people commented on how well she was dealing with the death of her only surviving relative. On the day of the funeral she wore her mother's dress. Her best friend commented on it, seeming to find it strange. It seemed perfectly natural to Samantha. So why did Anita have to say that to her in the gallery that day? Why did she have to show that compassion? Why couldn't people mind their own business? Much easier to do without them. Reilly wouldn't, didn't, would never make such demands on her. And suddenly, tumbling from this jumbled headlong reasoning, she knew. When Keith came in with the coffee, she said, 'Reilly lost his mother quite young.'

'What?'

'That's... I just know he did.'

But the observation was of no interest to Keith. 'You could have turned the light on,' he said primly.

'I don't like harsh lights.'

'Pull out that table for me before I drop this tray.'

Samantha did as she was told and Keith set down the tray and poured the coffee. Handing her a cup, he offered this comment (like a biscuit, she thought, something sweet to help the coffee down): 'I suppose I'd better tell you. I mean, I can trust you?'

'Of course. Tell me what?'

'Well...' Keith sighed hard. 'I don't mean to be evasive... I've had a difficult few months. We all have. Last year the work just flew out of the gallery – some days I'd sell three or four pictures to pissed City boys after their expense account lunches at L'Escargot or Edmund's or Little's – but people seem to be tightening their belts. And the Internet's changed the market. Suddenly everybody's a bloody dealer and the bargains are gone.'

'Yes. I did wonder.'

'And when it doesn't come in, it can't go out. What I mean is that if the gallery is not earning I don't have the wherewithal to go out and buy.

I'm not interested in contemporary. There are too few people I'd give wall space to, which means I'm at the mercy of auctions and people selling off private collections. That's how I work – that's how I've always worked… you were asking me about Reilly.'

'Yes.'

'It's only a temporary measure. I promise you. But the fact is that there are other sources of paintings. I don't mean the black market – you know, stuff stolen from churches, or museums or private collections – I won't touch that, I'm not a fence. I'm talking about pictures people have come across of which they don't quite understand the value… It's always represented a part of the business, I don't deny it – but the tougher the times…'

'And the Reilly?'

'This is particularly tricky.'

'Why?'

'Look, I'm going to get a brandy. I need one. Do you want one?'

'No. No, thank you.'

Samantha waited impatiently while Keith returned to the kitchen. She wanted to shake him; hold him and shake the story of Reilly out of him, but she couldn't afford to let him know the extent of her interest. Even admitting she had met Brian on his doorstep was dangerous, so she had been careful not to.

'So…' Keith returned to the room, took a sip of brandy and sat down beside her on the sofa. He then proceeded to explain the deal he had with Brian – whereby the builder would keep his eye open for suitable pieces, Keith would ask no questions, take everything he offered, and pay a good price up front. Reilly's picture (as she well knew) had come from a café

Brian was renovating and converting. Brian also brokered deals from contacts. Keith concluded by saying, 'But Reilly is a slightly different matter.'

'Why?'

'You've seen his picture – it's quite extraordinary. It'll sell, I know it will – I'm astonished he isn't better known.'

'What do you know about him?'

'Almost nothing. I looked him up in the usual places. I spoke to two or three of the large auction houses but they have no record.'

'So you know nothing at all.'

'Not quite. And this is why my conscience is a little troubled. This isn't about where Brian got hold of the picture – he says Antoniou told him to junk everything he found in the café during the renovation – it's about the ownership of it in a wider sense.' He took another sip of the brandy. The more he drank of it, the more sober he seemed to become.

'You mean it should be in a museum or a public gallery?'

'No. I mean it should probably be returned to his son.'

'What?'

'Yes. Brian let slip that the old boy still lives round here. There's not much goes on here that Brian doesn't know about.'

'But where? I mean, he must be nearly a hundred years old?'

'I don't know where – you'd have to ask Brian – well, actually, I'd rather you didn't ask Brian. As to his age – yes – apparently he's getting on a bit. I know nothing of his circumstances.'

'But he'd know everything – about what happened to Reilly, where his paintings are… if there are any other paintings, I mean.'

'What do you mean, "what happened to Reilly"?'

'Well, you said… You said yourself you couldn't find anything out about him. Surely there should have been some record if he was as good as you say he was.'

'Not necessarily. There are hundreds, probably thousands, of decent local painters who remain obscure and unknown. Doesn't mean they're no good, simply that they haven't had the breaks. And thank God for that – otherwise I'd be out of business.'

❧

Samantha left Keith's house shortly afterwards, remembering to collect the large envelope of gallery paperwork from the hallway table. Having taken it for granted that Reilly had no relatives, the news of his son was almost too much for her to take in. So when she returned to the street where she thought she'd parked Brian's van and it wasn't there she assumed she must have been mistaken. She tried the next street. But it wasn't there either. She returned to the original street and, this time, walked more slowly from top to bottom. Then she saw it, on the opposite side of the road to the one she remembered parking it on. She must have entered the road from the other end. The street was empty, but she checked a second time before she got out the keys and let herself in. This time she pulled away smoothly and was soon on the brightly lit high street. Seeing a sign for Paddington, she made a turn and headed home.

FOURTEEN

A Visitor From That Place of Memory

A CRY CAME FROM MOUNTJOY AT THE COUNTER: 'NO!'

Nimrod leapt to his feet. Amy Sykes turned from the man she was serving to see Mountjoy holding a newspaper. His hands were shaking. Two weeks had passed since Reilly's arrest.

'Why doesn't he allow us to visit him?' Mountjoy pleaded. 'Why? The poor fellow. He must be feeling so wretched.'

'Reilly?'

'Who else? Well, it's too late now. Too late.'

Amy Sykes returned to the counter, Nimrod trailing after her. 'What does it say?'

'Read it for yourself.' Mountjoy thrust the newspaper towards her but she gently pushed it away.

'Please. I can't. You read it to me.'

Mountjoy took a breath and began. 'This is Pardew's work, I'm sure of it: "The inquest into the circumstances of the mysterious Old Cross Canal crime ended yesterday when, at St Pancras coroner's court, the jury returned the following verdict – 'We find that, on the evidence presented to us, William Gower met his death by wilful murder, and that the evidence we have received is sufficient to warrant us in committing the accused for trial.' Dr Daffyd Thomas, the coroner, explained that this was equivalent to a verdict of murder against Thomas Reilly. Reilly, who was seated in court between two warders, heard the decision unmoved though it caused considerable excitement among the crowd both inside and outside the court."'

Amy Sykes reached for the support of a chair. Mountjoy's arms fell and the newspaper dropped as if the weight of it had suddenly become too much to bear.

'What does it mean?'

'It means that they consider Gower's death was no accident and Reilly is to stand trial for his murder. I must see him. Today. I must go now.'

'Will they allow you to see him?'

'Surely they must. He's not a convicted man. Surely he has some rights.' Mountjoy tore off his apron, hanging it on the peg on the wall behind the counter, and collected his coat from the adjacent peg. 'Please, attend to the coffee shop. Close it if you must.' He made for the door, Nimrod trotting close behind. But Mountjoy was stern. 'No, Nimrod. Not now. You stay here with Amy. Stay here.' He opened the door, triggering the bell, exited and closed the door, smartly trapping Nimrod inside. A moment later the bell jangled again, signalling the arrival of a customer, and Nimrod seized the opportunity to dash out between the man's legs before the door shut. Seeing Mountjoy crossing the street, heading for the omnibus stop, he followed.

❧

Mountjoy had been solicitous and had made up a bed for Nimrod beside the open fire in the coffee shop. In the course of the night the fire burned low but never went out, which meant that he didn't need to go in search of warmth. This was just as well. Mountjoy left him locked alone in the coffee shop when he closed up in the late afternoon, returning downstairs only once before he went to bed to allow him out to the street to stretch his legs and empty his bowels and bladder. On the first night of this new routine, having been let back in, Nimrod followed Mountjoy to the door behind the counter but Mountjoy closed the door against him. Nimrod gave a few barks – not full-voiced, just gentle reminders – but Mountjoy didn't respond, so he returned to the blanket laid out for him beside the hearth. Soon he was sharing the coffee shop with the night vermin. The coffee shop provided rich pickings. Mountjoy concluded each day by sweeping the floor, his cleaning routine enthusiastic but cosmetic. Having created a pyramid of dust, crusts, crumbs, ash, butts and rinds in the centre of the room, he set his broom against it and pushed it behind the counter, where it supplemented the pile from the day before and the day before that. He rarely returned to brush up the dusty trail he left behind. Only on a Friday night did he use the coal shovel to transfer the week's pile from beneath the counter to the street gutter, during which procedure much of the dust and debris fell from the shovel or was blown back in through the door. The benefit of this eccentric cleaning regime was that the gaps in the floorboards had been sealed against underfloor drafts by the years of debris that had accumulated there.

The mice came out first, emerging in rapid sorties from the skirtings. Nimrod stood, exerting his dominance. They, having already sensed his presence in the room, discerned no threat. Nimrod made a sudden move towards one but it maintained its course towards the counter. A year before, he would have chased it, perhaps playfully caught it in his jaw before releasing it. Two or three years before that, he would have trapped it and broken its neck. Now he was too old for such exertions.

The first rat emerged at midnight. Unlike the mice, which lived decorously and tidily within the hollow walls of the coffee shop, the damp intruder had come from the sewers and had found his way in via the drains. Another followed. Two males; the first dominant. Just as Nimrod was aware of them, so were they of him. The leader approached Nimrod, nose high, whiskers twitching. He stopped just short of him and pressed his nose to the floor, sniffing deeply. The scent he picked up from the floor led him past Nimrod to the skirtings, and then, using the wall to navigate, towards the counter. The other visitor had vanished elsewhere. In such company dogs are reluctant to sleep. Only when Mountjoy arrived in the early morning to light the range and prepare the breakfast did the intruders scatter and Nimrod finally settle back onto his blanket.

❧

The Omnibus laboured to a halt. Mountjoy was the first to board. He took a swift look inside the bus, but chose to climb the open staircase to the top deck. By the time the other passengers had got on Nimrod had reached the stop. The platform was high but a step beneath it halved the distance from the pavement. He had got as far as the step when the bus pulled away, and then the conductor's boot loomed towards him, sending him sailing through the air to land heavily onto the street. Hoofs clattered towards him. Raising himself to his feet, he limped towards the kerb, the steel-rimmed wheels of a brewery cart passing barely a foot away.

❧

Mountjoy drew his coat around his shoulders for warmth. He was sitting at the front of the open deck of the bus. The lower deck would have been more comfortable but when he boarded he couldn't face going inside. The bus soon reached King's Cross and passed the railway terminus. Then they were over the canal. They were beneath the railway viaduct when a goods train crossed it. The smoke from the locomotive drifted down and Mountjoy found himself in a fog. As the smoke cleared, up ahead he saw the grim prison emerge. Mountjoy knew he should have visited before but he had been waiting for word from Reilly. After two days he knew word would not come, but still he waited. When Amy said she was going to visit he advised against it. If Reilly wanted to see them he would let them know. Reluctantly, she agreed.

Mountjoy got off the bus and waited for it to pull away before crossing the Caledonian Road. The prison was huge: huge in the way its exterior wall dominated the street, huge in the way the sombre building behind it bullied everything else from his mind. He made his way towards the gate and when he got there he rang the bell and waited.

❧

In a cell high in the prison Reilly whipped charcoal across the paper on his knee. Like a maniac he dotted and drew, smudging the sharper lines into shadow with a flick of the edge of his hand. Frantically he set down the details of his cell, as he had done many times over the past two weeks: no reflection, no corrections; a snapshot, nothing more. Today his eye was drawn to the three-legged stool and the small table beneath the shaded gas jet. When he arrived on the wing, contrary to his expectations, Reilly had found the cell to be light. Against the left wall was the large funnel of a bright copper hand-basin. At the far end, a water closet. Built into the corner by the door there were three triangular shelves on which he was expected to keep his utensils, mug and soup box. His hammock and bedding were rolled together and stood on end on the top shelf. The room was illuminated by a window, high in the far wall, crossed with a wrought-iron bar. The prison wing, too, was bright, light flooding down in celestial beams from the glass gallery of the roof and from the tall windows in each end wall. The cells were stacked in three layers and connected by narrow iron balconies. Reilly's was on the topmost level.

Being on remand, Reilly had been allowed to keep his own clothes, but they had been taken temporarily from him when he arrived. He suffered the indignity of a bath, a body search and an inquisition from the doctor. He had been told he could send letters, receive visits and was offered reading materials. He declined the opportunity to write but had asked for his copy of Leonardo's notebooks, which they had yet to bring. A sketch pad and charcoal arrived courtesy of his solicitor. He had not asked for either. Had he been offered them he would have declined, as his solicitor knew he would. From their brief acquaintance, Reilly had been impressed by the elderly, shabby-suited Rushden. His vagueness was a cover for a sharp mind, although Reilly suspected that it wouldn't be many years before the vagueness was less studied, the mind less sharp. They had met on the morning of his appearance in front of the magistrates. Rushden had expressed surprise at his arrest because of the scánt nature of the evidence against him. It had been Rushden who had arrived in person after the coroner's inquest to report the results. He was apologetic and in the face of it Reilly had felt obliged to show an optimism he did not feel.

Reilly heard the spy-hole in the door open and shut. The door swung open. 'Visitor,' the warder said. 'Step out.'

Reilly took his pad and charcoal to the shelves before following the frock-coated warder into the vast open space of the wing. Forty feet across the void he saw the mirror image of his own gallery and ahead of him a bridge spanned the balconies. From the walkway they took the metal steps to the ground floor of the wing. There were no other prisoners out on the landings but Reilly could hear them. The wing was busy with the sound of looms rattling behind closed doors and the tapping of the shoemakers. When they reached the pristine asphalt floor of the hall, Reilly waited for the warder to unlock the door. They entered a large circular chamber, walked down another long corridor, the floor there as spotless as the rest of the prison, and then Reilly was marshalled into a small room and told to be seated. The warder took a chair by the door and lapsed into stillness. A moment later Reilly heard a voice in the corridor. A voice he knew. He turned to see Mountjoy walk in. The pain and sympathy on Mountjoy's face was too much to bear. Remaining seated, Reilly turned away. Tears welled in his eyes. Mountjoy approached him and laid a comforting hand on his shoulder.

When Reilly had composed himself he and Mountjoy faced each other across the table. The warder, affecting not to listen, waited in a chair by the door as still as a museum curator.

'I'm sorry, Reilly. I read about the coroner's inquest and I had to visit,' Mountjoy said.

'Yes. Rushden was good enough to come yesterday and tell me in person.' Having stifled his tears, Reilly was curt. To survive the ordeal he had been armouring his emotions, allowing himself no excursions into the past. Mountjoy had arrived from that place of memory, damaging the work he had done so far.

'Your solicitor?'

'He's a good man. I have no choice but to put myself in his hands. Doubtless he'll be calling on you to speak on my behalf.'

'Of course. But surely if we can find the murderer then there will be no need for you to be put on trial.'

'The police consider they have found their murderer. That's why I'm here, Mountjoy.'

'Then we must make our own enquiries. Surely somebody must know something.'

'If, indeed, he was murdered, which, despite the inquest, I still doubt.'

'So we leave it to the court?'

'I have no choice.'

There was then a moment of silence, which Reilly broke: 'You might be interested to know I've been sketching. In charcoal.'

'Have you?'

'I feel the need to work fast. Get something down as quickly as I can, like a photograph. The constraint of time is good for me: no reworking.

The technique is secondary. It's… I find when I'm working like that I can… lose myself.' Reilly's eyes drifted around the room as if he was seeing it for the first time. When they returned to Mountjoy his gaze was more intense.

'Tell me if I can bring you anything to make your life more tolerable,' Mountjoy offered.

'There is nothing. How is Nimrod?'

'He misses you.'

'How do you know?'

'I… I can see that he does.'

'Is he off his food?'

'No.'

'Do you allow him out?'

'Whenever he likes.'

'And how often is that?'

'Three or four times a day.'

'For how long?'

'Anything from five minutes to thirty.'

'Good. And he sleeps where?'

'By the fire. In the coffee shop.'

'Alone?'

'Yes.'

'I see. And the exhibition? Has anything been sold?'

'No.'

'Nothing?'

'I'm sure it would have done but I took the paintings down.'

'You closed the exhibition?'

'Yes.'

'For what reason?'

'I... had to make a decision. I assumed you'd want the exhibition to wait until your release.'

'Until my release?'

'Yes.'

'Or my hanging?'

'Please, Reilly. I thought it best.'

'To take my pictures down?'

'Yes.'

As the interrogation continued, Reilly's voice grew shriller, Mountjoy becoming increasingly concerned over Reilly's state of mind. He had seen him in the fever of creativity before but his energies had always been directed at the work in progress. Now it was Mountjoy himself who was the target and Reilly was unrelenting. '...So the paintings are safe?'

'Of course.'

'Dry?'

'Yes. Dry, safe, covered. Trust me, Reilly. I have your best interests at heart, as I always have.'

'Have you?'

'Of course.'

Reilly gave the statement some consideration. Then he pounced: 'And this imprisonment is in my best interests?'

'...Reilly, forgive me. If they would allow me to take your place, I would.'

'My best interests? My paintings – all of my life's work, stored safely in your care? My freedom removed? The threat of a hanging?'

'If you want to blame me for this, then do. I can feel no more wretched than I already do.'

'Please don't visit again.'

'…Reilly…'

'And return my paintings to my lodgings. You may choose four canvases for your trouble and in payment of my debt to you. I will instruct Rushden on how I want to dispose of the rest. He will contact you. Please prepare them.'

'Reilly, there's really no need.'

'Do as I ask.'

Mountjoy nodded. 'Of course.'

'I would also ask that you find a suitable home for Nimrod: one in which he will not be alone at night. There's a policeman, Portch – you met him – who I'm sure will take him in.'

'I'm happy to look after Nimrod.'

'But is Nimrod happy to be looked after by you?'

'Reilly, I understand your anger, but please…'

'Thank you for all you have done, Mountjoy, but all I ask now is to be left in peace.'

Reilly stood with such suddenness it caught the warder by surprise. Had he attacked Mountjoy the man would have been too slow to intervene. Immediately he ordered Reilly to sit down. Reilly complied. The warder opened the door. Mountjoy rose, looking one final time at his old friend, hoping for some sign of reconciliation, but Reilly wouldn't meet his eye. Mountjoy walked out and Reilly was returned to his cell, where he took up his sketch pad and charcoal and began frantically to capture the barred window and the afternoon light.

Mountjoy returned to the coffee shop. He would have preferred to spend an hour or two in his own company but he wanted to prepare Reilly's paintings for collection. Although he had assured the artist that his work was safe, he was concerned that the room in which he had stored them was a little damp. What he dreaded most was relating the details of the sorry meeting to Amy Sykes. He had intended to tell Reilly about Amy's circumstances but there had been no opportunity. He understood Reilly's show of anger, in part believing that it had been manufactured for some benefit to them both. But it saddened him. And he would miss Nimrod. He had done his best for the creature. Having never owned a dog, how was he to know they expected company as well as food and lodgings? When he pushed open the door of the coffee shop Amy greeted him with the news that Nimrod was gone. It seemed a fitting end to a dreadful day.

Nimrod limped through Old Cross, eventually returning to the lodging house, where he sank to the pavement beside the front step and waited for Reilly to return. As the afternoon wore on few people passed the house, but each time he heard footsteps approach he looked up with hope. Nobody paused to stroke him. A boy, having emerged from the lodging house, spat at him. Occasionally a cab went by. The light faded and he was hungry. Had he been in Reilly's company he would have alerted him to this by standing. If that failed he would approach the empty bowl and look towards it. If Reilly was so caught up in his work that he still didn't pay attention he might try a bark, and this would always be enough to draw the master from his seat. Having fed Nimrod, Reilly would usually take the opportunity to prepare himself a cup of tea, and once Nimrod had dispatched his food, Reilly would sit with him, his hands idling the fur at his neck, while he silently ruminated on his work in progress. When the maestro returned to the easel it would always be with renewed vigour.

When night fell and Reilly hadn't shown himself, Nimrod moved on, returning to the high street where the butcher was sweeping out his shop, the grocer closing his shutters. At the public house the trapdoor to the cellar was open and a leather-aproned drayman was rolling a barrel towards it. Three young men were noisily arguing at the door. One of them won the argument by knocking the hats from the other two, then led them boisterously inside. Nimrod dropped down into the gutter and ploughed along it, nose close to the ground. Among the butcher's sawdust there were some small scrapings and trimmings of fat that had spilled from the sausage bucket. He finished what he could find in two or three bites. Now he was beside the public house from which the voices spilled out, and the smell from the beer pumps and slops tray was tantalizing. He sat by the door and waited, and when the next customer entered the public bar Nimrod scurried in ahead of him.

The room was noisy with beery voices competing for attention. It was early in the evening and the conversation was, as yet, good-natured. The air was grey with cigarette and pipe smoke. Logs were stacked precariously on an open fire, and looked likely to spill from the grate onto the slate hearth, which was dusty with ash. Nimrod found a way through the forest of ankles, searching for a place among the chaos where he could rest in safety. He passed through a door and found himself in the snug bar, where a woman sat at a small, circular table, one of four that crowded the small room. Sitting beside her, slumped against the wall, was a large man in a brimless hat and a crude suit buttoned to the neck, eyes closed, snoring with aggression. His skin was pocked, as if he had taken a face of shot. The woman was conducting a conversation with the girl behind the bar. When she saw Nimrod she broke it off.

'Hello,' she said, both in greeting and recognition. 'Come here.' She clicked her fingers and Nimrod approached her. The smell among her petticoats was strong. The man beside her shifted and snorted in his sleep.

'I know you, don't I?' the woman said. Nimrod came to rest on her foot. She called to the barmaid, 'It's that little doggie I was telling you about. You know…? How strange.'

'Oh. That one.' The girl replied, going to the sink behind the counter. 'Give him this.' The woman stood and took an ashtray from the barmaid. She set it on the floor beside Nimrod who drank the water gratefully.

'We were talking about you,' the woman confided to Nimrod. 'You mangy thing. And now you're here.'

The girl behind the counter went off to serve someone who had called her from the public bar.

'Sit down here,' the woman said, patting the floor beside her. Nimrod understood and obeyed. Sleep beckoned and he gave in.

He was awakened later by the woman's hand petting his head. The room was a different place; the smoke was thicker, the voices harsher. There was a threat in the air. The man who had been asleep against the wall was standing over them both, leering down towards the woman, offering a hand. She took it, stood with some difficulty and followed him out and through the bar. Nimrod trailed after them into the cold street. They turned left, down an alley. They went through a gate, crossed a damp yard, climbed some unlit steps. Nimrod marked the route by scent – stale rainwater, cats, rats, human piss, a fox recently passed, human shit, horses, decaying meat, rotten vegetables, sweat. Soon they were in the woman's room and the man was lying on the bed, the woman tugging at his clothes. He was reaching for her but she kept pulling back out of his reach. Then he sat up and she was made to comply with his wishes. When it was over, the man slept and the woman came to sit in the single chair beside the unlit fire. She had tugged the cover from the bed to shroud her nakedness. Nimrod rose from where he had rested and settled beside her. She stroked him in the way Reilly stroked him when he was working. The room was cold, there was little in the way of comfort, but for the time being at least, he had found a sanctuary.

FIFTEEN

All Hell Let Loose

SAMANTHA DROVE BRIAN'S VAN, LOADED WITH REILLY'S PAINTINGS, to Paddington and then, once she was in the vicinity of home, trusted her sense of direction to lead her there. There were no parking spaces close to the flat so she double parked, switched on the hazard lights and set about unloading the paintings. Samantha co-rented a flat on the second floor of a medium-sized Victorian house. She had sole use of a bedroom but shared a small kitchen, living room and a bathroom with another girl, Lillian, a heavy-eyed gothic creature whose father visited two or three times a week. The arrangement suited Samantha because Lillian rarely emerged from her room. When she did, they occasionally argued over her untidiness, but the rhythms of their lives were compatible enough. Having never known her own father, Samantha envied the girl her father's visits and the reassuring and kindly way in which the man spoke to her (sometimes she listened at the bedroom door). He never failed to bring a present, but frustratingly it was always in a plastic carrier bag so Samantha never knew what he'd bought. When Lillian first arrived her father took Samantha aside and pressed a business card into her hand, asking her to call him anytime, day or night, if she was in the least bit concerned about his daughter. He owned a mini cab, he said, and was often at work. He offered a wink. David Geoffrey (the name on the card) was a man who, it was apparent, left much unsaid. But, at three o'clock that Monday morning, Samantha knew she could trust that Lillian would be safely in bed. She took tablets and slept soundly.

In two journeys Samantha emptied the van of the paintings and the newspapers. Her intention had been to return the vehicle immediately to Old Cross and come back by taxi. It was an expense she would just have to bear. She returned to the living room, knelt on the carpet and untied the ropes securing the sheets around the pictures. The first she had already seen. It was the portrait of the young Reilly in a conservatory, hiding, looking imploringly from the frame towards the viewer. She was grateful to be in his company once again and set the board against the wall. The colours warmed the chilly room. She knelt beside the second board, loosening the knot with excitement, feeling the rough gluey hemp against her fingers. Soon the ropes were laid out in a cross on the floor beneath the board. She then peeled back the sheet, undressing the painting. The picture was face down, the title written on the back in heavy pencil: '*Nimrod's Shadow*'. Nimrod. The name was familiar. No. It wouldn't come. She lifted the board and turned it face up on the floor. The picture showed a young woman reclining on a rough bed in a poor room. At the bottom right of the frame was the shadow of a small dog. It was then Samantha remembered: Nimrod: the nameplate on the stuffed dog she had left at the café: Nimrod. Perhaps another clue to Reilly. It would be dawn in three hours. She would go back to the café, collect the wooden case, and bring it home again in the taxi.

This time she climbed into the van with confidence, started the engine with a deft twist of the key and drove away without stalling. The warm cabin smelt of Brian. He was more real here than in that cold hallway, almost a comforting presence. She sharpened her focus on the task of driving through the sleeping city. In what seemed like minutes she was back at the café – the parking space had not been taken – and unlocking the door with the Yale key. The lights were off and there was no sign anybody had been in since she had left nearly eight hours before. Inside it was cold. She made her way through the dark, but switched on the hallway lights once she had closed the stairway door to the café behind her. She climbed the stairs and paused on the landing to wait and listen, but the building was silent. After another set of stairs she was facing Brian once again. The dark patch beneath him seemed to have solidified on the floorboards. His face had drained of colour. His eyes looked like they had never seen. Fear crept up her back. She shivered and then found she couldn't stop. 'I'm sorry,' she said. 'I'm so sorry.' Her hands began to shake. Her heart beat fast.

Samantha turned away and faced the ladder. She was afraid. She had seen films in which the dead had reached out their hands and touched the living. She paused half way up the ladder so she could look down and check that Brian was still on the floor. She went on. The loft was freezing. On her last visit she had hastily re-covered the display case, but now she unveiled it with care and this time she looked at the stuffed creature with respect. Reilly's hands might have stroked the fur of this old dog. She tried to lift the case but it was heavy so she pushed it along the floor with her foot to the edge of the loft hatch, then returned to switch off the light.

The only way she could see to get it down was to descend a few rungs of the ladder, pull the end of the case towards her and try to bear its weight when it tipped. She was halfway down and struggling to stop the case falling when she heard something below her. For a moment she froze, but then she found the strength and soon she had Nimrod safely on the landing.

'Brian? Is that you?' she heard from the café below. A woman: young, a rough Essex voice; unsure. 'Do you know what time it is, love? It's after three… Time you were home… You shouldn't be working this late.'

The woman waited for a response. Samantha had no choice but to stand as still as she could.

'Brian – are you up there?'

Footsteps on the stairs now. Another call, less tentative, this from the first floor landing: 'Brian, if you're pissing around I'm going to be very cross with you.'

Samantha looked down at the body. There was nothing to cover it with. What could she do? The obvious solution was to hide in the front room, wait for the woman to discover Brian's body and hope that, in her hysteria, she would run from the café to get help, at which point Samantha could make her escape. The only other option was to confront her on the stairs: play the injured party; pretend that she had been asleep in an upstairs room and the woman had woken her. But, knowing Brian as she did, Samantha suspected the woman might imagine she had some involvement with him, which would complicate matters still further.

'I'm coming up now. All right...?' The woman paused to light a cigarette. 'I'm on my way up.'

Leaving Nimrod on the landing, Samantha stepped carefully around the body, pushed open the door to the room at the front of the building and went in, closing the door behind her. The room, borrowing light from the street, had been used to store materials: bags of plaster and cement, several sheets of plasterboard, boxes of nails, tools left haphazardly on the floor, a portable generator. On a table in the bow window was an electric kettle, a carton of milk and three teacups, beside it was an old armchair and, beside the chair, a newspaper.

'I'm coming up now. Last chance. All right?' The woman, having lit her cigarette, had found some confidence now. She was angry with Brian for putting her through this – for making her get out of bed in the middle of the night, for leading her into this cold, dark building alone.

Samantha pressed her back to the wall. If the woman came into the room, the opened door would conceal her. She waited, tense, as the footsteps approached. Her hands continued to shake. She felt an acid pain in the pit of her stomach.

For almost a minute after the footsteps paused there was silence. Then she heard the creak of a floorboard as the woman knelt down (to check for a pulse?). Another creak as the woman stood again: then, 'You stupid bastard. Stupid bastard...' Footsteps down the stairs, unhurried, almost carefree, and then the woman was gone.

When Samantha finally arrived home the taxi driver agreed to carry the case containing Nimrod up the stairs to her flat. She paid him and tipped him five pounds. He seemed to want more but she had no more to give him. When he was gone she looked around the living room at the bounty she had collected that night. One of the canvases was still to be unwrapped. The newspapers were on the chair. She would save them for her return from work. She was afraid that if she slept she would never wake, so she changed her clothes, showered and then, as she sometimes did, set off to walk to work, hoping the exercise would revitalize her.

At half past six the city was being prepared for the day. A man with a mop and a galvanized, wheeled bucket was washing down the pavement outside McDonald's. Two window cleaners with wiper blades were performing choreographed sweeps on a clothes shop window, each stood on a six-foot ladder which tapered up to a point. One of them called hello to Samantha. A street cleaner in a donkey jacket and woollen hat was piloting an electric truck along the pavement. Water spat forcefully from long horizontal nozzles. A filthy pigeon sauntered in its wake, taking swift pecks at the shallow pools of water. On Tottenham Court Road a man with a power hose was blasting chewing gum from the paving stones. Outside a women's clothes shop an articulated lorry was parked on double yellow lines with its back doors open and the rear platform lowered. Inside it, in the ribbed interior, a bright bazaar of dresses and coats shrouded in what looked like cobwebs. When she looked into the window of the clothes store, she could see three well-dressed women on their knees, thongs visible, frantically stripping cellophane from the deep drift of dresses. Next door, at the coffee shop, the dawn shift in caps and aprons was standing in a semi-circle round a young shirt-sleeved man. He was evangelizing to his international crew, and they were listening to him without – so far as Samantha could judge – any sense of irony. When she reached the gallery she allowed herself to relax. She sank into the chair, laid her head on her arms, and slept.

❧

She was awoken by the telephone. Fear thundered through her heart. But then she remembered she had already taken the call she had always dreaded – nothing could cause her more pain than that.

'Samantha. It's Keith,' she heard. He was gleeful. Far too gleeful for the morning.

'Oh,' she managed, wiping a gritty speck of sleep from her left eye.

'All hell's been let loose round here.'

'Really?'

'Are you quite all right? You sound half asleep.'

'No, there's… somebody in the gallery. I'm just keeping an eye on her.'

'A nutter?'

'I don't think so. I'm just keeping an eye.'

'Good. Anyway, I'm telling you this because it might be germane. There's been a death in the district.'

'Who?'

'Brian. The builder I was telling you about last night. Apparently he was working in the café round the corner, fell down a ladder and landed on a hammer which went straight through him. Punctured his lung. Terrible.'

'Terrible. But why might it be germane?'

'Well, as I said, it was Brian who supplied me with the T. F. Reilly painting, and a few others. He also acted on behalf of others.'

'All right.'

'I mention it only because if there are any calls to the gallery relating to Brian, tell them to call me on my mobile.'

'I will.'

'It's all terribly exciting. I thought you'd be more interested. Not that I'm not grief-stricken, of course. But between you and me it seems that there are suspicious circumstances.'

'Really?'

'According to a very reliable source, the police think it might not have been an accident.'

'Why?'

'Well, apparently when Brian was found, there was some kind of display case by him with an animal in it. When the girlfriend returned with the police, it was gone. Somebody, therefore, had been in the building – and if someone was in there, then… you see?'

'Yes. I see.'

'Call me if anybody calls and do give them my number. Is she still there?'

'Who?'

'The nutter.'

'Oh. No. She's gone.'

'Good. Well, I might pop in tomorrow. I feel the need of an excursion.'

'Do you think the police will want to talk to you?'

'I can't imagine so. There's no reason for them to know of my association with Brian, so I think it's unlikely, and I can trust that you won't mention it, can't I?'

'Of course.'

'I can trust you?'

'Yes.'

'Good. Well, cheerio, then.'

'Goodbye.'

'…Oh, just one more thing.'

'Yes?'

'You remember we discussed Reilly's relative?'

'Yes.'

'Well, the truth is, afterwards, I felt rather guilty. I mean, the old boy doesn't have any claim on the picture Brian sold me but I thought it might be interesting to speak to him. After all, he might have more.'

'So you don't feel guilty, you just want to get hold of more of Reilly's work?'

'Well, we are sharp this morning, aren't we?'

'I thought you were doing something nice, that's all.'

'Somebody has to earn the money to pay your wages, Samantha.'

'I know. I'm sorry.'

'Mm. Well, I've made a few enquiries and I know where I can find him.'

'Where?'

'A sheltered housing scheme on Canal Street. I'll pop in and see him at some point.'

'When?'

'I don't know. Is it necessary for you to know all of my movements?'

'No. Of course not.'

'Well, then. Goodbye.'

Samantha was left listening to the dialling tone. She turned and faced Reilly's painting. He had whispered to her once again. He was keeping her busy. He had a son. Now she must find him before Keith got there and spoiled everything. Once she had thought she loved him. Now she wondered if hate was too strong a word for what she felt. Samantha's time at the gallery was coming to an end. Her life was set to change again. She had three of Reilly's paintings at home, and had no intention of leaving the one in the gallery to any casual buyer who might take a fancy to it. She would remove it that night and add it to her collection. Then she would find Reilly's son. She felt that somehow Reilly was beginning to guide her. Now she must learn to trust him.

SIXTEEN

Reilly in the Dock

LIKE MOST SUCCESSFUL BARRISTERS, MR HARRY CRAWFORD'S personality was large enough to dominate the courtrooms in which he appeared. He displayed a gourmet's relish for his profession. His girth was wide, but looked as though it might have been the result of theatrical padding put on for effect because his face was that of a thin man. He had developed a sonorous tone over the years to counter the sobering effect the courts (in this case, the Central Criminal Court at the Old Bailey) had on those who attended there but otherwise lived anonymous and blameless lives. Harry Crawford stood as counsel for the prosecution in the case against T. F. Reilly. Having made his opening statement, he invited Chief Inspector Macreadie to the witness stand. The men had done business before and fell into an easy rhythmic exchange – nothing was hurried or forced, every response as elegantly judged as the question that provoked it. A music-hall duo could not have worked any better together.

Winter light illuminated the court from the large, high windows. The room was designed in such a way that much of that light was directed towards the figure in the dock. Paled by fatigue and three months' confinement, Reilly watched Crawford and Macreadie set out the case against him. Occasionally Reilly's attention shifted towards the jury to see how the testimony was being received, or to the judge, Sir William Reynolds, who seemed to be not at all interested in the proceedings, rather to be going through his documents for the following trial. He did, however, Reilly saw, occasionally note something down. This reassured him. His solicitor, Rushden, had explained on more than one occasion that the legal system existed to prevent the false imprisonment of the innocent as much as to expedite the prosecution of the guilty. Reilly's faith in the system was, however, already being dented by the combined efforts of Mr Harry Crawford and Chief Inspector Macreadie. So much so that Reilly began to wonder, and not for the first time, if there was some vested interest in his conviction.

Crawford and Macreadie worked chronologically through the events following Gower's death, the discovery of the wallet, the relationship between the penurious artist, who lived on the charity of a coffee-shop owner, and the critic Gower, who had been lured to the artist's lodging house. It was suggested that to avoid suspicion falling on the artist it was necessary for the robbery and murder to take place elsewhere, and the canal was chosen for the purpose. In Macreadie's version of events, the exhibition of the artist's paintings was nothing more than a ruse to draw Gower to the district and then to divert suspicion following his disappearance. What could seem more innocent than an artist displaying his work? The reason Gower was carrying so much money, Macreadie had established, having interviewed a colleague of the critic's, was that he was a well-known purchaser of fledgling artists' work. This was, he was careful to admit, not entirely selfless on the critic's part, though Macreadie conceded he was unqualified to comment further on the complex relationship between critical acclaim and commercial worth.

'Why, then,' Crawford suggested, 'did Reilly not simply sell his paintings to Gower and save him the trouble of murder?'

'I would not wish to speculate on that but it seems unlikely that Reilly's efforts would have been worth anything approaching the one hundred and fifty pounds Gower was carrying.'

Reilly was grateful for Macreadie's sneering dismissal of his work. For the first time that day his mood shifted from anxiety to anger. Also, for the first time that day, he was aware that the judge was looking directly towards him. How long he had been watched, he did not know, but Sir William Reynolds seemed content to let him know that his anger had been recognized and he took it to be a good sign. Finally, after nearly an hour, Crawford relinquished the floor to Reilly's defence counsel to begin the cross-examination of Macreadie.

Rushden had introduced Reilly to the barrister Graveney seven days before. The three men, of similar backgrounds (somewhat less lofty than those of Crawford and Macreadie), might in other circumstances have passed the afternoon convivially. Rushden would have offered the voice of age and experience, and the barrister Graveney the occasional astringent observation that, though shocking, the other men would have been hard pushed to argue against. Graveney had only five years' service on the circuit but came recommended by Rushden. The youngish man inspired confidence in Reilly but little affection. His brusqueness put him in mind of the journalist Pardew. He was making his way up the ranks of his profession and it was cases such as Reilly's that would earn him the attention he needed to further his career. He was clean-shaven, elegant-looking (it was an interior elegance he had, not simply down to his clothes), jet-black-haired. Although he would have no trouble attracting female companionship he was not the kind who would offer much in the way of tenderness, which, Reilly well knew, would further increase his allure. Unlike Crawford's, Graveney's elegance was undiminished by his wig and gown. Crawford's costume looked threadbare, shapeless and borrowed; Graveney's sharp, new and tailored.

During the course of the meeting Graveney had made it clear that he considered the case against Reilly to have no merit. There was nothing beyond the wallet to link him to Gower. There was no real motive; nothing in Reilly's history that would suggest he was capable of killing the critic. In short he saw little reason for Reilly to worry. His only concern was that at St Pancras Coroner's Court Dr Daffyd Thomas had found sufficient evidence of murder. Had he not, of course, Reilly would now be a free man. But it was the suggestion by the coroner that this amounted to a verdict of murder against Reilly that worried him. Graveney explained that he had no right to make such an assertion. The case against Reilly was sufficiently weak that in Graveney's opinion the police should still be looking for somebody else.

When Graveney stood he took some time to look towards Macreadie before beginning his cross-examination. Macreadie was the one to break the eye contact. He took an exasperated look towards the judge who, at that moment, again had his head down.

'...A hundred and fifty pounds,' Graveney began, and then paused for effect. Wisely, Macreadie did not rush in to fill the silence. He was wily and well aware Graveney was toying with him. 'A sum, Chief Inspector, far exceeding what you consider Reilly's paintings to be worth?'

'Yes, indeed.' Macreadie turned to the jury, his sneer inviting them towards the same conclusion.

'You don't hold Mr Reilly's works in high esteem?'

'I don't. But, as I say, I'm not a critic.'

'Indeed not. Unlike Mr Gower, who was widely acknowledged to be a critic of some repute.'

'Yes. There's no disputing that.'

'And for a man of Mr Gower's stature to take the trouble to travel from Regent's Park to Old Cross we must assume he considered it to be worth his while.'

'We must?'

'Of course.'

'That is your assumption. And hardly a great distance after all.'

'A reasonable assumption I would suggest, based on the fact that the two men had met before when Mr Reilly's work was exhibited in a summer exhibition.'

'An assumption nevertheless.'

'Based firmly on the fact that Mr Gower was so taken by Reilly's painting that he wrote to the artist on a number of occasions.'

'Correspondence is conducted for many reasons. Without seeing these letters I wouldn't wish to speculate on how taken Mr Gower was with Reilly's pictures. Have these letters been presented in evidence?'

'Sadly, they no longer exist. But a well-respected critic travelled to Old Cross to value the work of an unknown artist. I think we can allow that Mr Gower was confident his journey would not have been wasted.'

'Again, you can allow what you wish.'

'Chief Inspector Macreadie, this is not about what either you or I allow. This concerns the work of a serious artist and an absolute value of his worth. In your opinion, which as you admit is valueless, the thirty-seven paintings comprising Mr Reilly's exhibition were not worth the one hundred and fifty pounds carried by Mr Gower. We do not know how Mr Gower valued them – but on the evidence of his encouragement of Mr Reilly, their continued correspondence, and Mr Gower's visit to Old Cross we can be confident that Mr Gower held the artist in some esteem. This being the case, the motive for Mr Reilly robbing and then murdering Mr Gower is removed.'

But Macreadie did not share Rushden's confidence, and the exchange between the two men continued. Reilly felt that neither man had won the exchange. He tried to put himself in the mind of a juror and concluded that Graveney had done enough to salvage his reputation. Having done so, the motive for robbing Gower was therefore diminished, if not removed altogether. The wallet was less easy to explain away, as he had always known it would be, and Graveney chose not to dwell on it, which, in Reilly's eyes, was shrewd. When Graveney sat down lunch was called by Sir William Reynolds, who wore the expression of a man who had been well entertained by the distractions of the morning.

Reilly was taken down a set of steps, allowed to use a lavatory, then shown into a small, sparse cell furnished with two chairs and a table. Shortly afterwards, lunch was delivered to him. He was hungry and set about the cold beef with relish. It was the first meal he had taken outside the prison for three months and although the food inside Pentonville was by no means bad, it seemed always to taste the same, as if the vats it had been prepared in somehow drew out the flavour. Contrary to what he would have expected, life in prison had given him an appetite he hadn't had on the outside. Without the distraction of a work in progress he found himself looking for something else to fill the void. He tried to read but lacked concentration. He slept sufficiently well at night, so could not pass the time that way. There was no work to be done as only the convicted prisoners were allowed to use the looms. He did, however, try to complete a number of charcoal sketches each day and found that his technique was improving. The governor, on one of his regular visits to the wing (he was an enlightened man), had even gone so far as to ask if he'd be happy for some of the sketches to be framed and exhibited in the prison library. Reilly said that he would be more than happy, but only when he had been granted his freedom.

Ten minutes after Reilly had put aside his plate, Rushden appeared with Graveney, they having finished their own hurried lunches in a public house. Graveney wanted to reassure him that the morning's proceedings had gone as well as he had expected. Reilly sensed his caution. Graveney was making no promises. There was a long way still to go. There would be surprises from both sides. When Reilly was led back up into the arena of the courtroom his senses were assaulted by the light, the chatter and the bustle. Having spent so much of his life avoiding drawing attention to himself, he found it curious that he didn't dislike taking the centre of the stage as much as he imagined he would. Creativity is as all-encompassing as serious illness. Without a work in progress there were facets of Reilly coming to life that had remained dormant for many years. It seemed also to be the case that his habitual melancholy had retreated.

❧

'Baaaah… baaaaaaaaah… baaaaaaaaah!'

'Stop it, Lol, you'll frighten him.'

'I'm tryin' to make it bark, Daisy.' The bullet-headed man, now dressed and out of bed (although his collar and cuffs remained undone), was standing above Nimrod and had been trying to provoke a response from him for the past fifteen minutes. The woman had gone out to fetch some bread so she had not seen him lift Nimrod by the scruff of the neck and hurl him against the wall. Nor had she seen him kick him hard in the ribs. Nimrod chose not to bark nor bite the man. Instead he tried to dodge out of his reach and remain there. Now, thankfully, Daisy had returned.

'I don' see no point in dogs,' Lol said.

'He probably don't see no point in you.'

'He pissed and shit on the floor.'

'Should have let him out. You could have mopped it.'

'Is it raining out there?'

'It's damp. Not raining.'

'Cold?'

'Not too cold.'

'Can't stan' the cold.' The man stumbled towards the door. It seemed as though he was still drunk; perhaps he was never sober. He lifted his heavy waxed coat from the floor and pulled it like a burden he was obliged to bear around his shoulders. The stale odours of the public bar spilled from the stiff folds of the fabric.

'You left my money?'

'On the table.'

When Lol reached the door he turned once to look towards Nimrod, then he was gone, his heavy, uneven footsteps crashing down the stairs. He stumbled. There was a curse. Another door slammed and there was silence.

Daisy went to the table. A pause. She lifted a plate, she pushed aside a book. Fractiously she moved the candle aside. 'Bastard!' she called, biting the back of her hand. 'Where's my money!'

Nimrod backed away. The woman knelt and peered beneath the bed, reaching blindly into the darkness. Her hand came out empty. She stood, dusting down her knees. 'That bastard.'

Daisy opened a small wall cupboard, shifted something aside, then pulled out a corked bottle. The liquid inside was clear. She took the bottle to the table and poured a large measure into a tea cup and then she drank it down. She sighed with the release.

'Here,' she ordered. 'Come sit with me.'

Nimrod approached and settled at her side. She took a drink. He felt her nails at his neck. 'Bastard,' Daisy said. The nails pinched harder and soon they met through the skin of Nimrod's neck.

❧

As had been evident in what she had revealed to Pardew several weeks before, Annie Cole was a nervous woman. Her nerves had been scrambled by the discovery of the body in the canal close to her home and they were getting the better of her now. Like a doctor reassuring a nervous patient, Harry Crawford was careful to employ no terms that would intimidate or alarm his witness. His demeanour was such that, as he leaned towards Annie Cole, despite the distance between them, she was drawn to focus her attention on his face. He hoped this would put from her mind his wig and gown, the rows of shuffling, whispering figures in the public gallery, the reporters on their bench, bored and shifty, the table with its mystifying array of leather-bound books – more words than the nervous woman imagined she would speak, or should rightly be spoken, in a lifetime – and the slight, tall man in the dock. His presence, among all the other distractions in the room, was the one she fought to resist the most. But it was his fingers she was drawn to, and the white marbles of his knuckles as he clenched tight against the bar. They put her in mind of her own; of the way she conducted herself, as she faced the rigours of her daily life.

'Your room looks out over the canal, does it not?' Crawford was leading her gently back to the beginning of her testimony. It had begun to seem to all in the court that the woman, undoubtedly younger than the fifty-odd years she appeared to be, could barely remember her name. They were becoming restless. To win any case Crawford was well aware he needed to convince not only the jury but also those in the public gallery, and to convince was first to entertain. Failing that, it was necessary at least to maintain the interest of the crowd.

'Yes, Sir,' Annie Cole said, snatching at the word, holding on to it. 'Yes, it does look out over the canal.'

'And from the window you can clearly see the towpath?'

'Yes. I can clearly see the towpath, Sir. From my back window.'

'And you were drawn to the window on the night of Mr Gower's death?'

'I was, Sir.'

'Explain to me what then happened.' Crawford smiled reassuringly, as though they had rehearsed this moment, which indeed they had.

'Oh, well I was embroidering, Sir, and I heard this splash and I went to the window and I looked out.'

Crawford's reassuring smile slipped a little. 'You went to the window and you looked out?'

'I did, Sir. I looked out and then I lifted the window to see better.'

'And what did you see?'

'I saw a man running away, away from the bridge.'

'And nothing else?'

'No, Sir.'

'Nothing?'

'Oh, yes, Sir.'

'What else did you see?'

'A dog, Sir. Sitting on the bank. Still as you like.'

'A dog?' By the tone in his voice, it was clear to all in the room that this was news to Crawford.

'Yes, Sir. A dog.'

'Well, let's put that aside. I'd like to return to the figure you saw on the towpath if we may. You say he was running away?'

'I did.'

'Running quickly?'

'Yes, Sir.'

'A young man, then?'

'I wouldn't know, Sir. It was too dark to see.'

'Perhaps from the speed at which the young man conducted himself…?'

'Oh yes, Sir, an old man wouldn't… conduct himself at such a speed…'

Having heard the unwelcome news about the dog, and been concerned what else Annie Cole might now choose to remember, Crawford thanked the woman and relinquished his position to Reilly's counsel. He had called Annie Cole to establish Reilly's presence on the towpath on the night of the murder; anything else was an unnecessary distraction.

That Graveney was capable of charm Reilly saw for the first time as he stood, straightened his robes, and turned towards Annie Cole. Graveney began by apologizing to the witness that he was going to cover similar ground to that covered by his learned friend, and then asked her to explain, exactly, what she could see from the window of her room.

'The canal, Sir,' Annie Cole said.

'Very good. I understand, from the newspaper reports, that your steps are lit?'

'Yes, Sir. Two steps up from the bank. I have a light above my door.'

'Wise, I would suggest. Given that the canal towpath is otherwise unlit.' Graveney turned to the jurors, inviting them to applaud her wisdom.

Annie Cole was encouraged. 'It's dark, Sir, at night. I don't tend to walk out at night after dark. But I have occasion to return home after dark in the winter. Not by choice, you understand.'

'I understand.' Graveney offered Annie Cole another reassuring smile. They were on the same side. 'So, you were in your room, at your embroidery and you heard a splash?'

'I was. Yes. And I did. Yes.'

'And being a concerned citizen you went immediately to the window. You raised it, and you saw a young man running away along the towpath. You tell us you also saw a dog on the canal side, sitting "still as you like".'

'Yes, Sir. Just looking into the black water.'

'On the dark towpath?'

'Yes, Sir. After dark it was.'

'But the dog was visible?'

'Yes, Sir. He was.'

'How was he visible? By the light of the moon?'

'No, Sir. There was no moon.'

'How then?'

'By the light, Sir, from the colour works.'

'From the colour works?'

'Yes, Sir. From the windows of the colour works, which are by the canal. They work late, sometimes all night, and the bank behind the works is lit.'

'So, by the generosity of the light from the colour works, you clearly saw the dog, and you clearly saw the man, who was standing beside the dog?'

'Oh no, Sir.'

'No?'

'No. He was not by the dog at that moment. He was running off along the bank, away from the bridge.'

'I see. Beyond the range of the light from the colour works?'

'Yes, Sir.'

'But within the range of the street lamps?'

'No. There are no street lamps other than those on the bridge.'

'The towpath, then, is lit further along?'

'No. There are no lights on the towpath.'

'Ah. A passing barge, then, and on it, a bargeman with a lantern?'

'There was no barge, Sir.'

'So how did know it was a young man?'

'By... by the speed, Sir, the speed at which he was... conducting himself.'

'A figure – at best a shadow – in the darkness, running quickly away from you on a dark, moonless night, with no other illumination... You would confidently identify that figure as a young man? More that that – as the young man in the dock? Bear in mind the seriousness of this case before you answer.'

Now that Annie Cole's attention was being steered towards Reilly she allowed herself to meet his eyes for the first time. Perhaps, in her thirty-eight years, she had unwittingly looked into the eyes of a murderer. She had certainly seen much cruelty. But there was none at all in Reilly's guileless face. 'No, Sir,' she said. 'I could not.'

'Very well. But you would nevertheless confidently identify the figure as a young man rather than, say, a child – perhaps the owner of the dog running for help – or a young woman?'

Annie Cole seemed to have been struck mute.

'Would you answer the question?'

'I could not confidently identify the figure as any of those things, Sir. No. I could not.'

'Thank you.'

And Annie Cole stepped down. She returned to the conversation with Graveney many times over the following weeks but she could never pinpoint the moment when the friendship between the two of them came to an end. Perhaps she had failed him in some way. It seemed to her that however decently you lived your life, every day the world found ways to inflict new cruelties.

❧

At roughly the time Annie Cole was leaving the court, Nimrod was following Daisy back through the streets of Old Cross to the public house. Through the morning he had sat beside her as she drank and wept and worked up a mournful anger at her impoverished circumstances. She provided nothing to assuage his thirst or his hunger.

'Bastard! Where is he?' Now they were inside the public bar, where several of the previous night's customers were back in residence. In hats and coats to ward off the afternoon chill, they were engaged in laying down those important early drinks which, if applied carefully, would provide the kindling for several hours of serious inebriation. The task involved serious concentration; the regulars turned their backs on the interruption and returned to the job in hand.

'Lol! Where are you, you thieving bastard?' Nimrod followed Daisy through into the snug, which was empty. There was fresh sawdust on the floor, the brass pumps gleamed, the fire was newly set but unlit and the bar smelt of disinfectant. The barmaid, drawn by the racket, came out from the back room to see what the commotion was about.

'He's not here,' she told Daisy quickly. 'He hasn't been in. You'll have to leave or the governor'll be down.'

'If you see him, you tell him I'm looking for him. You tell him he owes me.'

'I will, Daisy. I promise.'

'I'm short. You tell him I'm short.'

'I'll tell him.'

'You make sure you do.'

'What about…?'

'What?'

'What you was talking about.' The barmaid gestured towards Nimrod. 'The case has started. They're talking about nothing else on the high street.'

'Don't want to get involved. Told you.'

'But if you're short. You know. A few pounds. Come in useful 'til that bastard pays up.'

'And how will that make me look?'

'When did you ever care?'

'You don't know how much I care. Nobody knows.'

'You think about it. Who needs to know?'

And then they were outside again, Daisy leaning against the wall and weeping.

❧

PC Portch cut an elegant figure on the stand. His height and quiet authority lent him a charisma possessed by neither of the two previous witnesses. The jurors found themselves sitting up a little straighter, mimicking the straight-backed way Portch conducted himself. They were reassured by the constable. Should they ever be in need of help he was the kind of figure they would be most glad to see. Crawford had chosen to save the policeman's appearance until after Annie Cole. He was well aware of the impact this would have and he knew, as the first day drew to a close, that it was Portch's words that would remain with the jury until the following morning. If they dreamed that night, as jurors tend to do, Portch would be the figure they dreamed of.

Having established Portch's credentials, Crawford had invited him to explain the first time he had come across Reilly and Portch had recounted his visit to Mountjoy's.

'You explained that you were investigating the disappearance of Mr Gower?'

'I did. I spoke both to Mr Mountjoy and Mr Reilly.'

'Did either mention the discovery of the wallet?'

'No. It was mentioned by neither man.'

'Was there an acknowledgement of Mr Gower's visit to Mr Reilly's studio?'

'Yes. It was, by Mr Reilly's account, a convivial visit. A business meeting. He told me that Mr Gower left at seven o'clock in the evening and that was the last he saw of him.'

'And how would you describe Mr Reilly's demeanour on that day?'

'I would describe his demeanour to be typical of a man facing such questioning.'

'Which is?'

'Cautious.'

'Cautious?'

'Yes. He volunteered no more information other than that which was asked of him.'

'You discussed his profession?'

'We did.'

'And what impression did you gain?'

'He said he lived as many artists do, relying in part on the charity of others.'

They discussed what Portch had learned of Reilly's financial affairs and Crawford then steered him through his second visit to the coffee shop, at which time he had seen a change in the two men. They then arrived at his first visit to Reilly's lodging house.

'Describe the circumstances in which Mr Reilly both works and lives.'

'He lives in a single room, directly beneath the roof, at the top of a lodging house.'

'A well-appointed room?'

'The light is good, the room poor.'

'What was the purpose of this visit?'

'That morning the body had been discovered in the canal. Mr Reilly had been seen on the bank with Mr Mountjoy. I went to ask if, in the light of the discovery of the body in the canal, there was anything new he recalled about the visit of Mr Gower. Sometimes the memory is jogged by such events. He told me there was not. I further explained that no wallet had been found on the body.'

'His response to that?'

'He made no response.'

'Cautious?'

'Sir?'

'You suggested when you first encountered him, he was cautious. Would the same be true of this visit?'

'Less cautious.'

'You then returned later that day, with Chief Inspector Macreadie, to arrest Mr Reilly?'

'We returned to question him further, having been informed by Mr Pardew of the conversation over the wallet.'

'Mr Pardew being a journalist.'

'Indeed, and having heard Mr Mountjoy and Mr Reilly discussing the matter on their way to the canal.'

Portch was then asked to confirm the details of the interrogation following the arrest, much of which had been dealt with by Macreadie, and was then thanked and handed to Graveney.

'I'm interested in the dog,' Graveney began, directing the remark more towards the jury than Portch. 'What can you tell me about the Mr Reilly's dog, Constable Portch?'

'A persistent fellow,' Portch said.

'Indeed?'

'Yes. Scrabbling away at the chimney breast he was when I visited him.'

'I understand that you discussed the dog with Reilly?'

'I discussed the issue of my son being after owning a dog and sought his advice, which he gave.'

'And when you questioned Mr Reilly at the police station I understand the issue of the dog was again raised?'

'It was.'

'Because Mr Crawford chose not to raise the issue either with Chief Inspector Macreadie or with you, perhaps you'd be kind enough to remind us of the importance of the dog to Mr Reilly's defence.'

'Under questioning Mr Reilly suggested that his Jack Russell, Nimrod's his name, found the wallet on the canal bank the night Mr Gower died and fetched it back to his room.'

'Absurd, of course. Clearly absurd.'

'Well, I wouldn't say so.'

'You wouldn't?'

'No, I wouldn't. Not having seen the little fellow.'

'You'd say it was feasible that Mr Reilly's dog could have brought the wallet back with him to his room?'

'It's possible.'

'Possible?'

'Yes.'

'And then hidden the wallet for a number of days?'

'Indeed.'

'There was, as has already been established, a dog on the canal bank on the night of Mr Gower's death.'

'Yes.'

'And if, therefore, the figure on the bank was not the defendant – then the case against him is significantly weakened.'

'If the figure on the bank was not the defendant. It comes down to the issue of the wallet and how long it was in Mr Reilly's possession.'

'Explain what you mean by that.'

'If he came across it in all innocence, as he tells us he did, I'd suggest he would have brought the wallet immediately to the police station. That he didn't is a clear indication of his guilt.'

'Really?'

'Yes.'

'Foolhardy, but not necessarily criminal. A man comes across a wallet containing a hundred and fifty pounds, surely he can be allowed a few day's reflection on how that money might change his circumstances before returning it to the police – which finally he did.'

Graveney and Portch continued in a similar vein, neither giving ground, until Sir William Reynolds drew the day's proceedings to a close.

❧

When the cell door was locked behind him that night, Reilly took Leonardo's notebook from the shelf in his room (Rushden had finally arranged for it to be delivered to him), carried it to his stool, and opened it at random. He told himself that he would draw a lesson from the page he had chosen. Borrowing the light from the gas jet he read: 'When clouds come between the sun and the eye all the upper edges of their round forms are light, and towards the middle they are dark, and this happens because towards the top these edges have the sun above them while you are below them; and the same thing happens with the position of the branches of trees; and again the clouds, like the trees, being somewhat transparent, are lighted up in part, and at the edges they show thinner.'

That night he dreamed not of Portch but of Nimrod, imagining his weight across his knees while he slept.

SEVENTEEN

Gridlock

FOR HALF AN HOUR, IN THE STREET OUTSIDE THE GALLERY, THE traffic had been at a standstill. Sewer replacement works combined with a traffic accident had gridlocked the area. It was from the radio of an old green Volvo in which an elderly man was patiently smoking a pipe that Samantha heard the four o'clock Greenwich Time Signal. On the fifth pip the telephone rang in the gallery. She knew it would be Keith so she left the answerphone to deal with it. Keith, however, chose not to leave a message, which was not like him, so two minutes later when her mobile phone began dancing epileptically across the desk she answered it.

'Well, you're a dark horse, aren't you, Samantha?' Keith began.

'Am I?'

'I didn't tell them, of course. I thought I'd give you the opportunity to explain yourself to me first.'

'Explain what?' The man in the Volvo was looking towards her now, as though he was eavesdropping on their conversation.

'The game's up, girl.'

'Game?'

'I know you saw Brian the night he died. Exactly how you know him I'm still trying to work out. Were you in cahoots from the start?'

'Of course not.'

'So you don't deny you saw him. I suppose that's something.'

The man in the Volvo was irritating her now. He was not only staring at her but also smiling, expecting her to smile back. She turned aside so she wouldn't have to meet his eye. 'How did you find out?'

'The police found my envelope in his van. The bills and admin I gave you to take back to the gallery, remember? It was in the passenger footwell. They were very specific about that. Footwell is such an ugly word, isn't it? Anyway, I told them I'd asked Brian to deliver the paperwork to the gallery for me because I'd been unwell. That was why it was in his van. Don't you think that was good of me?'

'Yes.'

'I'll tell them the truth eventually, of course. Probably. But first I want you to tell me exactly what's going on and why the envelope was in the van.'

'All right. Not now. Tonight.'

'Tonight? What do you take me for, Samantha? I'm not a complete fool. As soon as you put the phone down you'll be gone. Out of the country I shouldn't wonder. No. I want you to tell me now.'

'I'll tell you tonight, Keith. You'll have to trust me.'

'Trust you!'

'I don't really think you have any choice, do you? As you say, I could put the phone down now and disappear. You don't have any power to stop me.'

'Power? My word. You are a determined mite, aren't you? Funny. I thought I was a good judge of character. I didn't have you down as being capable of anything as interesting as this. Did you kill him?'

'Don't be ridiculous. I'll explain it all later. Come to the gallery… and don't tell the police.'

'And why shouldn't I?'

'Because then I'll tell them that the three paintings of Reilly's I have are Brian's. They'll take them and you won't be able to sell them.'

'More paintings?'

'Yes. And they're beautiful – and much bigger than the one you have here.'

'I'll be there at five thirty.'

'All right.'

Samantha put down the phone. She knew she had to think fast, and tried to remember if she had ever given Keith her address. She was sure that she hadn't, but he did have her mobile phone number so she could be traced that way. The flat was, therefore, no refuge from Keith or the police. She had never had any intention of defrauding the gallery but there was no question in her mind that Reilly had chosen her to be the custodian of his paintings. This, she considered, gave her a moral right of ownership. She would remove the Reilly painting from the gallery, go back to the flat where she would collect the other three pictures and the other items she had brought down from the café loft, and then take everything to Old Cross, where she would find Reilly's son. From there, Reilly would guide her next step.

Samantha took the painting from the wall, carried it carefully to her desk and wreathed it in bubble wrap, which she secured with brown tape. She then fetched her coat from the cupboard, turned off the computer and the lights and left the gallery for the last time. For a moment she considered leaving a note of apology for Keith. He had, after all, been decent enough to give her a job. But there was nothing she could say to him that would make him understand why she felt she had more right to Reilly's painting than he did. When she had double locked the gallery door she posted the keys through the letterbox. With Reilly's painting under her arm she set off for the Tube. The traffic on the street remained at a standstill. At the sound of a horn she looked round to see the driver of the Volvo waving to her. Her eye caught a sudden movement on the pavement opposite the gallery, but it was just a man in a green Barbour jacket leaning closer to the restaurant menu in its miniature glass-fronted coffin.

Keith, having been watching the gallery from the vantage point of the doorway beside the restaurant, took evasive action when Samantha turned. He had waited to see in which direction she would make her escape after the telephone call. His intention was to give her twenty or so yards' start and then follow her. Keith had little faith in the police. The moment the two young constables arrived at his door that morning he made the decision not to reveal anything to them but to go to the gallery and confront his employee. He knew, however, that she would lie and so refined his plan with the phone call. Keith's hunch, knowing Brian as well as he did, was that he and Samantha had been working together to scam him. His assumption was that Brian had tipped her off about the job in the gallery. Once she was established there they would steal a few paintings, empty the safe, she would vanish and the connection between the two of them would never be guessed. This made greater sense when he replayed the original telephone conversation with Samantha in which she had virtually insisted on coming round to his house. Had he not been debilitated by illness, he would have spotted the con immediately.

She was at the end of the street now. Then she turned left and was out of sight. Keith set off after her at a half jog.

❧

The gates of the Tube station were shut. Samantha joined the fringe of the milling crowd. From an intermittent loudspeaker a voice announced that the station was temporarily closed due to overcrowding at platform level. On a normal day Samantha would have waited and soon been penned in as the crowd swelled behind her. She would have gone to that faraway place in her mind where she could take refuge from boredom and the trials of everyday life. But today was not a normal day. She would take a taxi. There was no question that the life Reilly had mapped out for her would mean she was financially secure. She got a momentary glimpse of the balcony of an elegant villa which overlooked the Mediterranean. She was lying on an immensely comfortable bed. The sun was warm on her face. She had no fears and no anxieties. The ache inside her was cured.

Samantha turned, and as if she had been doing so all her life, stepped to the edge of the kerb, raised her arm and a black cab immediately pulled up. She jumped in the back, gave the man in the tweed cap her address, and he sped away.

❧

Keith saw the taxi drive off as he turned the corner. In panic he looked for one he could hail in pursuit. There were two buses held by the lights. Behind them was a black cab but by the time it reached him it would be too late. The traffic was still heavy but it was beginning to move. Then, in the distance, he saw that Samantha's taxi had been caught in the queue waiting to cross Cambridge Circus. Beyond it the traffic was stationery. He sprinted towards the black cab and for the first time in his life he gave thanks for the clogged transport arteries of the capital.

❧

'Lost them,' Samantha heard from the driver. His disembodied voice came from an invisible speaker.

'Good.'

Unbeknown to Keith, she had spotted him as dashed for the cab. The figure in the Barbour coat had stuck in her mind. There had been something familiar in it. She then recalled that when Keith called her she could distinctly hear the news from a car radio and the outdoor sounds of the city. And when she pieced the clues together she suddenly knew that he had been watching her when he made the call. Keith knew she would run, he just didn't know where. He was inside her head now. She would have to be on her guard from now on.

'Where to now?' the driver asked her. They had made a brief stop at the flat to collect the paintings and some of her belongings and then fled north.

'I need a hotel. Somewhere close to Old Cross. Not too close and not too expensive. Do you know of anywhere?'

'Plenty, love. Leave it to me.' They took the next exit ramp from the urban motorway and ten minutes later pulled up outside the kind of grim establishment only a tourist would use. A blue neon sign advertised vacancies and televisions in every room. It would suit Samantha for the time being. She had no intention of staying there for long.

By the time she had paid off the driver she had only twenty pounds left in her purse. He had helped her inside with the luggage and the paintings, which were now arrayed around her on the bed. A corner of the stuffy, small room was partitioned into a tiny bathroom with a noisy fan and a shower with mouldy grout between the tiles. The lavatory, shower basin and sink were a mustard colour. The carpet was pink. The room smelled of strawberries, the fragrance emanating from a circular plastic device plugged into the wall. It didn't entirely mask the stale smell of cigarettes.

Samantha's phone rang. She found it beneath a newspaper. Keith again. He had called three times in the past half hour but had left no message. She turned off the phone and tossed it back onto the bed. Then she undressed and took a shower. Afterwards she lay on the bed wrapped in a scratchy hotel towel. She turned on the TV. The picture was jumpy except on the American channel showing international news. She left it on for the companionship, the sound turned down. Out of curiosity she switched on her phone and checked her messages. There was of course one from Keith. His voice was calm and focused, she could hear the engine of the taxi behind him as he travelled home. There was no preamble. 'All right. So you got away. But you won't evade me forever. Don't underestimate me, Samantha. Nobody steals from me and gets away with it. I'll find you. You really don't want me as an enemy. And by the way I haven't called the police yet. I'm saving that as a last resort. Why did you kill him? A lover's tiff? I'm angry at myself. I should have seen it coming, but there you are. I trusted you. You were very plausible. Congratulations. Anyway, see you soon. Have no fear.'

Samantha deleted the message. The next she knew she was waking up, cold and naked on the bed, the towel having slipped off during her nap. When she opened her eyes the first thing she saw was the television. A woman had replaced the man behind the brightly lit news desk. It was a little after nine o'clock at night and Samantha was hungry. She had read books in which people staying in hotels picked up the phone and blithely called room service. It had always seemed an extravagance, but it was preferable to wandering around an area she didn't know looking for a cheap place to eat. Besides which she had already established that soon she would have no money worries. She picked up the bedside phone and dialled reception. A woman answered in a thick East European accent. Samantha asked if it was possible to have some food delivered to the room and was put through to the kitchen. A boy answered, another East European. She repeated the request. He volunteered sandwiches in broken English. It was past nine o'clock, the magic time after which hot food was unavailable. She accepted the offer and was told the sandwiches would be brought up to her room. She dressed in preparation for his arrival and cleared up the room, putting the paintings against the wall and tidying her discarded clothes into the wardrobe. When the room was straight and she paused to look round it her confidence faltered. This wasn't her room; her life. What was she doing in an anonymous hotel surrounded by stolen paintings, pursued by a man, wanted by the police? In panic she tore the wrapping from the nearest picture and the colours of Reilly's world flooded the room. The young Reilly stared up at her with his imploring gaze and she knew again where she was and why she was there. She did, however, feel the need for a familiar comforting voice. It was a moment when, had her mother still been alive, she would have telephoned her and they would have spent ten or fifteen minutes idly chatting. It came as something of a shock to Samantha to realize that had she been feeling like this a day or so before, she would have called Keith and he would have fulfilled her mother's role.

Had she been at home she would have opened her book and read under the standard lamp for two or three hours. It was too late to go looking for Reilly's son tonight. She did, though, have the newspapers she'd brought from the café loft. She retrieved the carrier bag from the wardrobe and took it to the bed, kneeling on the coverlet and tipping the newspapers carefully out. She opened the first one and a paragraph immediately caught her eye. Her heart stilled. She read: 'Approaching the gallows in the execution shed in the prison yard, the prisoner was somewhat unnerved by the site of the noose and the sudden sounding of a loud horn of a tourist coach passing the prison. Ellis later declared he was afraid the condemned man was going to faint and got the execution over in just 25 seconds, which is believed to be a record.'

There was a knock at the door. She opened it to find a boy, sweat-smelling, sixteen or seventeen years old, tall and acned, in a black shirt and trousers, carrying a white plate with a single white-bread sandwich on it. The utilitarian sandwich was covered in cling film. She thanked him and took the plate from him at the door. He seemed to be waiting for something but she didn't know what it was so she closed the door. She ate the stale sandwich sitting on the bed, helping it down with a glass of tepid tap water from the bathroom. She regretted not ordering any chocolate. No meal was complete without something sweet. The sandwich was soon finished. It was not yet half past nine but she was tired. She pushed aside the newspapers and lay down, and before she knew it she was asleep.

EIGHTEEN

Mountjoy Takes the Stand

ALL WHO PLAY A PART IN A CRIMINAL TRIAL ARE EXPOSED BY THE process. Faced by the full glare of attention from the jury and public gallery, the scrutiny of the defendant, officials and clerks, bravado soon crumbles. Mountjoy's life had been lived decently and without pretension and as he took to the stand what was exposed of him was a dignified individual in a good suit, a new collar and highly polished boots. Amy Sykes had encouraged him to show a handkerchief in his top pocket but he argued that it gave the wrong impression. The eye would be drawn to that flash of white and a shrewd juror would ask himself why the witness was trying to distract attention from his face.

Harry Crawford was in full flow. He was at his best in the mornings. The first day had largely gone well for him although he regretted the unexpected mention of the dog at the canal side. To open the second day he had called Mountjoy to the stand. The statement he had made to the police revealed a sober individual who showed a great respect for the truth. This, Crawford trusted, would act as a balance to any inclination he might feel towards couching his answers in such a way that would show Reilly in a good light. Ten minutes had passed since Mountjoy had been called and they had now reached the moment when Gower's name was first mentioned in the coffee shop.

'The defendant asked you to make contact with him?' Crawford asked.

'He did,' admitted Mountjoy.

'Why?'

'I was happy to do so.'

'I'm sure you were but did it not strike you as odd that he should have asked you?'

'Not at all.'

'You considered the behaviour typical of the defendant?'

'I would say so.'

'To act as his unpaid agent?'

'That's not how I chose to see it.'

'In the light of subsequent events does it not now strike you differently?'

'How?'

'How?' Crawford echoed. 'Well, for one rather important reason: because there was then nothing to link the defendant with the critic's visit to his room. He could therefore argue that he had nothing to do with summoning him to the district. Had his name not appeared in the victim's engagements book there would have been nothing to link the two men.'

'He could argue that. But he does not.'

'Does he not? We'll come to that, I'm sure. But you were unsurprised by the request?'

'I was a little surprised.'

'For what reason?'

'For the reason that I understood that Reilly and Gower were not on the best of terms.' Only now did Mountjoy allow himself to look towards Reilly. He saw, with some distress, that his friend looked pale and unshaven; his hair had been cut short. Reilly was directing his gaze at a point somewhere just below the top of the dock. It was evident, however, from his expression that he was listening intently. Although Reilly had lived alone with only Nimrod for company, he had never presented himself to Mountjoy as a vulnerable or lonely figure. Today he gave the impression of being both.

'Not on the best of terms?' Crawford pressed.

'Only in that I think he found the attention following the summer exhibition damaging to his work.'

'The attention drawn to him by Mr Gower?'

'Yes.'

'He discussed this with you?'

'He did. But only in terms of his work.'

'This is an important point. Explain exactly what the defendant had to say about Mr Gower.'

'As far as I remember he threw away a number of paintings following the exhibition, giving the reason that he felt that he was painting for Gower's approval and not for himself. He needed to keep his mind clear. Which it wasn't.'

'Interesting, then, that we are being invited to understand that Mr Gower was a champion of the defendant's work.'

'Oh, he was a champion. He was a great champion of Reilly. He is a genius – in my humble opinion.'

'In the humble opinion of a coffee-shop owner, Reilly is a genius.'

'I may not be a respected critic, Sir, but I'm not a fool.'

'Of course. Forgive me if I implied that you were.' Crawford made a courtly bow towards Mountjoy. 'But you understood that there was no love lost between the two men?'

'Only in terms of Reilly's work.'

'But Reilly's work – by which we should take it you mean his paintings – was important to him?'

'There is nothing more important in the world.'

'So we can assume that anything that came between the artist and his work caused him displeasure? Distress?'

'Yes.'

'And the artist was poor? Financially, I mean. We're not discussing his artistic merit, here.'

'Yes. He was.'

'Eager, then, to persuade you to exhibit his work to pay off his debt to you.'

'Not initially.'

'No?'

'He came up with the idea for the exhibition only recently.'

'Did he?'

'Reilly is a true artist. He knows nobody judges his work more harshly than he does.'

'And as a result he preferred to live off your charity and remain in obscurity?'

'He does not live in obscurity in his own mind.'

'Which man does? But I'm interested that despite his debt to you, initially he resisted the offer of an exhibition.'

'He didn't resist it. It was never mentioned.'

'But recently persuaded you to hold one?'

'Yes. But I was happy to agree to it.'

'And why would you suggest that it took him so long?'

'I think he felt it was time he paid off some, if not all, of his debt to me.'

'Were you pressing him for payment?'

'No.'

'And it was at this time that Mr Gower's name was brought up.'

'Later.'

'And when was the issue of the wallet raised?'

'Reilly brought it to the coffee shop a day or so before the exhibition.'

'And explained how he came across it?'

'He told me that Nimrod had found it on the canal bank, and brought it home with him.'

'Nimrod being the somewhat eccentric name of his dog?'

'Yes.'

'And you believed him?'

'Why should I not have done?'

'You were unaware of the deceased's disappearance at this point?'

'I was aware that Gower had disappeared, not that he had passed away.'

'Why did Mr Reilly bring the wallet to you do you think?'

'To ask my opinion as to what he should do with it.'

'And what was your opinion?'

'That he should take it to the police station and hand it in.'

'And he agreed?'

'He did.'

'Nevertheless, despite seeking the opinion of a valued friend, he kept the wallet.'

Mountjoy nodded. Until this point, the exchanges between the two men had been proceeding at speed. Crawford chose this moment to pause, allowing Mountjoy's admission to settle in the minds of the jurors before asking: 'How well do you consider you know the defendant?'

'I know him as well as he allows himself to be known.'

'"As well as he allows himself to be known." Explain what you mean by that.'

'I have known many men. I serve coffee and food to two hundred or more each week. I could confidently tell you which of those men are content, which are happy, burdened, grateful… I can see it. But Reilly is different.'

'Go on.'

'…He lives in a world different to ours, a world of imagination. Although he walks along our streets and we see him and speak to him, he's often there, away in that other world.'

'Secretive?'

'Not through choice.'

'You would, therefore, be surprised to learn that he murdered Gower?'

'More than surprised.'

'More surprised than learning he had not taken the wallet to the police station? More surprised than the ludicrous story of his dog finding the wallet on the canal bank, bringing it back to his room and hiding it for two days? You've provided an elegant portrait for us of the artist – for which we are grateful – but in so doing I would suggest you've drawn a picture of a man quite capable of cold murder for financial reward – and capable of carrying on afterwards as if he was entirely innocent.'

'That was not my intention.'

'I'm sure it was not.'

❧

Nimrod spent the second night with Daisy as he had spent the first: cold, hungry and afraid. She woke with a scream before dawn and within seconds was off the bed and reaching for the bottle on the table. But the bottle was empty. She hurled it against the wall. It shattered. A shout came from the other side of the wall. Daisy shouted back. A child began to cry. She went to the fire, which had burned out many days before, and peered down at the grey ghosts of coal. Then she seemed to notice Nimrod cowering on the floor beside the hearth, tense, ready to back away.

'Here.' She clicked her fingers. Nimrod, shaking, his eyes firmly on her, did not move. 'Come here,' she said gently, and only then did Nimrod approach. 'I didn't mean to hurt you, little dog. I'm sorry. Come sit with Daisy.' She took the seat by the unlit fire and gathered Nimrod onto her knee. There she napped until the sun came up, and this time when she woke she stood with the shock of it, spilling Nimrod from her lap onto the floor.

'Come. Come.' She gathered up her shawl from the bed and out they went.

The streets were busy, the shops open, the roads crowded. It was a chilly morning. Frost powdered the untramped gutters and lay white in the shadows. Daisy passed through the busy people on the pavements with similar purpose, though she had none but to escape from the damp and cold of her room. She dashed through Old Cross, Nimrod at her heels, turned at the water pump that marks its northern boundary, and dashed back, all the while muttering to herself. She paused so often to ask if anyone had seen Lol that it became a refrain: 'Have you seen Lol? Have you seen Lol? He owes me money, he does. He owes me money.'

One man she stopped said he had heard Lol had left town on business, at which Daisy laughed, saying she couldn't imagine what that business could be as Lol had never, in all the years since she had known him, done an honest day's work. The man, encouraged by this, admitted that he suspected the business Lol was engaged in was not of the legitimate kind, but if it worked out for him then he'd be back within the week. He wished success on this venture as, like Daisy, like many others in the district, he was owed money by the fellow.

Learning that she was in same boat as others in Old Cross could have heartened Daisy, but it did not. And how much, after all, was she owed? Sufficient for a bottle of gin, a loaf of bread, a sack of coal. Enough for a day's consolation, nothing more. There was money to be had, she well knew. She had resisted it. All of her instincts told her it was wrong. But she was cold and hungry and too sober. The choices she had once had were no longer available to her. She was no longer young. Men like Lol still wanted her, for which she was grateful, but it would not be long before she would have to earn her living another way.

They reached the coffee shop and paused at the door. Daisy dallied, unsure whether to enter. Finally she did, and the moment the door was open Nimrod dashed around her legs and made for the shelter of the counter.

'Nimrod!' Amy cried, lifting Nimrod into the air and pulling him tight into her bosom. 'You're so cold!'

Soon he was back in his basket beside the fire, which was high and fierce. Amy fussed and fetched him water in a bowl, and watched while he drank it. She gave him food, of which he ate little. The plate was left beside him. Finally, he was lifted and a blanket placed beneath him. Amy laid him on it and folded the cloth around him.

Having attended to Nimrod, Amy turned her attention to the visitor, a raddled young woman she had seen about the area many times. 'He's not here,' Amy told her tersely in response to her enquiry about Mountjoy.

'When will he be back?'

'After he's finished at the Bailey. Why do you want him?'

'I've information that might be of use to him.'

'About the case?'

'He's a friend of Reilly's, ain't he? Some say his only friend.'

The hard-eyed exchange continued; no pretence from either woman that this was anything but a business transaction. 'You can tell me. I'm Reilly's friend.'

'I'd rather save it for him.'

'I don't know how long he'll be.'

'Then I'll come back. He'll want to know this – trust me. Trust me he will.'

'Come back at five o'clock. The door'll be locked. Ring and he'll come down and let you in.'

'I will.'

When the woman left a man stood and followed her out, pausing to toss a few coins onto the counter. Amy remembered the journalist from a few months before, when he had asked her questions about Reilly and she had answered them without pausing to wonder what lay at the root of his curiosity.

❧

When Graveney cross-examined Mountjoy he worked hard to repair the damage that had been done to the defence case. Reilly, Mountjoy was happy to concede, was flawed. Which artist wasn't? Graveney asked. And perhaps it went beyond that – could it not be argued that without flaws no man can be an artist? Crawford had been quick to infer criminal characteristics when in truth all Reilly exhibited was an artistic temperament. There was no animosity between the artist and Gower and no vested interest in luring the critic to Old Cross simply to rob and murder him. Mountjoy was encouraged to admit that he would have supported the artist financially for as long as he needed support. He was not calling in the debt, and therefore Reilly's financial situation was no more dire that it had been in the past. In fact there was an opportunity for it to be improved should the exhibition prove successful. As for the issue of the wallet – yes, Reilly had ignored Mountjoy's advice. For a few days he allowed himself the fantasy of life as a rich man – but what could be more human than that? If greed is a criminal trait then we are all guilty. By the end of the morning session, the jury were left with the picture of a firm but uneven friendship between two decent, strong, but quite different individuals.

Reilly took his lunch alone in the cell beneath the court. He was not visited by Graveney and Rushden. At a public house in Cock Lane the men were busy discussing the strategy for the final afternoon. The prosecution had not called Amy Sykes and the two men were debating whether to call her blind for the defence. On balance, Graveney decided against it, arguing that Crawford could use the fact that she was carrying Reilly's child to strengthen his motive for robbing Gower. It seemed likely that Reilly would be called the following morning, and by tomorrow afternoon his fate would be known. Rushden was uneasy. He had come across occasional cases like Reilly's when the outcome was as dependent on the character of the defendant as the case against him, and he was unsure how strongly Reilly would appeal to the jury. Graveney reassured him, but then, as the men set about their lunches, they fell silent, and they remained so after they had finished and took the brisk three-minute walk back to court.

Reilly had long since resigned himself to fate. Since he was a child part of him had always been detached, sometimes observing himself, sometimes the world around him. In the cell beneath the court he took refuge in that part of himself now, setting down his knife and fork, awaiting the moment when he would be taken back upstairs. He was there, he now knew, to play a role. No matter that he had not yet been questioned, he was aware that the jurors were often trying to read his face in an attempt to judge his reactions to the revelations of the witnesses. That was why he had found it so hard to look at Mountjoy. It pained him to see how such a decent man was being manipulated by Crawford into betraying him. He felt no animosity towards his old friend, just a deep sadness that circumstances had brought them to this. Whatever the outcome of the trial his life would be changed. He would no longer be the carefree artist living in his garret, concerned only about his work in progress.

The afternoon session began briskly. It took a few moments for the public gallery to settle when the journalist Pardew took to the stand. The man had the presence of a villain and the audience sensed drama. He looked towards them without fear, his eyes ranging along the rows, searching for the detail he would use when later he reported on the case. But today he had been relieved of his reporting duties, which is why he had called at Mountjoy's coffee shop on the way to the Old Bailey. His instincts had led him there, and, as so often in the past, had been proved right. He had overheard the conversation between Daisy and Amy Sykes and had followed her out when she left. After some persuasion she had agreed to meet him after she had seen Mountjoy. She had been suspicious of him, refusing to divulge the reason for her visit there, but suggesting that, for the right price, she would have something to tell him later.

Harry Crawford's voice boomed like a ceremonial cannon across the room, silencing the court: 'Mr Pardew, perhaps you could begin by telling us your profession.'

'I earn my living as a journalist, Sir.'

A man in the public gallery laughed.

'And a writer, too, so I understand?'

'I contribute to journals such as the *Fortnightly Review*, yes.'

'Explain how you first came across the defendant.'

'It was on the day of his exhibition. I had been assigned by my editor to report on it.'

'A routine story, well within your capabilities.'

'I had no great expectations.'

'At what point did that change?'

'I had an appointment with Reilly in the coffee shop but spent an hour in the district beforehand. Whilst there I took the opportunity of speaking to a number of people who knew the artist.'

'They were aware of him?'

'Without exception.'

'And how well disposed were they towards him?'

'I gained an impression that he was treated as many artists are – with suspicion in some quarters, envy in others. All knew him, or of him, and all had an opinion.'

'A good opinion?'

'Generally not.'

'For the benefit of the defendant would it perhaps be fair to allow those opinions to be ascribed to a general prejudice against artists?'

'It would.'

'You later met the defendant in the coffee shop?'

'I did.'

'Were you prejudiced by what you had heard about him?'

'As a journalist I am always curious to learn how reputations are earned, but generally disappointed by the reality.'

'Did Mr Reilly disappoint?'

'Not at all. I found him engaging. He was eager to discuss the exhibition, less eager to discuss the issue of the greengrocer's daughter, Amy Sykes.'

'Why should you wish to discuss the greengrocer's daughter with him?'

'I had met Amy Sykes that morning, and during the course of the conversation had learned she was carrying Reilly's child.'

'Which you considered relevant to the story you were writing about him?'

'Indeed.'

'But he was unhappy to discuss this?'

'He was. But we were soon interrupted by the news that a body had been discovered in the canal.'

'You were talking to the defendant when that news was delivered?'

'I was.'

'At that moment there was, of course, no suspicion of Reilly's involvement.'

'No. There was not. But when the messenger boy came in with the news I remember Reilly and Mountjoy exchanging a look.'

'A look?'

'Yes. It seemed odd, which was why I noticed it at the time, but it was later that I returned to it.'

'It was known, of course, that Gower was missing by then?'

'Yes, and I assume the defendant and Mountjoy could not have failed to wonder if the corpse was that of the critic.'

'And when you returned to the look that was exchanged between the two men…'

'Concern? Fear? Shame? It's not for me to suggest what that look conveyed. However, what I would have expected from Reilly was shock, or, at the very least, surprise. But, as I say, on hearing the news, Reilly's eyes immediately went to Mountjoy.'

Pardew then described how the café emptied. It was during the procession towards the canal bank that he had overheard the discussion about the wallet.

'You were close enough to hear this conversation clearly?'

'I was close enough to hear enough of the conversation to understand what was being discussed.'

'What did you hear?'

'Mountjoy suggesting that Reilly should have disposed of the wallet. Reilly agreeing and assuring him that he would do so at the earliest opportunity.'

'Dispose of the wallet?'

'Yes.'

'Not "return the wallet to the police"?'

'No, Sir.'

'Which would perhaps have been the obvious course of action for an innocent man to take.'

Nothing he heard that day surprised Reilly. If anything, he had expected worse from Pardew. What he relayed was an accurate rendition of the events of the day. Unfortunately for the artist, a bald relaying of the facts did his case no favours. That night, as he was returned to the prison and was escorted from the yard to the wing, he felt compelled to pause to look up at the sky. The warder allowed him a moment, knowing that, as men tend to do as their trial draws to a close, he was contemplating his fate and savouring a few rare moments in the open air. Reilly thanked the man and they continued to the wing.

❧

Mountjoy had stayed in court to hear Pardew and remained there until the end of the day. When he arrived back at the coffee shop he found Amy Sykes sitting beside the hearth cradling Nimrod in her arms like a newborn baby. The establishment now closed, she was lit only by the glow from the fire. Mountjoy rushed to her, knelt and embraced them both.

'He came back,' Amy told him. 'But he's so cold and he won't eat.'

Nimrod's eyes were closed. For a moment Mountjoy wondered if he was dead, but as he watched him he saw his chest rise and fall.

'Poor fellow. Poor fellow.'

Mountjoy drew up a chair and encouraged Amy to sit on it. He took Nimrod from her as she stood, but she then insisted on taking him back. With Nimrod on her knee she listened as Mountjoy reported on the events of the day, concluding that it seemed likely that the following day the verdict would be given. Then it was Amy's turn.

'A woman came here. With Nimrod. She said she wanted to see you.'

'Did she say why?'

'She said she had some information about the case and you'd want to hear it.'

'Why would I want to hear it?'

'As a friend, she said. As Reilly's friend she said you'd want to know. I told her to come back at five.'

Mountjoy glanced at the clock on the wall. 'But it's gone five.'

'She didn't seem the dependable kind.'

'Perhaps she'd be better off dealing with Reilly's solicitor. You should have encouraged her to speak to Rushden.'

'I don't think that's her way. She was after money. I don't think she had Reilly's interests at heart,' Amy said, her dull tone reflecting her mood.

Nimrod woke as Amy stood. She carried him through space, up a cold staircase and into another room where she laid him in front of a new fire. Again he slept, though the distance between sleep and wakefulness was becoming shorter and shorter.

❧

After leaving the court Pardew took a cab to Old Cross for his appointment with Daisy. She had agreed to meet him outside the public house at half past six. The journalist arrived at six and decided to pass half an hour inside, a glass or two of port to warm him, a newspaper to pass the time. He took his glass to the table that afforded him the broadest uninterrupted view of the bar. Whether or not on duty he could never resist watching people go about their private lives. Few held any secrets from him. The product of an unhappy marriage, with a histrionic mother and a distant father, he had always been sensitive to the moods of the household and had assumed the gift to be a common one. It was only as he matured into adolescence that he realized his father had neither the ability nor the interest in judging the temper of his wife, or, indeed anyone around him. His mother, on the other hand, lived as if all of her nerves were exposed to the world. A door slamming in a distant street would be enough to send her to bed for the day with an attack of the vapours. But Pardew's gift was also a curse. He could not control it, nor switch it off. Hence, as he sat, surveying the chaotic human dramas that were unfolding in that dismal, smoky room, he turned to his newspaper, forcing himself to close his ears to the harmonics of pain.

One voice, however, he could not block out once it started, shrill and demanding from the snug bar. It tormented his nerves like the sound of two cats fighting. It was a voice he knew, indeed the voice of the woman he expected to meet outside the public house in twenty minutes' time. She had told him she was to see Mountjoy first; it seemed she had been detained. Pardew waited the twenty minutes until the appointment and then slipped outside. He did not expect the woman to join him, but he wanted to give her the opportunity. It would make his job easier if she came to him but, as he had anticipated, after fifteen minutes she still hadn't emerged, so Pardew went back inside.

The air was now humid and thick but the warmth was welcome after his wait on the street. He pushed to the bar and bought another glass of port. His arm was jostled as he accepted his change. Turning to confront the man at his side, he was met with the dull eyes of a belligerent drunk, so he backed away. He didn't fancy his chances in a fist fight with any of the men in that room.

Pardew took his glass and waited beside the opening to the snug bar. There was no door, just a twisted metal hinge from which the door had been wrenched. The room was small and filled by four circular tables. Daisy was at the corner table, the back of her seat firmly against the bar. She was sitting with a thick-set man in a brimless hat and a huge waxed coat. The man had a bunch of her hair in his fist. In a brutal show of affection he was using it to pull her head forward, he then relaxed his grip and her head slumped back. He did it again and again, Daisy's head rocking back and forth, back and forth, she laughing stupidly at the game they were playing, happy to be in Lol's company once again.

Pardew watched. Ugliness he found compelling. He had no intention of approaching the woman while she was in the bar but he was content to wait in the hope that at some point in the evening she might find herself alone. The opportunity arose twenty minutes later when Daisy's companion, tiring of the game, stumbled to his feet and made his way towards the Gents'. Pardew wasted no time. As soon as the man was through the door, he approached Daisy's table. He chose not to sit, but watched as she looked up at him, fighting to focus on his face. Her body swayed, her eyes were half closed. She shook her head, trying to rid it of the fog of booze.

'It's you,' she finally managed.

'We had an appointment, Daisy,' Pardew encouraged as he would have done a child to perform a party piece.

'I know. Then Lol came back. Now I don't need to see you so you can go away.' She worked hard to express each thought with clarity.

'I thought you had something to tell me.'

'No, Mister, I had something to tell Reilly's friend. I can't recall why I had to see you. It don't have nothing to do with you. I don't like you, anyway.' Daisy's hand went to her glass. She lifted it and manoeuvred it with enormous concentration towards her mouth. The gin seemed to give her strength. 'You'd better not be here when my Lol gets back.'

'But I'm only here to help you,' Pardew said.

'Help me! That's a laugh.'

'But I am, Daisy,' Pardew cajoled. 'I'm here to help you with the law.'

'I don't need no help with the law.'

'But you do. Surely you realize that.' Pardew chanced a look over his shoulder but Lol still hadn't emerged from the Gents'. He knew his time was limited and he would get no further opportunity with Daisy.

'How do you work that out?'

'You asked to speak to Mountjoy about Reilly. I can only assume in connection with the current murder case. You have information.'

'What if I do?'

'Surely you're aware that you're legally obliged to reveal that information. If you withhold it, you could end up in a similar predicament to Reilly.'

'I never said I had no information.'

'Yes, you did, Daisy. You said it quite clearly.' Pardew smiled. 'I'm a journalist, my dear. It's a trustworthy profession. I took a note of what you said. The police trust my word. And if I tell them we've been talking and you told me you know something about the murder then they'll bring you in.' Pardew smiled again, but then he felt the weight of a huge hand on his shoulder blade.

'What's this one after?' Lol asked Daisy.

'I'm speaking to Daisy about legal matters,' Pardew said. He tried to squirm round and offer Lol his hand but the anvil weight remained on his shoulder. 'My name's Pardew, I'm a journalist.'

'What does he want?' Lol seemed to have no interest in what Pardew might have to say for himself.

'He wants to help me. That's what he said he wants.'

'With what?'

'With... with something I know.'

'Sit down,' Lol said, forcing Pardew down onto a stool, then taking the chair he had vacated before leaving for the Gents'. 'Now tell me what this is about.'

Pardew had no choice but to explain the reason he was there. The threat of violence hung in the air. He was aware that it was unlikely that Daisy had told Lol anything of her involvement with Reilly.

'Yeah,' Lol said sagely after Pardew had finished. 'The gentleman's right. If you know something you'd better tell it.'

'I was going to tell it, Lol,' Daisy offered eagerly. 'But not to the police. I was going to tell it to Reilly's friend. That's what I was going to do.'

'Why?'

'Because it's worth a quid or two, this is. You're the one that's saying I should never give nothing away for free. I was only doing what you told me.'

'What would it be worth?' Lol asked Pardew, and Pardew relaxed. Greed was a great leveller.

'Well, Sir, that depends on what the information is and what value the buyer might place on that information.'

'I told you,' Daisy said. 'It's important for that Reilly. If it saves his neck I'd say that was worth something, wouldn't you?'

'I'd say so,' Lol agreed. 'And perhaps this gentleman would be kind enough to tell us how you might get the best price for this information.'

'Oh, I'd need to know what that information was,' Pardew said. 'Only then could I assess its value.'

'Tell him, then,' Lol ordered her.

'Tell him?'

'Yeah.'

'But if I tell him then he can use it for himself. If I tell him now, he don't need to pay for it. He gets it free.'

'That's right, Daisy,' Lol said. 'That's right, now you say it. This gentleman wants it for himself and he doesn't want to pay for it. What you got to say about that?'

Pardew stood and took a step back, out of Lol's reach. He could see a clear path through to the door and he readied himself to run. 'I'd say what I said before. Unless I know what the information is I can't put a value on it.'

'And what's in it for you?'

'I was trying to help. That's all. My concern is that Reilly gets a fair trial.'

'Oh, you say that now,' Daisy said. 'You pretend to care about Reilly now. You don't take me in like that. I know you came here threatening me, trying to steal my information. Well, you can whistle for it, Mister. I ain't giving it to you and I ain't giving it to him and if he goes down then he can blame you. And I'll tell you something else, and I want you to listen hard. If the law comes for me then Lol comes looking for you and Lol always finds who he's looking for. Understand? Lol? That's right ain't it?'

Lol nodded. 'That's right, Daisy.'

Pardew took another step away. 'Very well. I understand. But if you change your mind you can find me at the newspaper or the Old Bailey.'

'Oh, I won't change my mind about you, Mister. I won't ever change my mind about you.'

Pardew dashed out of the public house, his heart racing.

NINETEEN

Deep Shelter in Camden Town

OLD CROSS ESCAPED RELATIVELY UNSCATHED FROM THE LONDON Blitz. It was, however, one of the districts hit, probably accidentally, in a raid which predated that sustained bombing campaign on the capital. On 24 August 1940, a bomb fell close to the canal, demolishing three houses on Canal Street and killing four adults and two young children. As soon as the bodies had been disinterred from the ruins the local children swarmed onto the rubble, dashing up and down the mounds and mimicking the manoeuvres of the planes that flew above them. Over the following weeks, weeds colonized the bomb site and seedlings took root, the greenery softening the sharp-edged foundations and fallen masonry. But then, a few years after the war had ended, a child fell through a rotten floor into what had once been a basement room, and the site was fenced off. The wasteland became increasingly forlorn, rubbish-strewn and forgotten as the years went on, and it wasn't until 1991 that the site was once again built on. The development, designated a sheltered housing scheme, was unfussy, the style if not the mustard colour of the brickwork chiming sufficiently with the existing terrace not to draw undue attention to itself. Many of the twenty-eight residents of the scheme were aware of the site's history (people born in Old Cross tend to die there), and at least one claimed to have seen the bomb fall and to have picked up hot shrapnel from the street. One had lost family to it. It was here, at the warden's door, that Samantha Dodd was now standing.

'I don't know if you can help me, but does a man called Reilly live here? I don't know his first name, I'm afraid.'

The warden was a lithe, athletic-looking man who, despite the cold, was dressed in a blue short-sleeved polo shirt, tracksuit trousers and budget training shoes. He appeared to Samantha a very capable type. Exactly the kind of man you'd want on the other end of your emergency alarm cord. But there was something slightly demeaning, she felt, about a grown man being a warden, almost as if he couldn't quite make up his mind what he really wanted to be.

'You're after Gerald, are you?' the man said. He wasn't unfriendly but there was little in the way of welcome in his tone.

'Gerald? Well, if Mr Reilly's name is Gerald, then yes, that's who I'm after.'

'Well, he's not here.'

'Is he away? I mean is he on holiday, or has he just gone out?'

'He's gone out. Up Camden.'

'Oh.'

'He goes there a lot. Some storage place. He takes his lunch with him. Makes a day of it.'

'Do you know exactly where in Camden?'

'Yes,' he mocked genially, 'I do know exactly where in Camden.'

Although she had not intended it, Samantha suspected the warden felt she was patronizing him. He gave her a sustained look, challenging her to ask the question, so she did: 'Well, would you mind telling me where I can find him?'

'I'll write it down if you like. Come in.'

The warden's room was cheerless and as cold as the street outside. It was dominated by several shelves of cleaning products and a tall stack of toilet rolls. There was a single comfy chair, a portable television, a telephone and, on a desk, an ancient computer. The warden opened a drawer beneath the desk and took out a sheet of scrap paper. He scanned it, and then handed it to Samantha.

'This is it. There's a phone number at the bottom.'

'Thank you.'

'When you get there, or if you get lost, call him and he'll fetch you.'

'From where?'

'You'll see. When you get there.'

'All right. Thank you.'

❧

Samantha took the Tube to Camden Town and when she was there bought an *A–Z* from a newsagent's by the Tube station. According to instructions on the piece of paper, the entrance to the storage depot was behind the car park of a large store. In less than ten minutes she was facing the sturdy door of the old building and dialling the telephone number she had been given. The eccentric brick building seemed to owe something to the London Underground school of architecture. Protruding from the front was a wide, flat-roofed single storey with a barred window at either side of the double doors. Behind and looming above that was a curved windowless wall and, rising from behind that, a tall, square, slatted turret. Samantha's excitement at meeting Reilly's son was tempered by her anxiety at leaving his paintings in the hotel room, but she had had little choice, having no intention of bringing them with her. The phone, however, was answered not by the slow, faltering voice of an old man, but by that of an impatient young man asking, 'Who's that?'

'I'm… my name is Samantha Dodd. I'm here to see Gerald Reilly.'

'Right. And is he expecting you?'

'No.'

'Well, I'll have to see if he wants to see you. He doesn't like to be disturbed. What do you want him for?'

'Just tell him I have some paintings of his father's. I'm sure he'll want to see me.'

'You outside?'

'Yes. I'm at the front door.'

'Wait there.'

Samantha waited and eventually the door swung open to reveal the young man she had spoken to on the phone. He was wearing the cap and civilian uniform of a private security company and holding his mobile phone and a packet of cigarettes in his hand. The peak of the cap was low over his eyes. 'Come in, then,' he said, without further greeting, and Samantha followed him through the door into the old air and towards the rear of the building.

'He's happy to see me?' she said to the man's back, more for the want of something to say than anything else.

'What?'

'Gerald Reilly. He's happy to see me?'

'Dunno. This way.'

Hurrying, the man led the way past a number of closed office doors. The building was unmodernized and unheated. They soon reached an ancient lift; around it were entwined two descending spiral staircases. The storage depot was, it seemed, entirely underground, the square turret at the rear of the building the head of the lift shaft. Samantha paused to look at a diagram on the wall that bore the title: 'Camden Deep Shelter'.

'What was this place for?' she asked the man, who was now on his way down one of the metal staircases. She could have found him in the dark by the stale smell of his aftershave.

'Home Office shelter,' he called back, his voice augmented by an echo. 'Built in the last war for civil servants.' The man continued down the staircase.

'And do you work here?'

'What?' The young man said with some irritation, stopping again, the echo of his last footfall on the metal step slowly dying.

'Do you work here?'

'Yeah. Something like that,' he said before going on, and this time Samantha followed him to the foot of the staircase. Another long corridor stretched ahead of them illuminated by a string of unshaded lamps.

'Not far now,' the man said, and set off along the corridor and past an open door. Samantha paused to peer into the room and saw a huge inert fan. 'Come on, I haven't got all day,' she heard from farther along the corridor.

She walked past further doors which were closed, some lavatories, and then they reached a crossroads in the passageway. The man continued ahead. Samantha's sense of direction suggested to her that the passageway seemed to be taking her all the way back to the Tube station she had come from. The farther they walked, the louder the rumble of Tube trains became. Perhaps there was an entrance at platform level through which they would eventually emerge. At a second crossroads the man turned left. 'Not far now,' he said over his shoulder as he climbed down another stairwell, this one narrower.

He waited at the bottom as Samantha caught up. A short way along the next passage he pointed to an open door and said, 'He's in there.'

'Thank you.'

'I'll leave you to it.'

'Will you fetch me when I've finished? I don't think I'll be able to find my own way out.'

'If he doesn't show you up, I will.'

'Thank you.' Samantha approached the metal door and paused at the threshold of the room. It was long and narrow and lit by a single unshaded bulb. Inside were several dexion shelves of box files. There was no sign or sound of anybody working in the far recesses. She took a step inside and called: 'Gerald, are you in there?' She paused, waiting for a reply, then took one more step in before calling again. It was then that she heard the door swing shut behind her and a bolt being thrown home.

Distantly she could hear footsteps retreating rapidly along the corridor and then the dull clanks as the young man climbed the metal stairs.

'Thank you, Reilly,' Samantha said out loud. 'Thank you.'

On a square table she found the note: 'Poor Samantha. You really should be less predictable. I knew you'd go looking for Reilly's son sooner rather than later and wardens are terribly underpaid. Scream all you like. Few people use the shelter. It's a marvellous place, isn't it? Very cheap and very secure. I've stored my valuable paintings down here for years. Not in the room you're in, I hasten to add. That hasn't been used since the business that hired it went into liquidation. I've had a poke through the boxes but it's tedious stuff. You're welcome to pass the time doing the same. You're very close to Camden Town station, by the way, so you can picture the people going about their daily lives as you slowly starve. Can you hear the trains? You must admit that it serves you right. Did you really think you'd get away with stealing from me? The saddest thing is that I don't think anybody will ever miss you, will they? Fondest regards, Keith.'

Keith was in the gallery when he took the call informing him that everything had gone to plan. He reassured the youth he had hired that it was only a prank and that he would release his friend within the hour, and instructed him to return the uniform to the theatrical costumiers he had hired it from. The youth sounded unconvinced. It had seemed like an easy way of making a hundred pounds but the longer he spent in the silence of the deep shelter waiting for the woman to arrive the less funny the prank seemed. Again, Keith promised the youth he would go straight to the shelter and let the captive out, telling him that there had already been one murder in the area that week and he didn't intend to add to the tally. When the call was over he looked at his watch. 10.35 a.m. He would let her stew for two hours and then release her. Once he had released her he would call the police and tell them where she was staying. It had been easy enough to trace her, having noted the number of the cab she was travelling in the day before. Fifty pounds to the cabby he had used, a quick call to control, and he had the address of the hotel she had been dropped at. He had considered visiting her in the middle of the night but he wanted her out of the room when he retrieved Reilly's paintings. He nevertheless had a grudging admiration for Samantha Dodd. She was clever. She had outsmarted him once and he didn't want to risk her outsmarting him again.

Closing up the gallery, Keith flagged down a cab to the hotel at which Samantha had spent the night. He shivered with revulsion as he walked into the reception and rang the bell on the veneered counter. He would rather die than stay in a place like it. It reeked of bad food and poverty. He explained to the surly Pole who arrived at the desk that he had been asked to collect some paintings from a client and handed over his business card. The moustached woman took it and looked at it then laid it down if it was a bargaining counter. Keith feigned impatience, explaining that he had a cab outside and he really needed to get away. The woman made a brief, token protest, but it was clear she didn't really give a damn about protecting her guests or their property. She turned, took the key from the rack, slammed it onto the counter and returned to the back office. Keith picked up the key and took the tiny lift to the second floor.

He opened the door to Samantha's room. The bed had yet to be made. A nightdress lay across the rumpled counterpane but the room was tidy. Keith lifted it to his nose and took in Samantha's fragrance. He [illegible] down again, straightening it on the counterpane. Keith could see the four canvases leaning against the wardrobe and, beside the wardrobe, a wooden display case. If he had been in any doubt about Samantha's involvement with Brian's death, the presence of the case ended it. He carried the canvases to the taxi, then returned for the case. Before he closed the door he took one more look around the room and felt a momentary pang of desire for the woman who had spent the night there. It was gone by the time he reached the lift.

Having taken the case containing Nimrod and the paintings back to his house, Keith realized that over two hours had passed. Samantha would surely doubt that he actually intended to leave her in there until she starved to death, but as time went on wouldn't she begin to wonder? But why should he let her off lightly given the problems she had caused him? Let her stew a little longer. Going without food for a few hours would do her good. He would let her out after a decent lunch. He owed it to himself.

The lunch lasted longer than he had expected and he left the restaurant, a bottle of wine the worse for wear, at three fifteen. Samantha had now been captive for nearly five hours. What if she needed to use the toilet? How disgusting would it be if she had had to go in that stifling, airless room? It was definitely time to release her. But something held Keith back from hailing a cab. If anything had gone wrong and something had happened to his captive he didn't want a cabby snitching to the police that he had been dropped off at the shelter. It was boring and he resented using public transport, but he would take the Tube.

He arrived at the shelter at a little after four. The main door was not locked, as it tended not to be (despite the stern instructions on the notice-board inside to the contrary). There was, as always, no evidence of anybody in the offices close to the door and no sign of anybody inside. He took the spiral staircase to the lower level, crossed the crossroads, followed the corridors and eventually found himself outside the bolted door where he waited and listened. Samantha would have heard his foot-steps on the staircase and he was surprised she didn't immediately call to him to let her out. She was stronger than he'd expected her to be and again he felt a grudging admiration for her. He put his ear to the door. There was no noise from inside the room, just a faint vibration through the metal from an electric motor. Perhaps the captive was asleep. Should he knock before he entered? No. Too ludicrous. He drew back the bolt. It squealed. He pushed open the door. The room was in darkness. Surely the youth had left on the light. He had not wanted Samantha to suffer the terror of being left in the dark.

'Samantha. Time to come out. Keith's here, my dear. The game's over… Samantha.'

Keith took a step inside. The light from the corridor made a fan nine or ten feet into the room. He walked to the edge of the light and called again.

'Where are you?'

'I'm here,' she whispered. 'Here.'

The voice chilled him. It sounded half mad. Perhaps she had gone insane. But the source of it was hard to place. He stepped further into the room.

'Where are you, Samantha?'

'I'm here, Keith,' she said, this time full voiced. No question now where the voice was coming from. Keith turned and saw her behind him, framed by the door. But the glimpse of Samantha's broad silhouette was fleeting. The door was slammed and he was left in the darkness as the bolt was rammed home.

'I didn't leave you a note, Keith,' he heard. 'Because I knew you wouldn't be able to read it in the dark.'

'Let me out, you little minx.' Keep it light, Keith told himself. Play it for a game and she might just play along.

'No. I'll never let you out. Reilly warned me about you. I can't afford to have you out here spoiling things for us.'

'Reilly?' Keith called through the door. 'What do you mean "Reilly"?'

'He's with me. He's looking after me now.'

'He's what? What on earth are you talking about?'

'Goodbye, Keith.'

'Samantha!'

As she walked away Samantha heard Keith calling her name four more times, each time with decreasing conviction. When she was out of the shelter she looked to the skies and thanked Reilly again. It had, after all, been him who had warned her to be on her guard, who had turned her mind back to the moment the warden had given her the sheet with the address on it. Why should he have had the address written on a scrap of paper in his desk drawer? Why did it come so easily to hand? It was at that moment that Keith's face came into her mind. So, after leaving the newsagent's, having bought the *A–Z*, she had called Anita and told her exactly where she was. Anita had reluctantly agreed that if she didn't call back within the hour she would take a taxi to the shelter and come and find her. There was no call. When Anita tried Samantha's number she couldn't get a connection. Mr Tubman had not been happy to let her out of work but she had told him it was a medical emergency. When she reached the shelter she tried several corridors before she heard the rhythmic tapping of metal on metal. She followed the sound to a door. Behind it she found her friend. Anita was concerned that Samantha seemed not to have been in the least disturbed by her imprisonment. She had insisted it was just another test she had to go through. 'A test? What test?' Anita asked her. 'And who locked you in?' She felt, having gone to so much trouble on Samantha's behalf, she had a right to know. But all she seemed to want to talk about was a man called Reilly whom she seemed to have become involved with. Her eyes were too bright. Her thoughts flowed too freely. All Anita could do was listen, her own concerns, her own life of no interest at all. Friendship, in Anita's opinion, was a trade and she was still waiting for her return. When she left, she was not reassured by her friend's reassurances.

Samantha returned to the Tube station and took a train for Old Cross. She had passed what she hoped would be the final test. First Brian, now Keith. In the great scheme of things their lives were worth sacrificing to bring Reilly's art to the world's attention. Now she would find Reilly's son, and this time nothing would stand in her way.

TWENTY

The Trial of a Rat for the Murder of a Chick

LONG BEFORE DAWN REILLY WOKE TO THE WHISTLE OF A LOCOMOTIVE and the limerick rhythm of goods wagons passing over the viaduct. When the train was gone the silence, or what passed for silence in the prison, returned. The glass in the galleried roof creaked; a man cried out in his sleep, a door was hammered by the fists of a terrified inmate, a mouse scuttled across the floor. Reilly tried for sleep but it would not come. He chose not to fight it but, instead, to enjoy the relative peace of the prison, running through the events of the previous two days in his mind as he had done many times before. At the beginning of the trial, when the jurors were sworn in, he had chosen a particular character to focus on, a youngish, open-faced everyman who declaimed the oath clearly and proudly before taking a seat (offering his hand to be shaken by his fellow jurymen) towards the left of the front rank. Reilly soon became acquainted with the man's repertoire of expressions. He seemed a sympathetic, studious character, being most moved by Annie Cole, whose ordeal on the stand he watched intently, rarely taking his eyes from her. By this, the third day, Reilly considered he knew the man quite well and could have made a decent stab at describing his circumstances (unmarried, poor, keen to better himself and studying to do so) and his character (honest, impressionable, prone to occasional bouts of melancholy). Unfortunately, Reilly was at a loss to know how the man's reaction to the witnesses would translate into a view on his own innocence or guilt. Only occasionally did the man look in his direction, seeming almost embarrassed to do so. Reilly turned his mind away from the trial and towards Amy Sykes. He would know his fate soon enough and if he was to be set free then the first thing he intended to do was find Amy and ask for her forgiveness. He had been cloistered from the world for too long and his relationship with Amy had suffered for it. He was a lucky man in that she still seemed interested in him, but perhaps that had changed in the three months he had spent away from Old Cross. The last time he saw her she had run from him – but was that because she was carrying his child? When he had the luxury of being a free man he had chosen to imprison himself in his poor garret room, but it had taken a spell in Pentonville to arrive at that understanding. Freedom, he now understood, is too often squandered.

Thoughts of freedom, of Amy Sykes, of Old Cross and, of course, the comforting memories of Nimrod were banished when the silence was shattered by the quarter-to-six hand bell summoning the early work parties. Five minutes later the bell was rung again, and then once more before doors were unlocked on the landings and footsteps started along the galleries. The first prisoners were leaving for the omnibuses that would transport them to the train for Portsmouth. When they were gone the silence returned for a few minutes more but Reilly, by now well versed in the prison routine, knew it wouldn't last for long. At six o'clock he heard the cry 'Unlock!' and the immediate response of the prison officers who moved smartly from cell to cell with their keys. Reilly's door banged open. He was aware of the swift cold glance of the officer, a quick, simple assessment: is the man in the cell alive or dead? He stands in his flannel drawers. He is alive. Leaving the door open, the officer moved on. On the other side of the wing the cells remained locked. They would be opened only when the cleaning had been completed on Reilly's gallery.

Reilly collected his clothes, glimpsing the black hood of the night over the glass-galleried roof. He re-entered his cell. The door was banged shut and locked. As he dressed he heard the warder's cry for the cooks, bakers and cleaners and pictured the smart response as they dashed eagerly from their cells to begin their day's labours. Would he be so eager to comply if the verdict went against him and he was returned to Pentonville? The regime was run with precision. Having been confined for actions deemed criminally non-conformist, the men serving time there seemed to take a perverse pride in displaying their newfound conformity.

Having dressed, Reilly swept out his cell. At half past six the bell rang again, signalling that work on the wing should commence. Immediately the clatter of the looms started up. There would be little respite from it as the day went on. Reilly's door was opened again. An officer held out a dustpan. Reilly emptied the meagre dust he had collected from his own pan into the officer's. The officer turned and discharged the dust from his pan into a tin-lined basket carried by a following prisoner. Reilly dropped his pan onto the slate floor of the gallery where it would be collected. His door was locked and he was left again in grateful solitude until his reverie was broken by the seven o'clock bell that signalled the double-locking of the cells.

When the trap in Reilly's door opened at half past seven he thrust his tin cup through the hole. When he pulled back the cup it was full of steaming cocoa. An unseen hand deposited a small loaf on the trap shelf. Reilly took his bread and cocoa to his stool and ate his breakfast as slowly as he could. He had learned to eke out any task. Although this was less important now the trial was on and his days were full, it was a habit he had picked up in the first endless days of his captivity. After he had eaten his bread, Reilly took a careful look around his cell for what he hoped would be the last time.

What Reilly had taken to be the night when he glanced towards the prison ceiling that morning was actually the underside of a thick covering of snow. The creaking of the glass roof was the sound of the metal frames protesting at the extra weight they were bearing. When Mountjoy rose from his bed at half past four he immediately felt the chill in the air, but it wasn't until he was downstairs in the coffee shop that he noticed the snow on the window ledges and the translucence of the reflected light from the street, even in the pre-dawn. He stood at the window and looked out at the snow continuing to drift slowly down. The tracks and hoof marks of a passing cart were soon covered. It was while he was contemplating the gentle scene, allowing himself a few moments of idle reflection on the day ahead and the prospects for Reilly, that Mountjoy remembered he had left Nimrod in the upstairs parlour. With the fire stirred back into life in the coffee shop he could bring him down and settle him in the warmth. So, after emptying half a scuttle of fresh coal into the grate, Mountjoy went upstairs to the parlour. He could hear Amy dressing in her room, humming quietly to herself as she tended to do in the mornings. As always, Mountjoy was comforted by Amy's presence. He would miss the serenity she brought to the life of the coffee shop when she left; the unexpected encounters with the fragrance of her perfume lingering in the rooms she had been in.

The parlour curtains were drawn, the air in there, always tainted by the cooking smells from below, stale. But that morning there was a sharp, unfamiliar tang of ammonia in the air too. Mountjoy pulled open the curtains, gathered his courage and turned slowly to face the fire. At that moment Amy appeared at the parlour door, tying her apron. Nimrod, it seemed, had managed a few steps in the night. He lay on his side on the threadbare rug at the centre of the room. His open eyes were like black beads. From their respective sides of the room Mountjoy and Amy approached him, both lowering themselves to their knees on the rug, Amy taking Mountjoy's arm for support, the child she was carrying already adding a noticeable burden. Mountjoy reached out to touch Nimrod's head. It was cold. He felt Amy's hand on his own shoulder. Awkwardly, still kneeling, they embraced.

In the night, the pain in Nimrod's limbs intensified, then softened and finally went away, leaving him free to walk towards the light. When he reached the parlour rug he lay down and his legs twitched in one final phantom movement before falling still. Death, as it often does, had treated him more courteously than life.

❧

When Reilly was brought up the stone steps into the court he took a moment to look around the public gallery. He recognized a few faces as having been there from the first day but he was shocked to see Mountjoy among them; shocked without being able to understand why. It seemed perfectly understandable that his old friend should want to attend what was expected to be the final day of the trial, but Mountjoy seemed out of place: a statue, sitting stiff and formally among the shifting, leering ghouls. Their eyes met. Reilly inclined his head in greeting. Soberly, Mountjoy did the same. And then Reilly saw Amy. He had not noticed her before because he had not expected to see her there and had assumed the pregnant woman at Mountjoy's side to be a stranger. Her hair was longer than when he had seen her last. She, too, was dressed formally (the pathos of it pained Reilly), and she was holding herself with great composure. Gone was the shy Amy who lived in fear of her father. Here was a woman who sat as if she had every right to take her place in the public gallery. Reilly smiled towards her. Muscles he had not used for a long time tightened in his face. Amy lifted her hand from her lap and made two quick clenches of her palm. Then Reilly saw her look to Mountjoy for reassurance and he understood where she found her confidence. He felt a swift flush of jealousy. Casting his eye around the rest of the room, Reilly spotted Pardew among the journalists, waiting contemptuously (he had seen it all before) for the proceedings to begin. Portch, too, was in the court, as was Macreadie. The snow had made its presence felt in the room. Not just in the gritty puddles on the gallery floor and the salt-edged patches of damp on leather boots, but in the white weight that freighted the sky outside the tall windows. And it had begun to fall again, making the world new. Anyone pausing to listen as they walked through the courtroom would have heard that it was the favourite topic of each conversation, the sum of which melded into the general untidy hubbub that dimmed only when the judge appeared in the court, stately in his robes.

The proceedings began. Graveney rose to his feet and invited Reilly to the stand. Reilly left the dock and walked the short distance to the witness box, watched closely by the twelve jurors, the journalists and the eager crowd in the gallery, all in their own amateur way, looking for signs of innocence or guilt. But Reilly's short passage was unremarkable; neither spry nor laboured. He took the oath and waited for Graveney to begin, which he did in an unexpected way by drawing Reilly's attention towards the snow and asking him if he found inspiration in such conditions.

'Of course,' Reilly said. 'What artist would not find inspiration in the quality of the light?'

'You chose your lodgings because of the light?'

'I did.'

'A simple room?'

'Simple, yes.'

'You have no need for luxuries?'

'Only the luxury of food and privacy and time. Friendship, too. That is a luxury I am privileged to have.' Reilly looked towards Mountjoy.

'Tell me something of the training of an artist.'

This was easy, Reilly thought. I can answer these questions without fear. 'My training? Or training in a general sense?'

'Whichever you choose. The members of the jury have heard a considerable amount about your work and reputation but I think many would be intrigued to know how one goes about becoming an artist.'

'If I can be allowed to borrow from the writings of Leonardo da Vinci?'

'Please.'

'He suggested that the artist as a youth should first learn perspective, then the proportions of objects. Then he should copy from some good master, to accustom himself to what he called "fine forms". Then from nature, to practise the rules he has learnt. Then, for a time, he should study the works of various masters and finally get the habit of putting his art into practice and work.'

'And that is how you learned?'

'That is how I began to learn. Every day I work I learn something more, but as I learn I also forget. Artists rarely continue to improve as time goes on. Perhaps they become more technically adept but in so doing they lose a freshness of eye.'

Before Graveney could continue Harry Crawford embarked on a noisy coughing fit, which was effective in drawing the attention of the entire courtroom in his direction. Between coughs he waved his pristine handkerchief theatrically around his mouth, fought for breath and apologized for the interruption, but by the time it was over, the spell Graveney had been trying to cast was broken – the fact acknowledged by Crawford by an apologetic wave of his hand and a quick, shameless smile. Graveney had no choice but to return to the relative poverty of Reilly's studio, inviting him to describe it to the jury – which he did in some detail, and then asking him to explain the circumstances in which the wallet arrived in his room. He related it in the same way he had explained it to Portch and Macreadie, but the interruption had broken the rhythm of the exchanges between the two men and Reilly's assertion that Nimrod had fetched the wallet back from the canal, and then hidden it in the room, drew a rare laugh from the public gallery. This disheartened Reilly. He became vaguer in his responses, to the extent that Mountjoy began to wonder if his friend had lost all hope of being found innocent.

The morning went on interminably and when Graveney sat down and Crawford took over (his cough now miraculously cured), the prosecutor's task was an easy one. He had noted the points in Reilly's story the audience had found most amusing, and led him through them again, playing to the gallery and drawing an even bigger laugh the second time around. By the time Reilly came to explaining why he had chosen not to return the wallet, Crawford only had to gurn at his response to earn an easy guffaw from the crowd. There was nothing Graveney could do to help him, beyond praying for a miracle when Sir William Reynolds summed up the case for the benefit of the jurors. Towards the end, Reilly rallied. He was becoming tired of Crawford's game and found that if he took his time, and allowed a more significant pause between question and answer, he could retrieve some of his dignity. By the end of it, though, the fundamentals of the case against Reilly had not changed. The evidence – the possession if the wallet, his poverty, and his profession – all counted against him. All that stood against it was his character and what he hoped was the direct way he had tried to answer the questions put to him.

He was taken down shortly after twelve, but for the first time could not face the food put in front of him. Graveney, it seemed, had little appetite either. He arrived as soon as the plate had been put onto the table in the small cell. Reilly, while appreciating his bravery in facing him, wanted to spare him from what the barrister clearly considered his traditional obligation – the reassurance of his client – so Reilly asked him if it snowed still. Graveney replied that he didn't know. He hadn't noticed. When he left after five awkward minutes, Reilly was left wondering how wise it had been to be represented by a man who took no time to notice what the weather was doing outside the window. When he was taken up again after lunch to listen to the final addresses of both Crawford and Graveney, he heard very little of them, concentrating, as he was, on watching the snow falling. When Sir William Reynolds made his summing-up, pointing out discrepancies in the evidence (there were few), clearing the case of all superfluous matter, and directing the jury in the points of law that had arisen, Reilly had so removed himself that it seemed the judge was talking of someone else entirely. The jury were then sent away to consider their verdict. It was a little after three. Reilly went down the now familiar stone steps, taking one more backward glance towards Amy, who blew him a kiss across the room.

Reilly was locked into his cell, preparing himself for a long wait. It seemed likely, he knew, that the verdict might well not be arrived at that day, in which case he would be returned to Pentonville to face yet another night of confinement, of morning bells and calls and shuffling footsteps and whispered conversations between men who had learned to speak without moving their lips, and that terrible stench of too many men in close proximity; the stale reek of flesh that has not been allowed often enough into the open air.

But then, at four o'clock, just as he had given up hope, the guard outside his cell was summoned. The man immediately returned, unlocked the cell, and led him up the steps for the last time. Now the court was silent. Even Pardew forgot to affect nonchalance when the foreman of the jury was asked if the jury had reached a verdict on which they all had agreed. 'We have, Sir,' the earnest man replied.

'Do you find the prisoner guilty or not guilty of the murder of William Gower?'

'We find him guilty.'

'Prisoner at the bar, do you have anything to say why the sentence of death shall not be passed upon you?'

But Reilly was no longer listening. Thank God, he thought. Thank God it's all over, and at last I can leave that damned place and get back to Old Cross, back to Amy, back to Nimrod. He had been so sure of his acquittal that he hadn't taken in the words of the foreman, and the roar from the gallery could have been predicted whatever the verdict. It was only when Sir William Reynolds looked ominously towards him, placing the square of black silk on his head, that he understood the terrible truth. Somebody cried 'No!' from the gallery. Reilly looked up to see it was Mountjoy. But Mountjoy was struggling to support Amy, who seemed to have fallen into a dead faint. He was trying to settle her into her seat and the man on the other side of her was trying to help him.

'...Thomas Ferdinand Reilly you will be taken hence to the prison in which you were last confined and from there to a place of execution where you will be hanged by the neck until you are dead and thereafter your body buried within the precincts of the prison and may the Lord have mercy upon your soul.'

Before he was taken down, Reilly saw Pardew. Cool again. Removed again. Writing in his notebook, looking up, looking around, looking down, scribbling a quick phrase about the faces in the crowd: the handshake between Portch and Macreadie, the pleasure showing on the face of the Chief Inspector; the woman in a dead faint in the public gallery, the men supporting her into her seat; and the final sight of the shamed artist Reilly, head bowed, taken down the steps on his way to the condemned cell of the Model Prison, and thence – in three or four weeks' time – to his appointment with Mr John Ellis, hangman. 'And so the gallows' beam brought to Pentonville from Newgate will be put to good use once again,' Pardew reported when later that day he wrote up his final account of the trial. He would make sure to be included in the party of press allowed to attend the hanging, even if it would mean rising early that day. Some sacrifices were worth making.

❧

In a public house in Old Cross the verdict reached Daisy's ears, although, due to her state of inebriation, it took a while for the meaning of it to reach her brain. Lol delivered the news to her, having heard it from another man when he went to fetch a newspaper. When he told her he made a point of asking her if it changed anything.

'Change what?' Daisy asked him. 'What would it change?'

'Depends what it is. You know what he said. You tell me what you know and I'll tell you.'

'Nah, Lol. I know what you're trying to do. You just want to know for yourself. Well, I'm not telling you.'

'Come on, Daisy. Come on, darling. You tell Lol, now.'

'What's it worth?'

'You tell me what you know and I'll tell you what it's worth.'

Even through the cloud of booze, Daisy recognized Lol's tone had changed. All day he had been irritable. Money had been expected which hadn't arrived. A job hadn't come off. His pockets were empty.

'It's nothing,' she assured him, 'nothing.'

Lol went staggering out of the snug. How long it would be before he returned she did not know. Sometimes when he left he would be back two minutes later. Occasionally it would be weeks. But today she sensed it wouldn't be too long. He knew she had something that might be of value to him. Something that might be of great value. A small Jack Russell terrier had been the only other witness to what had happened that evening and when she recalled the night of Gower's death, the dog came to Daisy's mind. She remembered having tormented him and she regretted it. When Lol reappeared in the room she acknowledged to herself that the powerless make the cruellest torturers.

'Here,' Lol said, thrusting a small velvet-covered box towards Daisy.

'What is it?' she asked, looking suspiciously at it and refusing to take it from his hands.

'It's yours. A present.'

'A present? For me?' Daisy said, then repeated it louder for the benefit of the barmaid. The repetition had the desired effect. Three pairs of eyes were on the box when Daisy opened it to reveal the pearl necklace inside.

'Lol! Are they real?'

'Course they're real.'

'And it's for me?'

'Yeah.' Lol looked guilty behind him. 'Only don' go showing it off around the place.'

'Do it up for me,' Daisy said, draping the necklace around her neck and turning her back towards Lol. With heavy blunt fingers he managed to secure the fragile clasp. Daisy ran her palm flat from her throat to her breasts, feeling the tiny pearls, warm as flesh, turning against her skin.

'See? I do care for you,' Lol said.

Despite her inebriation, from the moment Lol arrived with the gift, Daisy was in no doubt what contract she would be entering into should she choose to accept it. But for a while she played him along, standing unsteadily and showing off her pearls to the barmaid, then going over to the mirror and admiring herself in it. She was born to wear pearls – where had it all gone wrong? In the reflection she could see Lol, waiting impatiently for his own reward. She knew she didn't have long. Lol had a notoriously short temper.

'All right,' she said, returning from the mirror and taking her seat again at the table. 'I'll tell you. But we share this.'

'A course we share it,' Lol reassured her. 'A course we do.'

'Stupid, really.' Daisy snorted a quick laugh through her nose. 'All that trouble for him.'

'So what happened? What did you see?'

'What I saw was this...' Daisy began, leaning towards Lol's ear and whispering, all the while her palm flat against her pearls, protecting them should he try to snatch them from her when the story had been told.

ꙮ

Meanwhile, in another part of Old Cross, a young man was going about his macabre work in the large back room of the premises that bore the legend: 'W. Stewart, Bird and Animal Preserver'. His secondary occupation, dentistry, was not advertised. The unheated shop was so irregularly visited that W. Stewart worked there alone. The doorbell would summon him if he was ever needed by a customer in the front. In the small street window was a large display case housing a rat, a field mouse, a barn owl, a tawny owl, a ferret, two cockerels, a sparrow hawk, a magpie, a shrew, a mole, a vole and a hedgehog. The animals were arranged around a miniature court room, the title of the tableau 'The Trial Of A Rat For The Murder Of A Chick'. The rat was flanked by the two cockerels, the barn owl playing the role of the presiding judge.

The back room of the premises was much larger than the shop itself, with two tall doors giving onto a narrow cobbled lane (ensuring the room was even colder than the shop). It was dominated by a large work table, at the end of which was an iron vice. Countersunk into one end of the table was a sheet of glass that the taxidermist used for the skinning of birds. Against the wall was a large, lead-lined vat containing a salt and alum solution, above it a pulley for lowering and raising larger animal skins. On a sturdy shelf, awaiting collection, was a stuffed crocodile wrapped in brown paper; on the floor his latest creation, a small chimpanzee carrying a miner's lantern, an owl mounted upon its shoulder.

W. Stewart was a neat man, precise in his work, dress, attitudes and manners. He was often to be seen paring the cuticles of his immaculate nails with a knife. Arranged neatly on the work table, in size order (and gleaming), were two pairs of scissors, three bone scrapers, a currier's knife, a bone-saw, several pairs of cutting pliers and a large needle. There was also a large cotton cloth for mopping up the fluids. Today, obedient in death, Nimrod lay on the taxidermist's table, and from his rear leg, with a pair of curved scissors, W. Stewart was carefully, almost tenderly, coaxing off the skin.

TWENTY-ONE

The Haunting of Pederusa

'WHERE ARE MY PAINTINGS?'

Having left Keith imprisoned in the Camden Town deep shelter, Samantha arrived back at the hotel. She was intending to change before returning to Old Cross to find Reilly's son but when she got back to her room she discovered the theft of the paintings. Now she was facing the intransigence of a Serb woman across the hotel reception desk. The previous receptionist's shift had finished and she had gone home.

'Paintings? I do not understand.'

'There were four paintings in my room,' Samantha explained carefully. 'They are now not there. The room is locked. I want to know where they are.'

'I am sorry. I do not know the whereabouts of your paintings.' The woman shrugged with Balkan indifference. As far as she was concerned, given the traumas of her recent life, the loss of a few paintings was of little concern to her.

'Well, find someone who does. Speak to the woman who was on earlier.'

'She has gone home.'

'Phone her.'

'I do not have her cell phone number.'

'That's simply not good enough.'

'These paintings were of value?'

'Of course they were,' Samantha said, glimpsing some hope.

'Then it was inadvisable to leave them in your room.'

'Look. Will you please get the telephone number of the other receptionist. Otherwise I'll have no choice but to call the police.'

The woman gave a slow, weary sigh of defeat and went, unhurriedly, into the back office. The sound of a laser printer was briefly audible. Returning with a sheet of A4 paper, the woman laid it between them on the desk. 'I have discovered her number here on this sheet of administration.'

'Call her.'

'Yes. Thank you.' The woman picked up the phone and glanced down at the sheet. 'If you will allow me to do so this is what I am going to do now.'

When she had dialled the number, the woman's eyes returned sullenly to Samantha before suddenly igniting: 'Hi Alicja…? Yeah, Radmila… No, baby. No… No.' The small talk went on for a few moments longer than Samantha considered necessary before the issue of the paintings was raised by the receptionist. Listening intently to the reply she nodded twice, then told Alicja to hold. Covering the receiver with her palm, she said, 'A man he came and took them.'

'What man?'

'Wait please.' The woman relayed the question to the telephone, then reported the answer: 'A businessman. He told Alicja he was collecting them for a client. He left his card but Alicja I think threw it away.'

Keith, Samantha knew at once. She should have guessed. Not an opportunistic thief after all. 'Ask her if the man was thin, with thin hair, in his forties.'

'Hi Alicja? Yes. The guest she wants to know if the man was thin with thin hair, and forty years of age? Yeah?... Yeah? Ok, baby. Wait one more moment please.' This time she turned the phone against her shoulder. 'Yes. She says he was thin with thin hair.'

'Right.'

'Is there anything else I should ask Alicja?'

'No. That's all. Make up my bill, please, and call me a taxi.'

'And no police?'

'No. No police.'

'OK. I will make up your bill.'

'Thank you.'

'And thank you too, *pederusa*.'

The telephone conversation continued while Samantha waited for the lift. There was laughter at her expense but she was beyond caring. The likelihood was, she thought, as she packed her suitcase and gathered up her bags, that Keith would have taken Reilly's paintings home. Keith would have no further use of his home so it was as good a place as any to stash her belongings for a while. If necessary she would spend the night there after finding Reilly's son. Reilly seemed intent on drawing her back to Old Cross. Perhaps that was where her new life would begin – in the place it had ended for him. Only when her taxi passed the café and she saw the police cars outside did Samantha remember Brian. She could conjure up neither regret nor sympathy for him but she knew she would have to proceed with caution. She could not trust that Keith hadn't called the police and told them of her involvement.

Emptying the cab of her belongings, she paid the cabby and waited for him to drive away before crossing the road and walking several houses down the street to Keith's. It was a small deception but she was beginning to think like a fugitive – if her description was published in connection with Brian's death she didn't want the taxi driver to lead the police immediately to Keith's front door.

The spare key was hidden where she had found it before, beneath the damp doormat. She opened the door and hurried in. Soon she had everything safely inside the front room, where she was gratified to see the four paintings Keith had stolen from her (technically three, as he owned one of them, but it was a distinction she was no longer prepared to make). It was getting late and a decision had to be made whether to visit Reilly's son or settle in for the night, get some rest, and make an early start the following day. Having experienced the decline of her mother she knewthat the elderly tended to be at their best in the mornings and treated any night visitor with deep suspicion. Samantha, therefore, decided to allow herself the luxury of a long bath, a decent home-cooked meal, and a night in front of the fire. Reilly was encouraging her to have some time off and she was glad of it.

She was grateful but not entirely surprised to discover that Keith's towels, stacked neatly in the airing cupboard, were fluffy and smelled of fabric conditioner. His underpants were folded neatly over a clothes horse.

Here was a man accustomed, perhaps resigned, to living on his own. The water that thundered from the big old taps was hot and there was plenty of it. While the huge Victorian bath filled and the steam obscured the mirror she opened a new bar of Keith's expensive soap, which she had found in the cupboard over the sink. She smelled it. Sandalwood. Having tested the water she stepped into the bath, lay back in the neck-deep water, closed her eyes and soon she was asleep.

She awoke an hour later in a bath of tepid water, which had robbed her of her body heat. Her spirits and temperature were restored when she dried herself with the large, lush towel she had left over the bathroom radiator. Choosing not to dress, she wrapped herself in another large towel and carried the stack of her clothes to Keith's bedroom before going downstairs to the kitchen, where she found a variety of pastas in a cupboard and several jars of pesto. By nine o'clock, having washed up, she was ready for bed and, after glancing through a tame pornographic magazine she found on Keith's bedside table, she turned off the light and fell immediately into a deep sleep.

She was awakened by a sound in the room late in the night. Reaching out for the bedside light she thumbed the switch but nothing happened. A floorboard creaked and she knew there was somebody in the room. She sat up, pulling the quilt to her chin, and focused on the shape at the end of the bed. Her heart beat fast. The shape was very still and as her eyes adjusted to the light she discerned that it was wearing a tall hat, and a long frock coat. The figure smelled of damp and earth.

'Reilly? Is that you?' Samantha asked.

The figure slowly turned and left the room. She heard footsteps on the stairs and then a door opening on the ground floor. She clambered naked from the bed – a flash of pink in the black – picked up the towel she had discarded on the floor, and went to the top of the stairs. From there she saw the figure, now carrying the display case containing Nimrod, pausing at the open front door. Without turning, without closing the door, he left the house. Samantha dashed to the window and saw him walking away in the direction of the canal. When he was out of sight she ran barefoot down the stairs and closed the front door, then returned to the bed and lay down. She did not expect to sleep but she did. When she woke the following morning her first thought was that Reilly had come to her in a dream. But Nimrod was gone from the front room and there were muddy boot prints across the carpet. She had no doubt that he would return for her. Tonight she would be ready for him.

TWENTY-TWO

The Topping-Shed Barber

AMONG CRIMINALS, BETWEEN INFAMY AND FAME THERE IS NO distance awarded by morality. The condemned man becomes the only prisoner on the wing considered to have discharged his debt to society. But it goes beyond that. The consensus is that society, in fact, now owes a debt to him, because whatever the crime he has committed, society is preparing itself to inflict a greater injury on him. Within a month the services of John Ellis, a barber from Rochdale, would again be required in what was colloquially known as the Topping Shed of Pentonville jail.

After the sentence had been passed on Reilly, Graveney and Rushden had made a brief visit to the cell beneath the court. The elderly Rushden seemed to have been aged even further by his experiences, and Reilly, forgetting his own woes, gave the man his chair. Despite his heavy coat, Rushden shivered with the cold and when he sat he occupied himself massaging the thin, white fingers of his right hand with his left. Graveney announced that it was a terrible day indeed, the worst day of his career, and even went so far as to wonder whether the life of a barrister was for him. It was left to Reilly to offer reassurances to the two men that they had done all they could. Graveney suggested an appeal, explaining that a recent change in the law now allowed for it, but Reilly told him he wanted to get the matter over and done with as quickly as was possible. He asked Rushden to visit him in Pentonville to help him put his affairs in order and asked about the storage of his paintings. Rushden admitted that they had, as yet, not been collected from Mountjoy's. This irked Reilly, but he hid it, turned to Graveney and told him he should on no account give up a profession to which he was so obviously suited. The men left Reilly somewhat meekly, like father and son, Graveney encouraging Rushden to take his arm for support. Reilly's warder, who had heard the exchanges, told him that it wasn't uncommon for a barrister such as Rushden to throw himself at the mercy of his client when the verdict had gone against him, and normally he knew it was a ruse, but Graveney he knew to be an honest man. Had Reilly concurred with him, the warder was in no doubt that Graveney would have given up the profession the following day.

Reilly, having little future of his own to look forward to, was unsure why he found himself troubled by Graveney's career. But, beyond doing all that he could for Amy, he had little else in mind. As he returned in his chains to prison, this led him to contemplate that his former life had been concerned with nothing but the future, with his work; his reputation. Soon all that would be left of him would be his paintings. If his child was to know him at all then it would be through that body of work. He had hoped that Rushden would advise him on how he could best preserve it, but he now wondered if Rushden was the right man to advise him on anything. Perhaps it was best to leave the paintings in Mountjoy's care. At least Mountjoy had a genuine appreciation of their worth.

Reilly arrived back at the prison a little after seven. Work on the wing had ended and the men were locked in their cells for two hours of reading or contemplation before the gas to the cell jets was cut, plunging them into darkness. The news of the verdict had arrived ahead of him. Despite the efforts made inside the prison to restrict communication, information flowed freely. Reilly had witnessed conversations between men who seemed to be able to talk without moving their lips. He had seen the dinner-cans with notes scratched on by nail, and he had heard the coded knuckle taps on the cell walls. But the silence of the prison that night was broken only by the swift whispers of bristle against the asphalt; a work party of two prisoners was brushing sawdust from the floor of a wing following the repair of a door frame. Reilly's approach was signalled by the clinking of the chain that linked his wrists and the two men turned their heads towards him. Through the circular eyeholes cut into the hat brims obscuring their faces Reilly could see a deadening; a sympathy. Who, he wondered, would design such a terrifying uniform? Why was it necessary to make every man in there look inhuman? The effect of this, on that night, as Reilly was taken to Condemned Cell Number One, where he would never be alone, and the lights never extinguished, was that he felt he was being welcomed by two sentries of hell.

Reilly's misery would have been compounded had he been aware of Amy's plight that night. After collapsing in the court, Mountjoy and another man had supported her to the street, each taking an arm over their shoulder, and there she waited while a cab was summoned from a nearby stand. On the swift journey home through the white, snow-prettied streets, her temperature rose. Mountjoy loosened her coat but she shifted and fought him. In her fever she began talking to Reilly, imploring him to forgive her. Mountjoy tried to soothe her but she became more and more distraught, and then he found that the only way he could calm her was to take Reilly's role and assure her that he understood, and forgave her, indeed did not blame her. She took his hands and clasped them between hers and then took them into her mouth as if they were ice and she was suckling water.

When they reached the coffee shop the cabman stepped down and helped Mountjoy support Amy up the stairs to her room. Once there, Mountjoy confided to the cabman he was afraid to leave her. The man understood – he was a compassionate man – and agreed to fetch the doctor. He would hear of taking no fare for it. While they waited Amy moaned and shifted beneath the sheets. She was too hot, too cold. Her clothes were constraining her. She pushed off the sheets then kicked them away and Mountjoy could see the blood beneath her soaking deep into the mattress. At that moment he heard the bell and dashed downstairs to let in the doctor, explaining the circumstances to the young man as they climbed the stairs. 'Sheets, please, and hot water, and you may leave us,' the man said, draping his coat on a chair, opening his Gladstone bag, kneeling beside the bed and taking Amy's hand. 'And close the door. Please knock when you return.' Gratefully, Mountjoy pulled shut the door and went to fetch what the doctor had asked him.

In the coffee shop he boiled a large kettle and when the water began to rattle in torment inside the heavy pot his own misery rose and rose until he could contain it no longer. It washed out of him, in huge, heaving sobs from his chest; in hot salty tears that flowed from his eyes and continued to flow each time he wiped them away with the back of his hand. He cried for Reilly, for Amy, for Nimrod, for the terrible curse that seemed to have been cast by him over the lives of the people he loved. It was all because of him. Reilly's debt to him was small. He should have refused his offer to repay it, and had he not agreed that Reilly could exhibit his paintings, Gower would never have visited Old Cross. Had the events not been set in train by that visit, then Nimrod would not have been living in the coffee shop and would not have run away. Reilly would not have been convicted for murder, Amy would not have witnessed it and would not now be needing the services of the young doctor. But hanging malevolently over it all was Pardew. However bad their wounds, the poison had been injected by the hack. Without the sly reporting of the events of the day of the exhibition, the legally cautious insinuations of motive, would the case have been brought against Reilly? Perhaps so. But would it have succeeded? By no means as likely. Pardew's reporting had led to a hunger, an expectation, that could be sated only by a hanging.

When the kettle finally came to the boil Mountjoy's tears had stopped, but he could not rid himself of the dread that burdened his chest. He poured the water into a jug and carried it carefully towards the stairs, glimpsing two figures at the window: a tall brute of a man with a pocked face wearing a huge coat and brimless hat and a slight woman with a white-powdered face from which peered wary eyes, copious unkempt hair, and a huge expanse of cleavage decorated by a rope of pearls. The man, by a swift sideways cock of his head, indicated the door should be opened, but Mountjoy had no intention of allowing two vagabonds onto his premises at such a late hour. Ignoring the man, he carried the jug of water up two flights of stairs and placed it outside the door of Amy's room. He waited, hearing the doctor speak, then the fevered, quick voice of Amy. He knocked.

'Not now,' the doctor said with easy authority. 'Please leave the water and the linen at the door.'

Mountjoy fetched the linen and left it beside the water and returned to the coffee shop where he found the two figures still at the window. The woman was now leaning her back against the glass and was stamping her feet against the cold, the man was continuing to look in through the blinkers of his hands. Seeing Mountjoy cross the room he banged on the glass with his palm and gestured again towards the door, this time raising a fist. Wearily, resigned, Mountjoy slid back the bolt and stood aside as the man bullied his way in, shouting for the woman, still outside, to follow him.

'What do you want?' Mountjoy said, retreating behind the counter. 'I have little money on the premises and the coffee shop is closed.'

'Hear that?' Lol asked Daisy. 'He thinks we're here to rob him, when all we're here for is to help.'

'That's right, Lol. That's right,' Daisy said, without conviction. The day was already abandoned to drink, her only concern now to get to her bed before the cushion of it slipped away.

'State what your business is, or leave,' Mountjoy snapped. 'I warn you, I have no patience tonight.'

'We heard about your friend an' we unnerstand why that might be so,' Lol said, doffing his hat in mock sympathy. 'But what Daisy has to tell you has a bearing on that gentleman, don't it, Daisy?'

Daisy nodded.

'This is Reilly, I assume?' Mountjoy said.

'Who else?'

'Go on.'

'First, the terms. What would you say a man's life is worth?'

'As I said. State your business or leave.'

'An unnert and fifty pound?'

Mountjoy left the counter, strode quickly to the door and opened it. 'That's enough. Please leave.'

'Tell him, Daisy,' Lol said, not shifting from his place at the counter. 'Go on. Tell him.'

'Your friend, Reilly,' she said. 'I was there that night.'

'What?'

'When the man drowned in the canal.'

'Drowned?'

'I saw it. I was there.'

Seeing they now had Mountjoy's full attention, Lol said, 'So let's all sit down and talk about it, shall we?' Lol took a seat beside the fire. He patted the seat of the chair beside him with his calloused palm. Dutifully, Daisy joined him. Mountjoy closed the door, bolted it and reluctantly went over to join them. And there he heard the story of the night of Gower's death.

'So what's a man's life worth?' Lol said, when Daisy had finished. 'An unnert and fifty pound?'

Mountjoy finally understood. The cost of Reilly's life, the price of Daisy's statement to the police. How would she explain that she had not come forward before? There would be a way. Would she go forward without the bribe? Of course not. But where would he find a hundred and fifty pounds? Was that not what Gower had carried with him? But who did he know who could raise such a sum? Mountjoy's eyes, ranging around the room, came to rest on a newspaper on the counter.

'Very well,' Mountjoy said, standing. 'I'll have your money for you. Though to profit in such a way from a man's misfortune is despicable.'

'It is,' Lol agreed, leading Daisy out. 'It certainly is.' As they walked out of the door, Mountjoy realized the brute believed he had been paid a compliment.

He remained by the low fire until the doctor came down, his coat on, his Gladstone bag in his hand.

'Stay with her and if her fever worsens, send for me,' the doctor said, walking briskly towards the door.

'Is she…?'

'It's all over.'

Mountjoy nodded and the doctor took his leave.

❧

The following morning Mountjoy closed up the coffee shop at ten and went in search of Pardew, leaving Amy in her bed. The fever had passed but she was weak and had no appetite either for food or company. It had not snowed again and the only evidence of the previous day's fall was in the filthy ledges of ice in the gutter and the white patches on sun-sheltered roofs. Although Mountjoy felt some guilt at leaving Amy alone, he was grateful to be away from the coffee shop, away from the court, and in the company of people whose concerns and fates he was unaware of. Even Sykes, who glowered at him when he passed his shop, did not dampen his spirits. The offices of the newspaper were in the adjoining borough and

Mountjoy walked there, during which time he diverted his worry over Reilly by concentrating his thoughts on the route he was taking and the winter sun now climbing above the buildings and imposing brightness but little warmth onto the narrow streets.

Above the impressive frontage of the newspaper offices, silhouetted against the static white sky, was a statue of Caxton. A series of sculpture panels over the lower storey windows illustrated the processes involved in producing a newspaper. Mountjoy went beneath them, feeling inclined to duck his head. Once inside, he explained his business to the man at the front counter who went off to relay it to Pardew. The man returned soon after, raised the flap in the counter and Mountjoy followed him through a half-glassed door into a gloomy, tall-ceilinged back room where several young men, all of whom seemed to be smoking, were lounging at their own tables, each of which was illuminated by a measly pool of light from an electric table lamp. The room had the feel of a gentleman's club the morning after a good party. But it was cold, and all of the men were wearing coats. One of them was pecking at the keys of a mechanical typewriter and, besides the occasional cough, the tiny percussive explosions of the typebar against the platen were the only sounds in the room. Pardew's table was closest to the editor's office, which ran along the left wall of the building, monopolizing all of the natural light from the windows. Inside it, Mr Henry, senior in age and status, was visible at his desk in his morning misery, also smoking. As Mountjoy was led between the tables, his presence provoking little interest from the journalists, he spotted Grubb at a school desk in the far recesses of the room. Grubb's desk had no electric light, but it did have a candle. The boy was hard at work in the gloom copying capital letters from a work book onto a sheet of lined paper, his concentration signalled by the folded rosy end of his tongue protruding from his mouth. The effort he was using to guide his quill was immense; the boy was holding it as though he was afraid that if he let it go it would fly up towards the ceiling and be lost among the cocoon of dense cobwebs between the rafters. As Mountjoy approached Pardew he saw Grubb slide down from his chair, take his paper from his desk and cross the room ahead of him. The boy arrived at Pardew's table first and Mountjoy, having been acknowledged by a brief nod from the journalist, waited behind him. Pardew took a quick look at the sheet of paper, cuffed the boy on the head (Grubb seemed to be expecting it and barely flinched), and said, 'Very, very scruffy. Do it again.'

'Yes. Do it again, Grubb,' another man called, laughing.

'And again. And again,' called another.

Grubb sighed, looked at Mountjoy without any sign of recognition and returned to his miserable perch to continue his work.

'Mountjoy, what brings you here?' Pardew drew himself stiffly to his feet and held out his hand. He was wearing fingerless gloves.

'A proposition,' Mountjoy said. 'Some advice. Perhaps both.'

'Grubb!' Pardew called, 'Bring Mr Mountjoy your chair.'

'No, it's not necessary,' Mountjoy said.

'Oh, but it is. The boy has to learn. Don't you, Grubb?'

They waited while Grubb carried over his chair and deposited it resentfully beside Pardew's table. 'With good grace, Grubb,' Pardew chided. 'Good grace.'

'Sorry, Mr Pardew.'

'Now go off and fetch us all some coffee. Do you want coffee, Mountjoy?'

'No, thank you.'

'Bring one for Mr Mountjoy in case he changes his mind. And be quick about it.'

Pardew dropped a number of coins into Grubb's cupped hands and the boy set off wearily towards the door.

'I said be quick about it,' Pardew called, chasing him and planting a kick on his backside, prompting Grubb to break into a run as he left the room.

'You have my sympathies. Of course that goes without saying,' Pardew said as he returned, took his seat and lit a cigarette without offering one to Mountjoy.

'Reilly didn't do it.'

'Your continuing loyalty to him is commendable,' Pardew said slyly.

'You know very well he didn't.'

'I think it's fair to say that the verdict was greeted with some surprise by all. Graveney gave a good account of himself, didn't he? But I understand there's to be no appeal.'

'No appeal?'

'Apparently not.'

'Then how long is it likely to be?'

'Before he's hanged?' Pardew said brightly. 'Well, assuming the judge has not recommended mercy, once the Home Office has received the case papers, a report will be written for the Permanent Secretary and the Home Secretary. Reilly's sanity will be assessed, and if he's judged to be *compos mentis* then three weeks.'

'Three weeks!'

'Sometime in the week following three clear Sundays after sentence. Tuesday, Wednesday or Thursday, that's the form. Better for Reilly to be put out of his misery, wouldn't you say?'

'No. I wouldn't say.'

'Believe me, if there is no hope of a reprieve, for his own sake, the condemned man is best hanged as quickly as is possible... You mentioned some advice?' Mountjoy could be of no further use to Pardew, Reilly's newsworthiness being over until the hanging, and he was eager to get him away.

'Yes.' Mountjoy shook away the awful vision that had just lodged itself in his mind. 'Some advice about Reilly's paintings. I thought you'd be the man to speak to.'

'They remain unsold?'

Mountjoy was gratified to see that Pardew's interest had been fired. 'Of course. We took them down when he was arrested. I have them upstairs in the coffee shop.'

'There was no exhibition?'

'No.'

'I see. And you'd like me to tell you what you should do with them?'

'Oh, I know what should be done with them. They must be sold.' Pardew nodded. Mountjoy went on. 'I thought you might advise on where we might get the best price.'

'I'm flattered that you came to me. But I know very little about the art market.' Pardew waited for Mountjoy to contradict him, but he didn't. 'Did you have a figure in mind?'

'Reilly is keen to provide for Amy Sykes as well as he can. I think two hundred pounds is a fair sum.'

'Two hundred pounds? I very much doubt Reilly's work would attract that kind of money.'

'Really?'

'He has no reputation.'

'Reilly is a fine artist. He will paint no more paintings. On that alone he deserves a decent price for his work. There is, of course, as you will be aware, the other aspect to it, which would surely not count against him.'

'The paintings of a condemned man,' Pardew reflected, picturing the headline. 'Yes, no doubt of that. No doubt at all…' He came out of his momentary trance. 'You're a clever man, Mountjoy.'

'Am I?'

'Yes. You didn't come here seeking advice.'

'No?'

'You came here offering a story.'

'Perhaps,' Mountjoy agreed.

'Because a story along the right lines would do no harm to Reilly's market value, would it?'

'You've seen through me, Pardew, as I knew you would.'

'And I'm going to write that story for you. Reilly's reputation depends on it.'

'I'm sure he'll be very grateful.' Mountjoy waited.

'And what's more, Mountjoy,' Pardew said, 'I'm going to find the one hundred and seventy myself.'

'One hundred and seventy?'

'Yes. A fair price, wouldn't you say?'

'You're offering one hundred and seventy pounds today?'

'That is my offer.'

'For all of the paintings?'

'And for the report.'

'And the story will appear when?'

'In a matter of days. After which time I will take possession of the paintings. I mean it wouldn't do if I was to be seen profiting from my reporting of Reilly's misfortune, would it?'

'Of course not – considering how charitable your intentions.'

'Indeed.' Pardew leaned forward and held out his hand. Mountjoy took it with only the smallest of hesitations.

From the moment Reilly was returned to Pentonville he was not allowed a moment of solitude. Condemned Cell Number One, where he was now confined, was larger than his previous cell to accommodate the two or three warders who now attended him at all times. It was, Reilly learned from the first shift, an unpopular duty because the men were confined for eight straight hours behind bars, their sole duty to ensure the prisoner didn't do the job the hangman had been employed for. Reilly had never contemplated suicide but the constant scrutiny he faced from his sullen attendants pushed him closer to it than he had ever been.

On the second morning, as he chewed on his breakfast bread, Reilly's teeth encountered a lump in the doughy flesh. It was his habit to eat with his back towards his warders, so they didn't see him spit the lump into his palm. He had expected it to be a beetle or the tiny skull of a mouse, both of which he had found in his food before. Instead he discovered a warm coin of folded paper. Reilly palmed it and finished his meal. It took him an hour of surreptitious work to unfold the paper, which he concealed inside the newspaper he had been given. When he later opened the paper he found a printed sheet that read: 'Instructions to be observed in burying the bodies of executed prisoners. 1. All the clothing, with the exception of the shirt or similar garment, will be removed from the body which will be placed in a coffin made of half inch wood, deal or pine. 2. The sides and ends of the coffin will be well perforated with large holes. 3. Lime will not be used. 4. The original size of the plot of ground will be 9 feet by 4 feet, and the grave will be from 8 to 10 feet in depth. 5. When the coffin has been covered by 1 foot of earth, charcoal to the depth of three inches will be thrown into the grave, which will then be filled in. The top coffin will be not less than four feet below the ground surface…' Whatever cruelty had been intended by passing such a document to Reilly, it did not touch him until he read the sixth instruction: 'Arrangements will be made for the grave sites to be reused in sequence, in such wise that no grave shall be used over again until seven years have elapsed…' He was to die. He would not see his child. His child would have no stone at which he could mourn him. Reilly had fondly imagined a sun-warmed plot in a small, remote churchyard, the plot beside his father and mother, perhaps. At least he had outlived them. They had not seen his shame. He took down his charcoal and paper from the shelf and began to sketch. In the absence of a grave and a stone he set about his own epitaph.

TWENTY-THREE

Reilly's Ghost

THERE WAS NOBODY OUT ON THE NIGHT-TIME STREET TO WITNESS it, but the figure dressed in ersatz gravedigger's garb could barely conceal his glee. It took Keith all the willpower he could muster to walk as slowly as he could until he knew he would be out of sight of his house. The boot prints he had made on his carpet were, he thought, a particularly masterful touch (although it had pained him to soil his new Hessian carpet, he'd brought a bag of mud along with him for the purpose). And the gravedigger's fragrance had worked well. It was the eager young girl in the costume-hire shop who had asked him whether he'd given any thought to how a ghost would smell. He admitted he had not. She said they had a new range of fragrances especially for the purpose, so he added an extra five pounds to the thirty-five pounds he'd shelled out to hire the 'Authentic Victorian/Edwardian gravedigger's costume'.

Keith had spent only two hours in captivity before being released by the youth he'd employed to imprison Samantha. The youth was not in the least surprised to find the room still locked when he returned there. He went back to the Deep Shelter late that afternoon because he hadn't trusted Keith and had no intention of being party to a criminal act. He was, of course, shocked to discover not the woman behind the locked door, but Keith, who fell on him in gratitude, paid him fifty pounds in lieu of an explanation and then set off for the police station.

Keith was in no doubt that Samantha had no intention of ever releasing him. She was clearly insane and prison, or some secure psychiatric institution, was probably the best place for her. Before he reached the police station, however, Keith changed his mind. In the current climate of crime and understanding he knew there was no guarantee that Samantha Dodd would be punished. More likely was that she would be left to the mercy of counsellors, then released into the bosom of an understanding and forgiving community in receipt of a weekly stipend. That was no good. He wanted Samantha to suffer the terror he had suffered in those two hours of incarceration. That she had kept him in the dark was a particularly nasty twist (which, strangely, he almost admired her for – it showed a degree of cruelty he found quite appealing). Nevertheless, it was necessary for Samantha to pay for what she had put him through (no recognition, of course, that he had done the same to her). She was clearly obsessed, perhaps possessed, by Reilly, so why should Reilly not appear to her?

But, having watched her sleeping, the sheets having fallen away from her, he realized (or acknowledged for the first time) he was attracted to her. And it wasn't simply because it had been nearly five years since he had had a woman in his bed. He found her genuinely alluring, with a kind of mature sexuality he liked. He had no time for skinny models. Give him a big girl any day; give him cruelty, the sneer of a lip, the threat of the whip. Seeing her lying there, pink, luscious and naked (and wearing the fragrance of his best soap) stirred him.

Keith had suspected that Samantha might be holed up in his house. He had begun to understand how her mind worked. After his release from the shelter he had waited across the street for a while, confirming his suspicions. It was there he formulated his plan and, with that in place, he went in search of a local room for a couple of nights. He was returning there now but the display case with the stuffed dog in it that he was carrying was a burden. It was heavy, aesthetically appalling and of no value whatsoever. Coming across a half-full builder's skip, he hefted it in, hearing the gratifying crunch as the glass shattered and the frame fractured. By four o'clock he was in bed, the gravedigger's costume on its hanger at the back of the door. With thoughts of Samantha Dodd's lush body making his heart race, he obliged himself to sleep.

❧

Samantha woke late the following morning having slept well for the first time in many weeks. After dressing she made herself a cafetière of Keith's good coffee, then walked the short distance to the housing scheme on Canal Street where, finally, she hoped to meet Reilly's son. Old Cross was hers now and it was with the confidence of one who had every right to be there that she knocked on the warden's door. When he opened it (wearing a well-ironed yellow polo shirt today), she could immediately see his embarrassment. How much he had been involved in Keith's ruse she didn't know, and didn't want to know. She tried to make this clear by the way she asked to see Gerald Reilly, adding that she hoped he wasn't again spending the day in Camden.

'You're after Gerald again, are you?' the man said jovially, as if her previous visit had been a great success. 'Yes, you'll find him in. Just go across the courtyard and he's in number eight. You'll see the number on the door.'

By the time Samantha had thanked the warden, his door was shut. She glimpsed him lurking behind it as she walked along the side of his office and through the archway that led to the courtyard around which the two-storeyed buildings were grouped. Each ground-floor flat had a patio door giving onto a small terrace, almost large enough for two garden chairs – only one if the clashing of elbows was to be avoided. There was a strip of neat grass around the block-paved courtyard, at the centre of which was a circular fishpond. She paused to peer at the flashes of orange and silver between the shifting pondweed. Water tinkled like coins from the pond filter. All of the flats faced the courtyard, giving the impression that they were hunched together, shoulder-to-shoulder in solidarity, backs against the outside world. A stern, remote square of sky loomed far above. As Samantha continued across the courtyard she could see shadows shifting in the interiors of the flats. One of the residents ogled her nakedly: a woman framed by her patio door, wearing a pink house-coat, a headscarf and holding a teacup. She waved. Samantha waved back.

Number eight was a ground-floor flat, tucked into a corner. The door numeral was large, as were the no-nonsense door fittings and the bell. There was a handrail up the short, gentle gradient. Samantha pressed the doorbell, expecting it to issue an ugly electric buzz or a slow two-tone chime, but she could hear bells pealing cheerfully and ironically inside the flat. Without further preamble the door was opened briskly by an elderly man. Gerald Reilly was not as decrepit and old as she had expected. He looked closer to seventy or seventy-five than a hundred. He was stylish rather than fashionable, his charcoal grey cardigan (cashmere, she noted) and grey trousers looked as if they had been well tended, as did his scarlet suede tasselled loafers; the dress of a retired architect, perhaps. Gerald Reilly had a goatee beard and full head of longish hair, both silver white. He seemed kindly; curious, rather than perturbed by the unexpected visitor.

'Can I help you?' Reilly said in a soft, courteous voice, and Samantha promptly burst into tears.

Ten minutes later, she was sitting in Reilly's sitting room which looked out, not as expected, over the courtyard (that was the bedroom), but over the canal, along which a narrow boat was proceeding towards the bridge, its speed so sedate it was barely troubling to throw a wake behind it. A man stood stiffly behind the wheel while a black Labrador dashed from bow to stern and then back again, covering twice the distance of the boat. It had taken Samantha five minutes to regain her composure. She had fought hard to stop crying but each time she did and embarked on an explanation, the tears began again. By then she was already ensconced in Gerald Reilly's flat and sitting on Gerald Reilly's favourite chair (from which he had removed his morning *Telegraph*). He was now in the kitchen, calling to her to put the rug across her knee because, he said, sometimes he found a rug across the knees a great comfort in times of distress.

'So… here.' Reilly returned to the sitting room with two mugs of tea, one of which he held out for Samantha to take. As he did so, though, he seemed to change his mind and diverted the mug onto a coaster beside her. 'Drink it when it's cooled,' he said. 'I don't have any brandy to offer you, I'm afraid.'

'Oh, I don't need brandy. I'm really so sorry. So sorry.'

'My dear, never apologize either for tears or laughter; neither can be helped.'

'You're kind. I knew you would be.'

'I'm intrigued that you know who I am.'

'Well, sort of. I know who your father was.'

'My father?'

'T. F. Reilly. The painter.'

'Yes. I know who he is and what he once did. I'm rather astonished that anyone else does. I don't believe I've ever heard him described in such a way before – as a painter, I mean.'

And with that Samantha finally managed to complete the explanation she had been trying to offer since she arrived on Gerald Reilly's doorstep. She told it all, from the moment she caught sight of the painting in Keith's gallery, to the discovery of the paintings by a local builder (she edited Brian out) to the newspaper articles about Reilly's trial, to her belief that Reilly had somehow reached out to her across the century. She stopped short of mentioning that his ghost had visited her in the night, and she was careful not to reveal that the owner of the first painting she encountered was now entombed deep below the streets of London in a wartime shelter where he was, even now, starving to death.

'How extraordinary,' Gerald Reilly said after she had finished. 'This is extraordinary. So some of his paintings survived? In a café, you say?'

'Yes.'

'He had a great friend in Old Cross. Perhaps that was the source of the paintings.'

'Mountjoy. Yes. He was mentioned in the newspaper reports of the trial.'

'I see. Well, I would be intrigued to see his paintings. All I have are a few charcoal sketches.'

'No paintings at all?'

'None.'

'Well, where are they? I mean there was mention of an exhibition in the newspaper, so I assumed there were others.'

'Oh there were – there were many more. But not now.'

'Do you know what happened to them?'

'I think I do. But perhaps we should first make a trade.'

'Trade?'

'I'll show you Father's sketches if you promise to bring his paintings for me to see.'

'Of course. I'd be happy to.'

Reilly stood and went into the bedroom, where he could be heard opening the wardrobe.

'I always intended to get these framed, but to be honest they reflected a period of his life which was rather shaming.' He reappeared with a large artist's folder of stiff board tethered closed by black cord. He laid the folder on the floor, undid the bow and lifted open the top board. They both then looked down at the sketch, which was a church graveyard, the church in shadow in the background.

'That's beautiful,' Samantha said.

'This is the grave of my grandparents. Oddington in Gloucestershire. The church, St Nicholas's, has some extraordinary wall paintings. I visited there many years ago.' He touched the paper with his fingertips. 'It's one of a number of sketches my father did when he was in prison, all of which represented something of the family history. Here...'

Gerald Reilly lifted off the top sketch with care and laid it on the floor. The second was a house, seen from the rear, built of large blocks of Cotswold stone, with mullioned windows and a tiled roof.

'This was my grandparents' house. Where my father lived throughout his childhood. My grandmother died when he was young – ten or eleven, I think. And my grandfather raised him alone after that, though I don't think he did a particularly good job of it if the truth be told. He was a difficult man.'

'What did he do?'

'Grandfather? A gentleman farmer, which means any number of things but I think in his case is meant that he employed other people to do the work.'

'I've seen this house before.'

'You've seen it?'

'Your father painted it. Again, from the back, but he's in the picture in a greenhouse, I mean I assume it's him – there's a young boy. He seems to be hiding. That's the impression you get.'

'And does it have a title, this painting?'

'Yes. *The Crime.*'

Reilly nodded slowly. '*The Crime.*' He lifted it off, revealing another sketch. This was a young man, bent over a cell table, drawing. The picture was crude; it was clear that the artist had failed to catch the study's facial nuances, but there was something in the way he had represented the stance of the subject that his character could be inferred.

'This is not by my father,' Reilly said. 'It was among the other sketches. I assume it's a study of my father working, perhaps by another inmate, or perhaps by one of the warders. It's not very good.' Reilly turned his head towards Samantha, whom the picture had rendered speechless. '...As I say, this was not done by my father... Are you all right?'

'Yes. I'm sorry,' Samantha said, composing herself. 'It's just that I've never seen an image of him as an adult before. I mean I've pictured him and he came... no, it doesn't matter. The fact is that it's just quite a shock seeing it.'

'I don't think there's anything extraordinary about it.'

'No. I suppose not. Except for the fact that it's him, alive, drawing, in that terrible place and he seems oblivious to everything around him.'

'Alive, yes.' Reilly returned the sketch to the folder and closed it. 'That's enough, I think, for today.'

'Yes. Of course,' Samantha said, disappointed, registering the change in Reilly's tone. Perhaps she had pushed him too hard. 'Thank you for letting me see his work. I'll bring the paintings for you.'

'Incidentally, who owns those paintings?' Reilly asked as he led her to the door.

'Well, I suppose I do.'

'And how exactly did they come to be in your possession?'

'Through the gallery. Where I worked. Somebody offered them and… and we bought them.'

'You understand my curiosity?'

'Of course.'

Gerald Reilly opened the door. Samantha went out into the courtyard. 'I'm sorry for the state I was in when I arrived,' she said.

'I told you. There is no need to apologize,' he said, but Reilly was no longer smiling. 'You'll come tomorrow?'

'Yes.'

'I'll expect you at ten.'

'Can I ask you one more thing, Mr Reilly?'

'Of course.'

'Do you believe in ghosts?'

❧

Keith had intended to spend all day in the bed and breakfast. He did not want to ruin his plan by running into Samantha on the street, but at eleven o'clock there was a pounding on the door, and the landlady's voice informed him that she had to clean the room and expected him out of it within fifteen minutes. Further, that she didn't expect him back before three because she was going out and didn't like her guests roaming about the place when she wasn't there. Under normal circumstances Keith would have chosen a more salubrious place to stay. The room was oppressive and he was already beginning to wonder how he could bear a day's confinement in there. He dressed and called a cab company to take him to the gallery – which was the one place he thought it unlikely that Samantha would risk visiting again.

After spending a day there (bar two hours for lunch) clearing the backlog of mail, and curtly answering the cheerful questions of a time-wasting elderly woman who seemed to think he had nothing better to do, Keith returned to the bed and breakfast, buying a bottle of decent Chianti on the way. He drank the wine watching the early evening television, and didn't fight it when the alcohol lured him to sleep. He had no intention of visiting Samantha before midnight.

He woke at eleven and watched a rehash of the news he'd seen four hours earlier, then he dressed, drinking the remainder of the wine. The costume had been advertised as a typical gravedigger's garb, but, to Keith's eyes, the three-quarter-length coat looked rather too militaristic for such a lowly profession. He did, however, like the collarless shirt and the loose breeches, while the boots (which would have doubled as pantomime pirate boots, with sagging knees) rubbed his heels. The wig looked like it belonged to a sailor. Putting his wine glass down on the bedside table, he completed his wardrobe by spraying some of the gravedigger's fragrance over his coat and into his wig. He then faced himself in the mirror and some lines came into his head from a text he had studied at school. They seemed to suit the occasion so he said them out loud: 'I am thy father's spirit, / Doom'd for a certain term to walk the night, / And for the day confined to fast in fires, / Till the foul crimes done in my days of nature / Are burnt and purged away. / But that I am forbid / To tell the secrets of my prison-house, / I could a tale unfold whose lightest word / Would harrow up thy soul, freeze thy young blood…'

❧

Keith arrived at his home a little after one and waited on the far pavement, watching it. The downstairs curtains were open and the room was dark. The curtains in the upstairs front bedroom were closed. Keith approached the front door, slid the key quietly into the lock and let himself in. The house was warm. Samantha had kept on the heating (how dare she, when he was so careful not to use too much gas). He closed the door carefully behind him and paused in the hallway to listen. The central heating boiler popped. Keith climbed the stairs and paused again when he reached the top. The door to the front bedroom was ajar. He crossed the landing and pushed it open. A figure was discernible beneath the duvet. Keith had given little thought to how he would proceed once he had got into his bedroom, he had assumed that inspiration would strike when he got there. The previous night he had been lucky. A creaking floorboard had woken Samantha. As he had hoped, she had been immediately taken in by his dress and all he had had to do was stand there silently looking menacing for a while, before leaving in as ghostlike a way as he could manage. Tonight, however, probably due to the heat in the house and having eaten well at his expense, she was sleeping soundly. Keith tried a ghostly moan but it sounded ludicrous in the silence of the room, so he stopped. He took a step closer to the bed, hoping he would tread again on the loose board and Samantha would awaken. He found the board and it creaked but still the figure did not move. Keith moved closer to the bed. The figure was still. It was then he heard a movement behind him and felt a weight against the back of his skull. The blow lacked conviction and although the pain was sharp it felt like little more than a cut in the skin. Keith turned to defend himself, parrying the next strike with his raised forearm.

'Will you please stop it!' he managed. He had not been in a fight since school and it was all very undignified, particularly because he knew that the attacker was Samantha (who, having packed the bed with pillows, had been lying in wait for him behind the door) and therefore a woman, and therefore he should not fight back. She tried one more lunge with what Keith now knew was his bedside lamp, which made him more indignant because it had taken him months to find a light with a shade that matched his new duvet and it was now probably damaged beyond repair.

'Stop it!' he said as he would have done to a dog, wresting the lamp from his assailant and throwing it onto the bed. But Samantha seemed to be in some kind of mania because now she threw herself at him, her full weight pushing him back onto the bed. She fell on him, her hands around his neck, her thumbs on his windpipe and her hot face close to his, engulfing him in the overpowering fragrance of sandalwood.

'For God's sake, woman. Get off!' Keith cried, but the feeble attack continued.

Who is to say when the assault became an embrace? Perhaps it happened at a different time for them both, but Keith felt, as he was in the process of being strangled (ineffectually, it has to be said), he had every moral right to reach up for his assailant's breasts, and almost as soon as he did so the hands were released from his neck (surprise? delight?) and, then, after a pause, began tearing at the buttons of his gravedigger's collarless shirt (damn the deposit, Keith thought). He felt her hot lips pressed against his and responded. He went beyond thought.

Keith engaged enthusiastically with Samantha that night ('Sam', he heard himself calling out at one point), but he did so suspecting that she was not engaging with him but with the romantic figure of a long-dead artist. He, however, was happy to enjoy Samantha without any erotic mental embellishments. When they fell back, exhausted, neither spoke. They then took it in turn to visit the bathroom, and by some tacit agreement both returned to the bed. The light remained off. They reached for each other in the darkness and lay entwined in the dank bed, naked, both smiling; shocked, sated, but strangely still aroused. The events of the night were as much of a surprise to Keith as they were to Samantha, she being a virgin, and he virtually so, despite a long, sexually frustrating affair with a troubled sculptress who, shortly after they parted, found the courage to undergo a sex change operation and now went around using the name Harold.

Morning could have been awkward if either had felt any regret for the previous night. Neither did. Keith woke first, remembered, and rolled over to face the woman in his bed, whose arm was across his waist. The movement woke her.

'You stole from me,' Keith said, kissing Samantha's nose.

'You imprisoned me,' Samantha responded.

'But I would have let you out. You imprisoned me, too, and tried to starve me to death.'

'You pretended to be a ghost, knowing how much Reilly means to me.'

'You tried to kill me with my best lamp.'

'You took me against my will.'

'You took me against mine.'

'Then we're even.'

'Perhaps.'

❧

It was agreed by Keith that Samantha would keep to the arrangement she had made with Gerald Reilly, but take only one of his father's paintings with the promise to return with the others at a later date. She walked the short distance to Canal Street, the painting under her arm, her mind burdened with so many conflicting emotions over Keith and Reilly that there was no room in it for her concerns over how she had parted from Gerald Reilly the previous day. Was this what Reilly had intended all along – that his paintings would eventually lead her to Keith? It was, after all, Nimrod who had tipped her off about what Keith was up to. She had found him lying in the gutter on her return from Gerald Reilly's, having been ejected from the skip where Keith had dumped him. Reilly's ghost would surely not have abandoned his beloved companion in a builder's skip. There was a logic to it she found appealing and although she would never in the past have considered Keith to be a suitable partner, she was hard pressed to imagine anybody being suitable – anybody, that is, meeting her mother's strict criteria of suitability, none of which the woman had ever applied to herself (background, income, expectations). Even in death Samantha was constrained by her mother. There – for the first time she had expressed it – that woman who had controlled every waking moment of her life, right down to the thoughts she was allowed to have about her. 'Honour thy father and thy mother': her favourite, and oft quoted, commandment. Samantha would gladly have honoured her father had she ever met him. Well, her mother was dead, and she had been cremated in the way she had asked to be cremated and her friends had been invited and Samantha had put on a good show for them. That was it. She had honoured her. Her responsibilities to her mother were therefore now at an end. Small wonder her father left. Perhaps one day she would find him. Perhaps, in Reilly, she had found a preferable version of him.

She had reached Gerald Reilly's door and was now ringing his bell. As he had done the previous day, he opened the door immediately, but this time he looked at her in a different way. Was it possible, Samantha wondered ('Sam', perhaps she would call herself Sam now), that somehow he knew what she had been up to the previous night? Well, it was her business. Nobody else's.

'You brought the paintings?' Gerald Reilly asked, looking disappointedly at the small, brown-paper-wrapped package she had under her arm.

'I brought one. I didn't want to damage the others. They're bigger. But this one is easy to carry.'

'Mm,' Reilly said, disapproving. 'And where are the others?'

'At Keith's. He doesn't live far away. They're quite safe.'

'Keith Blake's?'

'That's right. You know him?'

'You'd better come inside.'

'Thank you.'

There were two police officers in the living room: a young woman with expensively cut and streaked blonde hair and a slightly older man who looked as if he hadn't slept for a few days, and who had a beetroot-coloured rash on his neck that drew the eyes away from his face. When Samantha looked at his hands she also saw an angry rash there, so she deduced a nervous skin complaint. The policewoman approached her and took her arm rudely.

'Oh,' was all Samantha managed to say before the policeman cautioned her, using words she last remembered hearing in a Saturday night TV drama. They seemed as ludicrous and stagey then as they did now.

'I'm arresting you on suspicion of the murder of Brian Scott. You do not have to say anything but it may harm your defence if you fail to mention when questioned something which you intend to rely on in court. Anything you say may be given in evidence.' As he spoke, he scratched the skin of his right hand with his left, but then he pulled his hand away with what looked like an enormous amount of willpower. Perhaps he was aware of the absurdity of the words he was obliged to use; perhaps that lay at the root of his skin complaint.

'All right,' Samantha said, because everybody was looking at her as if they expected her to say or do something. The policeman then took charge of Reilly's painting, promising Gerald Reilly, not Samantha, that he would return it when he could, while the policewoman continued to hold her too firmly by the arm.

When the formalities had been completed it seemed to be Gerald Reilly's turn: 'I don't think you quite understand how inappropriate it is for you to have my father's paintings,' he said, with an anger that seemed out of all proportion to anything that had taken place since she arrived at the flat. Samantha could only assume that it had been stewing since her visit the previous day.

Reilly went on: 'I can't bear the thought of you touching them. I would like them all returned to me.'

'I don't think *you* understand,' Samantha said, 'how much I've been through for these paintings.' She had not been at all surprised to find the police in the living room; she accepted it in the same way as what had happened the previous night, as if Reilly was creating such episodes to illuminate the drabness of her life, to show her an alternative reality in which she could choose to live. Gerald Reilly's anger concerned her more than the arrest. It seemed so unfair.

'However much you've been through,' Reilly said, 'I can assure you it pales in comparison with my father's experience.'

'Of course. I'm not saying it doesn't. I know what happened to your father,' she conceded. 'Some of it, anyway.'

'How?'

'I told you. I read about him in the newspaper. The trial, the prison, the… everything. You can have the papers. Please don't think badly of me.'

'Everything was taken from him by people like you. I can't tell you how angry that makes me.'

'But you don't understand! I never wanted the paintings for myself. I always intended getting them back to where they belonged. Keith didn't care. He would have sold them. And Brian didn't have a clue what they were worth. He just wanted to make money out of them… I'm on your side. Honestly.'

She noticed the policeman taking out his notebook and jotting something down. Then they took her away.

Having closed the door, Gerald Reilly went immediately to the bedroom and watched Samantha being led away across the courtyard. All the while she was looking back over her shoulder towards the flat, hoping for some sign that he had forgiven her, but even had he wanted to, there was nothing he could now do for the unhappy girl who had barged into his life without warning.

On the way to the police station it came to Samantha that perhaps Reilly had intended this all along. Could the paintings be cursed in some way? She tried to warn Keith of her suspicions when she was allowed to make a call.

'What on earth are you talking about?' he said, 'And where are you?'

'I'm at the police station. I've been arrested.'

'You?… Arrested? Where?'

'At Gerald's. They were waiting for me.'

'Oh, Christ. Well, it wasn't me who tipped them off.'

'I know it wasn't. It was Gerald.'

'This is dreadful. I've bought some chicken for supper. I thought we could… What I mean is… are you all right? I'll come down there.'

'I don't think they'll let you see me.'

'Have they charged you?'

'No. I've seen a nice man who said he was the custody officer. He says I can have a drink if I like. I'm waiting to see a solicitor.'

'Don't say anything until he comes.'

'About what?'

'About Brian. About anything. And for God's sake don't mention how I came by the painting.'

'All right.'

'Not that there's anything illegal about it, of course. You sound very calm about it, I must say.'

'Yes. I feel calm. I'm just upset about Gerald. He thinks I'm some terrible person who was only interested in him because of his father's paintings.'

'Does that really matter now?'

'Yes. It does. It matters more than ever now.'

'You're a strange creature, Samantha.'

'...Will you leave me now?'

'No.'

'But I might be sent to jail.'

'Then I'll come and see you.'

'But it might be years.'

'Then so be it.'

TWENTY-FOUR

Death Watch

DEATH WATCH, REILLY LEARNED, WAS A LOTTERY INTO WHICH EVERY warder in the country was unwillingly entered. When a prisoner was condemned to death the names were drawn, and those unlucky enough to hold a winning ticket were summoned to their governor's office and informed that they were to pack a bag and take a train to Pentonville where they were expected to stay until the execution had been carried out. They were then allowed a few days' leave. Warders up and down the country lived in dread of such a duty. The three shifts of men who accompanied Reilly in his spacious and eternally lit cell were a surly lot. They grumbled at the confinement, at the heat, at the cold, at the food, at the unfriendliness of people they encountered on the streets of London and at the military regime of the prison. Each shift had its own distinct brand of discontent, but Reilly found one of the three more tolerable than the others, and that was solely because of the presence of a young man called Jebb, who had come from Parkhurst, and who it would have been impossible not to take to. Jebb was a farmer's son, well used to hardships. The young, well-built man had thick, straw-like hair and skin so reddened by the outdoors that it never lost its ruddy blush. Confinement seemed no burden to him; he considered it a small price to pay for the meals provided for him each day. His family had suffered genuine hunger and real poverty, and each day that he had food in his stomach was, he said, money in the bank against that time in the future when he was convinced he would again face starvation. Reilly felt some kinship with Jebb and often, as he sketched, the young man sat with him, attentive and courteously silent unless Reilly prompted him with a question or an observation. Jebb was the only man among the nine who acknowledged that he had a character beyond that of a condemned man. He seemed so keen to learn from Reilly that the artist encouraged him to try his own hand with the charcoal. By the second week a bond had been forged between the two men to such an extent that the inmates of the cell had become divided into two parties.

The fact that Jebb had made himself unpopular with his colleagues didn't seem to concern him. His physical presence gave him an authority that few would have seen fit to challenge. When he left the prison at the end of the day he lodged alone in a widow's house in King's Cross. Jebb told Reilly he walked everywhere (he couldn't afford cabs and omnibus routes were a complete mystery to him) and arrived most mornings with reports of epic all-night trudges across the city to see some sight he had heard or read of. He never used a map but had an unerring sense of direction and seemed to have little need for sleep. For the past three nights he had, he said, visited the docks. What he got up to there he didn't say.

Reilly was drawn to Jebb for his character and his eagerness to learn, but also because he could see in the man an unfulfilled promise; an expectation that life had something more to offer him. It became Reilly's mission, in the few days he had left to him, to nurture something in Jebb, so when the warder finally, awkwardly, tried his hand with Reilly's charcoal, Reilly encouraged him – suggesting he choose the face of one of the men in the room to sketch. Jebb chose Reilly. The result, which Jebb eagerly held up both for Reilly and the other warders to see, was greeted with bellows of laughter from his colleagues, one of whom said that it looked more like a cauliflower than a human face. It was, Reilly admitted, not the best likeness, but as a first effort it was not at all bad. He had expected Jebb to take the ragging in good humour but for the remainder of the day he sulked and refused to talk either to Reilly or to the other warders.

The following day, on entering the cell, Jebb made no mention of it. Reilly assumed he had made his peace with the other men on their way up.

'Can I sit with you?' Jebb asked.

'Very well,' Reilly said, laying his newspaper aside.

Jebb drew up a chair. 'It was them,' he said, in a whisper, gesturing to his colleagues. 'They made me seem foolish in front of you.'

'Jebb, they didn't.'

'It doesn't do. Doesn't do at all.'

'Think nothing of it.'

'I waited for them last night,' Jebb said. 'Outside their lodgings. If one had come out alone…'

'Then what?'

'Then they'd have learned what it means to mock me.'

Reilly was obliged to take his exercise after the other men in the prison had finished theirs. A man under sentence of death is granted no further association with any other inmate. Of the five sites employed for exercise in the prison, the yard outside B Wing was never used for condemned men, it being the location of the topping shed. But Reilly asked Jebb to seek permission for him to visit it. He was curious, he said, to see where the hanging would take place. The governor said he could imagine no reason why Reilly should not be granted this simple wish and he asked Jebb to accompany him. They walked out into the yard that same afternoon. A light wind whipped round as if it, too, was imprisoned there. Reilly enjoyed the chill against his skin. He was eager to make the most of the elements in his last few days. Above the yard loomed a grim tenement of soot-stained bricks at whose windows the faces of several children could be seen peering down at them. Pale-faced, they looked like the ghostly spirits of the men who had had their lives taken from them at the gallows. It had been a long time since Reilly had seen a child and it put him in mind of Amy Sykes, which provoked a sharp pang of anxiety because Rushden had not yet visited him, as he promised he would, to go through his affairs.

As they circled the yard he and Jebb were discussing Leonardo's notebooks, which Reilly had encouraged the young man to read during the interminable hours of waiting. It seemed he had not only read them but memorized certain passages. He recited one as they walked, their footsteps matching the pace of his delivery: 'The space between the parting of the lips and the base of the nose is one-seventh of the face. The space from the mouth to the bottom of the chin is the fourth part of the face and equal to the width of the mouth. The space from the chin to the base of the nose is the third part of the face and equal to the length of the nose and to the forehead.' He turned to Reilly, soliciting his approval.

'I'm sure you have that right. But it's one thing to know it. Another to apply it.'

'You're more critical than the others, I swear you are,' Jebb said.

'It's not a criticism, simply an observation, Jebb. Don't take things so much to heart.'

Jebb remained grim faced.

They had passed the topping shed for the third time. The reason Reilly had asked to use the yard was not simple curiosity over the site of the hanging; it was because he hoped that if he could make the place familiar to him then the pain he would suffer on the day itself would somehow be lessened. Jebb, irritated by Reilly's dismissal of his recitation, fell silent, and so they continued to troop round without exchanging a word, Reilly sometimes looking up at the tenements, sometimes up at the cells, and then for a while casting his eyes down towards his boots.

'I didn't kill Gower,' Reilly said. It had taken him a week to lead up to this. He knew it was unfair on Jebb, because it pushed him back into the role of warder when he had been generous enough to play the role of companion.

'I've rarely met a man who admits to the crime he's serving time for.'

Reilly waited for some assurance that Jebb believed him, but none came. Instead he said, 'When I came here I took the place of another man.'

'What do you mean?'

'Another man was down for duty here.'

'You wanted to come to London?'

'Manchester would have done just as well. I was curious to meet a condemned man. Didn't matter where.'

'I see,' Reilly said, uneasily. 'Why?'

'Wouldn't you be?'

'I... I don't believe so.'

Again they fell silent. Jebb spoke first. 'The sketch of the house you did yesterday?'

'Yes?' Reilly said, expecting some technical question to follow.

'You lived there?'

'Yes. I lived there as a child.'

Jebb nodded.

'Why do you ask?'

'And the churchyard. A family plot?'

'Yes, my mother was buried there – and, later, my father.'

'Would you ever wish to visit that place again?'

'Of course. But that's why I sketched it, because I have visited it in my imagination.'

'And where else would you choose?'

'Oh, I think Paris, for a few days, and Old Cross of course. I should like to go back to the coffee shop and say goodbye to Mountjoy, and Amy, and... and I should like to walk along the canal with Nimrod one last time.'

Jebb nodded, as if in approval. 'Last night I went down Ratcliffe Highway again. It's a fine place.'

'I don't think I've ever heard it called that before, Jebb. You're a braver man than I am. I've never been to the docks.'

'I saw ships of every nation: steamers and cutters and barges. A whole forest of masts. I went aboard a Polish trader at the invitation of the second mate. His English was good, if a little comical. More than five hundred tons she was. He said it would take three days to unload her and then she's away again to Norway, and then to Poland.'

'You should take care. The docks are no place to visit at night.'

'But that's just the time to visit. The jacks seem mainly honest. They make no pretence of friendship. Not like these bastards in here. Respect is earned by honest work, not clever words. And the women… I've never known such women.'

'Then perhaps you should go to sea.'

'Oh, I intend to go to sea all right,' Jebb said. 'I spoke to a shipping agent in a pub close to the bridge. He said vessels lose able hands every time they come into a port like London. It was him who introduced me to the Polish fellow.'

'Well, I'm glad, Jebb. This place would be the death of you.'

'As it will be the death of you…' Jebb said slowly. 'But when I say I intend it, what I mean to say is that I intend it soon.'

'How soon?'

'She sails on Friday.'

'Friday!' The word echoed around the courtyard. Reilly repeated it, more quietly: 'Friday?'

Jebb nodded.

'Well, that's excellent, Jebb. At least one of us will escape this dreadful place soon. Have you had permission from the governor?'

'I've told nobody.'

'But surely there are formalities.'

'I'm sure there are. But when I walk out of that gate I have no intention of ever returning.'

'How long have you been considering this?'

'A week. A year. Since I first looked out at St Catherine's lighthouse sitting upon my father's shoulders.'

'I admire your courage, I really do.'

'You do?'

'It's a bold man who takes his destiny into his own hands.'

'Every man's destiny is in his own hands.'

'Perhaps not every man's,' Reilly said soberly as, again, they faced the topping shed. Beside it was the small graveyard. Even after death the condemned were segregated.

Jebb looked over his shoulder to ensure they were still alone in the yard. Then with lowered voice he spoke urgently. 'Word is they've set a date for the hanging. The governor's been waiting for your solicitor because by rights he's the one who should tell you. Only he's not well. That's why he's not been in.'

'Tell me.'

'You want to know?'

'Yes.'

'Eight days' time. Tuesday. 8 a.m.'

Reilly nodded, seeing the face of a clock in his mind. He tasted his lunch at the back of his mouth. He made to continue round the yard but then Jebb laid a hand on his arm, holding him back.

'Wait,' Jebb said. 'I'm not finished.'

Reilly had never seen such seriousness on the face of his jailer.

'I said I visited the docks.'

'Yes. I heard you.'

'Well, it was for a good reason.' He paused. 'I spoke to the master. There are free berths on the Polish vessel. He'll take us both if we work our passage.'

It wasn't a good joke, given the setting, but Reilly laughed for the first time in many weeks. However, when he looked at the other man he saw Jebb was deadly serious.

❧

In the week following his visit to the newspaper office, Mountjoy continued to await the money from Pardew. He was aware that the journalist was waiting for the right moment to publish the story on Reilly's paintings, judging when it would have the greatest influence on their value. When, on Tuesday morning, the news came through of the date of the hanging, a week hence, he anticipated a visit from him at any moment. He had had no further communication with the ruffian Lol but that surprised him less. The impetus lay with him to secure the money and he knew at which pub he could find him when the time came.

On the same morning, shortly before eleven, the messenger boy Grubb burst into the coffee shop. Away from the oppressive newspaper office, Grubb reverted to the eager child Mountjoy had encountered on the day Gower's body had been discovered in the canal. His hair seemed recently to have been brutally shorn, with barely an eighth of an inch of it remaining on his skull. The effect was to make him look even more imbecilic than he had done before. Seeing Mountjoy working at the range, he dashed up and spewed out the garbled message. 'Mr Pardew wans to know if you're about this afternoon at four as he wans to come an talk to you about the business he said he discussed with you when you came to see him at the office.'

'He's coming this afternoon?'

'This afternoon and I'm to tell him directly and Mr Pardew don't like to be kept waiting so I said I'd tell him what you tells me.'

'Four o'clock would suit me very well,' Mountjoy said. Grubb absorbed the reply with a nod of his head, turned heel and dashed towards the door. Mountjoy stilled him with a call: 'Are you hungry, Grubb?'

The boy paused, his hand on the doorknob. Like a hungry dog spying a joint cooling on a counter, he made the calculation: illict food versus punishment. Like a dog, his solution was to choose the immediate comfort of food in his stomach; the punishment would just have to be the price he paid for it.

'I am.'

'Then take a seat, Sir. And I'll attend you shortly.'

'I'll 'ave to be quick as Mr Pardew is waiting for me to bring him back the reply and his coffee.'

'Don't worry, Grubb. I'll give you some cake to sweeten Mr Pardew's temper. You can tell him you had to wait for me to return from the grocer's.'

'He won' want to know that. He'll say I'm not telling him the truth. Mr Pardew always knows.'

'Then tell him I insisted you wait. That's the truth, isn't it?'

'Suppose it is.'

'Very well, Grubb. Then I insist you wait and eat. Now take a seat and rest yourself for a while.'

Grubb took off his cap, trooped to a seat by the window and sat down. As Mountjoy prepared his breakfast he watched the boy's eyes range round the table. Picking up the salt pot, he tipped it into his palm and watched the formation of a tiny pyramid.

'Grubb,' Mountjoy called, 'please don't waste the salt.'

Grubb righted the pot and tipped the salt from his palm onto the table. He licked his first finger and began dabbing it up. Mountjoy had every sympathy for the boy and he had hated to see him being bullied by Pardew and his cronies, but he was coming to see that there was something profoundly annoying about him that perhaps provoked them.

'Grubb,' Mountjoy called again, 'make yourself useful by clearing the tables.'

Grubb, conditioned to responding immediately to orders, left his seat and collected the empty plate from the man at the next table. He also tried to take the man's coffee cup, but he had not finished with it and there was a short struggle as Grubb and the man both had hold of it and it went back and forth between them. Only when the man said, 'Will you let go!' did Grubb release it, the coffee slopping out onto the man's trouser leg. 'You fool!' the man shouted and aimed a blow at Grubb's head, but the boy ducked out of his reach. They then both looked towards Mountjoy for mediation. Mountjoy barked at Grubb to return to his table and not to move from it until he was told to, and took the coffee pot and a damp cloth to the man's table for him to mop the coffee from his trouser leg.

For the next five minutes Grubb managed to sit still. He had been given an order by an adult and therefore complied. Mountjoy judged that he'd prove to be a useful employee if kept on a tight rein. He did, however, feel that the boy would perhaps have more prospects with Pardew if he could survive the miseries of the newsroom apprenticeship. While Grubb was eating his breakfast, using his fingers as often as his knife and fork, the door opened and Mountjoy saw a tall, neat-looking man enter, carrying a large, paper-wrapped parcel in his arms. He went over to help the man through the door, only then recognizing him as William Stewart, the taxidermist.

❧

When Pardew arrived at the appointed time, Nimrod had been put in pride of place, at a cleared space at the end of the counter. Pardew stared at it with a distaste he didn't bother to mask, then asked to see the paintings, and Mountjoy led him upstairs to the back room.

'Good,' Pardew said, rubbing his hands. 'If you'd be good enough to allow me a few minutes I'll make some notes.'

Mountjoy was loath to leave him in such close proximity to Amy Sykes. Her hatred of the journalist had not diminished over time; she continued to hold him solely responsible for Reilly's imprisonment. But since losing the baby Amy rarely emerged from her room, and when she did, it was only for brief periods. Mountjoy tugged the door shut, leaving Pardew to his work, and returned to the coffee shop. Pardew emerged an hour later declaring himself satisfied. He told Mountjoy he could expect to see the story the following day and had made arrangements for the paintings to be collected at ten o'clock and the money delivered. Once again he offered condolences for Reilly's plight, and looked again at Nimrod's case, this time reading the nameplate aloud: 'Nimrod.'

'Nimrod, yes,' Mountjoy said.

'"Let us leave him standing here, and not speak to him in vain: since every language, to him, is like his to others, that no-one understands."'

Mountjoy was none the wiser. He thanked Pardew and Pardew left.

❧

There was little time for reflection; little time for discussion. From the moment Jebb made the offer in the exercise yard Reilly felt his life had been handed over to the young man and he had no further say in it. He had, of course, protested that the sacrifice Jebb was making on his behalf was too great. Jebb assured him that it was not and that he would be very grateful if Reilly would waste no further time in discussing the matter. Jebb said that from the first time he sat beside the artist as he worked he made the decision that he would do all he could to save his life. Reilly was innocent. Hanging him was wrong. There was no more to be said about it. If the authorities would not reprieve him then Jebb would take the matter into his own hands. Reilly accepted Jebb's offer, though he remained unsure of his motives and felt that the longer he knew Jebb the less he understood him. But he had so successfully conditioned himself to accepting his fate that he had lost all joy, all hope, everything that makes life tolerable. Now he very much wanted to live.

They had made two further circuits of the yard, Jebb talking all the while, Reilly saying very little, listening intently. The ship sailed early on

Friday. They would need to be out of the prison on Thursday. Any earlier and there was a greater risk of being caught. They would hide until dark and then walk through the night to the docks. Exactly how Jebb intended to get Reilly out of the prison he would reveal later. It was important for both of their sakes that when they now returned to the cell they should continue as they had done over the previous two weeks. It was Reilly who suggested that perhaps they should pretend a certain distance had grown between them. It would be more useful if Jebb could ingratiate himself with his fellow warders. That way, if there was anything to be learned, Jebb would more likely be party to it. Jebb agreed that it seemed like a sensible plan, although he felt it was not within his nature to pretend a friendship he did not feel and he didn't want to make his fellow warders suspicious by a change in his demeanour. Reilly suggested a compromise: that Jebb would remain within the proximity of the two other men and eavesdrop on them. If challenged, he would admit that he had become tired of Reilly's company, wanted nothing more than to return to Parkhurst, and would be glad when the hanging had been carried out.

The plan was agreed. When they returned to the cell, Reilly's main concern was over his provision for Amy Sykes. Not that his estate amounted to much. His father's death had left him with land but also with considerable debts. Reilly had wondered at the time why his father did not grieve for his mother, only later realizing that, being the man he was, his grief took a more self-destructive form; almost wilfully, he dismantled the farm that had provided the family's livelihood for so many generations. But what little was left would need to be secured for Amy. There was no time now to deal through Rushden who, either through illness or shame, seemed to have renounced all responsibility for Reilly. He would need to see Mountjoy and explain it face to face. He knew Jebb would consider a detour too dangerous, but that was just what he intended. He would visit Old Cross once more before taking leave of it for the final time.

TWENTY-FIVE

The Visits

TWICE KEITH HAD CHANGED HIS CLOTHES. FOR A SECOND TIME HE undressed. The third outfit he studied in the full-length bedroom mirror – chino trousers, casual linen jacket, open-necked shirt – seemed no more suitable than the formal suit and tie and the informal jeans and T-shirt he had discarded, but he decided it would just have to do. Having never visited anybody in prison before, he was unaware of the protocol. Would he be strip-searched? Would they shine a torch up his arse? Would he face the humiliation of a full cavity search by a burly man wearing disposable gloves? He changed his underpants just in case.

Samantha had been in prison for a week. Bail had not been granted on the grounds of the seriousness of the crime and the uncertainty over the state of her mental health. She could offer nothing in the way of motive or explanation to her young solicitor. She explained that to help her, Samantha needed to help herself. But she simply smiled and told her that it was probably her fault that Brian had fallen through the loft hatch. Had she not been there then temptation would not have been put in his way. She had shoved him and he had plunged to his death. Out of desperation the solicitor had called Keith and implored him to go and try and talk sense into his girlfriend.

By the early afternoon Keith was standing in a rag-tag line of what he categorized as underprivileged people waiting for a door to be opened to let them inside the prison. The queue was formed largely of women and children. None of the women seemed to have come alone, unlike the men, two of whom stood smoking in solitude. The only other male visitor looked to be the age of somebody's grandfather; he was standing politely and respectfully at the head of the line with a similar aged woman. They could have been in a Post Office awaiting their pension. Several times Keith checked that his wallet remained in his inner pocket and was careful not to make eye contact with anybody else in the queue, most of whom he judged could have turned a vicious tongue on him in an instant. The children – all of whom seemed to have single-syllable Christian names – seemed unaffected by their surroundings. Some of them had been set loose in a small fenced play area in which there was a sandpit and a single plastic swing. Keith watched intently for signs of depravity but discerned no more anarchy in there than in any other park he had wandered through.

The prison door opened. The children were called from their play and were assimilated into the queue. Keith followed the woman in front, carefully watching and copying what she did, before being allowed into a large, featureless anteroom with plastic chairs against the walls and posters warning of the punishments they could expect for smuggling in drugs or alcohol. He followed the example of the others and put his mobile phone, his loose change and his wallet into a locker, removed the key and put it safely into his inner pocket. There was then an uneasy silence broken only by the children. A woman leaned towards him. He recoiled, driven back by her presence and her perfume until he understood she was offering some advice.

'Your first time?' she said.

'Yes. It is.'

'It's shit in there. And I'm not just saying that.'

'Oh,' Keith said, beyond which he felt there was nothing to say.

'Wife is it?'

'No. She's… girlfriend.'

'Remand?'

'Yes.'

'Her first time?'

'Yes.'

'Poor love. I hope she's strong. Keep back some change in your pocket. You're allowed to buy them a cup of tea and a bar of chocolate inside.'

'Oh. Well, thank you,' Keith said, and returned to the locker to retrieve some money.

As soon as he had sat down again the door at the far end of the room opened. Immediately everybody stood and began to file slowly into what looked like a large gymnasium set out for an exam. There were three long rows of equally spaced square tables, a chair on either side. On a raised podium at the far end, two elderly women sat beside a tea urn smiling benevolently at the visitors. For a moment Keith wondered if they were a theatrical drag act, but then realized these were the unpaid guardians of the tea and chocolate. He chose a table closest to the window wall in the row that seemed to be most in favour. The two solitary men, however, seemingly without reference to each other, both sat at tables as far away as they could from the others, then settled and waited, expressionless, at a loose end without a cigarette to occupy their hands. Keith could not have denied that he felt a vicarious thrill from being inside the prison. He had expected it to feel like school, with the attendant stomach-cramping agonies of not belonging. Only as an adult did he finally fit into the world. But, despite the similarity to a school room, he felt none of his old terrors re-emerging. He had liked the stern, masculine woman who told him to remove his chewing gum. There was a glint in her eye that showed she relished the power. Nor did he really mind the company of the rough-tough women visitors. As soon as they had walked through the door together from the outside world they had formed an immediate bond, us against them – the screws who made the lives of our loved ones a living hell. He took in all he could so he could later relate it as a story in which he would play the role of unwitting hero.

The room seemed suddenly to become filled with women in fluorescent bibs. There were shouts, whistles, people standing, embraces, children hoisted into the air, tight hugs, tears and chaotic, painful greetings. And then Samantha was manifested at his table, smiling a quiet beatific smile and when Keith saw her face he could not help but shed a few tears. It was, he said, not like him. Not like him at all.

'Oh, Keith,' Samantha soothed. 'It doesn't matter. But don't cry for me.'

He stood and they embraced, each drawing something from the contact of the other. Then they sat and faced each other across the table. Samantha's emotions seemed to have been quietened by her period behind bars.

'Have they put you on tablets or something?' Keith asked her.

'Why do you say that?'

'I don't know, Samantha, I...'

'Well, they haven't. I saw a doctor and she asked if I was having trouble sleeping, and I said I wasn't, and she said that if I was she'd give me something for it.'

'But are you sleeping?'

'No. I haven't slept for days. I don't need it any more. You can do so much more if you don't need to sleep.'

'Tea,' Keith said, wanting suddenly to be away from her. 'I must buy you tea.' Tea would solve everything. 'Would you like a cup – and chocolate? Apparently it's allowed.'

'That would be nice.'

'Anything in particular?'

'No – just...' and then Samantha remembered the other person she had been not so long ago – though of course it seemed a lifetime before – the earnest, overweight girl who trotted off each lunchtime for her sandwiches and chocolate. 'Just something plain – like milk chocolate. No nuts.'

'All right. I won't be long.' Keith stood. But before he went to join the queue he reached out his hand and touched Samantha's face. Samantha took his hand and kept it pressed against her cheek. 'Are you sure you're all right?' he asked her.

'I'm fine. Honestly. Better than fine. It all makes sense now, you see. Everything.'

'Does it?'

'Yes.'

Keith joined the lengthy queue for tea. The regulars, knowing the system, had scurried up to the women at the platform as soon as they had welcomed their loved ones. Keith's wait was long. Three times he telegraphed his apology and annoyance back to Samantha with grimaces, and each time he did he saw that she was watching him, in fact seemed never to have taken her eyes from him. Perhaps that was what love meant – that once in the presence of that person you had no choice but to stare at them in adoration. He tried to convince himself that was the case as he waited in the queue behind a woman with badly dyed blonde hair and a purple T-shirt and jeans – the outfit inadvisable, he told her in his mind, as she was too fat to carry it off. When he turned for the fourth time towards Samantha he finally understood what it was he saw on her face. It was the evangelistic expression of someone who had seen the light. It wasn't to him she was showing her adoration, she was hoping to convert him. Keith felt a chill pass through him. Darling Samantha needed help.

'I'm sorry.' Keith apologized to the tea woman, having reached the front of the queue. She smiled as if to suggest she understood the burdens he was carrying. 'Two teas and a bar of that chocolate please.'

He carried the tea over to the table, the chocolate balanced at an angle across the saucer. Samantha took the cup from him and he sat down.

'"It all makes sense now,"' Keith said. 'You said, "It all makes sense now."'

'Yes.'

'What did you mean?'

'Oh, Keith, don't look so worried. It's sweet, but please, don't worry.'

Keith tried to lighten his expression. 'I'm not worried. I'm just… you know, curious.'

Samantha tapped her nose; a gesture of secrecy. 'I never thought I'd ever be sent to prison. I don't know what my mother would have said.'

'Is it terrible?'

'Not terrible.'

'Surely it must be.'

'Not in the way you'd expect. It's funny not being able to do exactly what you want, and to go exactly where you want to go, but you soon learn what you can do and so you adjust.'

'I mean you hear such awful things,' Keith prompted. 'Brutality, bullying, people spitting in food, all that funny stuff in the showers.'

'Yes.'

'Yes?'

'Well, it isn't nice. People do get bullied, and not just by the staff. And you have to block the gap under your door so the rats can't get in. You soon get used to the mice. It's not nice. The toilets, especially. But I didn't expect it to be.'

'That's just awful.'

'I don't know. They seem to leave me alone. If I killed a child, or hurt a child that would be different, but I just killed a man, so I'm all right.'

'That's how it works, is it?'

'They think I'm strong. They think he got what he deserved.'

'Yes, well that's all very well but you didn't kill him, did you? You've got to get out of this state of cheerful victimhood, Samantha.'

'I'm not a victim. Just as Reilly wasn't a victim. You can only be a victim if you choose to be.'

'We're not talking about Reilly now. We're talking about you.'

'But we are. Don't you understand?' Samantha leaned forward, her eyes gleaming. 'That's what I meant when I told you it all made sense.'

'What?'

'Oh, Keith, sometimes you're so dim. When you get home, read the newspapers I found in the attic. Then you'll understand.'

'Will I?'

'I promise.' She smiled forgivingly. 'This chocolate's lovely. Thank you. Do you want some?'

'No. You have it.' Keith took a look around the room. 'So have you made any friends here?'

'Not really. I probably could if I wanted to.'

'And when are you seeing your solicitor again?'

'Tomorrow, I think.'

'Well, she's made me promise to talk some sense into you, so at least try to give her something to work with, otherwise you're going to end up behind bars for a considerable length of time, and you don't want that do you?'

'Of course not. But it's not going to happen.'

'It is going to happen. Don't you understand?'

'Reilly found a way out, didn't he?'

'Did he?' Keith said soberly.

Samantha took his hand. 'I can see it in your eyes, Keith. You think I'm mad. Well, I'm not. Trust me. I understand now, all right? I thought

I hated Reilly. I thought he'd betrayed me, leading me to Gerald and having the police arrest me – but that was exactly what was supposed to happen... Stop looking at me that way.'

'I can't help it, I'm sorry. How can you possibly say that being arrested is in your best interests?'

'That's the wrong question.'

'And the right question?'

'There isn't a right question. This is how it worked. Reilly needed help to get his pictures back where they belonged, and now they are, or they will be. He used me to do that for him, and on the way he took me on this wonderful journey. In return he taught me all kinds of things. He showed me I needed to leave my job and come and work for you. He led me to Brian, and he helped me escape when Brian died. He showed me what it was like to be in prison in that shelter and how I couldn't live like that. And then he led me back to you and showed me how to love and be loved – like he was loved – and when I was confused he sent dear Nimrod to make me see more clearly. And now I'm in here, in prison, which is where he was at the end. All I have to do is trust him and follow his example. That's all. I stopped trusting him, but now it's all right because I trust him again. Don't you see?'

'Not really.'

'You will. Because you played a part. You just don't realize how he's guided you, too. You will if you allow yourself to listen to him. But don't think badly of me. It's all for the best. I'm happy now. Happier than I've ever been.'

'Samantha, how could I ever think badly of you?'

'I'm glad you said that, Keith. Kiss me.'

Keith leaned across the table and their lips met. When they pulled apart Samantha stood and walked briskly to the door, where she waited to be let out. There was still over half an hour of visiting time left, but their time together was at an end.

❧

When Keith got home he looked again at Reilly's paintings. He had hung them temporarily in his front room, replacing three smaller canvases that had been in there. Due to their size they overwhelmed the small space, and Keith felt crowded by them; each one seemed to clamour for his attention. But at the same time he drew some solace from them. As he looked at one, and then the next, seeing the face of the young Reilly staring through the broken greenhouse glass towards him, he tried to put himself in Samantha's mind. In the pleading face of the child she had found a message, the message had given her a purpose which, to that point, her life had lacked. But what possible purpose could she now have found that would lead her to accepting her imprisonment without protest? Reilly had been imprisoned for a crime he did not commit. How could a lesson be drawn from that?

Samantha had encouraged him to read the newspapers she found in the attic, assuring him that when he did, he would understand. He thought it unlikely but made himself a pot of tea, brought the tray (with the biscuit tin on it) into the front room, sat down in the armchair, and slid the newspapers from the carrier bag. The first one contained the report of Reilly's arrest. The second one was dated August 1917 and didn't seem to carry any reference to Reilly in it at all, although there was a short paragraph on the death of a popular local coffee shop owner at Ypres. The third, which was dated April 1912, again had nothing in it which referred to Reilly, although it did contain a report of the hanging in Pentonville of a poisoner called Frederick Sedden who had persuaded a wealthy woman to sign over several properties to him in return for an annuity for the rest of her life. He had killed her using arsenic. Keith took a sip of tea, helped himself to a digestive and read: 'Frederick Henry Sedden was hanged by John Ellis yesterday at the accustomed hour of 8 a.m.' He turned the page: 'Approaching the gallows in the execution shed in the prison yard, the prisoner was somewhat unnerved by the sight of the noose and the sudden sounding of a loud horn of a tourist coach passing the prison. Ellis later declared he was afraid the condemned man was going to faint and got the execution over in just 25 seconds, which is believed to be a record.'

Was it possible that she had skimmed the paper and believed this to be an account of Reilly's death? Was this the escape she had imagined for him? There was a knock at the door. The caller had chosen not to use the doorbell. Keith found an elderly, dapper man on the doorstep, with silver hair and a goatee beard, wearing a homburg hat and an expensive-looking, long, charcoal-grey coat.

'My name is Gerald Reilly and I think you have some paintings of mine.'

'Oh,' Keith said. His instinct was to protest and send the man away, but he was too weary for an argument, and his mind was too preoccupied. 'Come in. In the front room.'

'Thank you.' Reilly walked briskly into the house removing his fine leather gloves.

Keith followed him in and watched as Reilly approached the first canvas: the picture of Amy Sykes reclining on Reilly's bed. The old man smiled in recognition and nodded. He reached to touch the cold paint and his fingers made contact with the board. Keith knew that had Samantha been there she would have read Reilly's visit as a sign.

'Don't think badly of me.' When Samantha's words returned to him, Keith finally understood the awful conclusion of her logic. Perhaps he had known it all along.

'I must make a call,' he said and dashed to the phone in the hallway where he called directory enquiries. Given their usual ineptitude at finding even the simplest number he was surprised to be almost immediately supplied with it. He accepted the offer to be connected. Having expected to be talking to a woman, he was surprised when a young man answered the phone. Keith was brisk. 'My name is Keith Blake. I am a friend of a woman you have in custody there. Her name is Samantha Dodd. I have reason to believe she might be attempting to take her own life… I cannot tell you that… No, I do not know which wing she's on. I think you can probably find that out for yourself. But please do it quickly and then please call me back… Yes. Thank you.'

He gave his number and put down the phone. When he turned he saw that Reilly had joined him in the hallway. He was surprised to see that the old man looked as concerned as he felt.

TWENTY-SIX

Ratcliffe Highway

THE PENTONVILLE CAP THAT COVERED THE PRISONERS' EYES AND much of the face meant that Reilly's unshrouded face would be unfamiliar to many of the warders. The plan was that on the Thursday afternoon he, accompanied by Jebb, would exercise in the rope-yard beside the long entrance hall that lead to the courtyard and the main gate. After exercise they would take brief refuge in the doorway to the hall. Reilly would change quickly into the warder's uniform Jebb had for him. They would re-enter the corridor and turn right along the entrance hall, cross the courtyard and leave through the door in the main gate, as all prison officers did. Jebb assured him that the bored key-man wouldn't give them a second glance so long as Reilly had a set of keys to hand in at the office and, by return, retrieve his wooden tally. The uniform was easy to find. Jebb had a spare one at his lodgings. But the keys were the problem. Even the laziest warder guarded his leather cartouche box that contained them with his life. By Wednesday Jebb confessed he had still found no solution to it and when he and the two other warders arrived on the Thursday afternoon shift change, Reilly was alarmed not to see him carrying the promised bag with his spare uniform in it.

It was raining, which was all the excuse the other two warders needed not to accompany Jebb and Reilly out to Exercise Yard Number One. Instead they followed them as far as the entrance hall but went on to the officer's wardroom in the courtyard for a smoke, promising to come out as soon as they had warmed themselves. Jebb unlocked the door and he and Reilly took the short flight of stone steps down into the rope yard, bowing their heads against the rain. The area had earned its name by the long rope laid on the paved circle of brick set into the soil. The rope was knotted at distances of fifteen feet. When the men were out at exercise one would be stationed at each knot. When the order was given the rope would be raised, and at the command 'Forward!' the men would walk briskly around the yard until they were called to a halt. The rope was substantial and soaked through with the rain. On such days it calloused the palms. Jebb toed the rope to feel its weight, as he had a habit of doing, and it rolled a little before lazing back to stillness.

'I couldn't get the bloody keys,' Jebb said, from the corner of his mouth, though there was nobody who could possibly have heard him. 'Walk the circuit.'

They set off around the circumference of the rope. Jebb waited until they were at the point furthest from the corridor before he explained. 'But there's another way out of here. It's not fancy and there's no reason for it not to work. But it depends on you. You need strength for this; you need to play the role well.'

'Anything,' Reilly said. 'Just tell me what I need to do.'

'If it works you'll have your freedom within the hour. If not, you'll be here for the rest of your short life.'

'Tell me.'

'Before that, put this in your mind. We'll meet by the Royal Naval Rendezvous at eleven o'clock tonight. Any man there will know it. It's in the docks close by the mint. It's a small place. A Union Jack hangs from the first-floor window. Eleven sharp. I'll wait no longer than five minutes past the hour, and you do the same. Keep out of the way until then.'

'Of course.'

A few more paces in silence while Jebb allowed Reilly to take in what he'd been told. Next time he spoke with more intensity. 'I don't need to tell you that when you get out of here you run for your bloody life. Don't look back. Not for one second. Not even if you think you hear me calling you.'

'I won't.'

'We'll take two more circuits round here. On the third, when we come round to the door, I'll stop and unlock it and I'll give you this package.' Jebb tapped the chest of his frock coat with his palm. 'Are you ready?'

'Yes.'

'You need to know it. Not just say it.'

'I'm ready.'

The instructions continued as they completed the circuits. When they got to the door for the third time they climbed the steps. Jebb tugged a flat package from inside his coat and handed it to Reilly. Then he reached behind him, lifting the tail of his frock coat, and pulled out a pistol from where he'd hidden it, shoved into his belt in the small of his back. The metal of the weapon was blue-grey, the long wooden grip was ridged. It was an elegant-looking piece, Reilly thought. Too easy on the eye for the agony it was designed to deliver. Jebb pushed a lever forward and up, releasing the safety catch with an oiled click, then, by a sleight of hand Reilly was too slow to see, tugged another part of the weapon above the butt. Something clicked into place and Jebb handed the pistol, grip first, to Reilly.

'Here. Now mind this. You pull the trigger, it goes off. It doesn't need much help so take care. If you loose it off it'll make your hand sing. Be prepared for it. Understand?'

'Yes.'

'You have eight bullets in the magazine. I pray you won't need them. Now when you get out of here make sure you cover yourself up. You won't get far in that brown garb. There's a waistcoat and shirt folded flat in the bag.'

'Yes.'

'Remember where we're to meet?'

'Yes. Royal Naval Rendezvous. Eleven sharp.'

'Breathe deep… Now when we're through that door you're on your own. We turn right and you march me as your captive to the gate. We'll need to pass through the doors at the end of the corridor. They'll be locked. I'll unlock them, it'll be quicker, but if there's anybody in the corridor you'll have to take my keys from me and do it yourself. Are you ready?'

'I'm ready.'

'Now take me by the scruff and point the pistol at my cheek. Hold it there and by God look like you'd mean to use it. If the gateman thinks you're playing at it he won't open up. Make some noise. Push me about.

If necessary loose off a shot into a wall. If he hesitates put a bullet into his shoulder. Can you do it?'

'I think so.'

'Any doubt in your mind and you'll fail. Any doubt at all. Can you do it?'

'I can do it. Thank you, Jebb.'

'Save your thanks 'til later. You'll pay me back somehow. Are you ready? Because when this door is open it begins.'

'Yes.'

'Right. And good luck to you.' Jebb unlocked the door and pulled it open. 'Now,' Jebb said.

Reilly grabbed Jebb's shoulder, pushed the pistol into his cheek and ordered him forwards. He could see the fear in Jebb's eyes – and he held himself a little straighter, looking into his fear and finding anger inside it; reaching deeper into the despondency and despair he'd felt since the arrest, the unfairness of it all; the terrible travesty of justice that he had refused to protest. What would it have mattered what the men in there thought of him once he was dead? As an artist he had always been too concerned for his reputation. Artists paint for posterity and too often forget to live for the moment.

The corridor was empty so Reilly's ripe oaths were heard by no-one but Jebb. Reilly pushed him forward at a half run. They passed the Chief Warder's room and paused by the glass doors at the end of the corridor. Jebb looked around him, to check the corridor remained empty, pulled out his keys and unlocked the door. Then they were through, Reilly pushing Jebb ahead of him down the broad flight of steps into the cold, cobbled courtyard. The portcullis gates were ahead of them. An empty omnibus was parked facing the gates. The gates loomed above them, thirty feet away, twenty-five, twenty, and then Reilly saw Jebb's two colleagues emerge reluctantly into the chill from the wardroom at the edge of the courtyard. When they saw Jebb they froze. Instinctively Reilly turned Jebb towards them as a shield.

'Stay where you are or I shoot,' he called. The words seemed to hang in the air. One of the men raised his hands in surrender. The shout alerted the gateman who emerged from his hut to see what the fuss was about. He too stopped in his tracks. Reilly pushed on, his hand clenched tight on the fabric of Jebb's shoulder. They reached the gateman. The gateman looked into his eyes, then into Jebb's.

'Open the gate,' Reilly said with deadly calm and what the gateman had seen was enough because the door was opened. Reilly released Jebb and was through the rectangle of light into freedom. He ran and ran and ran.

❦

When he could run no more Reilly rested, panting, against an alley wall, his chest rising and falling, feeling the cold bricks against his flexing spine. He had crossed the Caledonian Road, run down a side street, then another, and stopped only when he thought his lungs would burst. Nobody seemed to have pursued him but he knew the alarm would have been raised and he couldn't linger for long. Tearing open the waxed paper package Jebb had given him he found a shirt and a waistcoat which he pulled on, then balled the paper and dropped it onto the alley floor. He wished he had asked Jebb how to make the pistol safe but he hadn't so he would just have to carry it with care. He waited a few more moments for his breathing to slow, then emerged from the alley at a walk and slipped into the innocent human traffic of the world as if he had every right to belong.

He had no money. It was the one thing Jebb had forgotten. He would just have to walk to Old Cross. With seven or eight hours before the rendezvous there was time enough and the air had never tasted sweeter. He could not have survived a long sentence. It would have killed him as surely as if he had been denied food or water. A woman passed, pushing a pram. From beneath the hood, he could see the child peering up towards the rain clouds. His cheeks were red. Reilly knew exactly what combination of pigments he would use to achieve that blush of red over flesh and he could have rendered those vertical brooding clouds in an instant. A bus passed by on its way to Paddington. The driver sat up proudly in his open cab, bouncing in his sprung seat. The engine was deafening but Reilly felt he could distinguish a hundred lesser noises contributing to the greater din. There were seven passengers against the nearside windows of the lower deck. He glimpsed them for only a second or two but, given a stick of charcoal, he could have rendered a recognizable representation of any of them. He was glad to feel his life back in his own hands, and only then remembered that it was not. He must be alert. He was a wanted man and there would already be police out looking for him. Reilly dropped his head, removed the smile from his face, slowed his pace. In short, he merged with the rest of the people going about the laborious business of their day. When he passed a flower stall outside St Pancras, with its metal buckets of daffodils, irises and delphiniums on the wooden stepped shelves, he affected not to notice but stole a breath of the fragrance and held it deep. His mind carried the image of the purple-flowered iris as he climbed the station steps and passed the entrance to the Midland Grand hotel. The flower was supplanted by a flush of desire for a bottle of Bass. He felt some irritation towards Jebb and it wasn't for the first time. Of course it was unfair. The man had saved his life and deserved his undying gratitude, but there was something about Jebb that had increasingly jarred with Reilly. He had been surprised at his display of petulance over the response to his sketch in the cell. No man likes to be laughed at in such a way, but he sulked for several hours and left the cell without any attempt at conciliation. The following day he arrived as if nothing had happened, sat at Reilly's side and waited for further instruction. He had a childlike selfishness about him. Yes, Jebb had undoubtedly saved his life, but he had enforced a friendship on him and saddled Reilly with a debt he would be repaying for the rest of his life. Of course it was unfair to feel anger towards him, but he felt it anyway.

Reilly walked through the archway into the vast, echoing space of the station and paused on the concourse looking up at the departure board, reading off the names of northern cities; no-nonsense names for no-nonsense places. He could only imagine them; he had visited none of them. The station seemed to be as good a place as any to pass an hour or so and he knew he could play the part of waiting traveller well. He had been to St Pancras several times before (it wasn't such a long walk from Old Cross), and the Gothic palace never failed to lift his spirits. In the summer he went simply to see the beams of midday light flooding cheerfully down through the roof. He could picture George Gilbert Scott, the architect, smiling over his drawings, daring the investors not to applaud his audacity by rewarding him with the contract. Each time Reilly visited there he fancied he could hear Scott's laughter echoing from the roof amid the shrill whistles of the guards and the lumbering percussions of the locomotives dragging their burdensome coaches from the long platforms, over the canal and away towards the sooty north.

Reilly tensed as he saw the two policeman enter, halt, and begin to make a methodical sweep of the concourse. There was no question they were looking for him, but no reason for their attention to be drawn to him if he kept his nerve. He turned his back on them, put his hands in his pockets and walked into the ticket hall where he joined one of the three queues. The silent queue moved a step forwards. Reilly chanced a look towards the concourse and was alarmed to see the two policeman walking directly towards him. He remained convinced that they had, as yet, not spotted him, but he turned away and his right hand found the cold grip of the pistol that was tucked inside his belt. He would not use it. Of course he would not. He was an artist, not a felon. Surely you needed to serve an apprenticeship in evil before you could draw an elegant German pistol in a public place and loose off a bullet towards a man in a uniform. But, perhaps having done so once, his apprenticeship would have been served and the second shot would come more easily. You could lose your virginity only once.

Reilly wanted to turn and see how close the men were, but if they were close then seeing a man turn towards them might just be what caught their attention. They would not know his face but they would have a description and all it would take would be for one of the men to notice the mud brown of his trousers and make the connection with the prison. He wondered whether he would get warning or whether the first he would feel would be a hand on his shoulder or a cuff around his wrist. But the two constables walked past him, moving purposefully towards a man at the head of the next queue. The young man, in a rough cloth suit, bore no facial resemblance to Reilly but he was of a similar height and build. Just as the man took his ticket from the hatch and picked up his suitcase the officers were on him. They stood close to him, bullying him with their proximity. Reilly could see that the man was guilty of something. But that was all Reilly allowed himself to see before leaving the queue, returning through the concourse, passing the grand exterior of the hotel and setting off up Midland Road towards Primrose Hill, where he had decided he would pass the three or four hours until dark.

He had chosen the park to wait because it was one of the few places he could legitimately lurk without money, but he was glad that he had. He was to leave London, perhaps forever – what better vantage point could there be but a bench on Primrose Hill to watch the light of the day dim over his city one last time? When the cold got too much he stood and walked to another bench. He relieved himself against a tree. He drank from a water fountain. The water was metallic but ice cold. It refreshed his cloyed mouth. When the daylight was finally gone and the first street lamps were lit, showing as mustard smudges against the dusk, Reilly drew himself stiffly to his feet and set off on the walk to Old Cross.

A clock struck seven as Reilly turned into the high street. He looked up and down but there was nothing that seemed out of the ordinary and no sign of the police. They could have been in hiding but he felt he knew the area so well he would somehow have sensed them. He crossed the road. A man he recognized approached him along the pavement. Instinctively he turned to peer into a shop window. The man passed him by. He had a hankering to visit his room even though he knew it was foolhardy, but his luck had held so far, and surely he was owed more. Soon he was facing the lodging house. For ten minutes he waited for one of the tenants to emerge but none did. There was a light behind the curtains of the ground floor room. He banged on the window with the palm of his hand. One of the curtains was lifted. The tenant, the young, myopic academic called Joseph, peered out. He saw Reilly but didn't show any sign of recognition. Reilly was not in the least surprised. Joseph's mind usually seemed to be on greater things.

'Will you let me in?' Reilly called. Joseph dropped the drape. Reilly went to the door and waited. He heard a door open inside, then the front door opened and before Reilly could thank him Joseph turned his back and pottered back to his room. Reilly tugged the heavy door shut and was plunged into a darkness whose landscape he knew only too well. He climbed the stairs, pausing at doors behind which he could hear the sounds of domestic normality. At his arrest he had been taken immediately to the police station and had not returned to his room to lock the door. It remained unlocked. He went inside. The cold was bitter and the air damp. He found a stub of candle on the table and felt around for some matches but their damp heads crumbled as he tried to strike them. The cold white light from the moon illuminated the room sufficiently for him to be able to look round it one last time. Nothing seemed to have been disturbed or taken, but there was nothing of value worth stealing. Perhaps the easel would have raised a few pounds but it remained to dominate the room, throwing a stern shadow over the floor. What had once been a loaf of bread was now something else entirely and had taken on a new liquid form. Reilly sat at the empty easel. His body assumed the stance of a painter. He reached for a brush and pinched the soft sable bristles. Gently they fell through the pads of his fingers. He set the brush back in its jar. With one more look around the room: at the mattress, the table, the wash stand, the rack that had once contained his boards, and a final glance up towards the moon through the soot-streaked skylight, he left the lodging house, taking his old topcoat with him.

Finally he approached Mountjoy's coffee shop, knowing now that the diversion to the lodging house had been to buy him time. It was well after seven and he was aware that the place would be closed. Reilly rang the bell. He waited. Nobody came. He rang the bell again and banged the door. Again, he waited. Still there was no sign of Mountjoy. The lights in the café were out but the fire was lit. Reilly leaned close to the window and looked in, though what he hoped to see in there he did not know. The booths, as he had expected, were empty, and there was no sign of any of his paintings on the walls. His eyes travelled further and rested on the counter. There was something unfamiliar perched on the corner where occasionally Mountjoy displayed a glass dome of pastries. The box-like object was glass fronted and inside it (Reilly stared harder, as if by forcing his eyes to focus he could make more sense of the darkness) – inside it was a stuffed dog.

'Reilly?' he heard. 'Is that you?'

Reilly turned slowly and there, on the far pavement, he saw Mountjoy and Amy standing side by side.

'How?' Mountjoy began, crossing the road. 'I don't understand how…?'

'I escaped,' Reilly said simply.

'Good grief.'

Then they were inside, Mountjoy talking, talking, reassuring Reilly that everything would be for the best and they still had time for a reprieve. 'A woman,' he said. 'She saw it all. She went down to the canal with Gower and saw him fall. She'll testify for you. We've just this minute returned from seeing her.'

But Reilly seemed barely to be listening. He could not tear his eyes from the display case and the terrible sight of Nimrod, robbed of his pride for eternity. Now Mountjoy was mentioning Pardew, and his interest in Reilly's paintings, and the sacrifice that had had to be made. And there was Amy, on the edge of it all, watching Reilly, and wishing just for a moment that Mountjoy would stop talking so she and Reilly could have one minute alone together. Because it all seemed to be too much for him. Much too much.

The story of the night of Gower's death, of which Mountjoy, Gower, Nimrod and Daisy all knew a part, was this:

Nimrod had accompanied the critic from Reilly's room when he left shortly after seven o'clock and had followed him along Canal Street. There they had paused while Gower spoke to a woman who had accosted him with an offer – a local tart called Daisy. It was after that conversation that the critic took the steps down to the canal towpath and Nimrod followed. It was not a route either would usually have chosen for their evening constitutional, Nimrod being something of a coward when it came to confronting rats, Gower preferring the safety of well-lit streets. Gaining confidence and wishing to stretch his legs, Nimrod had bounded ahead, but then stopped to examine a promising odour emanating from a leaking pipe that discharged from the colour works into the canal. He emerged onto the towpath just as the unsteady critic passed, Daisy having gone ahead, her scent leaving an invisible ribbon in the air. Gower failed to see Nimrod emerge. His walking cane struck Nimrod on the back. Nimrod yelped. The critic lost his footing, stumbled and fell sideways into the canal with a shout, which alerted Daisy to turn. Immediately he slipped below the water, his pale face turned up towards the dark, moonless sky. Nimrod stood attentively at the bank for a while, watching the mud settle and waiting for Gower to emerge. When he didn't, he looked towards Daisy, signalling to her with a hopeful wag of his tail. Daisy approached and peered, as Nimrod was doing, into the canal. But when the critic failed to surface she gathered up her skirts and was soon gone in a blur of stockinged flesh and petticoats. Nimrod then returned home, Gower's wallet clamped between his jaws. When he fell the critic had been removing a ten-shilling note from it to pay Daisy (he had no intention of letting her see the contents of his wallet, but he was generous with tarts, imagining it would guarantee discretion), which is why he failed to notice Nimrod emerge ahead of him, and why the wallet fell from his hands as he plunged to his death.

Having delivered elements of the above to Reilly, and it not having been received with quite the enthusiasm he had hoped, Mountjoy withdrew to the seat beside the fire, where he sat looking into the flames. Reilly laid his hand on the cold glass of the display case. Amy came to stand beside him and, after a pause, took him in her arms. But that was the only brief moment of tranquillity in the day because at that moment the door of the coffee shop opened and PC Portch walked in. He approached Reilly so casually that for a moment Reilly was mesmerized into surrender. But then he gently pushed Amy aside and drew the pistol. Portch, implacable as ever, raised his hands to the height of his shoulders, but continued his approach. 'I thought I might find you here,' Portch said.

'Stop there!' Reilly ordered him.

'You came back for the little fellow, did you? Sentimentality undoes more men than you'd expect.'

'Reilly,' Mountjoy pleaded, coming to life again. 'There's no need for this. I told you. I've found someone who'll speak up for you.'

'Have you now?' Portch said.

'And you can guarantee it'll earn me a reprieve?' Reilly demanded.

'Yes… Yes, I'm sure of it.'

'I doubt it. Portch? You know the law better than any man here. What do you say?'

'I say you should put the pistol down and return with me to the prison. You shoot me, whoever your friend has found to support you, it'll do your case no good.'

'They can only hang me once,' Reilly said. 'I have no intention of putting the pistol down.' The men faced each other. 'Stand aside… I said stand aside!' Portch moved aside. Reilly turned towards Mountjoy. 'I can't take that chance. Speak to Rushden if you can find the damned man. What little I have will be Amy's.'

'But Reilly,' Mountjoy pleaded, 'at least wait until you've heard the outcome.'

'And if it doesn't go in my favour?'

'It will. Trust me.'

'It's not you who I don't trust, Mountjoy. I've been waiting too long for other people to decide my fate.' He turned to Amy. 'I came to say goodbye.'

'Let me come with you.'

'I'd advise against it,' Portch said dryly.

'It's not just you, Reilly, who's been waiting... Let me come.'

'And live the life of a fugitive?'

'I'd be happy to live any life, so long as it was with you.'

'Touching,' Portch said. 'Deeply touching.'

Amy went to Mountjoy, now slumped in the chair as if the life had gone out him. She knelt beside him, took his hand and kissed his forehead. 'Thank you, Mountjoy,' she said. 'Thank you. You saved my life, too.' He barely stirred. He was to lose them both. The decision had been made. And Reilly now knew why he had returned to Old Cross.

❧

By ten they were at the docks. The pubs were dense with smoke and hectic with voices, the wharves were crowded with sailors, porters, pilots and clerks. Horse-drawn wagons of bales and barrels crunched over the cobbles. Cranes swung nets of cargo above them. There was danger and fascination everywhere. Amy clenched Reilly's arm tightly, fearful of letting him go, but the tall, lanky man striding proudly along in his old topcoat, which must surely once have been fashionable, and the handsome girl at his side seemed to belong there. Who knew where they were bound, who knew from which ship they had come?

A racket drew them to the bottle-bottomed windows of a curio shop. There they paused and saw, inside in the yellow light, an array of treasures brought from all over the world: ancient weapons of wood, brass compasses, old cutlasses, ornate tobacco boxes, ivory chess pieces, splendid uniforms on tailor's dummies. But most captivating of all, and accounting for the racket, were twenty or thirty cages of parrots, cockatoos, and macaws: the bounty of South America and the coast of Africa, all in riotous conversation, winding in and out their necks, calling oaths in voices borrowed from the men who had owned them, laughing and screaming and singing. Reilly and Amy stood rapt, watching these birds in their cages, and saw that one had flown free – a parrot – which seemed at one moment blue and another green depending on how close it flew to the lanterns. It circled the dim heights of the room, alighting on a shelf. The shopkeeper swung a broom to fetch it down. But then it took off again, and made another circuit, and then found a place to wait on the counter where a drunken man, laughing, made a grab for it but again it was gone, and now it had seen the door, and now the door was open. And now it had flown.

Afterwards:
The Life of Reilly

'IS THIS THE REILLY EXHIBITION?' ANITA ASKED THE YOUNG GIRL dressed fully in black, hungrily smoking a cigarette just outside the door of the crowded cafe. The wide window was opaque with condensation, the voices loud from within.

'Yes. Do you have an invitation?' the girl asked her.

'No, I'm sorry. I just read about it and I thought I'd come. But it doesn't matter. I didn't know you needed an invitation.' Anita turned to go, at which point a man appeared at the door.

'You can come in if you like. There's plenty of wine,' he said, hovering just inside the café. Anita knew who he was immediately but he didn't show any recognition of her. She and Keith had met only once before, under painful circumstances, so she wasn't entirely surprised. After all, she was one of the noticers of the world while he belonged to the much more elite sector of the noticed. Keith wouldn't have done for Samantha, though, of that Anita was sure.

'Well, that's kind of you. I won't stay long. My husband's outside. He drove me.'

'Ask him in. The more the merrier.' Keith looked out, along the street, as if he was expecting somebody.

'No, he's listening to the football. I don't think this is quite his thing. Anyway, he's only got his slippers on.'

'Slippers?'

'Yes.'

'Well, help yourself to a wine and have a look around. There's a price list somewhere.'

'Don't worry. I'll find it. Thank you.'

Having exhausted his interest in her, Keith wafted away to rejoin the scruffy young journalist he had been cultivating. Anita thanked, apologized and excused her way through the press of guests. Taking a glass of wine and a price list from the table (looking around to see if she had to pay somebody for the wine, but it seemed she didn't), she went to look at the paintings. The ones that were for sale appeared to be perfectly well executed but they didn't seem to her to be anything special. It was the paintings by Reilly she had come to see, having read about the exhibition in the *Evening Standard*. Although only monochrome, the reproduced image had caught her eye as she flicked through the paper on the bus on her way home from work. She knew it immediately; it was the picture Samantha had shown her at the gallery on the day she visited with the new girl for lunch. The new girl was no longer with the company. There was another one now, who was much nicer, and whom they continued to call 'the new girl' even though she'd been there several months.

A dapper elderly man came to stand beside her, almost at her shoulder. His hair was longish and silver and fell around the contours of his head as if he had been wearing it that way all of his life. Anita wondered if he was going to try and chat her up, but he seemed content to contemplate the painting in silence.

'It's by an artist called Reilly,' Anita explained.

'I know,' said the man.

'...I've never been to an exhibition before.'

The old man chose not to reply.

'It's a sad painting, isn't it?'

'Do you think so?'

'My friend said she thought something terrible happened to him.'

'I suppose it did. But then something terrible tends to happen to us all at some time or another.' He looked directly at her. 'Doesn't it?'

'Yes. I suppose it does.'

The man, gratified by the admission he'd extracted, left Anita and went to join Keith, laying a hand on his shoulder in what looked to be a gesture of much needed comfort. They looked over towards her and Anita wondered if they were worried she was gong to steal the painting or splash wine over it, but they then returned their attention to the door.

Anita read the short note on T. F. Reilly's life printed on the back of the price list. It began with an introduction to the tempera technique he used to paint, which sounded very involved ('To prepare egg tempera pigment egg yolk and a little water is required. Any egg white in the mix will affect the drying time of the paint so separation from the yolk must be complete. Once this has been achieved the sac is pierced and the yolk encouraged to flow into a small container. A little water is then used to dilute it. Pigment paste is applied to a glass or marble slab. To this is added the yolk and the mixture ground with a glass muller…'). She learned that as a young man Reilly had been prolific, but most of those paintings had been destroyed in a fire. An office boy had been suspected of arson. No motive was established; a grudge was suspected but not proved. The artist had been imprisoned in Pentonville for a crime he did not commit, fled the country and then apparently travelled for many years with a woman called Amy Sykes, the subject of one of the paintings on display (little was apparently known about this period beyond the fact that they stayed for periods in Toledo, Morocco, and Sicily). The couple never married, but she later bore him a son when, many years after his pardon, they returned to settle in Old Cross. 'There are sketches, but no extant paintings beyond the ones on display,' the note concluded, 'and the assumption is that he stopped painting in his early twenties. T. F. Reilly and Amy died in August 1940 when a bomb fell on their house close to the canal, early casualties of the London Blitz. Their son, Gerald, however, survived and we are grateful to him for the loan of the paintings in the exhibition.'

Anita contemplated the picture she had faced that day in the gallery. Autumn. A grey walled garden some time late in the day. A street light (on closer inspection a gas light), unlit. Muted colours of the autumnal garden. The promise of winter in the empty flowerbeds. Melancholy as life. The sadness she felt on facing the painting was less profound than it had been before. She remembered almost every detail of that hour she had spent with Samantha in the cold art gallery, sharing a lunchtime sandwich. Perhaps the memory lodged because of her anxiety over the behaviour of the new girl. She remembered she had a blister, and how the toe of her tights stuck to it when she took off her shoe. She remembered telling Samantha she should come to the Christmas party, even though she knew she never would. She remembered being concerned for her, with good reason, she now knew. Anita turned away. She had seen enough. Her husband was in the car listening to the football and she very much wanted to see him; to press a quick kiss to his cheek, which she knew he would wipe away and ask her, 'What was that about?' 'Nothing,' she would reply. 'Nothing.'

On her way out she paused to thank Keith for allowing her in. He was still standing beside the silver-haired man, and they were continuing to watch the door as if they were expecting an important guest who hadn't arrived. Keith thanked her for coming, but in a vague way that she didn't much like. Anita suspected she knew who he was waiting for, and she could have told him she wasn't coming. There was an element of cruelty in it but she'd brought a postcard along to show him, knowing Keith would be interested to learn where Samantha was. It was the third one she'd sent in as many months. She reported that she was still in Morocco, but was intending to leave soon for Toledo. She felt stronger. The scars were fading. She hoped Anita was happy. There was so much in her life for which she was grateful. Reilly had saved her life, sending his son to the hospital to visit her after she cut her wrists. He convinced her to protest her innocence but more than that he wanted to make something clear to her. Prison wasn't the end of Reilly's journey, it was just a pause; a transition to the most fulfilling years he would spend. If she took anything at all from his father's work it should be a message of hope, not despair.

Now Anita remembered Samantha's face when she looked at Reilly's painting on the gallery wall the day she visited her. To Anita, it was just a lonely path. To Samantha Dodd it was a window into a whole new world that existed beyond the sadness, beyond the constraints of a life she was no longer obliged to endure.